THE OTHER SIDE
OF SILENCE

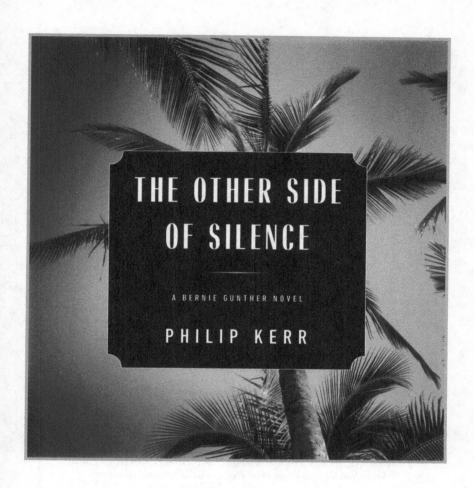

THE OTHER SIDE
OF SILENCE

A BERNIE GUNTHER NOVEL

PHILIP KERR

A MARIAN WOOD BOOK
Published by G. P. Putnam's Sons
New York

A MARIAN WOOD BOOK
Published by G. P. Putnam's Sons
Publishers Since 1838
An imprint of Penguin Random House LLC
375 Hudson Street
New York, New York 10014

Copyright © 2016 by Thynker, Ltd.
Penguin supports copyright. Copyright fuels creativity, encourages diverse voices,
promotes free speech, and creates a vibrant culture. Thank you for buying an authorized
edition of this book and for complying with copyright laws by not reproducing, scanning,
or distributing any part of it in any form without permission. You are supporting writers
and allowing Penguin to continue to publish books for every reader.

U.S. edition: ISBN 978-0-399-17704-0
International edition: 978-0-399-57469-6

Printed in the United States of America
1 3 5 7 9 10 8 6 4 2

Book design by Gretchen Achilles

To Jane, for all the happy years

He ruin'd me, and I am re-begot
Of absence, darkness, death: things which are not.

—JOHN DONNE, "A Nocturnal upon St. Lucy's Day"

THE OTHER SIDE
OF SILENCE

ONE

FRENCH RIVIERA
1956

Yesterday I tried to kill myself.

It wasn't that I wanted to die as much as the fact that I wanted the pain to stop. Elisabeth, my wife, left me a while ago and I'd been missing her a lot. That was one source of pain, and a pretty major one, I have to admit. Even after a war in which more than four million German soldiers died, German wives are hard to come by. But another serious pain in my life was the war itself, of course, and what happened to me back then, and in the Soviet POW camps afterward. Which perhaps made my decision to commit suicide odd, considering how hard it was not to die in Russia; but staying alive was always more of a habit for me than an active choice. For years under the Nazis I stayed alive out of sheer bloody-mindedness. So I asked myself, early one spring morning, why not kill yourself? To a Goethe-loving Prussian like me, the pure reason of a question like that was almost unassailable. Besides, it wasn't as if life was so great anymore, although in truth I'm not sure it ever was. Tomorrow and the long, long empty years to come after that isn't something of much interest to me, especially down here on the French Riviera. I was on my own, pushing sixty and working in a hotel job that I could do in my sleep, not that I got much of that these days. Most of the time I was miserable. I was living somewhere I didn't belong and it felt like a cold corner in hell, so it wasn't as if I believed anyone who enjoys a sunny day would miss the dark cloud that was my face.

There was all that for choosing to die, plus the arrival of a guest at the hotel. A guest I recognized and wished I hadn't. But I'll come to him in a moment. Before that I have to explain why I'm still here.

I went into the garage underneath my small apartment in Villefranche, closed the door, and waited in the car with the engine turning over. Carbon monoxide poisoning isn't so bad. You just shut your eyes and go to sleep. If the car hadn't stalled or perhaps just run out of gas I wouldn't be here now. I thought I might try it again another time, if things didn't improve and if I bought a more reliable motor car. On the other hand, I could have returned to Berlin, like my poor wife, which might have achieved the same result. Even today it's just as easy to get yourself killed there as it ever was, and if I were to go back to the former German capital, I don't think it would be very long before someone was kind enough to organize my sudden death. One side or the other has got it in for me, and with good reason. When I was living in Berlin and being a cop or an ex-cop, I managed to offend almost everyone, with the possible exception of the British. Even so, I miss the city a lot. I miss the beer, of course, and the sausage. I miss being a cop when being Berlin police still meant something good. But mostly I miss the people, who were as sour as I am. Even Germans don't like Berliners, and it's a feeling that's usually reciprocated. Berliners don't like anyone very much—especially the women, which, somehow, only makes them more attractive to a dumbhead like me. There's nothing more attractive to a man than a beautiful woman who really doesn't care if he lives or dies. I miss the women most of all. There were so many women. I think about the good women I've known— quite a few of the bad ones, too—whom I'll never see again and sometimes I start crying and from there it's only a short trip to the garage and asphyxiation, especially if I've been drinking. Which, at home, is most of the time.

When I'm not feeling sorry for myself I play bridge, or read books about playing bridge, which might strike a lot of people as a pretty good reason on its own to kill yourself. But it's a game I find stimulating. Bridge helps to keep my mind sharp and occupied with something other than thoughts of home—and all those women, of course. In retrospect it seems that a great many of them must have been blondes, and not just because they were

German, or close to being German. Rather too late in life I've learned that there's a type of woman I'm attracted to, which is the wrong type, and it often happens that this includes a certain shade of hair color that just spells trouble for a man like me. Risky mate search and sexual cannibalism are a lot more common than you might think, although more usual among spiders. Apparently the females assess the nutritional value of a male rather than a male's value as a mate. Which more or less sums up the history of my entire personal life. I've been eaten alive so many times I feel like I've got eight legs, although by now it's probably just three or four. It's not much of an insight, I know, and like I say, it hardly matters now, but even if it happens late in life a degree of self-awareness has to be better than none at all. That's what my wife used to tell me, anyway.

Self-awareness certainly worked for her: She woke up one morning and realized just how bored and disappointed she was with me and our new life in France and went back home the very next day. I can't say that I blame her. She never managed to learn French, appreciate the food, or even enjoy the sun very much, and that's the only thing down here of which there's a free and plentiful supply. At least in Berlin you always know why you're miserable. That's what Berlin *luft* is all about: an attempt to try to whistle your way out of the gloom. Here, on the Riviera, you would think there's everything to whistle about and no reason at all to be down in the mouth, but somehow I managed it and she couldn't take that anymore.

I suppose I was miserable largely because I'm bored as hell. I miss my old detective's life. I'd give anything to walk through the doors of the Police Praesidium on Alexanderplatz—by all accounts it's been demolished by the so-called East Germans, which is to say the Communists—and to go upstairs to my desk in the Murder Commission. These days I'm a concierge at the Grand Hôtel du Saint-Jean-Cap-Ferrat. That's a little bit like being a policeman if your idea of being a policeman is directing traffic, and I should know. It's exactly thirty-five years since I was first in uniform, on traffic duty at Potsdamer Platz. But I know the hotel business of old; for a while after the Nazis got into power I was the house detective at Berlin's famous Adlon Hotel. Being a concierge is very different from that. Mostly it's about making restaurant reservations, booking taxis and boats, coordinating porter service, shooing away prostitutes—which isn't as easy as it sounds; these days only American women can afford to look like prostitutes—and giving directions to witless tourists who can't read a map and don't speak French. Only very occasionally is there an unruly guest or a theft, and I dream of having to assist the local Sûreté to solve a series of daring jewel robberies of the kind I saw in Alfred Hitchcock's *To Catch a Thief.* Of course, that's all it is: a dream. I wouldn't ever volunteer to help the local police, not because they're French—although that would be a good reason not to help them—but because I'm living under a false passport, and not just any false passport, but one that was given to me by none other than Erich Mielke, who is currently the deputy head of the Stasi, the East German Security Police. That's the kind of favor that sometimes comes with a high price tag and, one day, I expect him to come calling to get me to pay it. Which will probably be the day when I have to go on my travels again. Compared to me, the *Flying Dutchman* was the Rock of Gibraltar. I suspect my wife knew this, since she also knew Mielke, and better than I did.

Quite where I'd go I have no idea, although I hear North Africa is accommodating where Germans on a wanted list are concerned. There's a Fabre Line boat that sails from Marseilles to Morocco every other day. That's just the sort of thing that a concierge is supposed to know, although it's much more likely that there are rather more of the hotel's well-heeled guests who've fled from Algeria than there are those who want to go there. Since the massacre of *pieds-noirs* civilians at Philippeville last year, the war against the FLN in Algiers isn't going so well for the French, and by all accounts the colony is ruled even more harshly than it ever was when the Nazis left it to the tender mercies of the Vichy government.

I'm not sure if the effortlessly handsome, dark-haired man I saw checking into one of the hotel's best suites the day before I tried to asphyxiate myself was on any kind of wanted list, but he was certainly German and a criminal. Not that he looked like anything less affluent than a banker or a Hollywood film producer, and he spoke such excellent French that it was probably only me who would have known he was German. He was using the name Harold Heinz Hebel and gave an address in Bonn, but his real name was Hennig, Harold Hennig, and during the last few months of the war he'd been a captain in the SD. Now in his early forties, he wore a fine, gray lightweight suit that had been tailored for him and black, handmade shoes that were as shiny as a new centime. You tend to notice things like that when you're working at a place like the Grand Hôtel. These days I can spot a Savile Row suit from the other side of the lobby. His manners were as smooth as the silk Hermès tie around his neck, which suited him better than the noose it richly deserved. He tipped all of the porters handsomely from a wad of new notes that was as thick as a slice of bread, and after that the boys treated him and his Louis Vuitton luggage with more care than a case of Meissen porcelain. Coincidentally, the last time I'd seen him he'd also had some expensive luggage with him, filled with valuables he and his boss, the East Prussian gauleiter Erich Koch, had probably looted from the city. That had been in January 1945, sometime during the terrible Battle of Königsberg. He'd been boarding the German passenger ship *Wilhelm Gustloff*, which was subsequently torpedoed by a Russian submarine with the loss of more than nine thousand civilian lives. He was one of the few rats that managed to escape from that particular sinking ship, which was a great pity since he'd helped to bring about its destruction.

If Harold Hennig recognized me he didn't show it. In our black morning coats, the hotel's desk staff all tend to look the same, of course. There's that and the fact that I'm a little heavier now than I was back then, with less hair probably, not to mention a light tan that my wife used to say suited me. For a man who just tried to kill himself I'm in remarkably good shape, even though I say so myself. Alice, one of the maids I've taken a shine to since Elisabeth left, says I could easily pass for a man ten years younger. Which is just as well, as I have a soul that feels like it's at least five hundred years old. It's looked into the abyss so many times it feels like Dante's walking stick.

Harold Hennig looked straight at me, and although I didn't hold his gaze for more than a second or two, there was no need—being an ex-cop, I never forget a face, especially when it belongs to a mass murderer. Nine thousand people—men and women and a great many children—is a lot of reasons to remember a face like Harold Heinz Hennig's.

But I have to admit that seeing him again, looking so prosperous and in such rude health, left me feeling very depressed. It's one thing to know that there are people like Eichmann and Mengele who got away with the most appalling crimes. It's another thing when several of the victims of a crime were your friends. There was a time when I might have tried to exact some kind of rough justice, but those days are long gone. These days, revenge is something of which my partner and I talk lightly at the end or perhaps the beginning of a game of bridge at La Voile d'Or, which is the only other good hotel in Cap Ferrat. I don't even own a gun. If I did I certainly wouldn't be here now. I'm a much better shot than I am a driver.

TWO

Between Nice and Monaco, Cap Ferrat is a pine-planted spur that projects into the sea like the dried-up and near useless sexual organs of some old French roué—an entirely appropriate comparison, given the Riviera's reputation as a place where great age and precocious beauty go hand in wrinkly hand, usually to the beach, to the shops, to the bank, and then to bed, although not always in such decorous order. The Riviera often reminds me of how Berlin was immediately after the war, except that female companionship will cost you a lot more than a bar of chocolate or a few cigarettes. Down here it's money that talks, even when it has nothing much to say except *voulez vous* or *s'il vous plaît.* Most women would prefer to spend time with Monsieur Gateau to Mister Right, although unsurprisingly these often turn out to be one and the same. Certainly, if I had a bit more cash I, too, might find myself a pretty little companion with whom to make a fool of myself and generally spoil. I'm enough of a feebleminded idiot now to be quite sure that I don't have what nearly all women on the Côte d'Azur are looking for, unless it's directions to Beaulieu-sur-Mer, or the name of the best restaurant in Cannes (it's Da Bouttau), or perhaps a couple of spare tickets to the Municipal Opera House in Nice. We see a lot of Monsieur Gateau and the firm, greenish apple of his rheumy eye at the Grand Hôtel, but he has his *confrères* at the nearby La Voile d'Or, a smaller, elegant hotel situated on a high peninsula overlooking the blue lagoon that is the picturesque fishing port of Saint-Jean-Cap-Ferrat. This three-story French villa— formerly the Park Hotel—was established in 1925 by an English golf champion named Captain Powell, which probably explains the old wooden putters on the walls; either that or they have a very challenging hole in the hotel's very elegant drawing room. That's usually where I sit down and drink gimlets and play bridge with my only three friends, twice a week, without fail.

To be perfectly honest, they're not what most people would call friends. This is France, after all, and real friends are thin on the ground, especially when you're German. Besides, you don't play bridge to make friends or to keep them either, and sometimes it helps if you actively dislike your opponents. My bridge partner, Antimo Spinola, an Italian, is the manager at the municipal casino in Nice. Fortunately he's a much better player than I am, which is unfortunate for him. Our usual opponents are an English married couple, Mr. and Mrs. Rose, who have a small villa in the hills above Èze. I wouldn't say I dislike either of them but they're a typically English husband and wife, I think, in that they never seem to demonstrate much emotion, least of all for each other. I've seen Siamese fighting fish that were more affectionate. Mr. Rose was a top heart specialist in London's Harley Street and made a small fortune treating some Greek millionaire before he retired to the South of France. Spinola says he likes playing with Rose because if he had a heart attack then Jack would know what to do, but I'm not so sure about that. Rose drinks more than I do and I'm not sure he even has a heart, which would seem to be a prerequisite for the job. His wife, Julia, was his nurse-receptionist and is by far the better player, with a real feel for the table and a memory like an elephant, which is the animal she most closely resembles, although not because of her size. She'd be a very good-looking woman if her oversize ears were not stuck on at right angles to her head. Crucially, she never discusses the hands she's just played, as if she's reluctant to give Spinola and me any clues as to how to play against them.

It's a good example to take when it comes to discussing the war, as well. As far as anyone knows, Walter Wolf—that's the name I'm living under in France—was a captain with the Intendant General's Office in Berlin, with responsibility for army catering. It's what you might expect of someone who's worked in good hotels for much of his life. Jack Rose is quite convinced he remembers me from a stay at the Adlon Hotel. I sometimes wonder what they might think if they knew their opponent had once worn an SS uniform and been the near confidant of men like Heydrich and Goebbels.

I don't think Spinola would be very surprised to discover I had a secret past. He speaks Ivan almost as well as I do, and I'm more or less certain he was an officer with the Italian 8th Army in Russia and must have been one of the lucky ones who got out in 1943 following the rout at the Battle of Nikolajewka. He doesn't talk about the war, of course. That's the great thing about bridge. Nobody talks about anything very much. It's the perfect game for people who have something to hide. I tried to teach it to Elisabeth but she didn't have the patience for the drills I wanted to show her that would have made her a better player. Another reason she didn't take to the game was that she doesn't speak English— which is the language we play bridge in because that's the only language the Roses can speak.

A day or two after the arrival of Hennig at the Grand Hôtel I went down to La Voile d'Or to play bridge with Spinola and the Roses. As usual they were late and I found Spinola sitting at the bar, staring blankly at the wallpaper. He was in a somber mood, chain-smoking Gauloises in his short ebony holder and drinking Americanos. With his dark curly hair, easy smile, and muscular good looks, he always reminded me a little of the film actor Cornel Wilde.

"What are you doing?" I asked, speaking Russian to him. Speaking Russian to each other was how we kept in practice, as there were few Russians who ever came to the hotel or to the casino.

"Enjoying the view."

I turned and pointed at the terrace and beyond it, the view of the port.

"The view's that way."

"I've seen it before. Besides, I prefer this one. It doesn't remind me of anything I'd rather not remember."

"That kind of day, huh?"

"They're all that kind of day down here. Don't you find?"

"Sure. Life's shit. But don't tell anyone here in Cap Ferrat. The disappointment would kill them."

He shook his head. "I know all about disappointment, believe me. I've been seeing this woman. And now I'm not. Which is a pity. But I had to end it. She was married and it was getting difficult. Anyway, she took it quite badly. Threatened to shoot herself."

"That's a very French thing to do. Shoot yourself. It's the only kind of French marksmanship you can rely on in a fix."

"You're so very German, Walter."

He bought me a drink and then looked at me squarely.

"Sometimes, I look in your eyes across the bridge table and I see a lot more than a hand of cards."

"You're telling me I'm a bad player."

"I'm telling you that I see a man who was never in army catering."

"I can see you've never tasted my cooking, Antimo."

"Walter, how long have we known each other?"

"I don't know. A couple of years."

"But we're friends, right?"

"I hope so."

"So then. Spinola is not my real name. I had a different name during the war. Frankly, I wouldn't have stayed alive for very long with a name like Spinola. I was never that kind of Italian. It's a Jewish-Italian name."

"It doesn't matter to me what you are, Antimo. I was never that kind of German."

"I like you, Walter. You don't say more than you have to. And I sense that you can keep a confidence."

"Don't tell me anything you don't have to," I said. "At my time of life I can ill afford to lose a friend."

"Understood."

"If it comes to that, I can ill afford to lose people who don't like me, either. Then I really would feel alone."

On the bar top next to my gimlet was a Partagas cigar box, which Spinola now laid his hand on.

"I need a favor," he said.

"Name it."

"There's something in there I'd like you to look after for me. Just for a while."

"All right."

I glanced around for the barman and seeing that he was safely outside on the terrace I lifted the box and peeked inside. But even before I'd flipped the lid open, I knew what was in there. It wasn't cigars. There's something about the twenty-three-ounce weight of a Walther police pistol that I would recognize in my sleep. I picked it up. This one was fully loaded and, to my nose at least, it had been recently fired.

"Not that it's any of my business," I said, closing the cigar box, "but this one smells like it's been busy. I've shot people myself and that was nobody's business, either. It's just something that happens sometimes when guns are involved."

"It's her gun," he explained.

"She must be quite a girl."

"She is. I took it off her. Just to make sure she didn't do anything stupid. And I don't want it around the house in case she comes back. At least until she returns my door key."

"Sure, I'll look after it. A good bridge partner is hard to come by. Besides, I've missed having a gun about the place. A house feels kind of empty without a firearm in it. I'll put it in the car, okay?"

"Thanks, Walter."

I stepped outside, locked the gun in my glove box, and went back into the hotel just as the Roses drew up in their cream Bentley convertible. I waited a moment, and then instinctively opened the heavy car door for Mrs. Rose to step out. He always drove them to the La Voile d'Or, but she always drove them back, having allowed herself just the two gin and tonics next to his six or seven whiskeys.

"Mrs. Rose," I said pleasantly, and gallantly picked up the green chiffon scarf she dropped on the ground as she got out of the car. It matched the green dress she was wearing. Green wasn't her color, but I wasn't going to let that interfere with my game. "How nice to see you again."

She answered, smiling, but I was hardly paying much attention to her; my mind was still on Spinola's girlfriend's gun while my eyes were now drawn to two men having an argument at the opposite end of the hotel terrace. One of them was a florid-faced Englishman who was often hanging around La Voile d'Or. The other was Harold Hennig. Automatically I opened the front door for Mrs. Rose before allowing myself a second look at Hennig and the Englishman, which revealed it was, perhaps, less of an argument and more a case of a smiling Hennig telling the Englishman what to do and the Englishman not liking it very much. He had my sympathy. I never much liked taking orders from Harold Hennig myself. But I put it quickly out of my mind and followed Jack and Julia Rose inside, and for the first time in a while Spinola and I beat them, which trumped everything until I went back to the Grand to cover for our night porter, who'd phoned in sick with a summer cold, whatever that is. I'd had a winter cold in a Soviet POW camp for about two years and that was bad enough. A summer cold sounds just awful.

I don't mind the late shift. It's cool and the sound of cicadas is as soothing as the night honeysuckle that adorns the walls behind the emaciated statues near the front door. Also, there are fewer guests in evidence with questions and problems to solve and I spent the first hour on duty reading *Nice-Matin* to help improve my French. At about one o'clock I had to go and help a very rich American, Mr. Biltmore, up to his fourth-floor suite. He'd been drinking brandy all night and had managed to empty a bottle and the bar with his obnoxious remarks, which were mostly to do with the war and how the French hadn't quite pulled their weight, and that Vichy had been a Nazi government in all but name. I wouldn't have argued with any of that, unless I'd been a Frenchman. As Napoleon might have said, but didn't, "French history is the version of past events that French people have decided to agree upon." I found Biltmore slumped in a chair and barely conscious, which is the way I prefer hotel drunks, but he started to get a little loud and unruly as I went to rouse him politely. Then he took a swing at me, and then another, so that I was obliged to tap him on the chin with my fist, just enough to daze him and save us both from further injury. That left me with a different problem because he was as big as a sequoia and just as hard to fold across my shoulder, and it took almost all of my strength to get him into the elevator, and then the rest of it to haul him out of the cage and onto his bed. I didn't undress him. As a concierge, the last thing you want is for a drunken American to regain consciousness when you've got his pants halfway down his legs. Amis don't take kindly to being undressed, especially by another man. In a situation like that it's not just teeth that can be lost but a job as well. On the Riviera, a concierge—even a good one, with all his teeth—can be replaced in no time at all, but no hotel wants to lose a guest like Mr. Biltmore, especially when he's paying more than fifteen hundred francs a night, which is about four hundred dollars, to stay in a suite he's booked for three whole weeks. No one can afford to lose thirty thousand francs plus bar bills and tips.

By the time I went back downstairs I was as warm as a Chinaman's pressing cloth. So I went back into the bar and had the barman make me an ice-cold gimlet with the good stuff—the 57 percent Plymouth Navy Strength gin they give the sailors in nuclear submarines—just to help the four weaker ones I'd already drunk at La Voile d'Or to take the strain. I hurried it down with my evening meal, which was a couple of olives and a handful of pretzels.

I'd just finished eating dinner when another guest presented herself at the front desk. And it was quite a present: lightly scented, sober, tightly wrapped in black, which left you a pretty good idea of what was under the paper, and with a nice little diamond bow on the front. I don't know much about fashion but hers was a sort of ballerina bodice-shaped dress, with one shoulder uncovered and, now that I looked at it again, not a bow on the waist at all but a little diamond flower. In her matching black gloves and shoes, she looked every bit as fine as Christian Dior's bank balance. Mrs. French was one of our local regulars, a rich and extremely attractive English lady in her forties whose father was a famous artist who'd once lived and worked on the Riviera. She's a writer by all accounts and rents a local house in Villefranche, but she spends much of her free time at the Grand Hôtel. She swims a lot in our pool, reads a book in the bar, uses the telephone a great deal, and then has a late dinner in the restaurant. Often she's alone, but sometimes she's with friends. A few weeks ago, Mrs. French seemed to be making a play for the French minister of national defense, Monsieur Bourgès-Maunoury, who was staying here, but that came to nothing. It seemed that the minister had other things on his mind—like the Islamic threat posed by the Algerian FLN, not to mention Egypt's cut-price Hitler, Gamal Abdel Nasser, and perhaps the anonymous woman who was in the room next to his. He's not a bad-looking fellow, I suppose; dark-haired, dark-eyed, perhaps a little oily, a bit small, and frankly a couple of leagues below where Mrs. French plays. I thought a nice brunette like her could do better. Then again, Maurice Bourgès-Maunoury is tipped to be the next prime minister of France.

"Good evening, Mrs. French," I said. "I hope you enjoyed your dinner."

"Yes, it wasn't bad."

"That doesn't sound nearly as good as it should be."

She sighed. "It could have been better."

"Was it the food? Or perhaps the service?"

"To be honest, neither one of them was at fault. And yet there was something lacking. With only my book for company, I fear it was nothing that can be easily remedied by anyone here in the Grand Hôtel."

"Then might I ask what it is you're reading, Mrs. French?" My manners have improved a lot since I started working in hotels again. Sometimes I sound almost civil.

She opened her crocodile-leather dispatch bag and showed me her book: *The Quiet American* by Graham Greene. My cop's eyes took quick note of the bottle of Mystikum, a sheaf of French francs, a gold compact, and a little purple screw-top tin that might have contained a powder puff but more probably contained her diaphragm.

"Not one I've read," I said.

"No. But I think you've probably forgotten more about how to render an American acceptably quiet than Graham Greene has ever learned." She smiled. "Poor Mr. Biltmore. Let's hope he puts his sore head down to alcohol tomorrow and not your fist."

"Oh, you saw that. Pity. I had thought the bar was empty."

"I was seated behind a pillar. But you handled it very well. Like an expert. I'd say you've done that kind of thing before. Professionally."

I shrugged. "The hotel business always presents a number of interesting challenges."

"If you say so."

"Perhaps I can recommend something else for you to read," I offered, hurrying to change the subject.

"Why not? You are a concierge, after all. Although in my own experience playing Robert Benchley is perhaps above and beyond the call of your normal duties."

I mentioned a book by Albert Camus that had impressed me.

"No, I don't like him," she said. "He's too French for my tastes. Too political, as well. But now that I think about it, maybe you could recommend a book about bridge. I'd like to learn the game and I know you play it often, Mr. Wolf."

"I'd be happy to lend you some of my own books, Mrs. French. Anything by Terence Reese or S. J. Simon would do, I think."

"Better still, you could teach me the game yourself. I'd be happy to pay you for some private lessons."

"I'm afraid my duties here wouldn't really permit that, Mrs. French. On second thought, I think you're probably best to start with Iain Macleod's *Bridge Is an Easy Game.*"

If she was disappointed she didn't show it. "That sounds just right. Will you bring it tomorrow?"

"Of course. I regret I won't be here to give it you myself, Mrs. French, but I'll certainly leave it with one of my colleagues."

"You're not working tomorrow? Pity. I enjoy our little chats."

I smiled diplomatically and bowed. "Always glad to be of service, Mrs. French."

In bridge that's what we call No Bid.

THREE

"Well, this is a pleasant surprise. Fancy meeting you here."
Just a few kilometers west of Cap Ferrat, Villefranche-sur-Mer is a curious old Riviera town full of tourists enjoying its hidden Escher stairways, high tenements, and dark, winding cobbled streets. It's a little like being in a Gallic version of a Fritz Lang movie, shadowy, secret, and full of awkward, fish-eye angles, perfect for a deracinated wanted man living quietly and under a false name. So it was surprising to bump into Mrs. French outside a bar on—of all places—the Rue Obscure, which is entirely vaulted over, like a crypt, and most reminds me of a part of old Berlin, which is probably why I go there. Alone. The

La Darse Bar is a crummy, sepulchral sort of place with sawdust on the floor and sticky wooden tables and looks like it's been in existence since the time of Charles V, but the house rosé they serve in earthenware pitchers is just about drinkable and I'm often to be found there, if anyone was ever inclined to look for me. Nobody ever had been inclined to look for me and so I couldn't help but feel that Mrs. French finding me in the Rue Obscure wasn't entirely the happy accident she claimed. She was wearing pink capri pants, a matching head scarf, a loose black sweater, and around her neck was a string of pearls and an even more expensive-looking Leica. Hers was the kind of carefree, casual look that women spend a lot of time in front of the mirror getting just right.

"Do you live around here, Mr. Wolf?" she asked.

"In a manner of speaking. I have a place on Quai de la Corderie. On the seafront." I wondered who among my colleagues at the GHCF might have told her where I lived and, more to the point, my habits, and quickly arrived at the name of Ueli Leuthard, who was my boss and, I knew, a friend of Mrs. French.

"You realize we're almost neighbors, don't you? My house is on Avenue des Hespérides."

I smiled. My house resembled the local jail. The houses on Avenue des Hespérides were large, well-appointed villas with several stories, sprawling gardens, and expensively uninterrupted views of the sea. Describing us as neighbors was like comparing a sea urchin with a giant octopus.

"I suppose we are," I said. "But what brings you along this street, Mrs. French? It's not called obscure for nothing."

"Taking pictures, like everyone else. When I'm not writing, I take photographs. I've even sold a few. And call me Anne, please. We're not at the Grand Hôtel now."

"That's for sure. You know, I wouldn't have thought there's enough light for a picture in here."

"This is the whole point of a good picture. To work with the available light and shade. To find definition and meaning in black and white where none seems obvious. And perhaps to illuminate a mystery."

She made it sound like being a detective.

"Well, aren't you going to buy me a drink?" she asked.

"In there?"

"Why not?"

"If you'd ever been through the door you'd know the answer to that question. No, let's go somewhere else." I dipped my head beside her ear for a second and sniffed loudly, for effect. "That's Mystikum, and I'd prefer to enjoy it because you're wearing it, not because it hides the smell of fish."

"I'm impressed. That you know my perfume."

"I'm a concierge. It's my job to know these things. Besides, I saw the bottle in your handbag last night when you showed me your book."

"You have keen eyes."

"Not for very much, I'm afraid."

She nodded. "I won't argue about going somewhere else. It does smell of fish around here."

"Good."

"Where shall we go?"

"This is Villefranche. There are more bars in this town than there are mailboxes. Which probably explains why the post is so slow."

"I've a better idea. Why don't we go to your house and then you can give me that bridge book?"

"I think I may have misled you, Mrs. French. When I said it was a house what I actually meant was a lobster pot."

"And you're the lobster, is that it?"

"Certainly. There's no room in there for much more than me and a local fisherman's hand."

"All right. Why don't you go home, fetch the book, and then bring it to my house? Avenue des Hespérides, number eight. We can have a drink there if you like. There's quite a substantial wine cellar I've hardly touched since I rented the place."

"Didn't the Garden of the Hesperides have some golden apples that were guarded by a never-sleeping, hundred-headed dragon named Ladon?"

"We had a guard dog, but he died. I do have a cat. His name is Robbie. I don't think that you need to worry about him. But if you'd rather not—"

"It's like this, Mrs. French, so you don't mistake me. We might easily become friends. But suppose we fell out again afterward? You want me to teach you bridge. There are drills. Homework.

26

Suppose I said you were not a diligent pupil? What then? Suppose I had to get rough with you when you played your hand all wrong? Believe me, it's been known." I shrugged. "It's just that like all lobsters I'm anxious not to get myself into hot water. Staff are discouraged from fraternizing with people who stay at the hotel and I wouldn't want to lose my job. It's not a great job but it's all I have right now. The movie business is a little slow down here since Alfred Hitchcock left town."

"Well, that's all right then. I never stay there. I hate staying in hotels. Especially grand hotels. They're actually very lonely places. All of the rooms have locks on the doors and I always find that rather claustrophobic."

"You're very persistent."

"I certainly wouldn't want you to feel uncomfortable, Mr. Wolf."

She winced, and I sensed that it was me who'd made her feel uncomfortable, which made me feel bad. That's a problem I have sometimes; I never like making people feel bad, especially when they look like Anne French.

"Walter. Please call me Walter. And yes, of course, I'd love to come. Shall we say in half an hour? That will give me time to fetch the book and to change my shirt. For a lobster it's the most painless way there is to change color."

"I think pink would suit you," she said.

"My mother certainly thought so when I was a baby. Right up until the moment she discovered I was a boy."

"It's hard to imagine that you had parents."

"I had two of them as a matter of fact."

"What I mean is you seem like a very serious man."

"Don't let that fool you, Mrs. French. I'm German. And like all Germans I'm easily led astray."

Back home I did a lot more than change my shirt. I washed, and combed my hair. I even splashed on a little Pino Silvestre that a guest had left behind in his hotel bedroom. I get a lot of my stuff that way. It smells like a mixture of mothballs and a Christmas tree, but it does repel mosquitoes, which are a real problem down here and it's better than my natural body odor, which is always a little sour these days.

Mrs. French's villa occupied a beautiful garden that was a series of lawned terraces that hung on the edge of the rocks above Villefranche and looked as if it had been landscaped by someone from Babylon with a head for heights. The semi-rusticated pink stucco house had a round corner tower and an elegant first-floor terrace with an awning. There was a pool and a clay tennis court and a guest villa and a caretaker's house with an empty dog kennel that was only a little smaller than the place where I lived. I took one look at the basket and the dog bowl and thought about applying for the vacancy. We sat on the terrace that faced the floodlit, aquamarine pool and she handed me a bottle of Tavel that matched the color of the stucco and helped take away the taste of my cologne.

Inside, the place was full of books and art of the kind that takes a lifetime to collect, or paint, depending on whether it's taste or talent you have, and since I have neither, I just stood in front of it all and nodded, dumbly, careful not to admit that I thought it was all a bit like Picasso, and which she might reasonably have taken as a compliment but for the fact that I can't stand Picasso. These days all his faces look as ugly as mine and it seemed unlikely that my face should be of any interest to a woman who was at least ten years younger than I am. I wasn't sure what she was up to; at least not yet. Perhaps she really did want me to teach her bridge, but there are schools for that, and teachers, even on the Riviera. Maybe I'm just being cynical, but she showed no real interest in the book when I gave it to her and it stayed unopened on the table for as long as it took us to finish one bottle and open another.

We talked about nothing in particular, which is a subject on which I am something of an expert. And after a while she went into the kitchen to prepare us some snacks, leaving me alone to smoke and go inside the house to snoop among her books. I brought one back to the terrace and read it for a while. But finally she came out and soon after that, to the point.

"I expect you're wondering why I'm so keen to learn the game of bridge," she said.

"No, not for a minute. These days I try to do as little wondering as possible. The guests tend to prefer it that way."

"I told you I'm a writer."

"Yes, I noticed all the books. They must come in handy when you're thinking of something to write."

"Some of them belonged to my father." She picked the book I'd been reading off the table for a moment and then tossed it back. "Including that one. *Russian Glory*, by Philip Jordan. What's it about?"

"It's a sort of panegyric about Stalin and the Russian people, and the evils of capitalism."

"Why on earth were you reading that?"

"It's like meeting a rather naïve old friend. For a while during the war it was the only book that was available to me."

"That sounds uncomfortable."

"It was. But you were telling me about why you're so keen to learn the game of bridge."

"How much do you know about William Somerset Maugham? The writer."

"Enough to know that he wouldn't be interested in you, Mrs. French. For one thing you're not young enough. And for another, you're the wrong sex."

"That's true. Which is why I want to learn bridge. I was thinking it might provide me with the means of getting to meet him. From what I've heard, he plays cards almost every night."

"Why do you want to meet him?"

"I'm a big fan of his writing. He's perhaps the greatest novelist alive today. Certainly the most popular. Which is why he can afford to live down here in such splendor at the Villa Mauresque."

"You're not doing so bad yourself."

"I'm renting this place. I don't own it. I wish I did."

"What's the real reason you want to meet him?"

"I don't know what you mean. Maybe you didn't notice it, but I have an entire collection of his first editions and I would dearly like him to sign them all before—before he dies. He is very old. Which of course would make them worth a lot more. I suppose there's that."

"We're getting warmer," I said. "But I'll bet that's still not the real reason. You don't look like a book dealer. Not in those pants."

Anne French bridled a little.

"All right then, it's because I have an offer from an American publisher called Victor Weybright to write his biography," she said. "Fifty thousand dollars, to be precise."

"That's a much better reason. Or to be more accurate, fifty thousand of them."

"I'd really like to meet him, but as you've observed I'm the wrong sex."

"Why don't you just write to him and tell him about the book?"

"Because that would get me nowhere. Somerset Maugham is notoriously private. He hates the idea of being written about and, so far, has resisted all biographers. Which is one reason why the money is so good. Nobody has managed to do it. I was thinking that if I learned to play bridge I might inveigle my way into his circle and pick up some conversation and some color. He'd never agree to meet me if he knew I was writing a book about him. No, the only way is to give him a reason to invite me. By all accounts he used to play with Dorothy Parker. And rather more recently with the Queen of Spain and Lady Doverdale."

"Bridge isn't the kind of card game you can just pick up and play, Mrs. French. It takes time to become good. From what I hear, Somerset Maugham's been playing all his life. I'm not sure even I'd be in his league."

"I'd still like to try. And I'd be willing to pay you to come here and teach me. How does a hundred francs a lesson sound?"

"I've got a better idea. What kind of cook are you, Mrs. French?"

"If it's just me, I tend to go to the hotel. But I can cook. Why?"

"So I'll make you a deal. My wife left me a while ago. I miss a cooked meal. Make me dinner twice a week and I'll teach you how to play bridge. How's that?"

She nodded. "Agreed."

So that was my deal. And in bridge the dealer is entitled to make the first call.

FOUR

For a couple of weeks my arrangement with Anne French worked well. She was a quick study and took to the game like a new deck and a dealer's shoe. She wasn't a bad cook and I even managed to put on a few extra pounds. Best of all, she made a hell of a gimlet, the kind you can taste and feel for hours afterward. This might even be why, once or twice, I got the idea she wanted me to kiss her, but I managed to resist the temptation, which is unusual for me. Temptation is not something I can easily avoid when it comes wearing Mystikum behind its rose petal ears and you can see its smaller washing still hanging on the line outside the kitchen door. It wasn't that I didn't find her attractive, or that I couldn't have used a little affection—or that I didn't like her underwear—but I've been bitten so many times that I'm as twice shy as the wild pigs that came into the trees at the bottom of her garden after dark and truffled around for something to eat. Shy and apt to think that someone might have a rifle pointed at my ear. Meanwhile, I continued going to La Voile d'Or for my biweekly game and my life continued along the same monotonous path as before. Life can be appreciated best when you have a regular job and a goodish salary and you can avoid thinking about anything more important than what's happening in Egypt. At least, that's what I told myself. But one night Spinola was drunk—too drunk to play bridge—and I was actually pleased because it gave me an excuse to call Anne to see if she wanted to take the Italian's place at the table. I was disappointed to discover, first that she wasn't at home and second that I was more disappointed than I told myself was appropriate, given everything I'd told myself and her about not getting involved with hotel guests. Meanwhile, the Roses drove Spinola home in their Bentley, which left me alone on the terrace with a last drink and cigarette, wondering if I should drive to Anne's house in Villefranche and look for her in case she hadn't heard the telephone or chosen not to answer it. It was the wrong thing to do, of course, and I was just about to do it all the same when an Englishman with a little dog spoke to me.

"I see you here a lot," he said. "Playing bridge, twice a week. I say, aren't you the concierge at the Grand Hôtel?"

"Sometimes," I said. "When I'm not playing bridge."

"It is rather addictive, isn't it?"

He was probably about forty but looked older. Overweight and a little sweaty, he wore a double-breasted linen blazer, a white shirt with overextended double cuffs and gold links that looked like a modest day on the Klondike, gray cavalry twill trousers, a silk tie that was the color of a South American jaguar, and a matching silk handkerchief that was spilling out of his top pocket as if he were about to conjure a bunch of fake flowers, like a cheap magician. He was the same man I'd seen arguing outside the hotel entrance with Harold Hennig.

"Hello, I'm Robin Maugham."

"Walter Wolf."

We shook hands and he waved the waiter toward us. "Buy you a drink?"

"Sure."

We ordered drinks, some water for the dog, lit our cigarettes, took a table on the terrace facing the port, and generally tried to behave normally, or at least as normal as you can when one man isn't homosexual and knows that the other man is, and the other man is fully aware that the first man understands all that. It was a little awkward, perhaps, but nothing more than that. I used to believe in a moral order, but then so did the Nazis, and their idea of moral order included murdering homosexuals in concentration camps, which was more than enough for me to change my own opinions. After the orgy of destruction Hitler inflicted upon Germany, it seems pointless to give a damn about what one man does in a bedroom with another.

"You're German, aren't you?"

"Yes."

"It's all right. I'm not one of these Englishmen who doesn't like Germans. I met a lot of your chaps in the war. Solid men, most of them. In forty-two I was in North Africa with the 4th County of London Yeomanry, in tanks. We were up against the DAK—the Deutsches Afrikakorps—which was the 15th Panzer Division in my neck of the woods. Good fighters, what? I'll say so. I sustained a head injury at the Battle of Knightsbridge, which ended my war. At least that's what we called it. Strictly speaking, it was the Battle of Gazala but one always thinks of it as the Battle of Knightsbridge."

"Why?"

"Oh. Well, that was the code name for our defensive position on the Gazala line: Knightsbridge. But to be quite honest there were so many chaps I knew in the 8th Army from Eton and Cambridge and my Inn of Court that it sometimes felt as if one was shopping in Knightsbridge. Not that I was an officer, mind. I joined up as an ordinary trooper. On account of the fact that I was a bit of a bolshie. And just to pay my own bar bills, so to speak. I never much liked all that damned officer malarkey."

He made it all sound like a long day in the cricket field.

"What about you, Walter?"

"I was well behind our lines and quite safe in Berlin. A man without honor, I'm afraid. Too old for all that. I was a captain in the Intendant General's Office. The Catering Corps."

"Ah. I begin to see a pattern."

I nodded. "Before the war I worked at the Hotel Adlon."

"Right. Everyone stays at the Adlon. *Grand Hotel*. The film, I mean. Vicki Baum, wasn't it? The Austrian writer."

"Yes, I think so."

"Thought so. I'm a writer myself. Books, plays. Working on a play right now. A comedy that's based on Shakespeare's *King Lear*. It's about a man who has three daughters."

"There's a coincidence."

Maugham laughed. "Quite."

"I suppose it would be too much of a coincidence if you were not related to the other Maugham who lives around here."

"He's my uncle. Matter of fact, he used to know Vicki Baum, when he was living in Berlin before the first war."

The drinks arrived and Robin Maugham grabbed his glass of white wine off the waiter's tin tray with the impatience of the true drunk. I should know; my own greenish glass had taken on the aura of the holy grail.

"He likes Germans, too. Willie. That's what we call the old man. Speaks it fluently. On account of the fact that before med school he spent a year at the University of Heidelberg. Uncle Willie loves Germany. He's particularly fond of Goethe. Still reads it in German. Which is saying something for an Englishman, I can tell you."

"Then we have something in common."

"You too, eh? Jolly good."

It was easy to see that Robin Maugham was a playwright. He had an easy way of speech about him, a talky, bantering sort of chat that concealed as much as it revealed, like a character you knew was going to prove much more consequential than he seemed if only by virtue of his prominence on the theater bill.

"You know, what with the bridge and the German, perhaps you'd like to make up a four at the Villa Mauresque one night. The old man is always keen to meet interesting new people. Of course, he's notoriously private, but I'll hazard a guess that the concierge at the Grand Hôtel—not to mention someone who worked at the famous Adlon—well, that person must be used to keeping a few confidences, what?"

"I'd be delighted to come," I said. "And you needn't worry about my mouth."

I thought about Anne French and what she might say when I told her I'd been invited up to the Villa Mauresque. It was possible she would perceive my invitation as an affirmation of her own strategy: to learn bridge in order to meet Somerset Maugham. But it seemed equally possible that she would see it as some kind of betrayal. And while for a brief moment I considered simply not telling her in order to spare her feelings, it seemed to me that my being there at all could only help to facilitate her own invitation. Alternatively, I might be her spy and report on how things really were at the Villa Mauresque, providing her with the color she needed for her book.

"But I feel I ought to read one of his novels," I said. "I'd hate

THE OTHER SIDE OF SILENCE

to have to admit that I haven't read any. Which one would you recommend?"

"A short one. My own favorite is *The Moon and Sixpence*. Which is about the life of Paul Gauguin. I'll lend you my own copy if you like."

Robin Maugham looked at his watch. "You know, it occurs to me that we could still make dinner at the villa. That is if you haven't already dined. Willie keeps a very good table. Annette, our Italian cook, is wonderful. Willie was in a good mood today. Rather absurdly, an invitation to the forthcoming wedding of Prince Rainier and Grace Kelly in Monaco seems to have left him as delighted as if he was getting married himself."

"I got an invitation myself but sadly I shall have to decline. It would mean finding all my decorations and buying a new suit, which I can ill afford."

Robin smiled uncertainly.

I looked at my own watch.

"But sure. Let's go. I don't mind interrupting my alcohol consumption with some food."

"Good." Robin drained his wineglass, scooped up the terrier, and pointed toward the end of the terrace. "Shall we?"

I climbed into my car and followed the Englishman's red Alfa Romeo up the hill and out of the town. It was a lovely warm evening with a light sea breeze and an edge of coral pink in the blue sky as if some nearer Vesuvius were in fiery eruption. Behind us the lightly clad myrmidons of Hermès filled the many waterside restaurants and narrow streets, while the miniature Troy that was the little port of Cap Ferrat bristled with innumerable tall masts and hundreds of invading white boats that jostled for undulating position on the almost invisible glass water, as if it mattered a damn where anyone was going or anyone came from. It certainly didn't matter to me.

FIVE

Approached along a narrow, winding road bordered by pine trees, the Villa Mauresque stood on the very summit of the Cap and behind a large wrought-iron gate with white plaster posts on one of which was carved the name of the house and what I took to be a sign against the evil eye, in red. It didn't slow me down and I drove through the gates in Robin Maugham's dust as if I had the nicest baby blue eyes in France. The place couldn't have looked more private if King Leopold II of Belgium had been living there with his pet pygmy and his three mistresses and his private zoo, not to mention the many millions he'd managed to steal from the Congo. By all accounts he had quite a collection of human hands, too, lopped off the arms of natives to encourage the others to go into the jungle and collect rubber, and I think the king could have taught the Nazis a few things about cruelty and running an empire. Unlike Hitler, he'd died in bed at the age of seventy-four. Once, he had owned the whole of Cap Ferrat, and the Villa Mauresque had been built for one of his confidants, a man named Charmeton, whose Algerian background had left him with a taste for Moorish architecture. I knew this because it's the sort of detail a concierge at the Grand Hôtel is supposed to know.

According to Robin Maugham, his uncle had owned the villa for more than thirty years. It was the type of place you could easily imagine a novelist writing about except that no one would have believed it, for the house seemed even more elaborate—inside and out—than I could have expected. Anne French was renting a nice villa. This one was magnificent and underlined Maugham's international fame, his enormous wealth, and his impeccable taste. It was painted white, with green shutters and tall green double doors, horseshoe windows, a Moorish archway entrance, and a large cupola on the roof. There was a tennis court, a huge swimming pool, and a beautiful garden full of hibiscus, bougainvillea, and lemon trees that lent the evening air the sharp citrus scent of a barber's shop. Inside were ebony wood floors, high ceilings, heavy Spanish furniture, gilded wooden chandeliers, blackamoor figures, Savonnerie carpets, and, among many others, a painting by Gauguin—one of those heavy-limbed, broad-nosed, Tahitian women that looks like she must have gone three rounds with Jersey Joe Walcott. Over the fireplace was a golden eagle with wings outspread, which reminded me of my former employers in Berlin, while all the books on a round Louis XVI table were new and sent from a shop in London called Heywood Hill. The soap I used to wash my hands in the ground-floor lavatory was still in its Floris wrapper, and the towels were as thick as the silk cushions on the Directoire armchairs. The Grand Hôtel felt like a cheaper version of what there was to be enjoyed at the Villa Mauresque. It was the sort of place where time and the outside world were not welcome; the sort of place it was hard to imagine could still exist in a ration-book economy that was recovering from a terrible war; the sort of place that was probably like the mind of the man who owned it, an elderly man in a double-breasted blue blazer that looked as if it had been made by the same London tailor as Robin's, with a face like a Komodo dragon lizard. He stood and came to shake my hand as his nephew made the introduction, and when he licked the lips of his thin, broad, drooping pink mouth, I would not have been surprised to have seen a tongue that was forked.

"Where have you been, Robin? We've delayed dinner for you, and you know I hate that. It's most inconsiderate to Annette."

"I dropped into the Voile for a drink and met a friend of mine. Walter Wolf. He's German and he's a keen bridge player and he was at a loose end so I thought I'd better bring him along."

"Is he indeed? I'm so glad." Maugham placed a monocle in his eye, looked directly at me, and smiled a rictus smile. "We d-don't see n-nearly enough G-Germans. It's a good sign that you're returning to the Riviera. It augurs well for the future that Germans can afford to come here again."

"I'm afraid you've got me wrong, sir. I'm not here for the season. I work at the Grand Hôtel. I'm the concierge."

"You're very welcome all the same. So, you play bridge. The most entertaining game that the art of man has devised, is it not?"

"Yes, sir. I certainly think so."

"Robin, you'd better tell Annette that we have an extra guest for dinner."

"There's always plenty of food, Uncle."

"That's not the point."

"I thought we could make a four with Alan, later."

"Excellent," said Maugham.

While Robin went to speak to the cook, Maugham himself took me by the arm and into the dark green Baroque drawing room, where a butler wearing a white linen jacket materialized as if from thin air and proceeded to make me a gimlet to my exact instructions and then a martini for the old man, with a dash of absinthe.

"I dislike a man who's not precise about what he wants to drink," said Maugham. "You can't rely on a fellow who's vague about his favorite tipple. If he's not precise about something he's going to drink then it's clear he's not going to be precise about anything."

We sat down and Maugham offered me a cigarette from the

box on the table. I shook my head and lit one of my own, which drew yet more of his approval, only now he spoke German—albeit with a slight stammer, the way he spoke English—probably just to show that he could do it, but given it was probably a while since he'd done it, I was still impressed.

"I also like a man who prefers to smoke his own cigarettes rather than mine. Smoking is something you have to take seriously. It's not a matter for experiment. I myself could no more smoke another brand of cigarette than I could take up marathon running. Tell me, Herr Wolf, do you like being the concierge at the Grand Hôtel?"

"Like?" I grinned. "That's a luxury I simply can't afford, Herr Maugham. It's a job, that's all. After the war, jobs in Germany weren't so easy to come by. The hours are regular and the hotel's a nice place. But the only reason I'm doing it is for the money. The day they stop paying me is the day I check out."

"I agree. I have no time for a man who says he's not interested in money. It means he has no self-respect. I myself only write for money these days. Certainly not for the pleasure of it." A tear appeared in his eye. "No, that went out of it a long time ago. Mostly I write because I've always done it. Because I can't think what the hell else to do. Unfortunately, I have never been able to persuade myself that anything else mattered. I'm eighty-two years old, Herr Wolf. Writing has become a habit, a discipline, and, to some extent, a compulsion, but I certainly wouldn't give what I write to anyone for free."

"Are you working on anything at the moment, sir?"

"A book of essays, which is to say, nothing at all of any consequence. Essays are like politicians. They want to change things and I'm not much interested in any change at my age."

A large and lumpish man with bad psoriasis and wearing a garishly colored shirt appeared and went straight to the drinks tray, where he mixed himself a drink as if too impatient to wait for the butler to fix one for him.

"This is my friend Alan," said Maugham, reverting to English. "Alan, do come and say hello to a friend of Robin's. Walter Wolf. He's German and we're hoping he's going to play a couple of rubbers with us after dinner."

The lumpish man came and shook hands just as Robin Maugham reappeared and announced that dinner was ready.

"Thank God," said Maugham.

"Ronnie Neame rang when you were in the bath," the lumpish man told Maugham. "It seems that MGM are going to make *Painted Veil* but want a different title. They want to call it *The Seventh Sin.*"

"Ugh." Maugham grimaced. "That's a fucking awful title."

"It's the seventh commandment," said Robin.

"I don't care if it's in the Treaty of Versailles. No one's shocked by adultery these days. Not since the war. Adultery's common. After Auschwitz, adultery's a minor misdemeanor. You mark my words: The film will make a loss."

We went into dinner.

Robin Maugham had not exaggerated; his uncle kept an excellent table. Dinner was eggs in aspic jelly, chicken Maryland, tiny wild strawberries, avocado ice cream—which I didn't care for—all washed down with an excellent Puligny and then an even better Sauternes. Afterward, Maugham lit a pipe, fixed a pair of horn-rimmed spectacles onto his nose, and led the way to the card table, where I partnered Robin and we played and lost two rubbers. The old man was a bridge demon.

"You're not a bad player, Herr Wolf. If I might give you a tip it's this: Never take a card out of your hand before your partner has declared. It preempts his play. Don't overreach for a card until it's your turn to play."

I nodded. "Thank you."

"Don't mention it."

When we'd finished playing cards Maugham sat next to me on the sofa with his legs tucked underneath him, revealing silk socks and sock suspenders, and asked me all sorts of personal questions.

"Are you married?"

"Three times. I've not had the best of luck with women, sir. The ones I married least of all. They're odd creatures who don't know what they want right up until the moment they decide on exactly what they do want, and when you don't give it to them right away, they're apt to get sore with you. The rest of the time, with the rest of the women I've known, it was my fault. My most recent wife left me because she didn't love me any-more. At least that's what she told me when she walked out with most of my money. But I think she was trying to let me down gently."

Maugham smiled. "You're bitter. I like that. Tra la la. Would you like another drink?"

"No, sir. I've had enough."

We talked a while longer until, at exactly eleven o'clock, W. Somerset Maugham declared that it was his bedtime.

"I like you, Herr Wolf," he said before he went upstairs. "Do come again. Come again soon."

SIX

Anne French was thrilled when, the following night at her house in the hills above Villefranche, I told her that I'd been up to the Villa Mauresque to have dinner and play cards.

"How exciting. What's it like? Is it very camp?"

"Camp" was not an English word I understood, and Anne had to explain.

"It's very English," she said, "although its origins are French, oddly enough. From the French term *se camper*, meaning 'to pose in an exaggerated fashion.' But in English we use it to describe anything outrageously or ostentatiously homosexual."

"Then, yes, it's very camp. Although I can't fault the old

man's taste. He lives very well. Everything is the best. There's a staff of about ten, including a butler and several gardeners. He doesn't eat a lot and doesn't drink much. Just talks and plays cards. Although there's no talk allowed when we're playing cards. He's a ferocious player. We're going to have to work hard to get you up to a standard where I can recommend that you take my place."

"Until then you can be my spy. The next time you go I want detailed descriptions of everything. Especially the house and gardens. Are there naked statues? Who still comes to stay? And find out what his opinions are on writers today. Who he rates. Who he hates. And his friend, of course. Do find out about him. By all accounts, the last one, Gerald, was a complete drunk and a rotter. Tell me, were there lots of boys? Was there an orgy?"

"No. That was disappointing. Maugham's friend and companion is a man with bad psoriasis named Alan Searle, who's also his secretary. Not obviously queer, unlike the nephew, who I'm surprised to find that I like. He's very genial and I think something of a war hero, on the quiet. It was all a very long way from Petronius." I shook my head. "If it comes to that, I liked the old man, too. Felt sorry for him. He's got all the money in the world, a beautiful house, famous friends, but he's not happy. Turns out we have that in common."

"You're not happy?"

I laughed. "Next question."

"Is he writing?"

"Essays."

"Oh. Nobody's interested in those. Essays are for schoolchildren. Did you get a look at his writing room?"

"No, but he told me you can see an exact reproduction of it in a television film called *Quartet* that was filmed in a studio three or four years ago."

"When are you going back?"

"I don't know. When they ask me, I suppose. If they ask me."

"Do you think they will?"

"He's eighty-two. At that age anything is possible."

"I'm not sure I agree. Surely—"

"Time is short for someone like that. Chances are, yes, they'll ask me again."

It so happened that it was the following night when I received a call at the hotel front desk asking if I might be free that evening; I was.

This time the great man was in a more expansive mood. He talked about meeting the Queen, and the many other famous people who'd been to the villa, including Churchill and H. G. Wells.

"What was Churchill like?" I asked politely.

"Looked like an old china doll. Very pink. Very doddery. Hair like spider's web. If you think I'm senile you should see him." He sighed. "It's very sad, really. Before the war—the first war—we used to play golf together. I made him laugh, you see. Lord, that must have been what—nineteen ten? Christ. Doesn't time fly?"

I nodded, and then for no reason that I can think of except that I wanted him to know I could, I quoted Goethe, in German.

"'Let's plunge ourselves into the roar of time, the whirl of accident; may pain and pleasure, success and failure, shift as they will—it's only action that can make a man.'"

"That's Goethe, isn't it?" said Maugham.

"*Faust*." I swallowed with difficulty. "Always chokes me a little."

Maugham nodded. "You're still a young-looking man, Walter. With a good twenty years of action ahead of you. But don't fuck it up, dear boy."

"No, sir. I'll try not to."

"I've fucked and fucked up a great deal in my life." He sighed. "Quite often of course they amount to the same thing. Seriously. I'd have been a knight of the realm by now if I hadn't fucked quite so egregiously. But then I expect you're used to that. You must see all kinds of egregious behavior down at the Grand Hôtel."

"Of course. But nothing I can talk about."

"The rich have time to fuck. But the poor only have time to read about it. They're too busy trying to make a living to fuck a lot."

"I expect you're probably right."

"And before the war, Robin tells me that you used to be the house detective at the Adlon Hotel in Berlin."

"That's right."

"You must have seen some even worse behavior then. Berlin was the place to be in the twenties. Especially for someone like me. My first play was produced in Berlin. By Max Reinhardt. At the Schall und Rauch cabaret theater. Tiny place."

"On Kantstrasse. I remember it. Sadly, I seem to remember everything. There's so much I'd like to forget but try as I might, it just doesn't happen. It's like I don't seem to be able to remember how. It's not too much to ask in life, is it? To forget the things that cause you pain. Somehow."

"Bitter and maudlin. I like that, too." He lit a cigarette from the silver box on the table. We were awaiting dinner and afterward the inevitable game of bridge. "I've remembered now. That's it. 'Funes the Memorious,'" said Maugham. "It's a story by Borges on just that very subject. A man who could not forget."

"What happened to him?" asked Robin.

"I've forgotten," said Maugham, and then laughed uproariously. "Dear old Max. He was one of the lucky ones. Jews, I mean. Got out in thirty-eight, and went to America, where he died, much too soon, in nineteen forty-three. Nearly all of my friends are gone now. Including the wonderful Adlon. My, that was a good hotel. Whatever happened to the couple who owned the place? Louis Adlon and his sweet wife, Hedda."

"Louis was murdered by the Russians in nineteen forty-five. With his riding boots and waxed mustaches he was mistaken for a German general." I shrugged dismissively. "Most of the Red Army were just peasants. Hedda? Well, I hate to think what happened to her. The same as the rest of the women in Berlin, I imagine. Raped. And raped again."

Maugham nodded sadly. "Tell me, Walter, how was it that you became the house detective at the Adlon?"

"Until nineteen thirty-two, I'd been a cop with the Berlin

police. My politics meant that I had to leave. I was a Social Democrat. Which for the Nazis was tantamount to being a Communist."

"Yes, of course. And how long were you a policeman?"

"Ten years."

"Christ. That's a lifetime."

"It certainly seemed that way at the time."

After dinner and a couple of rubbers, Maugham said, "I
want to talk to you in private."

"All right."

He took me up a wooden stair to his writing space, which
was inside a freestanding structure on top of a flat roof. There
was a big refectory table, a fireplace, and no windows with a
view that could distract a man from the simple business of writing a novel. A bookshelf held some favorite titles and, on a coffee table, a few copies of *Life* magazine. Another of Jersey Joe's
Tahitian sparring partners was up on the wall, but what with the
beam from the lighthouse at the southwestern end of the Cap,
it was a little like being on the deck of a ship of which Maugham
was the Ahab-like captain. We sat down at opposite ends of a big
sofa and then he came to the point.

"You strike me as an honest man, Walter."

"As far as it goes."

"One imagines that you wouldn't be working as a concierge
at the Grand if you weren't."

"Perhaps. But good fortune rarely walks you out the door to your car. Not these days." I shrugged. "What I mean to say is, we're all trying to make a living, Mr. Maugham. And if we can pull off the pretense that we're doing it honestly, then so much the better."

"You're an even bigger cynic than I am, Walter. I like you more and more."

"I'm German, Mr. Maugham. I've had a lot more practice with cynicism. We all have. It's the thousand-ton weight of German cynicism that caused the collapse of the Weimar Republic and gave us the thousand-year Reich."

"I suppose so."

"What can I do for you, sir? You didn't bring me up here to help me confess my sins."

"No, you're right. I came to tell you about a few of mine. The fact is, Walter, I'm being blackmailed again."

"Again?"

"I'm a rich old queer. I have more skeletons in my closets than the Roman catacombs. Being blackmailed is not so much an occupational hazard for a man like me as an existential condition. I fuck, therefore I am subject to demands for money, demands with menaces attached."

"Pay him, whoever it is. You're rich enough."

"This one is a professional."

"So go to the police."

Maugham smiled thinly. "We both know that isn't possible.

Blackmailers work on the same principle as the Mafia. They prey upon a vulnerable minority of people who can't go to the police. Their power is our silence."

"What I meant was, why tell me?"

"Because you used to be a policeman, and because I want your help."

"I don't see how I can be of assistance, Mr. Maugham. I'm a concierge. My detective days are long gone. I have a hard job seeing off the merry widows at the hotel, let alone a professional blackmailer. Besides, I'm a little slow on the uptake these days. I'm still trying to work out how you know I used to be a detective."

"You were ten years with the Berlin police. You told us yourself."

"Yes, but it was someone else who told you I'd been the house bull at the Adlon Hotel." I nodded. "But who? Wait, it was Hennig, wasn't it? Harold Heinz Hennig. I saw him arguing with your nephew in front of La Voile d'Or a couple of weeks ago. So that's his racket."

"Never heard of him."

"I forgot. He's not calling himself that anymore, is he? He's checked into the Grand under the name Harold Heinz Hebel. It was he who told you about me, wasn't it?"

"That's right. Hebel. He told my nephew about you. It was his idea that I should try to employ you, Walter."

"His idea?"

"He said he knew you from the war and that you were reliable. And honest. As far as it goes."

"That was nice of him. Not that he would know how to spell 'reliable' and 'honest.' The man is a criminal."

"I know."

"Well then, why take his recommendation? Why not hire a local man? A Frenchman."

"It's simple. You see, Walter, it's Harold Heinz Hebel who's blackmailing me."

"Now I really am confused."

"The fact is, Hebel's asking rather a lot of money for a compromising photograph of me and some other people. He wants me to feel that I can make a deal with him in complete confidence. He said you'd be the kind of man to make sure he kept his side of the bargain. And that you're not the type of man who would get nervous handling a large sum of money."

"Now I've heard everything. Blackmailers recommending detectives. Or ex-detectives. It sounds an awful lot like a salmon recommending a good poacher."

"It makes perfect sense when you think about it. A good deal isn't a good deal if either party feels he's been cheated. Hebel wants me to feel confident that I'm getting value for my money."

"I can't help you, Mr. Maugham. I like you. I liked my dinner. I feel sorry for you. But I'm just not able to help you."

"He said you'd say that. Hebel."

"He did, huh?"

"He said that I should let him know if you didn't want to help and then he could probably persuade you himself."

"Did he say how?"

Maugham smiled. "Oh my, yes. You're an interesting man, Walter. Or should I say Herr Gunther? Yes, you've had an interesting life. A career in the SS and the SD. Working for Dr. Goebbels, among others. You must tell me all about that sometime. It sounds quite fascinating. He said to tell you that if the French Sûreté were to find out that you're living down here under a false identity, you'd lose your job and you'd be deported back to Berlin, immediately, where the Americans would almost certainly hang you. For what reason, he didn't say. But I must admit it does sound serious."

"Fuck you," I said, and stood up. "Fuck you and your queer friend and your queer nephew."

"Actually I think we'll all be f-fucked unless we can work something out, Herr Gunther. Sit down. And let's talk about this s-s-sensibly." He nodded. "You know I'm right. So just calm down and think about what you're saying."

"Like I said before, Hebel is a false name, too. He could be deported." I sat down and lit a cigarette. I smoked it, too, but mostly I wanted to jam it in the old man's bloodshot eyeball.

"Perhaps. But he's willing to take the risk. The question is, are you willing to take the same risk, Herr Gunther? You've got a good job. With the prospect of making a little extra money from me. Shall we say a five percent handling fee? Why screw that just to bring him down?"

"Believe me, if you knew the man like I do, you'd know the answer to that question."

"Oh, I can believe it. The man is a snake. But, please, it doesn't have to be like this, Herr Gunther. All you have to do is agree to be my agent in this matter and all of this unpleasantness will go away. We can be friends. Don't you agree?"

"Is this him who's blackmailing me now, or you, Mr. Maugham?"

"Come now. I'm merely repeating what Hebel told me."

"Really? It strikes me that you've been on the end of blackmail often enough to know exactly how to apply a bit of pressure yourself."

"Maybe I do. For which you have my apologies, sir. But I'm a desperate man. You can take that to the casino and buy chips with it."

"Maybe you are desperate. But you can't trust this guy. Just because I'm the middleman doesn't change anything. Jesus, for all you know I'm part of the same scam. You don't know the first thing about me. How can you be sure that I'm not going to buy the photograph and then blackmail you myself? You can't. That's the thing about blackmail. It's a dirty business. Everyone's your friend right up until the moment they turn around and screw you."

"You make a good point. But I have no choice but to take the risk."

"Can I be blunt?"

"Be my guest."

"Everyone in the world knows you're queer. What of it? Does it affect anything? You've got your invitation to the royal wedding in Monaco. Has it crossed your mind that what you do in your bedroom really doesn't matter to people anymore?"

"That's true in France, perhaps. And Italy, certainly. But it matters a lot back in England. Homosexuality is a crime in my country and I should hate to be prevented from ever going back. Besides, there's rather more to the photograph than just my being queer."

I sat there smoking sullenly for several seconds.

"Ten percent. If I'm going to play agent I want a proper agent's commission. Ten percent."

"All right. Ten percent it is."

"So tell me about the photograph."

SEVEN

"B efore the war I worked for the British secret service," said Somerset Maugham. "Mostly I was based in Geneva. But some of the time I was stationed in what was then Petrograd. I shan't bore you with the details of my mission but I had a largish team of British agents under my control. Frankly, it's always been a business that attracted homosexuals, because queers are used to living their lives in secret—at least in England, where to be homosexual can still draw a sentence of up to two years in prison. Being silent about who and what you are is second nature to English queers. Things haven't improved a lot since the days of Oscar Wilde. That's why so many queers like Isherwood and

Auden went to Berlin in the twenties. Because it was a poof's paradise. And a good reason why I live here. Anyway, that's all by the by. I still have a lot of friends in SIS. Many of them, including Sir John Sinclair, the current head of MI6, were my agents. Besides, it's not the kind of business you ever really retire from."

I nodded grimly. "Don't I know it? I've been trying to retire from the detective business for years now, but it keeps dogging me."

"Yes. I am sorry about that."

"I doubt it."

Maugham stared into space for a moment and then adjusted his monocle. "Over the years since, I've done small jobs here and there for SIS," he said, continuing. "And I've welcomed friends and acquaintances at the Villa Mauresque. In nineteen thirty-seven, not long after I first bought this place, I had a number of friends to stay, including two boys just down from Cambridge University, who came down here in Victor Rothschild's Bugatti: Anthony Blunt and Guy Burgess. Subsequently they went to work for MI5: MI5 is the UK's domestic and counterintelligence agency. Blunt is rather less well known, at least to anyone outside of the world of fine art. But Guy Burgess is now infamous as a result of a press conference in Moscow just a few months ago when he and another man, Donald Maclean, were revealed to have been long-term spies for the Soviet Union—where they're both now living. You may have read about it in the newspapers. Anyway, Guy is, and always was, notoriously homosex-

THE OTHER SIDE OF SILENCE

ual. For that matter so is Anthony. And there's a photograph of us and several others lying naked beside my swimming pool. This is the photograph that your friend Harold Hebel is in possession of and which he is threatening to send to the press in England. I can't tell you the embarrassment it would cause me if it was revealed in the British newspapers that Guy and I were intimate. It's not just a question of our homosexuality, as I'm sure you can appreciate, Herr Gunther; it's also a matter of my loyalty to my country. I'm not a Soviet spy. Never have been. But given my service in Petrograd and my friendship with Guy, who knows the trouble the newspapers might cause for me? Certainly I had contact with people who worked for the Petrograd VRK and the Cheka—the forerunner of the KGB—when I was there. So you can see how vulnerable I am. Especially in America. Senator McCarthy hasn't just been going after Communists but homosexuals, too. The so-called Lavender Scare, for example. So. Visas to the United States might be withdrawn. Lucrative film contracts cancelled. MGM are making a film of one of my books as we speak. And United Artists plan to film a short story of mine next year. I may be the most successful writer in the world but I am not immune to public opinion. To say nothing of the embarrassment it might cause for my poor brother, Frederic, in England, who just happens to be the former Lord Chancellor. We've never been close, he and I, but I would like to spare him that, if I can. He's very old. Even older than I."

"Where did Hebel get this photograph?"

"There are a number of possible explanations. There were

several other men at that particular pool party who might have taken photographs: Dadie Rylands, Raymond Mortimer, Godfrey Winn, Paul Hyslop. But most likely it was my former friend and companion Gerald Haxton. I met Gerald during the Great War and we were together for the rest of his life. He died in nineteen forty-four. Gerald was a wonderful man and I loved him very dearly, but in spite of my generosity Gerald spent too much and was always in debt—mostly to the local casinos. In order to raise some extra cash he may have sold the photograph to a male whore called Louis Legrand with whom he was infatuated. Loulou was here a lot during the thirties, and many of the guests here at the Villa Mauresque—myself included—were his appreciative customers. He's in the photograph, too. He went to live in Australia after that, doing what I'm not entirely sure. But he turned up here a couple of years ago demanding money for some letters written to him by me and some of my more illustrious friends."

"And what happened then?"

"I paid him off. With a check."

"Who handled that business for you?"

"A lawyer in Nice. A Monsieur Gris."

"To your satisfaction?"

"Entirely. But before you ask I can't use him again. Unfortunately he died, quite recently."

"If Louis Legrand had been in possession of the photograph then surely he'd have used it at the time, wouldn't you say?"

"Yes, that's true. But I now suspect he might not have used it because he appears in it. Anyway, he was disappointed with his check, it has to be said, and threatened to come back with something 'more damaging.' My lawyer wrote him a letter informing Loulou that if he ever returned with more menacing demands for money we would certainly place the matter in the hands of the police. And since Loulou did have a conviction in France, for pimping, which is illegal in this country, he could easily have been deported."

"So, would you say it's possible that he decided to use the photograph at one remove and sold it to Harold Hebel?"

"Yes, I would."

"Do you have a print you can show me?"

Maugham went to his refectory desk and pulled open a drawer. He took out a largish black-and-white photograph and handed it to me, without hesitation or embarrassment, which, for anyone but him, would probably have taken some nerve. But at eighty-two I guess he was through apologizing or feeling ashamed of what he was.

It was a nice swimming pool; at each corner there was an ornamental lead pinecone, with a diving board at one end and, at the other, a marble mask of Neptune as big as an archery target. There was water in the pool, too. Gallons of it. I tried to keep my eyes on the water, but it was difficult. Any self-respecting satrap would have been quite satisfied with the swimming pool's obvious luxury and, quite probably, the many naked men and boys in various stages of arousal, who were grouped around the mask of Neptune and paying particular priapic attention to the god's open mouth. As obscene photographs go, it was up there with anything drawn by Aretino at his most provocative. I'd seen worse but not since the days of the Weimar Republic, when Berlin was the world capital of pornography.

"Who's who?" I asked. "It's a little difficult to tell anyone apart."

"That's Guy there," said Maugham. "That's Anthony. And that's Loulou."

"Boys will be boys, I suppose."

"Quite."

"Is he offering you the negative?"

"Yes."

"How much does he want for this?"

"Fifty thousand American dollars. In cash. For the negative and the prints."

"That's a lot of money for a holiday snap."

"Which is precisely why I want someone trustworthy to handle the matter for me. Someone who knows what the fuck they're doing. And who's not going to get too nervous or overexcited. Someone like you. At least that's what Hebel says. He tells me you have experience of dealing with blackmailers. Is that true?"

"Yes."

"In Berlin?"

"Yes."

"Would you care to tell me about that, perhaps? Just out of interest, I mean. If I'm going to give you five thousand dollars' commission I think I have a right to know what kind of service I'm buying, don't you?"

"That's the thing about blackmail," I said. "You'll soon find that you don't have any rights at all." I shrugged. "But sure. I'll tell you. Not that there's much to tell. This was quite a few years ago, mind, so unlike that photograph—unfortunately—the story's a little grainy now. It must have been January nineteen thirty-eight. Long after I'd quit the police, and a year or two after I'd left the Adlon. When I was working as a private investigator in Berlin and before—well, that doesn't matter. But there's one detail you know already. The identity of the blackmailer. You see, a leopard doesn't change its spots. The blackmailer was a man called Harold Heinz Hennig, but I fear you know him rather better as Harold Heinz Hebel."

EIGHT

BERLIN

1938

I'm being blackmailed."

"I'm very sorry to hear that, sir."

"My old adjutant told me you used to be a policeman and that now you're a private detective, and I decided that since we were old comrades that I might come to you for help."

"I'm very glad you did. It's been a long time, Captain."

"Twenty years."

"You look well, sir."

"Thanks for saying so, Gunther, but we both know that's not true."

Captain Achim von Frisch must have been in his sixties, but

he looked much older, desiccated even; his hair was pewter-colored and his once handsome face looked drawn and poorly shaven. He wore a dark gray coat with a thick fur collar, a monocle, and gray kid gloves, and he carried a silver-handled cane. But even the wax in his imperial-style, eagle's-wing mustache looked spent and dried up, and there was a strong smell of mothballs around his person. His manner was exactly what you might have expected of an old Prussian cavalry officer, stiff and courteous, but I remembered him as a kind man who'd cared deeply about the welfare of the men under his command of whom, in 1918, I had been one. It might have been twenty years since I'd seen him, but you don't forget that kind of comradeship. I'd have done anything for my old army captain. Once, he'd grabbed me by the collar of my tunic and pulled me clear as I blundered into a position on the line that was being scoped by an Australian sniper. A second later, a .303 bullet that was meant for my head hit the back wall of the trench.

We were in my suite of offices on the fourth floor of Alexander Haus. The premises were small but comfortable and I had a pretty good view of my old office window in the Police Praesidium on the opposite side of Alexanderplatz, where I'd spent many years as a detective until my politics obliged me to resign from the force. Thanks to the Nazis, the private investigator business was brisk—mostly missing persons. People were always going missing in Berlin under the Nazis.

My business partner, Bruno Stahlecker, lit his pipe noisily

THE OTHER SIDE OF SILENCE

and shifted uncomfortably on his chair, but he wasn't nearly as uncomfortable as poor Captain von Frisch.

"I think I would prefer it if it was just you and I talking about this, Gunther," he said.

"Herr Stahlecker is one of my operatives and enjoys my complete confidence. You can speak freely in front of him. I rely on him to carry out a lot of my investigative work."

"I appreciate that. However, I really must insist. This is quite difficult enough as it is."

I nodded. "Bruno, would you be kind enough to step outside for half an hour. Better still, could you fetch me a packet of Murattis?"

"Sure, boss, anything you say."

Stahlecker grabbed his coat off the hat stand and, still smoking his foul-smelling pipe, he went out into the bitter January cold.

When he'd gone, I lit my last cigarette, stoked the fire, tidied my paper clips, polished my fingernails, and waited patiently for Captain von Frisch to come to the point. Patience is the key with every client who is being blackmailed. They're so used to paying someone to keep their dirty little secret that it's almost unthinkable they should just break the silence and start talking about it, and to someone they haven't seen since the war.

"I don't mind telling you that the last five years have been hell," he said, and, taking out a handkerchief, he pressed it to the corner of his eye. "Often I have considered ending my life. But my old mother would be dreadfully upset if I did something like that. She's ninety. And I am forced to employ a nurse to look after me, such has been the decline in my health. It's my heart, you see. In time the worry of all this will certainly kill me. I just hope I don't die before she does. That would break her heart."

In his large gray military coat, which so far he had refused to remove—it wasn't a great fire, and he'd said he felt the cold, abnormally so—von Frisch resembled an old and venerable German battleship about to be scuttled at Scapa Flow and even now he let out such a profound and hopeless sigh that it was as if this badly damaged ship were already plunging through the depths to a watery grave on the bottom of the freezing North Sea.

"You should have telephoned, sir. Or written. I'd have been glad to come to your house. Where are you living these days?" I picked up my pen and prepared to write down a few details.

"Southwest Berlin. Ferdinandstrasse, twenty-six, in East Lichterfelde. Just around the corner from the S-Bahn station. Thank you, it's kind of you to say so, but the nurse is a sweet girl and I'd hate her to overhear anything of my own sordid past. A good nurse is hard to find these days. Although she is becoming rather expensive."

"Surely the baron is still a rich man."

"Not anymore. These terrible people have all but bled me dry."

"I see. Then perhaps you'd better just tell me about it."

He unbuttoned his coat and started to relax a little.

"I never married. Perhaps you knew that. And if you didn't then perhaps you can understand why I didn't, Gunther. When a man chooses not to marry he tells his mother that for all kinds of reasons he's never met the right girl, but mostly there's just one reason. The oldest reason of all. That there never could be such a thing as the right girl. If you know what I mean." He smiled thinly. "I imagine that it can't be the first time you've encountered this sort of thing."

"I understand perfectly, sir. During the Weimar Republic, when I was a cop at the Alex, I think I saw every facet of human behavior known to man. And quite a few that were unknown, too. Believe me, I'm immune to this kind of thing. Moral outrage is something only Nazis seem to suffer from these days."

This wasn't true, of course, but you have to say that to your clients or they'll never open up. I have just as much moral outrage as the next man, provided that man isn't called Adolf Hitler. According to the English *Daily Mail*—currently the best-selling newspaper in Berlin because it's the only paper in which the story appears—the Führer and most of the German High Command were currently exhibiting a great deal of outrage concerning the marriage of the minister of War, Field Marshal von Blomberg, to a woman of low birth and even lower morals named Erna Gruhn. Just how low was a matter of common knowledge in and around the Alex because Erna Gruhn was a prostitute and a former nude model. It was said the morals boys had a file on her that was almost as thick as von Blomberg's skull.

"In November nineteen thirty-three," began von Frisch, "I met a boy in the lavatories at Potsdamer Platz station. His name was Bavarian Joe and he was—well, he was—"

I nodded. "A warm boy for a cold night. I get the picture, Captain. No need to say any more about exactly what happened. Best get to the squeeze. I mean, the blackmailer."

"Following this liaison, while I was boarding a westbound train, another man got on and told me he was a police officer. I think he said his name was Commissioner Kröger. It wasn't. He isn't even a police officer, let alone a commissioner. Anyway, he said he'd seen exactly what had happened and threatened to place me under arrest for being a 175er, which is to say a homosexual. Then he offered to drop the charges if I would pay him five hundred marks in cash. I had about two hundred on me at the time so I handed this over and promised to take him to my bank the next day, where I would pay him the balance. And I did."

"Which bank was this?"

"The Dresdner Bank, on Bismarckstrasse."

I nodded and made a note of the bank, not that it was relevant, but most clients like to see you taking a few notes.

"I thought that was the end of it. But a few days later Schmidt—that's his true name, Otto Schmidt—returned with another man, who turned out to be a real Gestapo officer called Harold Heinz Hennig, who worked for Department II-H, which exists, I am informed, to investigate homosexuality. They asked me for more money—to be precise, another thousand marks. And once again I paid up. They said if I refused to pay they'd make sure I was sent to a concentration camp, where I'd be lucky to last the year."

"Cash?"

"Always. Small bills, too."

"Hmm."

"But this was just the start, and since then I have paid this pair of scoundrels a thousand a week, which at this present moment in time amounts to almost two hundred and fifty thousand marks. I'm afraid I could ill afford the taxi that brought me here this morning."

I whistled. Two hundred and fifty thousand marks is as attractive a figure as any you can see outside of a life class in the Berlin School of Art.

"That's a lot of money."

"Yes it is."

"Look, with all due respect, sir, this horse has bolted. I fail to see how it might help for me to help you close the stable door now."

"For the simple reason that I am now being blackmailed by the same people—or at least one of them, Captain Hennig—in an entirely different way and for an entirely different reason. Not for money. At least not for the moment. It's my silence that seems to be required right now. If it wasn't so tragic it might be funny. But this is where I need your help, Gunther. I assume that the Gestapo possesses a code of conduct. That corruption is frowned upon even among Nazis. Presumably this Captain Hennig has a superior, and one imagines he would hardly welcome the news of bribery in his own department."

"What's this man Hennig like?"

75

"Young, smooth, arrogant. Clever, too. Always plainclothes. Good suits. Buys his hats at Habig. Rolex wristwatch. Drives a black Opel Kapitän, which means I've never been able to follow him. We always meet in public places. And never the same place twice."

I nodded slowly. I don't mind trouble. It's an occupational hazard, but already this case was starting to look as if it might be more than the usual amount of trouble, which, in Nazi Germany, is always dangerous.

"As far as I can remember," I said, "II-H is run by two re-volting bastards, Josef Meisinger and Eberhard Schiele. The chances are that they're getting a large piece of everything this man Hennig's extorting from you. I'd be very surprised if they weren't. But Meisinger does have a superior he reports to. A man I know called Arthur Nebe, who's not entirely without princi-ples. It may be that he takes a dim view of these sordid activities. I suppose we might persuade him to get them to lay off."

"I hope so."

"But wait, you said they were now blackmailing you to keep quiet. If it's not too embarrassing, maybe you'd like to explain why. I'm not entirely clear about that."

"Actually, it's not embarrassing at all. Otto Schmidt spent time in prison. While he was there Schmidt informed some other people in the Gestapo that he had been blackmailing me for some years and the idiots managed to confuse me with the commander in chief of the army—Blomberg's number two, Col-onel General Freiherr Werner von Fritsch. That's Fritsch with a *t*, you understand. He's an officer of the old school and very definitely not a Nazi, so perhaps they are looking for an excuse to get rid of him. In other words, it would seem they have deliberately mistaken him for me in an attempt to smear his name and force his resignation from the army. And I am now being blackmailed to keep my mouth shut regarding what I know about this."

"By Hennig."

"By Hennig."

"And who's the officer in the Gestapo who's trying to pin this on General von Fritsch?"

"A commissar by the name of Franz Josef Huber. And a Detective Inspector Fritz Fehling."

"But it doesn't make any sense," I objected. "They're already trying to get rid of von Blomberg. Surely von Fritsch is best placed to succeed von Blomberg. Why get rid of him, too?"

"Sense? None of this makes sense. As far as I can see, dumb and unswerving loyalty to Hitler is all that matters to the Nazis. The question as it affects me is this: How far up the chain of command does this go? That is what I need to know. Does this knowledge that von Fritsch is entirely innocent extend all the way up the chain to Göring and to Hitler?"

"And if it did? What then, sir?"

"Just this. A military court has been appointed to hear General von Fritsch's case on March tenth in the Preussenhaus. It will be chaired by Göring, Raeder, and Brauchitsch, and the charges will relate to Paragraph 175 of the German Penal Code, which makes homosexuality illegal. Before then I need to decide whether, as a point of honor, I should insist on giving evidence and tell the court that it was me and not the general who was the subject of the Gestapo's blackmail. In other words, how much am I risking by taking on the Gestapo?"

"Off the top of my head I'd say that it's never a good idea to go toe to toe with the Gestapo. The concentration camps are full of people who thought they can be reasoned with. How ill are you, sir? What I mean is, can you travel? Have you considered leaving the country? There's no dishonor in running away from the Nazis. Many others have already done so."

"I might have done that," he admitted, "if it wasn't for my elderly mother. I might just find the strength to travel somewhere. But she certainly would not. And I could never leave her. That would be unthinkable."

"I can see you're in a difficult position."

"That's why I'm here."

"Look, have you spoken to General von Fritsch about this? I imagine he'd be quite interested in what you have to say."

"No, not yet. As I say, I want to find out how far up the chain this goes before I go out on a limb for the general. But if it should come to that, I'd prefer you to make the first contact with his legal counsel. I'm afraid I have little energy for waiting around the Bendlerstrasse to see him. I intend to retire to my bed the minute I return home."

"Do you know who his legal counsel is? I take it this is another senior army officer."

"Count Rüdiger von der Goltz. You'll find him at the Bend-lerstrasse, too."

"All right. But first I'll speak to Nebe. And perhaps also to Franz Gürtner, the minister of Justice. Perhaps he'll know what to do."

"Thank you." Von Frisch took out his wallet and opened it and thumbed two Prussian blues onto my desk. "From what your colleague told me earlier, this should be enough to secure your services on my behalf for one week."

"That's more than enough, sir."

The fact was, I'd have handled his case for nothing. But there was no point in arguing with the old man; Achim von Frisch was an old-school Prussian with a lot of pride and he'd no more have taken my charity than he'd have offered to clean my office or fetch my cigarettes.

After he'd gone I sat around and took the Lord's name in vain a lot, which only raised my blood pressure. Then Bruno came back with my Murattis and I had to smoke one right away and also take a bite of the bottle of Korn I had in my desk drawer. Then I told him what von Frisch had told me and he cursed a lot and took a drink, too. We must have looked like a couple of priests on holiday.

"This isn't a case," he said, "it's an unfolding political scandal. Take my advice, boss; leave it alone. You might as well look for Amelia Earhart as try and help this old Fridolin."

"Maybe."

"There's no maybe about it. If you ask me, you'd be putting

your head in the lion's mouth, with little prospect of getting it back with both ears. This is just the Nazis consolidating their grip on power. First the Reichstag fire, then the Night of the Long Knives when they murdered Ernst Röhm and the SA leadership, and now this—the emasculation of the army. It's just Hitler's way of telling the Wehrmacht that he's in charge. You know, I wouldn't be at all surprised if he makes himself the new minister for War. After all, who else is there?"

"Göring?" I murmured, not quite believing it myself.

"That fat popinjay? He's already too powerful for Hitler's taste."

I nodded. "Yes, you're right, of course. Too powerful and too popular with the people at large." I shook my head. "But I have to do something. In Turkey, Captain von Frisch saved my life. But for him, there would be a large hole in my head where my brains should be."

I'd handed Bruno the straight line for the joke and of course he did not disappoint; my business partner is nothing if not predictable, which, for the most part, is an excellent quality in a partner.

"There *is* a large hole in your head where your brains should be. There is if you take the captain on as a client."

"I already did. I gave him my word I'd try to help. Like I say, he saved my neck. The least I can do is try to save his."

"Look, Bernie, that's what happens in a war. It doesn't mean anything. Saving someone's life was just common courtesy in the trenches. Like giving a man a light for his cigarette. If I had

ten marks for every bastard's life I saved I'd be a rich man. Forget it. He probably has. It doesn't mean anything, Bernie."

"You don't mean that."

"No. All right. I don't. So, how about this instead? Survival
then was just a matter of luck, that's all. Why pay it any regard
now?"

I picked up my hat.

"Where are you going?" he asked.

"To Gestapo headquarters in Prinz-Albrecht-Strasse," I said.
"I'm going to find that lion."

NINE

FRENCH RIVIERA
1956

I sipped the perfectly mixed gimlet that Maugham's stone-faced butler had just brought up to the rooftop writing aerie and winced a little as I felt the navy-strength gin entering my hardening arteries like a good quality formaldehyde. Why else does anyone drink? Then I lit a cigarette, pulled hard on the filter, and waited for the sweet Virginia tobacco to deliver the coup de grâce to my senses after the dulling effect of the alcohol. Why else does anyone smoke? Meanwhile, a thin black cat had entered the room, and something about its stealthy, careful movements suggested that it was my own soul's dark relation, come to make sure that I didn't tell the old English writer too much. Never trust a writer, the cat seemed to be telling me; they write all sorts of things down. Things you didn't mean to tell them. Especially this one. He already knows your name; don't give him any more information. He'll use it in some book he's writing.

"I'd be grateful if you kept all that to yourself," I said. "Me being a former detective from Berlin. It's not something I want people to know about."

"Of course. You have my word."

"Anyway it's not a story in which anyone comes out with very much credit," I said. "Myself included."

"That's rather the point of a good story," said Maugham. "I dislike heroes at the best of times and I much prefer men with flaws. Believe me, that's what sells these days."

"Then the surprise is that I haven't been in a novel already. Seriously, though. In retrospect, I should have done a lot more to talk the captain out of his chosen course of action. But he was my old commander and I was used to doing what he asked. Which isn't enough of an excuse, really. But there it is. It's just another regret I have in the ten-volume apologia that's the story of my life."

"Ten volumes, eh? That sounds interesting."

"Big print, though."

"So what h-happened?" he asked. "In your story."

"Nothing good," I said. "It was a disaster for the captain, and in time for me, as well. It brought me back to the attention of General Heydrich, who, later that year, blackmailed me into returning to the police, which meant working for him and, eventually, the SD."

"Blackmailed? What did he have on you?"

I smiled. "Nothing in particular. Only the threat of extreme violence. That's the most effective blackmail of all. The Nazis had so many ways of threatening violence to a person that it's sometimes hard to remember that this was the German govern- ment we're talking about and not a bunch of Chicago gangsters. If I'd refused to do what he asked—work for him—I'd have been a dead man. No question. Heydrich always got what he wanted."

The cat blinked up at me with slow disbelief, as if question- ing the truth of that assertion. Cats just know when someone is lying or, in my case, bending the truth to suit my new persona. That's probably why I don't own a cat.

"And did you go to Gestapo headquarters? To put your head in the lion's mouth?"

"Yes. I met with Huber and Fehling. They were the two Gestapo officers who were charged with investigating the von Fritsch case. It was immediately clear to me that these two pos- sessed the arrogance of men who enjoyed the full confidence of people much higher in rank than themselves—Himmler, I think, and probably Heydrich, too. As you can imagine, they were less than helpful; they certainly didn't like the idea of their case against the general going up in smoke because Otto Schmidt was about to be proved an obvious liar. It was lucky for me that while I was there I actually saw their boss, Arthur Nebe. He didn't speak to me, but after he'd had a word with Huber, they decided to let me go. Nebe always had a soft spot for me, so I figure it was his call. All the same, I was warned in no uncertain terms that I was forbidden to make contact with Captain von Frisch again or with the general's legal counsel, Count Rüdiger von der Goltz. But I was always an insubordinate sort and I went to army headquarters anyway, where I spoke to another military judge—Karl Sack was his name—and put him in the picture. And it was he who informed the general's lawyers of my captain's willingness to give evidence against the Gestapo's star witness, Otto Schmidt.

"By then things were moving more quickly than I knew, and with a greater ruthlessness than even I could have conceived. Captain von Frisch had already been arrested at his home in Lichterfelde and taken into what the Gestapo laughingly called 'protective custody' at their Prinz-Albrecht-Strasse HQ. That usually meant something bad was going to happen, and it did. There they subjected him to a terrible beating from which he never really recovered. But he was immensely brave and refused to change his story—that he was the von Frisch who had actually committed the homosexual act in the lavatories at Potsdamer Platz station, not the general—and eventually they were obliged to let him go. Hennig made me and my partner come and fetch von Frisch from his cell in the basement of the Gestapo HQ, which I can still remember in awful detail. It's not the kind of thing you ever really forget.

"He was lying naked on the floor of the cell in a pool of blood and urine and, for several minutes, we thought he was dead. His whole body was as purple as a ripe plum—he was actually bleeding through his ears—and it was only when I touched him that he moaned and we realized that, incredibly, he was still alive. The Gestapo were very good at beating a man within an inch of his life, and sometimes nearer than that. A cursory examination of his body revealed he was suffering, probably, from several broken ribs, a broken collarbone, a broken jaw, and multiple contusions. All of his fingernails and several of his teeth had been torn out with a pair of pliers and one of his eyes was bulging horribly out of its socket. I'd seen men beaten before, but never as badly as that and certainly never one as old. Without a stretcher on which to carry him we were obliged to lift him out to my car in a filthy old blanket and only permitted to take him to the Charité Hospital on condition that we did not tell the medical staff the truth of how he had come by his injuries, so we were obliged to make up a real Bremen Town musician of a tale that he had sleepwalked his way out of the house and into the path of a tram. Not that they believed us, mind. They'd seen men, and women, who'd been beaten up by the Gestapo and SA many times before. How he'd resisted all of that and stuck to his story I'll never know.

"In spite of his injuries, somehow the captain managed to stage enough of a recovery for him to make it into the military court some five weeks later. On March second, nineteen thirty-eight, he gave his evidence and directly contradicted the story given by his original blackmailer, Otto Schmidt. The proceedings were an absolute farce. I sat and watched the whole thing in the Preussenhaus and even Hermann Göring looked embarrassed. Everyone could see he'd been badly beaten and everyone knew by who but somehow this evidence was ignored. Thanks to the captain, General von Fritsch was acquitted. But the mischief was already done, and while he retained his military rank he was not reinstated as commander in chief. He subsequently returned to his regiment and was killed during the invasion of Poland in September nineteen thirty-nine. There are some who believe he put himself in the way of a hero's death. And that would have been quite typical of a man of that background.

"After his dismally unconvincing performance in court, I heard Otto Schmidt was rearrested a couple of weeks later and taken to a concentration camp—probably Sachsenhausen—where I imagine he died wearing a pink triangle. Jews in the camps were forced to wear a yellow star. Homosexuals wore a pink triangle. It meant that the guards could devise punishments to fit the crime, as they saw it. Which must have been terrible. Because of the six million, it's usually forgotten that lots of German homosexuals also met violent deaths in the camps. The Nazis never seemed to run short of minorities to persecute."

"Dreadful," said Maugham. "It's tragic the number of queers who are blackmailed. You would think the very frequency of it would make it less tragic somehow, and that those of us with coarser frames could hardly bear much of it. And yet queers like me regard it almost as an occupational hazard. I often wonder what it is that other men seem to have against queers. I think it's the importance we attach to things that most men find trivial and the cynicism with which we regard the subjects the common man holds essential to his spiritual welfare. That and an abnormal interest in other men's c-cocks."

I laughed. "Yes, probably."

"And the poor old captain?" he asked. "What became of him?"

"His health was completely broken after the Gestapo's treatment. I kept up with him for a month or two after that, but then he was obliged to leave his house in Lichterfelde for lack of money and I'm afraid I lost touch with him. His eventual fate is unknown to me but it's quite possible he also ended up in a concentration camp for one reason or another. By then the captain's posh army friends were hardly in a position to prevent something like that from happening. Hitler had achieved his aims of becoming commander in chief and minister of War within the space of a few weeks. A few days after the von Fritsch verdict, Germany invaded Austria and von Blomberg and the von Fritsch case were immediately forgotten as almost all of Germany and Austria now hailed Adolf Hitler as the new Messiah. In Berlin not quite so much as in Vienna. In defense of my own city, I feel obliged to mention that left-leaning Berliners never took to Hitler the way the Austrians did. But that's another, longer story.

"Harold Hennig was demoted and later transferred to the security police in Königsberg; we met again when I was transferred there from Berlin, in nineteen forty-four, but again, that's another story, too. This man has been blackmailing men like you, sir, for more than twenty years. He's a professional and he knows what he's doing. We mustn't expect him to make any mistakes of the kind that were typical of the way the Nazis handled the case against General von Fritsch. He won't. In fact, it's my guess he intends to put the squeeze on me, in a smaller way than with you, sir. After all, he knows my real identity and a great deal of my true history. I'd say that he'll squeeze me not because he can make money out of me—I don't have much—but just because he can. With him it's a matter of inclination and habit. A way of demonstrating his power over another person."

"I'm sorry."

Maugham sipped his dry martini; I could smell the absinthe in his glass. It lent the cold vermouth and vodka a sort of corrupt edge, a bit like the inscrutable old man himself.

"Might I ask you a personal question?"

"You can ask but I may not answer."

"Have you ever killed a man?"

"Killing's legal in wartime. Or so we were often told."

"I'll take that as a yes. But do you think you could ever do it again?"

"It's like having a drink. It's hard to stop after just one. But it's a lot more difficult to kill someone than it ever seems on the pages of a novel."

"Ah, yes, where would art be without murder?"

"And yet it's a lot easier, too. Anyone who can slice a loaf can cut a throat. But it's been a long time since I pulled the trigger on a man. Believe it or not, I came down here to get away from all that."

"What I'm asking is if perhaps you could arrange for Herr

Hebel to have an accident. What I mean to say is that a car might easily knock him down. Or the brakes on his own car might be fixed to fail on some precipitous corner. There are plenty of those around here. I'd be quite prepared to pay you what I'm going to have to pay him, just to be sure that he's not going to come back and ask for more. I mean it. Fifty thousand dollars if you bump him off. At my age one is inclined to consider anything for a quiet life. Even murder. And frankly that isn't such a crime these days, is it? Not since the war. Look, all I'm asking is that you think about it."

"I know what you're asking, sir. And the answer is no. I'd much prefer to disappear again than have to kill our friend Harold Hebel. *Fiat justitia, pereat mundus.* Let justice reign even if the world should perish from it. That's just my version of the starry skies above me and the moral law within me."

"What's that—Kant?"

I nodded. "It's not because I care what happens to Hebel. I wish him as much ill as can befall any man. And there was certainly a time when I'd have cheerfully murdered him without a second thought. It's that I care about what happens to me rather more than him. I have no wish to add an eleventh volume to that ten-volume *apologia pro vita sua* I was telling you about before. Besides, you have no way of knowing what elaborate precautions a man like that has already taken with his life. He almost expects to be murdered. I daresay he has already sent a local lawyer an envelope that is to be opened in the event of his sudden death while he's down here in Cap Ferrat."

"That's a disturbing thought."

"It's certainly what I would do in his handmade English brogues."

"Yes, Robin noticed them, too. It's just too awful to be blackmailed by a chap who goes to the same shoemaker as oneself. At least Louis Legrand looked like what he was: a cheap little hustler. Apparently, this fellow looks like a successful businessman."

Maugham lit a cigarette and his eyes turned melancholy.

"Pity," he said with a touch of sardonic amusement. "That we can't kill him, I mean. I should like to have helped commit one truly criminal act in my life. Especially now that I am so highly regarded. It would have amused me greatly if I'd been able to attend the royal wedding while planning a murder."

"There's nothing to stop you killing him," I said.

"Even when I was in the service in Russia and I had to carry a revolver I was never much of a shot. And my eyesight is not up to much. So I'd be sure to miss. Unless it was a critic I was shooting at. I'm damned sure I could hit Harold Hobson, the theater critic, with no problem at all."

"Then one of your friends. Your butler, if he's as handy with a gun as he is with the gin. Or Robin, perhaps."

"If one had a revolver, one might almost suggest it to him," said Maugham. "But I'm afraid I wouldn't know where to get such a thing."

"Guns are easily obtained," I said. "It's the guts to use one in cold blood that are harder to find."

"I suppose so." Maugham thought for a moment. "Robin

could do it, I think. Kill Hebel, I mean. I'm certain he killed people during the war. Your people. He was mentioned in dispatches, you know. But on second thought he'd certainly botch something like a murder and leave a crucial piece of evidence behind: one of those monogrammed gold cuff links, perhaps. Or more likely his fucking business card. In many ways Robin is very unworldly. My fault, really. I've insulated him from the real world for pretty much all his life."

"Then you'd best not ask him in case he feels obliged to say yes."

"I think you're probably right."

"What happens now? Did Hebel explain if I'm supposed to make contact with him? Or if he'll make contact with me? And what about the money? Do you have that ready for him?"

"The cash is in my safe downstairs. And he said he would leave a note for you, explaining where and when he wants the money paid. The sooner the better, one imagines."

TEN

Sunday morning arrived as hot as a parboiled cicada. The Grand Hôtel's honey-marble lobby was air-conditioned so relentlessly, however, that I was glad of my thick morning coat even though it made me look like my grandfather, who was a civil servant and worked all his life at the Prussian House of Representatives in Berlin where, in 1862, he'd heard Bismarck give his famous "Blood and Iron" speech. I missed my grandfather. And for a moment I remembered how, when I was a small boy, he would take me from his house near Fischerinsel to visit the bear pit nearby. Behind my desk I must have resembled a bear in a pit, standing up on my hind legs whenever a guest came close in the hope that I might please them and earn myself a tip. Hotel guests drifted in, drifted out, drifted upstairs, drifted out to the swimming pool, drifted in to breakfast, lunch, and dinner and all in a variety of holiday costumes, some of which were almost as absurd and unsuitable as the black wool morning coat worn by a grand hotel concierge. A few of the guests even drifted off to the church in Beaulieu, but mostly they stayed put at the refrigerated hotel. I didn't blame them. It was too hot for religion but then, like many Prussians, I was always more pagan by inclination and background. For Bismarck it had been military spending—metaphorically, blood and iron—that had been the key to Prussia's significance in Germany; for me it was always the fact that Prussia had remained a total stranger to Christianity until finally it was conquered by the pope's Teutonic Knights in 1283. Ever since then, God has been punishing us harshly for the tardiness of our conversion to his church. Now, that's what I call a chosen people. It explained a lot of German history. It explained the impenetrable black forest that was my own dark soul, and it certainly explained my sense of humor, which was never very far away when giving the hotel guests directions, buying tickets for the theater, or handling an exchange of foreign currency, usually involving U.S. dollars. Americans always complained about the rate of exchange in spite of the fact they were the richest tourists on the Riviera that year. Americans were the richest tourists on the Riviera every year, a reputation that seemed to bring most of them a great deal of enjoyment but also had the effect of their paying almost twice as much as anyone else did and which the French unashamedly called *le tax américain*. Price gouging was one thing and you could hardly blame the cash-strapped French for giving in to the temptation to demand too much money in restaurants and taxis. Demanding money with menaces was quite another. In my book, blackmail is one of the worst crimes there is, since it can and does often last a lifetime, and I can still remember the enormous pleasure with which I learned that Leopold Gast, Berlin's most notorious blackmailer, had been sentenced to life imprisonment in 1929, after one of his many mostly female victims committed suicide, but not before writing a detailed letter to the police—a letter that later convicted him. Frankly, the guillotine would have been too good for a loathsome man like Gast. And it was with a similar degree of loathing that I now regarded Harold Heinz Hennig, aka Harold Hebel, as he walked nonchalantly across the hotel lobby to my station. He was smiling, too, like a wolf who'd just eaten the granny, which only served to exacerbate my hatred of the handsome, younger man. I caught a strong smell of cologne, noted the expensive Cartier gold watch on the tanned wrist of the arm resting on the desk, and found myself wanting to cut the limb off and make him eat it. It was with this pleasing image that I entertained myself while we spoke.

"Herr Hebel," I said in German, staring coldly at him like a porcelain dog. "What can I do for you?"

He put a manicured hand inside the breast pocket of his Savile Row jacket and withdrew a buff-colored envelope, which he then handed to me. "If you have a spare few moments, I was wondering if you might write a translation of this letter from French into German for me? My French isn't nearly as good as yours, Herr Wolf, and it contains some technical terms that are frankly beyond me."

These were the first words he'd spoken to me since January 1945, and it took all of my self-control not to remind him of this or to punch him in the nose. Hebel knew that, of course, but it was all part of a careful act that he should pretend he and I were almost strangers. His voice carried the rasping edge of a growl, like a big cat, or a guard dog.

"Certainly, sir. I'll get right onto it."

"Take your time, my dear fellow," he said affably. "There's no hurry. Sometime this afternoon would be just fine."

"Very well, sir."

"You can leave both versions in my room if you like. I'll pick them up tomorrow."

And then he went out into the fierce heat and handed a tip to the parking valet, who ran off to fetch his car.

I was on my mid-morning break before I opened the envelope and carefully read Hebel's typewritten instructions on how and where and when the blackmail money was to be paid. Then I went into the back office and called Somerset Maugham at the Villa Mauresque, and when his friend and secretary, Alan, fetched him to the phone, I told the old man to have the money ready for collection that same evening.

"He's made contact then?" Maugham was speaking German, which suited me fine; he seemed to like speaking German to me.

"Yes."

"What did you think of him?"

"The same thing I thought more than ten years ago. That I'd like to see him dead."

"The offer's still there."

"No, thanks. I don't care to murder anybody, Mr. Maugham. Even the people I don't much like."

"Can he be trusted?"

"No, of course he can't. He's a snake. But this is a big payday for him, and he'll want things to proceed without any problems. So, to that extent, everything should go according to plan. At least tonight. After that, your guess is as good as mine."

"How shall I pack it? The money, I mean. In a parcel?"

"A parcel would have to be unwrapped so the money could be counted. No, anything that slows things down tonight is to be avoided. A bag would be good. Preferably one that you don't mind giving away to a bastard like Hebel."

"Would a Pan American Airlines flight bag be suitable, do you think?"

"I don't know. Can that hold fifty thousand dollars?"

"I should say so."

"In which case, use it. Either way, have the money ready by seven o'clock. The meet is at eight. I'll bring the negative and the photograph straight to the Villa Mauresque, as soon as I have them."

"Fifty thousand dollars," he exclaimed grumpily. "Must be the most expensive fucking photograph in history."

"A picture can tell a thousand words. Isn't that what they say?"

"Christ, I hope not. Otherwise I'm out of f-fucking work."

"Look, sir, it's probably best that none of the words that this particular picture can tell are ever heard outside of a Turkish bathhouse or a novel by Marcel Proust. So you'd best reconcile yourself to paying up."

"That's easy for you to say, Mr. Wolf. Fifty thousand dollars is fifty thousand dollars."

"You're right. And I'll admit, fifty thousand pictures of Washington are fifty thousand stories I'd love to hear. So, don't pay him. Tell him to go to hell and take the flak. It's up to you, sir. But sometimes, when it's absolutely necessary, everyone has to eat flies."

"Suppose I give you the money and you drive straight for the Italian border? You could be in Genoa before midnight and on a boat to fuck knows where."

"And leave my wonderful job here at the Grand Hôtel? I don't think so. Every man likes to delude himself that he has some moral standards. For years I told myself that I was the most honest man I'd ever met. Of course, that was easy enough in Nazi Germany. But why take my word for it? Mark a few bills. Take a few serial numbers. I'd be easy enough to trace. I daresay even the French police wouldn't have too much of a struggle to find me or it. Come to think of it, do that anyway. You never know."

The rest of Sunday passed slowly as it often does, especially when there is an important task to be completed at the end of it. Hebel came back to the hotel just after lunch and went straight to his room without so much as a glance in my direction. He was a cool one, I'll say that for him. I went out to his car and searched it; there was a brochure from the perfume factory in Grasse and I concluded that this was where he'd been. Meanwhile, the small of my back had started hurting, which is not unusual when I've been on my feet for much of the day, and I was keen to get home and have a bath. But first I had an important job to do. As soon as Hebel went out again—around six—I took his key and went upstairs to search the German's room. I was nibbling around at the edge of his viperous person, keen to see what else he might have among his high-quality possessions that was potentially compromising to my vulnerable and easily compromised client. Letters, perhaps, or another photograph. It was my idea of room service. He had left nothing of value to him in the hotel safe, I knew, because I would certainly have known about it, and nothing in his car, either. That left his hotel suite and, perhaps, as I had suggested to Maugham, some local lawyer with a strong room and a weekly retainer. What I did find was surprising, although not in the way I might have expected.

ELEVEN

It was a nice suite atop the east wing of the hotel, just below a flagpole and the Tricolore, full of summer evening light and the smell of cut flowers, with a fine view of gently sloping lush gardens and, beyond, the deep blue sea. Anchored in the bay, the millionaire Greek shipowner Aristotle Onassis's yacht, the *Christina O*, with its distinctive yellow smokestack and naval frigate lines, looked like a brand-new *Argo* in search of some more modern and profitable golden fleece, as devised by Charles Ponzi, perhaps, or Ferdinand Demara.

I looked around the room. There was a big bed, a comfortable seating area, an en suite bathroom, and a sun terrace as long as the Champs-Élysées. On the walls were some French prints depicting anodyne scenes of the French Riviera that always made me think well of gloomier artists like Bosch and Goya, and a large bowl of fresh fruit. On top of a chest of drawers was Hebel's own portable Grundig tape machine. I switched it on and listened to a minute or two of bebop jazz, which I find is usually more than enough. There was an address book and a diary and a toilet bag filled with an optimistic number of condoms. Not unexpectedly, the closets and the drawers were home to a variety of fine clothes. But on top of a pile of neatly folded shirts from Turnbull & Asser I found an envelope addressed to Bernie Gunther, while under the rubble of socks and underwear was a nine-millimeter Sig, recently cleaned. It was a nice gun with a full clip and I was glad to see it there if only because it made me think Hebel wouldn't be carrying a weapon when I met him later, but it was the cheeky letter that interested me more and I wondered how I might read it without him knowing that I had. Obviously he'd been expecting me to search his room, which made me think I was probably wasting my time in there. So, after a minute of just staring at the position of the envelope on the top shirt—could there have been a hair I hadn't noticed that would tell him I'd been in that drawer?—I left it untouched exactly where it was. But on an impulse, and thinking I might use it to reason with Hebel later on, I took the gun, tucked it behind me under the waistband of my pinstripe trousers, and went downstairs again; he wasn't going to complain to anyone about my borrowing his gun, especially if it was pointed at his head. I rarely ever do anything on impulse, however, and almost immediately it was an impulse I strongly regretted.

In the lobby there were two plainclothes cops waiting for me and already making a silent inventory of my face, my manner, my morning coat, the way I walked—their eyes were all over me like ants. I knew they were cops because plainclothes always appear a little too plain in a grand hotel. Cops are the same the world over; they usually look as if they belong somewhere else, somewhere second-rate like the Soviet Union, or Alaska, where cheap suits, tight shoes, and creased shirts with yesterday's collars are almost standard uniform. These two looked like a couple of dull rocks in a silver punch bowl. I ushered them quickly into the back office in case they disturbed the chandeliers or Monsieur Charrieres, the hotel manager, caught a distressing sight of them. For a brief moment I thought they were there to speak to Hebel and wondered how long it would be before he tried to make a deal with them that involved me, but to my surprise, they were there to ask me about Antimo Spinola. They showed their greasy plastic identity cards and muttered their names through a blue cloud of French cigarette smoke, but I was hardly paying attention because I was now more worried that I might miss my appointment with Hebel than I was about any acquaintance I had with Antimo Spinola. The Italian could look after himself; or so I thought. There was five thousand dollars in it if I handled Maugham's blackmail money without a hitch—more than enough to buy a new car. Or a ticket to somewhere else; increasingly, somewhere else was a place I was keen to visit.

"How well do you know him?" asked one of the cops.

"Spinola? I play cards with him twice a week at the Hotel Voile d'Or in Cap Ferrat. He's my bridge partner. Which is to say, not well at all. Bridge is that kind of game. Too interesting for a lot of what-did-you-do-today talk."

"For how long have you played together?"

"Oh, perhaps a couple of years. As long as I've worked here, anyway."

"It's a beautiful hotel."

"Isn't it? So much beauty." I almost added, "But so much sadness, too. It's a beautiful, sad world, I think, that has some beautiful, sad people in it," only you don't speak to cops like that when they're asking questions. Not if you want them to leave you alone.

"Is bridge a game involving money?"

"It can be. But not for us."

"How did you meet?"

"We were introduced. I can't remember by who. Someone at the Voile perhaps."

"Two years isn't very long. Surely you can remember."

"You would think so. Perhaps the barman at the Voile. Maurice. Nice fellow. Good barman."

The questions were arriving fast now, like a boxer's jabs, snapped in from one man and then the other. I'd fought this bout and many others like it before, however; so I tucked my head down into my shoulder, lifted my left to cover myself against a sucker punch, and prepared to defend myself at all times.

"Were you ever at his apartment in Nice?"

"No. He never asked me."

"And the casino? Did you ever go there?"

I pulled a face. "I don't like casinos very much. For one thing, I don't have any money I can afford to lose. And for another, I don't care for the odds. And I haven't even mentioned the architecture. Most casinos look like opera houses and I never much liked the opera."

"Is money important to you?"

"Not especially," I lied. "As a matter of fact, I've always found it very purifying to be without much of it. Especially when you see what a lot of the stuff can do to people."

"What about Spinola? Is he short of money, do you think?"

"No. But then he hasn't showed me his checking account."

"Does he have any enemies?"

For a moment I thought about the gun he'd given me that was now on top of my lavatory cistern and then shook my head. All of a sudden I seemed to have so many guns and so little documentation for any of them. I felt like a forgotten armory.

"None that he's mentioned."

"What about friends?"

"That's what I say. What about them? Inspector, Spinola's my only real friend. I can't say if the same is true for him. I certainly hope not, because I'm not much of a friend."

"What about women?"

"He doesn't talk about them that much. He's careful like that. Too careful, perhaps. Because I imagine there must have been someone."

"Why do you say so?"

"Inspector, he's an Italian. And a good-looking Italian at that. Not to mention the fact he's unmarried. I can't imagine him letting those three things go to waste in a place like the French Riviera."

"And you're a German."

"What can I say? I've not been as lucky with women as he is, I expect."

"That's not what I meant."

"All right then, how about this. Germans and Italians—we have a habit of forming alliances. By the way, you have my apologies for the previous alliance."

"Where were you last night?"

"Last night? I had dinner at the Villa Mauresque. With Mr. Somerset Maugham, the famous writer. He's a very private sort of man, as I expect you know, but I'm sure he won't mind confirming my alibi. Assuming I need one." I lit a cigarette and paused, checking out their sweating, swarthy faces, which were almost as creased and nondescript as their clothes. "Look, would you mind telling me what this is all about? Is Monsieur Spinola in some kind of trouble? Is he all right? I think now would be a good time to tell me if something has happened. And why you're asking me all these questions."

Up to now we'd been doing just fine using the present tense; but then, the way cops do sometimes, they changed it, they went straight to the past tense with just a short, sharp delay that explained Spinola's current situation all too clearly. You might have said it was brutal except that there's no way to sweeten words like these; best just to spit them out like tacks.

"He's dead, I'm afraid. Monsieur Spinola was murdered. Someone shot him at his home late last night."

"We found your hotel business card by his telephone. And your name in his diary for tomorrow evening. The casino isn't open today so we thought we'd come and see you first."

Feeling the honor, I nodded slowly. "Tomorrow evening— that would be our regular game of bridge at the Voile. Shot? How? I mean, where was he shot?"

"Once, through the heart."

I kept on nodding but I was thinking about Hebel's gun now pressing against my kidney like a giant stone, and remembering that it had been cleaned and recently; you could still smell the gun oil in the muzzle. Not that it's difficult to get hold of a gun on the Riviera. There was a gun shop in Villefranche. And the French have the most relaxed gun laws in Europe. Hitler could have bought a gun without much of a problem. Easy enough after buying the whole French army.

"Do you own a gun, monsieur?"

"Me? No. Guns tend to frighten the guests. Even the Americans, oddly enough. Generally speaking, we find that we can make them pay their bills without too much of a problem."

"Was he scared of anyone? Did he seem upset about anything?"

"No."

"You don't seem that upset about the death of Monsieur Spinola."

"Oh, but I am. Good bridge partners are rather hard to come by."

"That's a pretty callous thing to say."

"Obviously you don't play bridge. Let's just say that I'm most upset about something when I appear to be taking it lightly."

"Any ideas as to who might have killed him?"

I smiled. Cops are the same the world over, always expecting someone else to do their thinking for them. It's a wonder that any of them ever managed to pass an exam at school without looking over the shoulder of the next boy. Then again, that's certainly one way of passing.

"No. I can't think of anyone. Least of all me. Given the way I play cards, it's much more likely that Spinola would have killed me. Look, why don't you ask the people at the casino? It strikes me that the kind of shady folk who operate these places, not to mention the ones who win and lose large sums of money—they're just the sort of people on the Riviera who kill other people without a second thought. There's organized crime in Nice, isn't there? Much of it centered around the casino. Maybe Spinola might have had a run-in with the local mafia."

"Rest assured that we will make every inquiry."

"Is that all?"

"It's enough, isn't it?"

"What I meant was," I said with true grand hotel patience and *froideur*, "do you require me for very much longer? Only, I have an appointment for which I'm already late."

"You won't try to go back to Germany, will you? Not until we've completed our inquiries."

The last time I had seen my home in Berlin it was just one tall, improbably perpendicular wall of blackened brick with three short floors somehow attached, like a giant letter *E*. No doors, no rooms, no roof, just the open sky, which was so crimson from the setting sun it looked as if it was the blood of all those who'd wasted their lives in the battle for Germany, which had felt like the end of the world. I remembered looking at it and thinking how much pain and murder there was in that red sky and how it would never be blue again. You could smell death on the wind, like the Last Judgment. Not that any of this mattered much now that the end of the world was so very much nearer than it ever was before.

"Go back to Germany?" I said. "To Berlin? No, gentlemen. That certainly won't be happening."

TWELVE

As I drove up the gravel drive, the tall green front door was opened by Ernest, the butler, and a moment later there was Maugham wearing an open-necked blue shirt, white linen trousers, and espadrilles. He was carrying a Pan American flight bag over one shoulder. I didn't get out of the car. I switched off the engine, wound down the window, and then Maugham leaned in. It was a beautiful deep summer evening—the kind of evening for talk of love, not blackmail money and an incriminating photograph.

Behind a hedge of thick pink and white oleanders I could hear the water trickling into the swimming pool, and the air was thick with the smell of orange blossom, which was preferable to the absinthe martini and the cigarette corrupting the old man's mephitic breath, which now poured over me like chlorine gas drifting across no-man's-land.

"Do you want a d-drink before you go?" he asked.

"No thanks. I'd best keep a clear head for the rubber I'm about to play with Herr Hebel. But I'll certainly have one on my return. In fact, tell Ernest I might have several."

"Of course. We'll even save some dinner for you."

He dropped the bag onto the passenger seat and, taking out a folded handkerchief, wiped his forehead, which was glistening with sweat. Robin appeared in the doorway, and then so did Alan Searle. Maugham sensed their lingering presence and glanced over his shoulder with a hint of displeasure, as if he were being minded like someone who was senile; he was anything but that.

"Where are you meeting him?"

"He's rented a room at the Voile. That was his suggestion, not mine. But it's neutral territory, you might say. Harder for me to lay any kind of trap for him there."

"Robin and Alan are both of the opinion that one of them should accompany you. And, more importantly, the money."

"Those aren't Hebel's instructions."

"I know."

"But sure, why not? As long as Robin or Alan stays in the car, I guess it would be all right."

"Aren't you a bit nervous?"

"No." But this was a lie. For some reason, I had a strange

feeling of foreboding, as if something dreadful was going to happen. I'd even started to question the whole damn arrangement. Was it possible that this was all some kind of elaborate setup designed to put me in the frame for Hebel's murder, which the wily old Englishman had somehow arranged separately? He was a supremely gifted author, after all, and it would not have been beyond his fertile imagination to have devised some labyrinthine plot. It certainly wouldn't have been the first time that I'd been played for a fool. After all, I had only Maugham's word that it was actually Harold Heinz Hebel who'd asked me to take charge of the handover. I even wondered if Spinola's gun was still sitting on top of my bathroom cistern where I'd left it and if Spinola's death was somehow connected to all this. A double cross in a woman is something you can never really hold against her; you have to factor it in, like the weather; it's just the way they're made. To my old-fashioned way of thinking, W. Somerset Maugham was like a wily old woman in so many respects.

"No? You surprise me. You're a man of very cool temperament, I must say, and I'm beginning to understand why Hebel thought you might be the right chap for the job."

"I'll be all right," I said. "I have a friend coming with me to make sure everything goes smoothly." And then, just to scare him a little, I flipped open the glove box and let him see the Sig that was in there.

"Christ, is that thing loaded?"

"Of course it's loaded. Without bullets guns are only good as paperweights."

"What I mean is, you wouldn't use that unless you had to, would you?" he said. "Unless your own life was in danger."

I grinned and lit a cigarette. "The other night you were in favor of me killing him, Mr. Maugham."

"I was. Still am. But not in cold blood. I suggested a car accident. I certainly didn't want you to kill him immediately after coming here to the villa. How would that look to the police? Besides, you said yourself he may have taken the precaution of lodging some kind of letter with a local lawyer that incriminates me, and perhaps even you."

"The gun's just an edge that he's not expecting," I said. "You see, it's his gun. I searched his room at the Grand Hôtel just before I came here and found it in his drawer. Which answers your question about how trustworthy he is. The man is a criminal." I glanced at my wristwatch and then back at Robin and Alan in the doorway. "You'd best make up your mind, sir. Do you want one of them to come or not?"

"Would it make a difference?"

"Not if I really was planning to take off with the money, no. Best they both stay here out of harm's way. Believe me, I know a lot about harm's way. It turns sharp left off the road to Shitsville when you're least expecting it."

I drove back down the hill to the port, which was still busy with small boats coming and going under the early-evening moon like bees collecting pollen. I parked the car near the harbor and walked up the slope of the esplanade toward the hotel entrance with the airline bag slung over my shoulder and the gun tucked underneath the waistband of my trousers. If anything was going to go wrong, I thought it best my car was elsewhere when it happened. The bell tower at the little church was marking eight o'clock as if time on the Cap was important. For anyone but me it probably wasn't. Red and pink people who looked as if they'd had too much sun were coming ashore and heading to the many restaurants in search of a good dinner, but it didn't matter at what hour they ate and really there was only one good restaurant and that was at La Voile d'Or. Although it was, perhaps, a little too formal for most tourists, which is probably why I liked it in the first place.

My first thought as I went through the front door of the hotel was not about Hebel or the money in the bag I was carrying, but of poor Spinola and how he and I were never going to sit down in the bar again and talk about nothing much before a friendly game of cards. I always felt alone, but suddenly the realization that I'd lost my one remaining friend hit me as hard as if I'd lost an arm or a leg. I liked Anne French, but I wasn't in any doubt that she was hardly a friend; she was just using me to get close to Somerset Maugham. I didn't mind that. People do what they have to do and what they think they have to do, and mostly there's no way around that. It certainly makes life interesting, if perhaps a little less enjoyable. I sighed as I realized I was probably going to have to tell the Roses that Spinola was dead and that our bridge evenings were at an end; and then I considered that I could ask Anne French to be my partner instead. She'd like that. Not as much as if I'd asked her to come and make up a four with Somerset Maugham, but then, she had to start somewhere.

I went to the front desk, where a man with a pimp mustache and a blue bow tie was reading the latest on the Tour de France in *L'Équipe*, although his girth told me it had been a long time since he'd ridden a racing bicycle. We knew each other. His name was Henri and, according to Spinola, he'd been in the Resistance, which was an organization that seemed to be growing all the time. Certainly it was twice the size it had ever been throughout the war.

"That's the newspaper that believed Captain Dreyfus was guilty of selling us secrets, isn't it?" I said.

Henri shrugged. "These days, there's no politics in it. Just cycling."

"In France? That is politics."

"You know, sometimes you are very French, for a German."

"I'll take that as a compliment. So is there another German here? Monsieur Hebel?"

"He's in room 28," said Henri. "Second floor. You're to go straight up, Monsieur Wolf."

I nodded. "You know Robin Maugham, don't you?"

"Of course."

"How well does he know Monsieur Hebel?"

"Well enough to have a drink with him."

"Once? Or more than once?"

"More than once, I should say."

I paused for a moment, wondering if I should tell him about

Spinola, and then rejected the idea. I wasn't in the mood to field a lot of questions to which I had no answers. All I wanted was to get the negative and the photographs and then leave without any complications.

"I suppose you heard about poor Spinola?" he said.

"Yes. The cops came to see me at the Grand, asking about our game tomorrow night."

"He was a nice man and a good customer. I'll miss him."

"Me, too. How did you hear?"

"I have a friend in Maréchal Foch."

The Avenue Maréchal Foch was where the Nice Commissariat of Police was headquartered.

"He's an inspector in the Police Judiciaire. He seems to think there was a woman involved."

"According to all your best writers, there usually is. But did he say why?"

"No. Only this and the fact that he was shot. With a small-caliber pistol."

"Maybe that's what makes them think it was a woman. The small-caliber pistol, I suppose."

"Monsieur, small or large, it makes little difference when the bullet goes straight through your heart. There was almost five liters of blood on the floor where they found him." Henri shrugged in that Gallic way, which is as eloquent as anything ever written by Voltaire or Montaigne. "I suppose that this is the end of your weekly bridge games with Mr. and Mrs. Rose. Pity. I shall miss you all."

I shrugged. "You know, Henri, there's an unwritten rule in bridge that when your partner gets killed you're supposed to try and find out who did it."

"Sounds more like the Mafia."

"It just makes it easier to replace a partner if you can find out why the previous one was killed. No one likes to take the seat of someone who's been shot."

"I can imagine."

"What I'm saying is that if your friend in the PJ finds out any more about what happened to Spinola, then I'd like to know about it. You know? For old times' sake. Italy and Germany. The Axis."

"And perhaps to even the score?"

"That was yesterday. Today, I'd just like to help, if I can. But to help, I need more information."

He nodded. "This I can understand. Sure. I'll ask him."

"Discreetly. I wouldn't like his answers to turn into awkward questions for you or me, or anyone else for that matter."

"Of course. And you can trust me. During the war we used to say that deliberation is the work of many, but action of one man alone."

"It's been a while since I saw myself in that light. But I am qualified in one respect. I am a man alone."

THIRTEEN

I took the stairs and walked along the thickly carpeted hall to room 28, where I knocked and waited patiently, although anyone observing the scene might have thought differently because of the gun I was holding in my hand—Hebel's gun. It was pointed straight at the door handle, a last-minute decision that was calculated to try and put an end to the blackmail right then and there.

The smile he was wearing as he opened up flickered for a moment as he backed away with his hands rising slowly behind his neatly combed head.

"No need for guns. What is this?"

"It's your gun. That's what this is." I kicked the room door shut behind me and tossed the Pan Am flight bag on the bed. "I thought you might recognize it."

"My gun?"

"Yes. It was in your drawer next to the note for me."

"Did you read it?"

"No. There's nothing you have to say that's of any interest to me."

"I see."

"No, you don't. This is not what you think, at all. I intend to search your room and make sure that I get the negative and all the prints—not to mention any other items you might be saving so you can squeeze the lemon again. That's just good business." I pointed the hole in the end of the gun at the carpet. "On your knees. It's been a while since I shot anyone just to wound them and I certainly wouldn't like to answer for the present state of my marksmanship, so you'd better not try anything."

Hebel knelt down at the edge of the bed and started to relax a little.

"Look, Gunther, I'm not armed. In spite of any evidence to the contrary, guns are always a mistake in this business. They're generally a sign that negotiations have failed."

"Is that what you call it? They'll be asking you to address the UN General Assembly next."

"There's very little here but do go ahead and search. You'll find the envelope with the prints and the neg on top of the chest of drawers. As I agreed with Herr Maugham. And I really don't have anything else for sale. Fifty thousand dollars—I assume it's in the flight bag—is a big score for me. Enough to retire on."

I found the envelope, and having established the promised contents were indeed there, I opened the drawers and generally had a good look around his room. It was a nice room, with a fine view of the harbor. Nothing as grand as the Grand, but nice and comfortable and tastefully decorated. I almost preferred it.

"One thing I learned with the Berlin police," I told him. "Money's like a state pension. There's never enough to retire on. Especially when you're a crook."

"I suppose you're not going to pay me now."

"That's the general idea, smart guy."

"But you still brought the money. You went to the house and fetched the money and now you're here. Which must mean— no, don't tell me that you're planning to keep it yourself?"

"I thought about it."

"Suppose I tell Mr. Maugham."

"Suppose I slap your mouth with this pistol. Dentists aren't so easy to find on a Sunday evening."

"You know we could split the money. Fifty-fifty. With my silence guaranteed."

"That would mean me becoming your partner. And that's not going to happen, not after what happened in Königsberg."

"Ah. I was wondering when we'd get to that." He shook his head. "Look, that was all a very long time ago."

"Hard to forget, though."

"Perhaps you should try. If you'd read my letter in the drawer at the Grand you'd have seen my apology for that. Not that this matters very much. We're all friends in Europe now, aren't we? Allies in the struggle against world Communism?"

"The way I figure it is this. With or without the fifty thousand dollars, you'll either come back with something else you want to sell, or you won't. A print you kept back. Or something altogether different. A letter, perhaps. Simple as that. My guess is that you will be back. Because you people always come back. I haven't forgotten the way you and that bastard Otto Schmidt squeezed poor Captain von Frisch for five years. I don't think you're the kind of leopard who knows where to buy a tin of paint or find a good plastic surgeon."

"Suppose I tell the police who you really are?"

"And suppose I tell them exactly how you know that? Involving the cops is bad for us both, and you know it. My guess is that we're both wanted men, in one half of Germany or the other. Frankly, you should be glad I don't put a hole in you, which is what you deserve."

"My dead body would be a little hard to explain."

"People have disappeared from this hotel before. During the war the Resistance met here."

"Oh. Well, it can't have been very effective, that's all I can say. I seem to recall this part of France was Nazi in all but name. Don't you agree?"

"I think it's time that you started answering the questions, not me."

"I've got nothing to say that you don't already know."

"I don't think so. When you squeeze a lemon, you flex your fist more than once."

"Not this time."

I picked up a pillow, folded it over the Sig, and pointed it at the heel of one of his handmade shoes.

"You're not serious."

"Let's start with where you got the picture."

"You know what these queers are like. Can't trust any of them."

"A name."

"Louis Legrand."

"Where did you buy it? Here in France? Where?"

"Here in France. In Nice."

"When?"

"A few weeks ago."

"Now tell me what else you have got on the old man, or I'll put one through your heel. It won't kill you, but you'll never walk again without the aid of a stick."

"Nothing. There's nothing else, I promise. Just the neg and the prints in the envelope. Since you have my pistol you've obviously searched my room at the Grand and I daresay my car as well. You know I'm telling you the truth."

"Stop wasting my time." I kneed him in the back and sent him sprawling onto the carpet. "We both know it wouldn't be in the least bit like you to bet everything on the one hand. That's not how your kind of salesman works. You squeeze the lemon until there's no juice in him and the pips have fallen out. So you're going to tell me where you've stashed the rest of your samples, or I swear you're only leaving this room in a wheelchair."

I pressed the muzzle of the Sig against his Achilles to underline my meaning; I don't know that I would actually have shot him, but he wasn't to know that.

"All right, all right, I'll tell you."

I let him up onto his knees again, but he was slow to get started so I flicked his earlobe with the Sig a couple of times to encourage his soul—assuming he had one—to unburden itself.

"I'd forgotten what a violent temper you have, Gunther. There's a fury in you I just didn't remember."

"You should see me when I can't find my cigarettes. So talk, before I give you an ear piercing you won't ever forget."

"There's a tape," he said.

"What kind of a tape?"

"A tape. BASF. AEG. I don't know. A sound recording."

"Of what, exactly?"

"A man speaking. You might say that it's a sort of confession."

"Who is this man?"

"Ah, now this is where it gets interesting."

I listened carefully as he started to describe what was on the tape. At first I was confused and then surprised, and then not really surprised at all. The whole thing sounded very clever. Too clever for an ordinary Fritz like me. Which is what I had half suspected all along. The only really strange part was that Hebel had decided to involve me in the whole rotten transaction. Then again, I seem to have a talent for finding trouble; it certainly seems to have no trouble in finding me. This couldn't have looked more like trouble if someone had erected the word in fifty-foot-high letters on the summit of nearby Mont Boron. After a while he could see his explanation had made a real impression on me and he felt confident enough to stand up and go and help himself from the bottle of schnapps on the bedside table and light a cigarette without me waving the gun in his face again.

"You want one?" he asked, and poured a short glass for me anyway. "You look as though you need one."

I took it from his hand and downed it quickly. It was good schnapps, cold as the Frisches Haff in January, and just the way I like it.

"Where is it now, this tape?"

"Safe. I'll let you have a copy tomorrow so you can deliver it to the Villa Mauresque where Herr Maugham can listen to it at his leisure. I'll even lend him my tape recorder so he can play it. Anyway, I expect he'll know what to do next. After that the old man will have forty-eight hours to raise two hundred thousand dollars. Shouldn't be too difficult given that he's already raised fifty thousand of it. Let's say that I'm letting you have the picture free as a sign of my good faith."

"You've come a long way since blackmailing warm boys in the lavatories at Potsdamer Platz station," I said. "I can see how you could squeeze Somerset Maugham. But this—this strikes me as foolhardy."

"Some lemons are bigger than others, but they'll squeeze

just as easily. I learned that from the Nazis. Hitler's grandmother was a practiced blackmailer, did you know that?"

"It doesn't surprise me."

When he'd finished talking I sat on the edge of the bed and thought things over for a minute or two before I spoke again.

"I'm not supposed to be here," I said.

"Certainly you are. I suggested to Herr Maugham that you would be the man best placed to help him. You're here because he needs you. And if it comes to that, so do I. You're a perfect cutout, Bernie. Reliable. Intelligent. With much to lose. Useful to me, and to Herr Maugham."

I shook my head. "What I mean is, I should be dead."

"All of us who survived the war were fortunate," said Hebel, and poured me another glass. "You and me perhaps especially so."

"Were we? I wonder. Anyway, I'm not supposed to be alive right now. A little while ago I tried to kill myself. I sat in the garage with the car engine running and just waited for it to happen. I'm still not exactly sure why I kept on breathing air and not Fina gasoline but, for a while, I understood what death really is. Of course we all know we're going to die. But until it happens, none of us really understands what it means to be dead. Me, I understood it, perfectly. I even saw the beauty of it. You see, Hebel, you don't die; death isn't something that just happens to you, no. It's like you become death. You're a part of it. All those billions who've lived and then died before you. You've joined them. And when you've felt that, it never goes away, even if you think you're still alive. Just remember that when all this is over. Just remember that it was you who chose to involve a dead man like me in your little scheme."

After that I told him we—by which I meant me and my client—would be in touch as soon as we'd listened to the tape. Then I collected the envelope with the photographs and the neg, the Pan Am flight bag with the money, pushed the muzzle of the gun under my waistband, and, without another word, left the room.

Downstairs in the hotel lobby, I returned to the front desk.

"When you speak to your friend in the PJ see what he can find out about a man called Louis Legrand."

"I already did," said Henri, writing down the name. "Speak to my friend, I mean. She left her scarf."

"Who did?"

"The woman suspected of Spinola's murder. I called my friend in the PJ and asked him, like you asked. Whoever it was shot him left a green chiffon scarf beside his dead body."

"Is that all? Now, with her underwear they might have proved something. Sexual behavior. Hair color. Who she likes for the Tour de France. Anything."

"It was in his hand. The scarf. Chances are she was wearing it when she shot him, at pretty close range, too. There was a powder burn on his shirt. So it must have been someone he trusted. That's what my friend says, anyway."

"Hmm."

"What does 'hmm' mean?"

"I'm not a detective. So it means I really don't know what to think about it, Henri."

Of course this was hardly a surprise, given everything else that was now crowding in upon my mind; my head must have looked like a stowaway's cabin on the ship in that Marx Brothers film. But most of the floor space was taken up with the realization that the whole thing involving Maugham hadn't been much to do with blackmailing him, at all. Not really. That had just been the hors d'oeuvre. Hebel had something else for sale. Something much more important than a photograph of some naked men cavorting around a swimming pool in 1937. That had been nothing more than a lure, designed to secure everyone's attention. To establish some credentials. Well, now he had them established, as if he had just presented them at the court of St. James while wearing white gloves and carrying a cocked hat with ostrich feathers.

"I did what you asked," he said resentfully. "He was a good man, Spinola."

"Sure, sure. I'll look into it, okay, Henri? Maybe I'll find something relevant. Maybe."

But somehow the name of the woman who'd shot and killed our friend Spinola seemed of lesser importance besides an elaborate plot to blackmail the British Secret Intelligence Service.

FOURTEEN

Up at the Villa Mauresque they were finishing dinner; at least they were until I showed up with the money and the photograph. For a while I let them all think I'd done a great job of getting back the prints and the neg and somehow the fifty thousand dollars as well. I couldn't have felt more popular there if I'd been Noël Coward wearing just a pair of sandals. I hadn't the heart to tell any of them that the whole thing had been merely the first act in an opera that threatened to be longer than *Tristan und Isolde*. So we sat on the terrace under the starry sky, watched by a Pekingese dog and a couple of blackamoor wooden bishops, and I ate some corned-beef hash and drank amarone and even permitted Somerset Maugham to put my hand to his pink, rictus mouth and say that whatever they were paying me at the Grand Hôtel, he would double it if I came to work for him at the Villa Mauresque.

"Doing what, exactly?" I asked.

The alligator eyes narrowed in their folds of brown skin as he considered the proposition. "I'm a r-rich man," he said, "and it strikes me that I need protection of some kind. Especially at my time of life. I might be kidnapped. Or blackmailed again. And there are always unwanted visitors at the front gates wanting a book signed. You have no idea. But if you became my security adviser, Herr Wolf, then I'd feel a lot safer. And not just me. My guests, too. Some very famous people come and stay here from time to time. Very famous and just as often even richer than I am. Charlie Chaplin, Jerry Zipkin, the Queen of Spain. And then there's my art collection. As you will doubtless have observed, I have paintings by Gauguin, Matisse, Renoir, Pissarro, Picasso, Toulouse-Lautrec, Bonnard, Monet, Utrillo. A man with a gun is just what the place needs most, I think."

"Who painted that one?" I said.

But Robin Maugham agreed enthusiastically. "This is a brilliant idea, Uncle," he said. "Your very own Simon Templar."

"You don't know the first thing about me," I said, with no idea of who Simon Templar was. "I am not a good man."

"Look around," said Searle. "There are no honors and decorations coming the way of anyone in this house."

"No, indeed," said Robin.

"I know that you returned with fifty thousand dollars I thought I'd never see again," said Maugham. "I think that b-be-speaks a certain devotion to principle."

"Then try this, sir. I'm not sure I could handle the predominantly male atmosphere up here at the villa. Pool parties and rent boys."

"We're much too old for all those shenanigans now," said Maugham. "Aren't we, Alan?"

"Speak for yourself," said Searle.

"What about you, Mr. Wolf? Is there anyone in your life? A woman, perhaps."

"You managed to make that sound queer," I said.

"It is," he said. "To us."

"I'm not interested in anything like that anymore."

"You sound exactly like a man with a broken heart," he said. "You fascinate me, Mr. Wolf. Who was the woman who made you so bitter?"

I laughed. "It took more than just one."

"Love is just a dirty trick that's played on us to achieve a continuation of the species," said Maugham. "That's what I think."

I shook my head. "It isn't like that at all, Mr. Maugham. It isn't something simply mechanistic, as you put it. Love and hate, human feelings and emotion, they're all the same God-given illusion. It's what convinces us that we're here and that we count for something in this universe. When we don't. Not for a second. Everything we feel and that we think—it's all the same cosmic joke. You should know that more than most people, Mr.

Maugham. You've been playing God and inflicting cosmic jokes on your characters for sixty years."

"I'd no idea you were a philosopher, Mr. Wolf."

"I'm a German, Mr. Maugham. For us, philosophy is a way of life."

I'd finished my dinner and now I asked him to show me the garden, and he took his pipe and I my cigarettes down to the grotto by the swimming pool, where there was a large Chinese bronze gong that sounded once a day to announce the cocktail hour. I'd missed that, of course, but Maugham had thoughtfully asked Ernest to prepare me a jug of cold gimlets and while we sat there, we talked and I drank myself into a slightly better mood. Or so I thought.

"One of the disadvantages to playing G-God," said Maugham, "is that I notice much more than most people. God is merely all-seeing. But I have other senses, too, and while my hearing may not be as good as it was, I can still detect a certain *weltschmerz* in your voice and manner that was not there before. Which is saying something, I can tell you. At the best of times you're just bone dry. But tonight you make Heinrich Heine sound positively full of the joys of spring. So then. It's not over, is it? With this man Hebel, I mean. It was kind of you to pretend it was, but there's something else he's got for sale. Something bigger than that photograph, I can tell."

"Yes, sir."

"Thank you for sparing the boys," he said. "That was decent

of you. They do worry so. But I think you'd better tell me now, don't you?"

"Yes, sir." I lit another cigarette. "It has to do with your friend Guy Burgess, again."

"He's not my friend, let's make that quite clear now, shall we? The man is an absolute scoundrel."

"Clear. Well, it seems that after he and his fellow spy, Donald Maclean, escaped from England in nineteen fifty-one, they traveled by boat to Saint-Malo, where they were met by KGB officers and then driven south to Bordeaux. There they boarded a Soviet freighter bound for Leningrad. According to Hebel, that's a voyage of several days, during which time they were debriefed, at length and separately, by KGB case officers as there was still some suspicion that the British had been complicit in the escape of these two traitors. Anyway, that debriefing was recorded on tape and it's one of these tapes that Hebel's now offering for sale. The unexpurgated confessions of Guy Burgess, is how Hebel described it to me. This is just one tape, but there are others being offered as part of the deal."

"Good God," said Maugham. "Dynamite, in other words. Absolute dynamite. The man was a Russian spy at the heart of MI5 for two decades. There's no telling what he knows."

"I think that's the point of the tape. He is telling. All of it. I haven't heard the tape but I'm to bring a copy here to you tomorrow, after it comes into my possession. He's even lending you the tape recorder to play it on."

"But what's this tape got to do with me, Walter? I haven't seen Guy Burgess in almost twenty years."

"Look, this is as much as I know about it, sir. Apparently, Guy Burgess is a drunk and his conversation on the tape—which was described to me as uncensored and wide ranging—includes the allegations that the British suspected he was a spy for years but let him go in order not to compromise relations with the Americans; that he was here for an orgy at the Villa Mauresque, in nineteen thirty-seven. And that immediately following this, Burgess joined the BBC and then MI6. It seems as if the photograph was just the lure to get you to bite. As a way of involving you."

"If any of this is true, how on earth did Hebel come to be in possession of this tape? And what the fuck does he want me to do about it? I'm not in the service anymore."

"Look, without hearing the tape, my opinion is this: The whole thing has been cooked up by the Russians to blackmail the British secret service using Burgess and you as cutouts. You're the back door to MI6 and MI5."

"Story of my life," muttered Maugham.

"Harold Heinz Hebel is possibly working for Soviet intelligence. The GRU. The KGB. Who knows which service? But it has to be a strong possibility that he came by this tape because the Russians gave it to him. He tells me he wants money for the tape or else he'll send it to the *New York Times*."

"How much money does he want?"

"Two hundred thousand dollars."

"Jesus Christ."

"I expect Hebel thinks you are best placed to pay the black-mail money yourself and then persuade—not to say blackmail—the British to pay you that money back. There's Hebel's security to think about, too. It's one thing blackmailing the British down here on the French Riviera. It would be something else to try it in London."

"Could the Russians really be in it for the money? Nothing else?"

"I don't know. Look, this isn't supposed to be a joke, but the opportunities for the USSR to trade with capitalist countries for some much needed foreign currency are limited. It just might be that extortion is their best export right now."

"And who better to extort money from than the British security services?" said Maugham. "It's like something out of a novel by John Buchan. Yes. I may not be in the security service loop anymore, but undeniably the last few years have been an intelligence disaster for my country. Richard Hannay may save the day for queen and country, but there are plenty of others who have managed to comprehensively fuck it up: Alan May, Burgess and Maclean, and the fellow now serving fourteen years in prison for handing all our atomic secrets over to the Russians—Klaus Fuchs. By all accounts, the American FBI thinks the British security services are a contradiction in terms, a laughingstock, and they're probably not wrong. A lot has changed since my own service in nineteen seventeen. We were good then. Formidable. Back then boys went up to Cambridge from their public schools to learn how to be lawyers and civil servants, not Russian spies.

Undoubtedly the British government would indeed prefer to keep all of this very quiet. Especially now there's a possibility of our two countries renewing their cooperation on atomic research. And while there's no danger of any of the British newspapers being permitted to publish any of these revelations, American papers are a lot harder to control. Two hundred thousand is probably cheap next to the price of what it's costing Britain to develop an atomic bomb on its own account. Having said that, two hundred thousand is a lot of money for me. A hell of a lot." He sighed. "Suppose I stump up the cash and the British refuse to reimburse me? What then? Some of these Whitehall people are very tight with money, you know. I mean, really stingy."

"Then you send it to the *New York Times* yourself."

"Would that make me a traitor? I don't know."

"I'd say a good lawyer might convincingly argue that you bought the tape to protect the interests of your country. But that your country let you down."

"Yes, there is that argument, I suppose."

I shrugged. "Wait and hear the tape. Who knows? Maybe you'll think it's someone else's problem after you've listened to it."

"Tell me about this man, Harold Heinz Hebel. What else do you know about him?"

"He's a rat who's giving rats a bad name."

"You already told me how he blackmailed that poor German captain, von Frisch, in nineteen thirty-eight. But you also said that you met him again, during the war."

"That's right. It was East Prussia. The winter of nineteen forty-four to forty-five. And that was the last time I spoke to him until this morning at the Grand Hôtel."

"I think that before we go any further you're going to have to tell me about that. In fact, you need to tell me all you know about our friend Harold Hebel. If I'm going to contact my friends in MI6 to ask for their help here, they will certainly need to know everything you know about this awful man."

"He's an opportunistic survivor who lives near humans and needs to be exterminated because he carries disease. He's a rat. A rat that deserves to be drowned in a bucket. Now, let me explain why. Let me tell you about what happened in Königsberg."

FIFTEEN

KÖNIGSBERG
1944–1945

I always loved Königsberg. The capital of East Prussia, it was a beautiful old city and, in many ways, very like Berlin. My mother was from Königsberg, and when I was a child, we used to go there to visit her parents, who ran a Viennese-style café and confectionery near the Kaiser Bridge, and occasionally, to take a beach holiday at the nearby seaside town of Cranz. But most of all I remember the Königsberger Zoo in the Tiergarten, which was one of the best in Europe and I can still recall, aged four, riding on the back of the elephant and seeing the bears. The bear pit at the zoo was even bigger and better than the one in Berlin. My grandfather owned a Mercedes-Benz—one of the first cars in Königsberg—and, to me, riding in the back of that car was almost as good as riding on the back of the elephant. Until they lost everything in the inflation of 1923 my grandparents were reasonably well off, I think. My grandmother was a good woman, always helping other people. There was a Jewish convalescent home in Luisenthal where she often took unsold cakes from the café and I used to wonder why it should have been this place that should receive her charity. Now I know why; she was herself half-Jewish. Much later, in 1919, my first wife and I went there on our honeymoon and we stayed in my grandparents' villa on the Upper Pond, which seemed to us like the last word in gracious living. We must have visited every attraction the city had to offer, including the Amber Museum—Königsberg is famous for its German gold, as amber is sometimes called— the Prussia Museum, and the zoo, of course, but mostly we just sat in the front garden and stared out at the pond. It was a very happy time for me. The war was over and I was still alive, with all my limbs intact, and in love. My wife adored the place and for a while we even thought about living there. In retrospect, I wish we had. Maybe she would have been spared the influenza that killed her not long afterward. The flu wasn't as bad in Königsberg as in Berlin. Fewer people to spread it, probably; there were only three hundred thousand people living there in the twenties, as opposed to the four million in Berlin.

My being sent to Königsberg in 1944 was supposed to be a punishment and feel like an exile from Berlin, but to me it felt like I was almost going home, especially as, until that summer, the city and most of East Prussia had been largely untouched by the war. As things turned out it was perhaps fortunate I was away from Berlin and out of anyone's mind when Count von Stauffenberg made his failed attempt at a coup in July 1944, otherwise I might have been swept up in the wave of executions that followed. More than a hundred kilometers to the southeast of Königsberg, Hitler came on German radio and announced he was alive, and if anyone was there to witness a demonstration of loyalty and affection—but only if they were—people breathed a great sigh of relief.

I was a lowly lieutenant, an officer attached to the 132nd Infantry Division and the FHO—the branch of German military intelligence responsible for the Eastern Front—and it was my job to help make meaningful assessments of Soviet capabilities and intentions, and communicate these with the army commanders on Paradeplatz. Those assessments were very simple: The Red Army was poised to annihilate us.

As an officer I was entitled to a room at the Park Hotel, on Huntertragheim Street and close to the Lower Pond. Built in 1929, the Park was the last word in modern luxury; at least it was until almost two hundred RAF Lancaster bombers turned up on two consecutive nights at the end of August 1944 and bombed the city to bits. Almost every building to the south of Adolf-Hitler-Platz, including the famous castle and the cathedral where Kant was buried, were destroyed or damaged. Thirty-five hundred people were killed and tens of thousands made homeless—a foretaste of the terrible fate that was soon to befall

Berlin. The upper floors of the Park Hotel and many of the men living on them disappeared in fire and smoke, but the second floor I lived on was spared and somehow the restaurant next door survived, too, which was just as well as it was one of the few places where German officers were allowed to take girls from the women's auxiliary services who, even in 1944, were sometimes strictly chaperoned.

There was one girl in particular, Irmela Schaper, a signals officer with the German naval auxiliary, of whom I was very fond. I had recently remarried, but that didn't make much difference to either Irmela or me since the city was more or less encircled by the Red Army and it was obvious to both of us that we were probably going to be killed. Irmela was a local girl. Her father worked for Raiffeisen Bank on Sträsemanstrasse not very far away from naval headquarters in the old seaport. I worked in the basement of what had been the post office close to Paradeplatz and we first met in a tobacconist's on Steindamm a short way north of there. We'd both heard that the cigarette ration had arrived in the city and went there simultaneously, only I got there first and bought the last packet. Not that these were much of a smoke, just a roll of cardboard and a few centimeters of inferior tobacco. It's hard to credit what we used to smoke back then. Anyway, she looked very smart in her double-breasted naval uniform, blond and buxom, which is just the way I like them, and as soon as I saw her I offered to share this last packet with her. I'm telling you all this because Irmela is the key to the whole story of what happened with Harold Heinz Hebel, or Captain

Harold Hennig as he then called himself. But you'll have to let me tell this story in my own way; I'm not a professional like you, Mr. Maugham; you'd probably tell me to start more fashionably in the middle instead of at the beginning. Well, maybe I can still do that.

"Ten each," I said to her, filling my cigarette case and then handing her the packet.

"That's very gallant of you," she said, and let me light one for her. She smoked it like a schoolgirl, hardly sucking the stuff in at all, and it made me smile, a little, but not so much that she might have thought I was laughing at her; that would have been impolite and foolish. Most women like to believe they're sophisticated, even when you're pleased that they're not.

"Don't be fooled. My armor is all rusted up and we had to eat my trusty white steed before he starved. If I tried to bow I'd probably fall flat on my face. Since the RAF left town my sense of balance isn't so good. My ears still feel like there's a brass band just around the corner."

"You mean there isn't? These days I don't hear so well myself. In fact, I may never sleep through a thunderstorm again without thinking Thor is an English bomb aimer in a Lancaster."

"As far as I'm concerned, 'sleep' is just a nice word in a fairy story. I'd like to believe in it, but experience and the Ivans have taught me different."

"Maybe we should get together for a drink one night and see who yawns first."

"It won't be me. I'm wide awake. You're the most interesting thing that's happened to me since I arrived from Berlin."

"Don't you like Königsberg?"

"As a matter of fact, I love it."

"It's my hometown. I used to live here."

"And now?"

"You call this living?"

"It's better than the alternative, perhaps. Well, now I know it's your hometown I love it even more."

"It was a nice place to live before the English decided to redecorate it."

"Let's not think about that now. What do you say we get a boat and you let me row you around Castle Pond?"

"Why would you want to do something so arduous on a warm day like this?"

"I don't particularly, but I can hardly offer to show you around your own hometown."

"Why not? Frankly, your guess about where anything is now is as good as mine. Yesterday I went for a walk along Copernicus Strasse before I realized it was Richard-Wagner-Strasse. I feel like a stranger here myself."

"It doesn't matter. The streets are all going to have Russian names soon. This time next year Richard-Wagner-Strasse will probably be Tchaikovsky Prospekt, or Borodin Street."

"That's a pleasant thought."

"Sorry. I'm an intelligence officer, but sometimes you really wouldn't think it."

"I think it's best to know the worst that can happen."

"That seems to be my job description."

"We could talk about it over dinner."

"That's the most pleasant thought I've heard in a long time. Where would you like to go? The safest place for dinner used to be the Blutgericht in the Castle courtyard basement."

"I know. Until they bombed it."

"Which leaves the Park Hotel."

"There's another place I know near the zoo on Erich-Koch-Platz."

I shook my head. "It can't be the Stadtkeller. That's closed, too."

"No, this is somewhere else."

"Not the naval nunnery."

Nunneries were what we called the dormitories where most of the women's auxiliary services were housed.

"No, but it's somewhere quiet, candlelit, with just the one exclusive table. Mine."

"I like the place already."

"After the bombing my parents left their apartment and went to live at their country house in Pillau. I stayed on. The auxiliary service commander thinks they're still living there."

"Which means that you don't have to keep the service women's curfew."

"Exactly."

"Nice."

"So. You're invited for dinner. It's canned stuff, mostly. But my father did have quite a decent selection of Mosels."

"Suddenly I seem to have quite an appetite."

"Shall we say eight o'clock?"

I glanced at my watch. "That's going to be the longest five hours of my life. What am I going to do with myself until then?"

"So go row a boat."

And that was it. I went to her parents' apartment in Hammer-weg Strasse for dinner. She cooked me a meal, I drank a couple of bottles of nice cold Mosel, and within a couple hours of me arriving there, we were lovers. That's how things were in those days. Implausibly fast. Uncomplicated. Nobody mentioned love or marriage or consequences. Nobody thought about the future because nobody thought they had a future. Really, you can't beat how easy life can be when you think there isn't going to be a tomorrow. Weeks passed like this and together, as winter arrived, we celebrated what we assumed might be our last few months on earth.

Irmela was tall and athletic. She was also highly intelligent, which was why she was working as a lightning maid in the naval signals section. She had to be intelligent to encrypt all communications using a special four-rotor code machine called the Scherbius Enigma before sending them. Before the war, she'd studied mathematics at Albertina University on Paradeplatz. The university was destroyed, like almost everything else in Königsberg, and while many people, including me, still took the risk of going into the remains of the university library in search of books—Gräfe und Unzer, the largest bookstore in Europe and opposite the university, had been completely consumed by flames after a napalm bomb fell through the glass roof—General Lasch, the military commander of Hitler's northern army, had his army headquarters in a bunker deep under the ruins. For several weeks I was just happy to see a lot of Irmela, who was an enthusiastic and noisy on-the-top kind of lover with considerable experience of men, which I came to appreciate. She knew I was married and didn't want anything from me except my company and my jokes, which in those days were a lot better than they are now. Experience has taught me that it's better to be serious, and I should know; I've tried and failed to be serious on thousands of occasions.

After the British bombing, the Russians halted their attack on the city for the winter and regrouped. Somehow the Alhambra movie theater on Hufenallee managed to keep going despite having been hit by a bomb, and while plays were no longer performed we often went there to see a movie, even though that always meant having to sit through newsreels telling us how well the war was going for Germany, and how victory would be ours in the end. Sometimes, after the film, Irmela would ask me if things were really as good as the Ministry of Truth and Propaganda described, which was a safe and secure way of asking if they were as bad as everyone said they were. Mostly I said that reports of mass rape and atrocities that stemmed from East Prussian towns nearer the Russian front were always exaggerated. But she knew I was lying and not because she thought that I believed in the final victory; she knew I was trying not to scare her, that's all. And one day toward the end of October 1944, she confronted my lies and evasions head on. Of course, she'd read some of the signals traffic about a place called Nemmersdorf, which was about a hundred kilometers east of Königsberg; she also knew that I'd been there to report on the situation for the FHO. We were in bed at her parents' place in Hammerweg Strasse at the time, and had just finished a particularly noisy bout of lovemaking.

"Christ," I said, "I hope the neighbors don't complain. Anyone would think I was raping you, or something."

That was the only time she hit me.

"Don't make jokes about that kind of thing," she said gravely. "I don't know a single girl in the auxiliary service who isn't petrified about what's going to happen when the Ivans turn up. You hear things. Bad things. Terrible things. We're all terrified."

"It's not as bad as people say."

"Liar," she said. "*Liar.* Look, Bernie, neither of us is a Nazi. The Gestapo aren't listening. Just for once don't spare my feelings. I know you're trying to stop me from worrying, but I also know you were somewhere near Nemmersdorf. Your name is on the report. You don't have to give me the details, only please tell me if anything of what I've heard about that place is true or not. If the Ivans really are as monstrous as people say they are. Or if the whole thing really is meant to deter us from surrendering. Which is the other rumor, of course. That the Ministry of Truth is trying to scare us out of surrender."

I lit a cigarette and helped myself to some of her father's brandy.

"Please," she said. "I need to know. Every woman in Königsberg wants to know what to expect. Particularly the women in the auxiliary services. You see, none of us in the auxiliary is particularly sure of our status as noncombatants. We're in uniform and are obliged to obey military orders but forbidden to use weapons and we're subject to civilian law. So where does that leave us? Will we be treated like civilians or prisoners of war? And will it matter a damn which is which when the Russians turn up? I don't mind dying. But I'd rather not be gang-raped before I die."

I didn't speak. How could I tell her what I knew? The things I'd heard from the few survivors of Nemmersdorf beggared description.

"Please, Bernie. Look, the word is that there were seventy-two women and girls in Nemmersdorf aged between eight and eighty-four. And that all of them were raped."

I nodded. "As a matter of fact, it's worse. Much worse than anything you've heard."

"How is that possible?"

"Raped, mutilated, and murdered." I paused. "All of them. Women crucified. Breasts cut off. Violated with vodka bottles. Your worst nightmare. What happened at Schulzenwalde was worse. There were ninety-five at Schulzenwalde. Dr. Goebbels is already organizing a team of Swiss and Swedish reporters and observers to go and see the place for themselves so he can tell the world's press that this is what Germany has been fighting against all along. Frankly, I think you can expect the newsreels to start getting worse from now on. They'll be telling the truth, in other words. As you say, their intention is now to deter us from surrendering. As if fighting on to the last is really going to make any damn difference."

"Why are the Russians doing this? I thought there were supposed to be rules on how you treat people in war."

"There are. It's just that we've treated Soviet POWs and Jews so very badly that we can expect no better treatment ourselves. There's a concentration camp to the west of here called Stutthof where more than a hundred thousand people—mostly Poles—are currently imprisoned. But we've been starving and murdering Jews there for a year."

Irmela nodded. "Which would fit with what we've heard in the signals. Naval captains have been complaining to their superiors here and in Danzig. Ships from the German navy have been used by the SS to take Jews to Stutthof from a camp called Klooga in Estonia. Apparently those prisoners were in a pretty bad way."

"Look," I said, "I think there's every chance we'll get all of the women and children out of Königsberg before the Red Army finally gets here. But before that happens, things in this city are going to get an awful lot worse."

One night, we were going to the Spätenbrau Restaurant on Kneiphöfsche Langgasse, near Cathedral Island. But en route we went to see the ruins of the cathedral and Immanuel Kant's grave, which was largely undamaged, mostly to give ourselves an appetite for life. Irmela knew a lot about Kant but was always kind enough not to tell me too much at once since I was an intelligence officer more by default than by aptitude. What I knew about Kant you could write on a spinning gas nebula. The cathedral itself was like a huge, empty skull found in the embers of a fire after some medieval execution. It was hard to know exactly what the RAF had been aiming their bombs at, since the nearest military target was more than a kilometer away. Or was it that they figured the only way to beat Germany was to be as bad as Germany? If so, then it certainly looked as if they had a good chance of winning.

"I always thought I'd get married in here," said Irmela as we wandered hand in hand around the ruins.

"Anyone in particular?"

"There was someone, but he was killed at Stalingrad."

"One of the lucky ones, probably."

"You think so?"

"We won't see most of those boys again. From what we know in the FHO, they're most of them working in Soviet slave-labor camps. If you ask me, your boyfriend was spared." I nodded. "So, let's you and I get married instead. In here. Right now. Come on. Why not?"

"Well, for one thing, you're already married," she said, "in case you'd forgotten."

"What's that got to do with anything? Besides, my wife is back in Berlin and I'll probably never see her again. Oh, and there's this for good measure: You say you love me and I certainly love you and I just happen to have a ring on my finger that will do for a ceremony until I can buy another. Besides, you'll probably be a widow before very long. And the blasphemy and bigamy certainly doesn't matter either since I'm going to hell already. If it makes you feel any better I'll take full responsibility for this when I get down there. I'll say, 'Look, it wasn't Irmela's fault, I persuaded her.'"

"You promise?"

"I can include that in the vows we make, if you like."

"We don't even have a priest."

"Who needs a priest in a Lutheran cathedral? I thought that was the whole idea of the German Reformation. To abolish priestly intercession. Besides, I can remember all the damn words. I've been married enough times already to know them by heart."

"You're serious, aren't you?"

"Under the circumstances I can't honestly see that God will mind very much. Frankly, I think he'll be glad that anyone can be in a ruin like this and still believe that the idea of God is even possible."

"I think he's possible, just not very likely," she said. "There were a hundred children killed in this cathedral when they took shelter from those RAF bombs. As a way of confirming that God doesn't exist it probably beats Nietzsche, don't you think?"

"In which case this will be like a second chance for him. For God, yes. A good way for him to get started in this city again. A chance to make it up to us. To show us that he really means something. You know, I'll bet we'll be the first people to get married in this church since that happened."

"You're mad, do you know that?" But she was smiling. "Why do you want to do this?"

"Because words matter, don't they? Most of the time I don't say what I mean just to keep from being arrested by the Gestapo. For once I'd like to say something that's actually important and mean it."

She nodded.

"I'll take that as a yes."

We were still celebrating our mock marriage—to be honest, it had seemed a lot more than a mock marriage at the time— with a horsemeat dinner in the Spätenbrau Restaurant when the devil put in an early appearance, as might have been expected after our lighthearted blasphemy. An unexpected bottle of extremely good Riesling arrived at our table, followed closely by its handsome donor, an SD captain whom, for a moment—it had been six years—I only half-remembered. But he remembered me, all right. Blackmailers need to have good memories. It was Harold Hennig, and to my irritation, he greeted me as if we'd been old friends.

"Berlin, wasn't it?" he said. "January, thirty-eight."

I stood up; he was a captain, after all, and I a mere lieutenant and it was a few moments before I connected him with the von Frisch case.

"Yes. It was. Gunther. FHO."

"Harold Hennig," he said, and clicked his heels as he bowed

politely at Irmela. "Well, Gunther, aren't you going to introduce me to this charming young lady?"

"This is Over Auxiliary—?" I was never quite sure of her non-military rank in the women's auxiliary and glanced at Irmela, who nodded back that I'd got this right. "Miss Irmela Schaper."

"May I join you both?"

"Yes."

"You look as if you're celebrating something," he observed.

"We're alive," I said. "That's always a cause for celebration these days."

"True." Captain Hennig sat down and took out an elegant, amber cigarette case, which he opened in front of us to reveal a perfectly paraded battalion of good cigarettes and then offered them around the table. "True. Where there's life, there's hope, eh?"

Irmela took one of his cigarettes and studied it like an interesting curio, and then sniffed the tobacco appreciatively. "I don't know if I should smoke this or keep it as a souvenir."

"Smoke it," he said, "and take another one for later."

So she did.

"Is this what the Gestapo is smoking these days?" I said, savoring the taste of a real nail. "Things must be better than I thought."

"Oh, I'm not with the Gestapo anymore," he said. "Not since the beginning of the war. I work for the Erich Koch Institute now."

"On the corner of Tragheimer and Gartenstrasse," said Irmela. "I know that building."

"Since the bombing we're rather more often found in Friedrichsberg."

"That must be nice," I said. "And a lot safer, too, I'd have thought."

Erich Koch was the Nazi Party gauleiter of East Prussia, and his huge country estate at Friedrichsberg, just outside the city, was the center of his commercial exploitation of the province, which, by all accounts, was completely unscrupulous. But his authority was absolute and General Lasch was obliged to give way to Koch's imperious demands. Even now the Erich Koch Institute in the city's Tragheim district was being remodeled—to a princely standard, it was bruited; while, at Koch's orders, a large number of civilian workers was soon to be put to work building an airplane runway on Paradeplatz, presumably so Koch could make a quick getaway in his personal Focke-Wulf Condor—and this at a time when there was a more pressing need to build the city's defenses for the Battle of Königsberg that was coming as soon as winter was over. Everyone assumed it would be the spring thaw of 1945 when the Red Army made its big push against the city. Right now, everything was frozen solid. Even the Russians. It was Erich Koch who had refused to consider the comprehensive and systematic plan proposed by General Lasch for the immediate evacuation of all civilians from East Prussia and who had placed his faith in building a wall—the Erich Koch Wall—in a place and to a construction standard that was of questionable value.

"The governor isn't in Friedrichsberg for reasons of his own personal safety," explained Hennig, "but because that's simply the best place to coordinate the defense of the city. It's not just Königsberg that's under threat but Danzig, too. Rest assured, the governor is looking after all our interests."

"I was sure he would be," I said, but everyone knew that Koch was looking out for his own interests most of all. I had a good idea that the Park Hotel where I was living was actually owned by the Erich Koch Institute and that the army was obliged to pay Koch four marks a night for every officer staying there, but I thought it best to confine my comments to general approval of the gauleiter. Koch was notoriously touchy and inclined to order the arrest and execution of anyone critical of his absolute rule. Public executions were common in Königsberg, with bodies left hanging from lampposts near the refugee camps on the southern side of the city where, it was believed, there was a much greater need for discipline.

"And what service do you perform for Governor Koch?" I asked Hennig, being careful not to mention blackmail and extortion.

He shook his head and poured some wine into a glass. "You might say that I'm his aide-de-camp. A military liaison officer. Just a glorified messenger, really. The governor issues an order and I have the job of conveying it to the military commander. Or anyone else who matters." He smiled at Irmela. "And what about you, my dear? I can see that you're in the naval auxiliary but doing what, may I ask."

"I'm in signals."

"Ah. You're a Valkyrie. A lightning maiden. No wonder this fellow Gunther is spending time with you, my dear. He always did like to stand a little too close to high voltages. In nineteen thirty-eight, he almost got his fingers burned. Didn't you, Gunther?"

"It's a wonder I have any fingerprints left," I said.

At this Irmela picked up my right hand and kissed my fingertips, one by one, and while I appreciated the tenderness of her gesture, I could have wished that she'd not done this in front of Harold Hennig, for whom all knowledge was power, probably. It wasn't that I thought he might tell my wife, but there was just something about him knowing about us I didn't like.

He grinned. "Well, we're all survivors, eh?"

"For how much longer, though," I said. "That's the question."

"A word of advice, old fellow," said Hennig. "There are only two people in East Prussia who still believe in the final victory. One of them is Adolf Hitler. The other is Erich Koch. So, if I were you, I'd avoid defeatist talk like that. I'd hate to see you end up decorating a lamppost for the edification of some foreign workers and refugees."

"It's horrible the way they do that," said Irmela.

"And yet it is hard to see how else good order is to be maintained in this city," said Hennig. "Iron discipline is the only way we are going to hold out for any longer." He shook his head.

"Anyway, I'm very glad to have left behind the Prinz-Albrecht-Strasse way of doing things. The Gestapo, I mean, with their torture chambers and knuckle-dusters. To be quite frank, I was never cut out for all that heavy stuff. Even with the law behind you, it's not for me."

His eyes glanced momentarily at me and I wondered if he'd forgotten how my partner, Bruno Stahlecker, and I had been obliged by him to fetch Captain von Frisch from Gestapo HQ after Hennig and his thugs had finished beating the old man half to death. But even if he hadn't forgotten about this and knew that I hadn't either, it was probably best I didn't mention it now. No one likes to be told that he's a loathsome piece of shit in front of a beautiful woman.

Hennig looked perfectly at ease, however, as if he'd been recalling his days with a student society given to displays of unruly behavior. He thrust his hands in the pockets of his riding breeches and pushed his chair back so that it stood on only two legs, rocking to and fro, and continued in this somewhat expansive mode, as if he was someone used to being listened to.

"But whatever you think of summary executions, my dear, I can promise you that the Russians will do much worse than we are capable of. I think it's only now that it's beginning to dawn on people just what we've been fighting for all along. The decline of the West faced with Slav barbarism. I mean, the historian Oswald Spengler was right. If anyone ever wanted proof of that, it's right here. Or at least a hundred kilometers east of here. I fear for the whole of European civilization if the Ivans conquer East Prussia." He chuckled. "I mean, I could take you to my office and show you a Soviet newspaper, the *Red Star*, with horrifying editorials that you could hardly credit might have been written. One in particular comes to mind now: 'Kill the Germans. Kill them all and dig them into the earth. We cannot live as long as these green-eyed slugs are alive. Today there are no books, today there are no stars in the sky; today there is only one thought. Kill the Germans.' That kind of thing. Really, it's quite shocking just how filled with hate for us these people are. One might almost think that they intended to drink our blood, like vampires. Or worse. I expect you've heard the reports about cannibalism. That the Red Army has actually eaten burger meat made of German women."

After Hennig's earlier warning about defeatism I wasn't disposed to argue that the Russians had been provided with good teachers in barbarism. But I did try to moderate his language a little. "I see no point in upsetting Miss Schaper with talk like that," I said, noticing that she had paled a little at the mention of cannibalism.

"I'm sorry," said Hennig. "Lieutenant Gunther is absolutely right. Forgive me, Miss Schaper. That was thoughtless and insensitive of me."

"That's all right," she said calmly. "I think it's best to know exactly what we're up against."

"Spoken like a true German," said Hennig. He turned in his chair and snapped his fingers at a waiter. "Bring us some brandy," he said. "The good stuff. Immediately."

A bottle of ten-year-old Asbach Uralt arrived on the table

and Hennig threw some banknotes beside it as if money meant nothing; and given that he worked for Koch, it probably didn't. The splash around Paradeplatz was that, with the help of the institute's ruthless manager, Dr. Bruno Dzubba, the diminutive Koch had amassed a personal fortune of more than three hundred million marks, and it was clear from the fistful of cash in Hennig's hand and the expensively tailored uniform he was wearing that some of this money was coming his way, at least in the shape of a generous expense account. Hennig uncorked the bottle and poured three generous glasses.

"Here's to happier subjects," he said and toasted Irmela's eyes. "Your beauty, for instance. I confess I am very jealous of Lieutenant Gunther. You will forgive me if I say I hope you have a friend who's a lightning maid, Miss Schaper. I should hate to be here for much longer without a charming young lady to spoil like Lieutenant Gunther."

"It's she who's been spoiling me, I'm afraid," I said.

"The mind reels at the very thought." Hennig downed his brandy and stood up. "Well, thank you for a delightful evening, but I'm afraid duty calls. The governor has to address the representatives of the People's Storm Unit here in the city tomorrow morning. Governor Koch has been appointed as their local commander. And I have to write his speech for him. Not that I have the first clue about what to say to them."

The People's Storm Unit was the new national militia that Goebbels had just announced—a home guard composed of conscripted men aged between thirteen and sixty who were not already serving in some military capacity. With a keen sense of humor most Germans were already referring to the People's Storm Unit as the Father and Son Brigade or, sometimes—and even more amusingly—the Victory Weapon.

After he'd gone—but not before Irmela had promised to introduce him to some of her female friends—I breathed a sigh of relief and then downed my own brandy.

"I can't fault his taste in alcohol," I said. "But I do hate that man. Then again, I hate so many men these days that I simply can't remember them all or exactly why I hate them, except to say that they're Nazis, of course. Which is as good a reason as any, I suppose. It's so much easier to know why you hate people now."

"But why do you hate him in particular?"

"Take my word for it, there's a good reason in his case. It's a righteous, holy thing to be able to hate a man like that. Love thy neighbor? No. It can't be done. The fact is I really do believe that Jesus Christ would have made a special exception in the case of Harold Heinz Hennig. And if not, then it's clear to me that it's impossible to be a Christian. Just as it's impossible to believe in a God who would let a hundred children die taking shelter in his church."

I paused for a moment and she kissed my fingertips again.

"Please, Bernie. Let's not talk about that anymore. I want to kiss every centimeter of you before I go to sleep tonight. And then I want you to do the same to me."

But I still had an itch that I needed to scratch. "That's another thing," I said. "I hate that he knows about us. That there's something between us now. It worries me. For a man like that, all knowledge is something to be used like a loaded pistol."

Irmela sighed and put down my hand. "You're crazy to worry about him, Bernie. Think about it. What possible harm could he do us? Besides, he's just a captain."

"Not just any captain. He's an extension of Erich Koch. Did you see the way the waiters in here fawned over him? The quality of his uniform? That amber cigarette case? Besides, the man used to be a blackmailer. Possibly still is, for all I know. The leopard doesn't change his spots. So maybe he's got something on Koch. Perhaps Erich Koch is the lemon who's being squeezed now. You know, I wouldn't be at all surprised. There must be a hell of a lot to get on a bastard like Erich Koch."

"You'll have to explain some of that. Why is Koch a lemon? I don't understand."

I told her all about the von Frisch case, to which Irmela very sensibly replied:

"But he's got nothing on you, Bernie Gunther. Or on me. Neither of us has anything to hide. Nor do we have any money to give him. Do we? Besides, there's a war on and there are more important things to worry about, wouldn't you say? You're worrying about nothing. If you're going to blackmail someone you only do it when there's a profit in it, surely?"

"Why is he here now?" I asked.

"It was a coincidence, that's all."

I sipped my brandy and then bit my fingernail.

"There's no coincidence with him. He doesn't arrive in your

life without there being a reason. That's not how it works with a man like that."

"So how does it work? Tell me."

But I could not. After the wine and the brandy, it was beyond my powers of speech to explain to her the sense of foreboding I had about seeing Harold Hennig again. For her to have understood how I felt about Hennig it would probably have been necessary for her to have returned with me to 1938 and seen poor Captain von Frisch's battered body lying in a pool of blood and urine on a cell floor. Looking back on it now I might have said it was like that picture by Pieter Bruegel popularly known as *Landscape with the Fall of Icarus*: I imagined an ordinary day in Königsberg—if such a thing was even possible; Irmela and me walking by the sea, hand in hand, enjoying the view and looking at the ships with innocent smiles on our windswept faces, but as oblivious to what is really going on in the picture as Bruegel's plowman or the lumpish shepherd staring up at the now empty gray sky. Meanwhile, somewhere in the corner of the canvas a tragedy unfolds, unnoticed by almost everyone. Hubris knocks us from the sky and we are both drowned in the freezing northern sea.

That's the thing about blackmail. You don't understand how it could ever happen to you until it does.

Winter came early that year. Snow filled the gray December air like fragments of torn-up hope as the Russians tightened their cold, iron grip on the miserable, beleaguered city.

Water froze in the bedroom ewers and condensation became ice on the inside of windowpanes. Some mornings I woke up and the bottom of the iron bedstead I shared with Irmela looked like the edge of the roof outside, there were so many icicles hanging off it. Defeat was staring us in the face like the inscription on a new headstone. Christmas came and went, the thermometer dropped to an unheard-of level and I more or less forgot about Captain Harold Hennig. Matters affecting our survival demanded more attention. Fuel and food ran short, as did ammunition and patience. The general opinion was that we could last for another three or four more months at most. Unfortunately, this opinion was not shared by the great optimist who had quit his wolf's lair in Rastenburg and was now safely back in Berlin. But Irmela and I had other things on our minds than mere survival, not least the fact that she was pregnant. I was delighted, and when she saw my own reaction so was Irmela. I promised, faithfully, that if by some miracle I survived the war I would divorce my wife in Berlin and marry her; and if I didn't survive, then something of me might, which would be some consolation at least for a life cut short, if not tragically—I could hardly claim that—then for a life that had been cut short of meaning. Yes, that was how I thought about the prospect of having finally fathered a child. Something of me would remain after the war. Which is all part of the butt-fuck that is life's grotesque comedy.

Then, one day in late January, and quite out of the blue, Captain Hennig arrived in a government car with an order for me to report to Gauleiter Koch on his estate in Friedrichsberg

THE OTHER SIDE OF SILENCE

and neither I nor my senior officers in the FHO had any option but to comply since the order was signed by Erich Koch himself. Not that I was in any way indispensable to my superiors. Only the most dimwitted intelligence officer could have failed to notice that the Russians were winning. But no one at FHO HQ ever looked at me the same way again; it was assumed among my fellow officers, not unreasonably, that I was another of Koch's larval spies.

We drove west out of the city, on the Holsteiner Damm, along the northern shore of the Pregel River and, after about seven miles, where the black river flowed into the even blacker Vistula Lagoon, we saw the house, which bordered one or two other palaces of lesser grandeur. Hennig had not told me why I had been summoned there by the gauleiter, about that he remained infuriatingly silent, but usefully he did explain that the house had been built by King Frederick III of Prussia in 1690 as a lodge for elk hunting, although as soon as I caught my first sight of it I formed the conclusion that a place of that size might more plausibly have been used as the base for a yearlong expedition to hunt woolly mammoths or saber-toothed tigers. Prince Bismarck would have scorned the place as too grand and, perhaps, too Prussian, but judging by the pretensions of Gross Friedrichsberg, I expect it was just right for the eldest son of Frederick the Great—who must have been justifiably worried how else he was going to live up to the enormous reputation of his father—and Erich Koch, of course. Given that the place was the size of Potsdamer Platz station, I imagine Koch must have thought it was the perfect house for a former railway employee like him.

Immediately prior to my leaving FHO headquarters with Hennig I'd been told that the Schloss Gross Friedrichsberg, as it was known to all who worked there—and it was indeed a huge estate, being several hundred hectares—was now owned by the East Prussia Land Company, lest there be any suggestion that Koch was enriching himself at the expense of the German people; the fact that Koch was owner of the East Prussia Land Company was probably just an unfortunate coincidence.

An immaculate butler ushered us through the front door and straight into the castle library, where Koch was waiting beside a coal fire that could have powered a class 52 steam locomotive for the DRG. To be fair, it was a very large room and it probably needed a big blaze in the grate to prevent the glacier ice from encroaching past the farthest sections of the bookshelves. The gauleiter was seated in a Louis XV–style gilt wingback chair that was as tall as a giraffe and only served to make him even smaller than he certainly was. With his toothbrush mustache and smart party tunic, Koch looked like a ration-book Adolf Hitler, and meeting him in the flesh, it was difficult to take seriously his very public assertions in the *Völkischer Beobachter* that the lowliest German worker was racially and biologically a thousand times more valuable than any Russian. I'd seen smaller Nazis but only in the Hitler Youth. And he looked about as racially valuable as the onanistic contents of a schoolboy's handkerchief. He stood up but not noticeably and then we saluted each other in the time-honored way.

"Thank you for driving out here," he said.

I shrugged and looked at Hennig. "Hennig did the driving, sir. I just admired the view. It's a nice place you have here."

Koch smiled sweetly. "No. It's not mine, you know. Would that it were. The East Prussia Land Company owns this lovely house. I just rent it from them. God knows why. These old Prussian houses cost a fortune to heat in winter, you know. I'll probably bankrupt myself merely trying to keep this place warm." Koch waved at a drinks tray. "Would you like a drink, Captain Gunther?"

"I've not often been heard to say no to a glass of schnapps," I said. "And it's Lieutenant Gunther now."

"Yes, of course, you had a difference of opinion with Dr. Goebbels, didn't you?"

"I was wrong about something. Made a mistake. I'm probably quite lucky to be a lieutenant, sir."

"That's all right." Koch grinned and poured us a glass of schnapps. "The doctor and I have never exactly seen things eye to eye. Prior to my appointment as the East Prussian governor I'm afraid he rather suspected me of having been implicated in the publication of a newspaper article that made fun of his physical handicaps."

There was only one handicap that I recalled, but it seemed foolish to disagree when all I really wanted was to get out of that place as soon as possible. The last thing I wanted was to be drawn into a twilight rivalry between these two little men. I tasted the schnapps, which was enough to promote an emaciated smile.

"How would you like to be a captain again?"

At that stage in the war, it was better to be the lowliest kind of officer there was. Being a general seemed like a responsibility that no one would have wished for. But I shrugged with an indifference that I felt could reasonably have been interpreted as modesty. Koch wasn't concerned with my feelings in the matter, however, and had already assumed that, like him, I was keen to advance in life and to profit wherever and whenever possible, and probably however, too.

"And you will be," he said. "I need only call your commanding officer, General Lasch, to make that happen."

"It's kind of you. But I wouldn't trouble yourself on my behalf. I've long ceased to believe that my future lies in the army."

"Oh, it's no trouble. I'm always glad to help someone who's fallen foul of Joey the Crip. Isn't that so, Harold?"

"Yes, sir," said Captain Hennig. "We don't like the doctor very much."

"Harold tells me that you were a policeman in Berlin before the war. A commissar, no less."

I finished the schnapps and let him pour me another, the way I like it, right to the brim, before putting that one down the tube, too.

"That's right." I was pleased to change the subject. Or so I thought. "But my maternal grandparents were from Königsberg.

I used to visit here a lot when I was a boy. I always liked coming to the old Prussian capital. You might almost say that for me this is a home from home."

"I feel much the same. I'm from Elberfeld, near Wuppertal. But this is where my heart now lies. In East Prussia. I love it out here."

I glanced around the library. All those books were making it easy for me to understand why he had such a foolish, sentimental attachment to the place. Books are precious. They can almost make you feel at home. In any other home but that one they'd have been used as fuel.

"When you came here as a boy, I bet you visited the old Amber Museum."

"Oh, yes sir. Prussian gold, they used to call it."

"Indeed. The world's major source of amber is the Samland. And Palmnicken, in particular. We've had Jews—mostly women— surface mining the stuff for the last few years. Tell me, do you like amber?"

I didn't, as it happened. To me, amber had always looked like nature's plastic, not in the least bit precious and no more than a curiosity at best. I couldn't ever understand why some people seemed to prize the stuff so highly. But since I felt we were now, perhaps, finally coming to the point of my being there, I nodded politely and said, "Yes, I suppose so. I never really thought much about the stuff."

"What else do you know about it?"

171

"Only that it's expensive. Which is where I stop knowing about anything very much. There's usually a tight hand brake on my thinking when there's a lot of money involved."

"As there is for everyone these days. We're all of us having to make sacrifices in this terrible war that was forced upon us by our ideological enemies. But Harold tells me that you are not without diversions in Königsberg. That there is a lovely girl in the naval auxiliary you've been seeing. What's her name?"

"Irmela. Irmela Schaper."

"Good. I'm glad about that. A soldier should always have a sweetheart. Don't you agree, Harold?"

"I do indeed, sir. Especially now that I've seen the girl. She's as sweet as a sweetheart gets."

"Before she stops being a sweetheart and becomes a wife, eh?"

Koch laughed at his own joke. But it was too near to being true for me to join him in a smile.

He went over to a desk as big as a Tiger tank and pulled open an enormous drawer. "Come over here, Captain," he said. "Come and see."

The drawer was full of amber objects—necklaces, brooches, earrings, cigarette holders, animal carvings; it looked like one of the many market stalls near the museum I'd seen when I was a boy.

"Please, pick something out for your sweetheart."

"I couldn't, sir. Really, it's very kind of you, but—"

"Nonsense," said Koch. "Whatever you think she'd like. A nice necklace, or perhaps a brooch. Or for yourself, if that's what you'd really prefer. Harold has a very handsome antique ciga-rette case. Not to mention a beautiful pair of cuff links that were originally made for Arthur Schopenhauer."

I'd have much preferred to have taken nothing; the idea of being in Koch's debt was horrible to me, especially now that I'd learned how some of the stuff was mined. And I couldn't help but think that much of what I was looking at had been stolen from someone else—from Jews, probably. But finally I could see I had no choice in the matter. I picked up a gold necklace that contained a large teardrop piece of amber and, holding it up in front of my eyes, let the firelight illuminate the perfectly pre-served insect it contained.

"Oh yes," said Koch. "Good choice. That's a Wilhelmine piece from before the Great War. Fascinating, isn't it? The way an insect from thousands of years ago should have become trapped by some sticky tree resin which then fossilized."

"Perhaps it will remind her of me," I said.

Koch took the necklace from my hand, wrapped it in a sheet of tissue paper from the same drawer like a local shopkeeper—evidently he'd done this kind of thing before—and then placed the object in my tunic pocket, as if he would brook no argument against his gift.

"Do you feel trapped, Captain Gunther?" he asked. "Like that insect?"

"A little, sometimes," I said carefully. I hadn't forgotten Hen-nig's words of caution about defeatism and the gauleiter's predi-lection for hanging defeatists from the city's lampposts. "Who doesn't? But I'm sure it's just temporary, sir. We'll break out of this encirclement before very long. Everyone thinks so."

"Exactly. Before the light there must first be the darkness. Is it not so? And now let me show you something else."

Koch led the way out of the library and into the hall, which seemed to have more antlers on display than a Saxon deer park—not to mention the whole arsenal of musketry that had probably put them there. As we walked across a marble checkerboard floor I felt as if I were a pawn about to make a move with which I strongly disagreed. I ought to have walked through the front door and all the way back to Paradeplatz. Instead I followed Koch to a door where a suit of Gothic armor stared at me with slit-eyed, steely disapproval. I should have been used to that, having once worked for General Heydrich.

We went down two flights to the basement and into an enormous darkened room where he struggled to find the light switch.

"Here, sir," said Hennig, "let me."

A few seconds later I was looking at a series of decorative panels, each of them half a meter in height, that were arranged along the room's walls. Some of these panels had imperial crowns and a large letter R on them, while others depicted hunting scenes; there were also ornate carvings—entwined imperial eagles, classical warriors, more imperial crowns, and mermen holding dolphins; and all of them made of amber. Frankly, there was a little too much amber in there for my taste; about a ton of the stuff. It was like being inside an enormous beer bottle.

"Tell me, Captain Gunther, have you heard of the Amber Room?"

"No, sir."

"Really? The famous Amber Room that was a gift from King Frederick William the First to his then ally, Tsar Peter the Great?"

I shrugged, hardly caring if Erich Koch thought me ignorant. I thought he was an outrageous crook who probably deserved to hang, and his opinion on anything—least of all my knowledge of amber and Russian history—mattered not in the least.

"Russians weren't so bad then, I guess," I said.

"That was before Communism," said Koch, as if I were the one German who might have forgotten 1917.

"Yes, it was."

"Well then, let's see. In 1701 Peter installed these magnificent panels in a special room in the Catherine Palace near present-day Leningrad, where they stayed until we liberated them a few years ago and brought them here to Gross Friedrichsberg. When it was still at the palace, the room was often described as the Eighth Wonder of the World."

I tried to look impressed, although my own opinion was that this wide-eyed, lazy description of the Amber Room must have been given by people who didn't get out very much. I was getting a little tired of Koch's reverence for the orange stuff, so I decided to hurry things along.

"Sir, might I ask what all this has to do with me?"

"You're going to help us get these priceless artifacts back to Berlin, where they belong."

"Me? How? I don't understand."

"Don't worry," said Koch. "We weren't thinking of making you hide them under your coat, Captain. No, we had something else in mind. Didn't we, Harold? Something a little more sophisticated."

"We're going to load them on a refugee ship that's due to leave the port of Gotenhafen in a few days' time," said Hennig. "The MS *Wilhelm Gustloff.* As you probably know, many of those ships are frequently targets for Russian submarines from the Baltic fleet operating out of the Finnish port of Hangoe. We thought it might help to guarantee the safety of both passengers and panels if the Russian navy was informed that one of their most important national treasures—which we may have to trade back one day—is on board that same ship."

"They might be rather less inclined to sink it," said Koch, as if I might have failed to understand.

"Informed? How? By postcard? Or would you like me to drive to the front and give them a letter?"

Hennig smiled. "Well, that would be one way. But we were rather hoping you might persuade that sweetheart of yours—the little lightning maid—to put out an unencrypted signal on an open frequency informing the Russians, indirectly, of the presence of the Amber Room on board the *Wilhelm Gustloff.*"

"Really," said Koch, "when you stop and think about it, this would be to the advantage of everyone."

"Persuade her? How? What am I supposed to tell her?"

"Only what we've told you."

"Need I remind you both that putting out a signal without encoding it using a Scherbius Enigma machine would be a court-martial offense? For which she could easily be shot as a spy. Or worse. You're asking her to break the very first rule of being a signals auxiliary."

"No, no, no," said Koch. "My authority as Prussian gauleiter supersedes all local military and naval codes and protocols. There would be no chance of this even getting near a court-martial."

"There are going to be as many as ten thousand people on that ship, Gunther," said Hennig. "Civilians. Women and children. Wounded German soldiers. The Russians might not care for *them*. But they would never attack if they thought by doing so they'd be destroying the famous Amber Room."

"Is it them you're worried about?" I asked. "Or these priceless bits of tree resin?"

"That's a little unfair," said Hennig. "This is, by any definition of the word, a great historical treasure."

"Then it beats me why you don't just give an order to our Marine War Office commanders in Kiel and have them put out a signal."

"For the simple reason that they're in Kiel," said Koch, "and more than seven hundred and fifty kilometers away from my authority."

"Besides," added Hennig, "if the Russians were to intercept an unencrypted naval communication from Kiel they'd assume it was some kind of trap. On the other hand if it comes from a small and, let's face it, unimportant naval station here in Königsberg, they'll conclude it's not been authorized by the Marine War Office and then be inclined to take it more seriously. That the person sending the message is someone desperate to prevent the loss of thousands of lives."

"And what happens if this cultural blackmail of yours doesn't work? What if the Russians aren't as keen on amber as you are, sir? What if they're not interested in preserving a national treasure? Let's face it, they haven't shown a great deal of care for anything else in this damn war. Haven't you heard of Stalin's math? If there are ten Russians and one German left alive at the end of this war he will consider it to have been won. They now own the international patent on scorched earth."

"Nonsense," said Koch. "Of course they don't want to lose the Amber Room. It was the fucking Ivans who disassembled it for transport to some Siberian shithole in the first place. They must think it's valuable. Our men got there only just in time to prevent that and shipped it back here to Königsberg instead."

I shook my head. "I'm sorry gentlemen. But I won't do it."

"What the fuck do you mean, you won't do it?" said Captain Hennig.

"I won't. It's a monstrous thing to ask of a girl like that."

"Says who? You? Fuck you, Gunther. This isn't just any beer cellar Fritz who's asking you for a favor, this is the governor of East Prussia."

"She's only twenty-three years old, for Christ's sake. You

can't ask a girl like that to disobey strict orders and take a risk not just with her own life but with the lives of thousands of people."

"You dumb idiot," said Hennig. "Call yourself an intelligence officer? I've seen scum in my toilet that's more intelligent than you."

"It's all right, Harold," said Koch calmly. "It's all right. Let's be civil here. Is that your final word, Gunther?"

Suddenly I felt tired—too tired to care much what happened to me now; it might have been the schnapps; then again the whole war felt like a lamppost that had been tied around my neck. Only, maybe it would be my neck tied to the lamppost.

"Yes it is, sir. I'm sorry. But I simply can't ask her to do this."

Koch sighed and pulled a face. "Then it looks as if you're not going to be a captain again, after all."

"I suppose I really don't care what happens to me."

Hennig sneered. "It also looks as if you're walking back to town."

"Gentlemen? After what I just heard? I could certainly do with some fresh air."

I didn't tell Irmela what had happened. I thought it best not to worry her. It's not every day in Nazi Germany you turn down a man as powerful as Erich Koch, and part of me expected that I might be arrested at any time and thrown into the concentration camp at Stutthof. They hadn't threatened me, exactly, and, more important, they hadn't threatened her, but I hardly thought they would just give up. Somehow I had to think of a way of preventing them from intimidating Irmela, and soon, too.

"Do you have to go to work tomorrow?" I asked her that night.

"Why?"

"I'm just asking, that's all. I was thinking maybe we could spend the time here together, alone."

"I'm on duty. You know that. I can't not just turn up. This is the naval auxiliary we're talking about here, not a Salamander shoe shop. Besides, they're relying on me. In case you had forgotten, there's a lot happening right now in the Baltic Sea."

We were in bed at the time, and sharing the cigarette now lying in the cheap imitation amber ashtray that was balanced on my chest.

"I understand."

"It's not that I don't like spending time with you, my darling snail. I do. These moments we have here are very precious to me. Shall I tell you why? Because I never thought I would have them. When you showed up in my life I had more or less reconciled to myself to ending my life here without ever having known the real love of a man."

"What about Christoph? The fellow who died at Stalingrad."

"We were lovers. But we weren't in love. There's a difference. Besides, he was just a boy."

"Nothing wrong with that if you're just a girl."

"I know you think that. And maybe that's what I was before.

But I'm a woman now. You made that happen. Without you I'd still be giggling in cinemas. You treat me like something precious. Like I matter to you. You listen to what I have to say like you genuinely care. I can't tell you what that means to a woman. That's all I ever wanted. To be heard by the man I love."

I was silent for a few moments after that. There's nothing quite like a few loving words from a woman to make a man quiet.

"Look," I said, "if anyone ever threatens me as a way of trying to get to you, then please tell them to go to hell. I'll take my chances. In this life and the next."

"What are you talking about?"

"I'm just saying. I'm not the one who's important here. You are."

"Yes, but why are you saying it?"

"There's a war on. People say all kinds of strange things when there's a war on."

"All right. I understand all that. Look, has this got anything to do with Captain Hennig?"

"No," I lied. "Nothing to do with him at all. As a matter of fact I don't think I've seen him since that night in Spätenbrau, on the day we were married."

"I couldn't let anything happen to you, Bernie," she said. "Not now. You're such a sweet man, do you know that? You've given me my life."

"Nonsense. It was yours from the beginning."

"It's true. No one was ever as kind to me as you've been. I don't know what I'd do without you."

"You have to think of the baby now. Not me. Do you understand? I'm not in the least bit important beside you and the child."

"I don't understand. Why are you talking like this?"

"All I'm saying is that I want you to be careful, Irmela."

"We're surrounded by the Red Army, by Russian fighters, there's no fuel and not much food, there are no secret weapons to rescue us, our homes are defended by the Father and Son Brigade, and you want me to be careful? You're ridiculous, do you know that? If I didn't love you so much I'd say you were going crazy."

"Maybe I'm just crazy about you? Did you consider that possibility? That's right. I'm mad about you."

"Well, that makes two of us who are mad. It's infectious, obviously. Give me another cigarette."

"In my tunic."

I hadn't intended to give her the amber necklace but she found it when she was going through my pockets looking for cigarettes and I hadn't the heart to tell her that it had been given to me by Erich Koch.

"It's beautiful," she said. "For me?"

"No, I was rather thinking I might wear it myself."

"I absolutely love it," she said, putting on the amber necklace immediately and bounding across her bedroom to look at herself in the cheval mirror. "What do you think?" she asked, turning to face me.

I had to admit it suited her very well, a conclusion that was made easier for me by the fact that she was entirely naked at the time.

"Yes, it looks good on you."

"You really think so?"

I smiled. "Yesterday's newspaper would look good on you, Irmela."

"It must have been very expensive," she said.

Once again I felt a little awkward when I failed to admit that it had been a gift from Erich Koch and very soon afterward I started to regret I hadn't told her the truth about the necklace, fearing Harold Hennig would do it for me and spoil things. There was no doubt about it. I had started to care for Irmela very deeply, much more than I could have imagined was even possible for a man of my age. I had no right to the love of a nice girl of twenty-three. I was almost fifty, after all; fifty years of fuckups and disappointments, which means that when you think you only have a few months of life ahead of you every minute seems to count, and every feeling becomes magnified, massively. I'd have done anything to protect her and the baby she was carrying, but it's odd how inadequate anything like that can begin to feel. The best part of me was probably gone forever, but I could still hope to look after her.

The next day, when I walked down to Paradeplatz as usual, I found myself tailed by a black Audi. With so few cars on the snow-covered, cratered roads it was easily noticed, like a large and shiny spot of ink on a white sheet of paper. It stayed about ten meters behind me, which was another reason to notice it. I'm a fast walker. There were three men in it I didn't recognize, but I knew that wouldn't last. An introduction was coming whether I wanted one or not. I just hoped the freemason's handshake wouldn't be too painful. I kept walking in the hope that the longer I kept walking the farther away I was taking them from Irmela's building but after another hundred meters I saw the futility of it, turned, slipped on the ice, almost falling over, and walked back to the car with as much dignity as I could muster. When I leaned down to the driver's window I almost fell again. One of the men in the car sniggered. I knew they were Gestapo even before he flashed his brass identity disk in the palm of his hand. Only the friends of Koch and the Gestapo could get that kind of joke or, for that matter, the petrol.

"You Gunther?"

"Yes."

"Get in," said the man with the disk.

I didn't argue. His wooden face had been argued with many times before, to no avail, and at least it was just me they were arresting. So I sat in the back of the Audi, lit a cigarette, listened patiently as their leather coats creaked against the car seats, and tried to think of all the other times I'd been picked up by the Gestapo and managed to talk my way out of it. Of course, things were very different now the war was almost lost. The Gestapo had always been good listeners but since July '44 and Count

Stauffenberg, they'd stopped listening to anything very much except the sound of tightly strung piano wire.

To my surprise we didn't go to the Police Praesidium on Stresemannstrasse, behind the North Railway station. Instead we drove a little farther east and stopped in front of the Erich Koch Institute on the corner of Tragheimer and Gartenstrasse, which was one of the last buildings in Königsberg still displaying Nazi flags. It added a nice touch of color to a city that had gone prematurely gray with fear and worry. Absurdly, some bandbox guards came to attention as the car drew up; they must have figured the only cars with petrol contained people who were important. The Gestapo even opened the car door for me and two of them escorted me through the cliff-high doors and up the marble double stairway, where a man was carefully fitting long, brass stair rods. At the top stood a tall plinth with a bronze of Erich Koch staring over the balustrade, like a satrap surveying his empire. Or maybe he was just checking that the stair-rods were being fitted correctly. Crystal chandeliers hung from the ceiling as if in imitation of the freezing weather outside, which made the blasts of warm air blowing from the vents in shiny new ceramic stoves all the more surprising. The institute was noisy with hundreds of foreign workers hammering and painting and redecorating, which seemed a little premature as the Red Army hadn't yet said which color they'd have preferred for 1945.

I was ushered along a corridor as big as a bowling alley where thick, new blue carpet was being laid and, for a moment,

I wondered if I was actually in the East Prussian School for the Blind in Luisenallee. It was the only possible explanation for so little foresight and so much obvious reluctance to face the truth. Amid the ignorant confusion of it all Harold Hennig was standing with his hands in his breeches pockets, his gray tunic open, as if he didn't have a care in the world, and quite probably he didn't. Every time I saw him I knew he wasn't ever going to be one of the unlucky ones without a comfortable chair when Ivan stopped the balalaika music. Seeing me he beckoned me forward and led the way into an office already carpeted but without much furniture, just a lot of fluff on the floor, a couple of chairs and a half-size desk on which lay his greatcoat and cap. A large portrait of a very pink-faced Adolf Hitler was hanging on the wall. Wearing a gray greatcoat with the collar turned fashionably up and a peaked hat, the leader was looking off into the middle distance as if trying to decide if the blue of the carpet matched the blue of his eyes. He needn't have been concerned. It was a cold blue with an affinity for black and a degree of darkness that Goethe understood only too well, and an excellent color match.

"Here's me thinking this is East Prussia," I said, "when the true state we're living in turns out to be Denial."

Hennig snorted with contempt, put his hand on my shoulder, which I didn't much like, and walked me over to the fireplace, where a log the size of a wild boar was sizzling quietly, just like my temper. From the mantelpiece he took down an amber box and flipped it open.

"Smoke a cigarette, Bernie," he said quietly. "Take the edge off your tongue."

I took one, lit it, and tried to stay inside myself for a few minutes longer.

He smoked one, too. I even lit the match for him. For a while all we did was blow smoke at each other. It was beginning to look as if we could get along really well.

"When the pathologists examine your dead body," said Hennig, "they'll probably find you had an enlarged mouth." He sighed wearily. "Nineteen forty-five, and you still haven't learned that you should talk only when words are safer than silence."

"I'm not going to change my mind about my girl," I said.

"You don't have a mind. Not to speak of. For a Fritz in intelligence, you're very fucking dumb. I thought the same back in thirty-eight. You were dumb to get mixed up in that business with von Fritsch. You must have known how it would all play out. Sure you did. An idiot could have seen how that was going to end. Himmler himself gave the orders to frame that fucking general. You were dumb to take that case."

"I took it because Captain von Frisch was my commanding officer in the Great War. And because I loved him."

"That's what I'm talking about. You were dumb. Principles are for people who can afford to have them, not for you and me. You were lucky to walk away from that case with your fingernails."

"Maybe. But I'm still not going to help you now."

"Yes, you are," he said. "And here's why, dumbhead."

He collected a file off the desk and handed it to me—a thin blue file on the cover of which was the official stamp of the Saint Elizabeth Hospital on Ziegelstrasse, and the name of Irmela Louise Schaper. I didn't have to open it. I already knew what was in it.

"One of the benefits of being the governor of East Prussia is that no one has any secrets from you. No, not the smallest thing. Not this small thing, certainly. Even doctors don't dare plead the usual code of patient confidentiality in Königsberg. And not when the Gestapo tell them otherwise. So. Your girlfriend is going to have a baby. Congratulations. I presume you're the father. Although some of those naval girls like to set sail with a big crew on board, if you know what I mean. And I do wonder what your poor wife will say when she finds out."

"You bastard," I muttered.

"Not me. But the baby, yes, almost certainly. Anyway, time will tell. Which—let's be honest here—is short. No, please don't talk, for once just listen, Gunther. Because this is no longer really about you, is it? Not anymore. To be frank, I only need you in case your girlfriend is sufficiently principled not to understand what's good for her. And her baby, of course. Let's not forget that little twinkle from your eye."

He fished a piece of grayish paper out of his breeches pocket and showed it to me. The paper was headed *Identity Pass for the MS Wilhelm Gustloff.* Irmela's name was printed on the bottom of the pass.

"Thanks to the generosity and understanding of the governor, all of the women in the women's naval auxiliary are to be given one of these. It's a special pass, printed on the *Wilhelm Gustloff's* own printing press. They've got everything on that ship; a swimming pool, movie theater, three restaurants, and, most important of all, the real prospect of seeing Germany again. Even now those auxiliary women are being told that they're the lucky ones. That they're to be evacuated from Königsberg. Today. Already they're breathing a sigh of relief. The good-looking ones at any rate. I should think many of them have already left the city by now since boarding commences on January twenty-fifth. Which is tomorrow. I say all of the women but as you can see this particular pass has yet to be signed by the governor. Or I. And until it is, it simply isn't valid.

"As soon as it is signed, both Miss Schaper and her unborn child, of course, can board the ship. But not until then. You see where I'm going with this, Gunther. Either she agrees to send the unencrypted signal—which I will supply, of course—and on an open channel, or she'll be the last naval auxiliary left in the city when the Russians turn up. After which I don't give much for her chances or the baby's. I'm sure I don't have to tell you of all people what the Russians are doing to our women. It was you who wrote the report on Nemmersdorf, wasn't it? How many women was it they violated? The Russian soldier seems to regard the rape of German women as a patriotic duty. I mean, they fuck like they're using a bayonet. So, I wonder how many Ivans she could take on before she lost that baby."

"You put that very nicely, Hennig. So nicely I wonder how I

don't see how many of your teeth I can make stick to my knuckles."

"You don't want to hit me, Gunther. That would spoil everything. For you. For your girl. And her invisible jockey."

I bit my lip, which was momentarily better than biting a senior officer. I wasn't sure what the military law on that one was, but I didn't think it was a ticket home on the MS *Wilhelm Gustloff*.

"And where will you be? When the ship sets sail."

"Oh, I'll be on the ship, too. Someone has to oversee the transport of the Amber Room back to Germany. I'm sure you agree it's much too valuable to let it travel by itself."

"I'm impressed. How did you manage that?"

"Let's just say that when the gauleiter was in the Ukraine—where he was also the governor, of course—he managed to spirit away the contents of four whole museums. And those are just the ones that I know about. I should say he now has an art collection to rival Hermann Göring's."

"And you threatened to tell Hitler or Himmler about them. Is that it?"

"It would have been my duty as a German officer."

"And Koch? What about him?"

"He's staying on in Königsberg. Bravely. As you might expect of a man like that. Right up until the very last minute, when I believe he has made plans to facilitate his own escape to a house on the coast and then on an icebreaker, to Flensburg. But you needn't concern yourself with the governor's safety. All you have to do is go and see your little lightning maid, show her this identity pass, and then tell her what to do. She won't even have to endure the scrutiny of her colleagues as she carries out this important duty for the governor. As we speak, she's probably the last one there. So, it couldn't be simpler."

"Suppose she says no."

"You'd better make damn sure she doesn't say no, hadn't you? Not if you want to be a daddy in eight months. As soon as I've seen her give the signal—yes, I'm coming with you, Gunther, just to make sure—I'll sign this pass and you can drive her to Gotenhafen yourself, where you can say your romantic goodbyes. I'm afraid there's no pass for you, my friend. Sorry about that. Not unless you're part of the submarine training division; we need those boys to crew the U-boats. Or unless you're badly wounded. Then again, I suppose we could always make that happen. Ordinarily, that might be the only alternative for a swine like you. For me to have those two thugs in the corridor take you outside and blow your brains out. But with you, Gunther, things are different, I think. You'd probably welcome a bullet in the back of the head. But failure to comply with the governor's orders will only result in you being assigned to the concentration camp at Palmnicken, where your duties will include assisting the SS to dispose of three thousand Jewish female workers. Which I imagine you'll probably think of as a fate worse than death. That's what I can promise you. So, as you can no doubt see, you really don't have a choice." He looked around the room as if he expected that the fluff and the chairs were going to back him up.

"Look, it's not so bad what I'm asking you to do here. Anyone would think that I want something really difficult. All I'm trying to do is preserve the lives of everyone on that ship."

"Including yours."

"Naturally including mine. In a few months' time, when the war is over, and you're dead or in a Soviet labor camp, and Irmela and I are safely in Germany, you'll wonder why you didn't cooperate sooner. The fact is, we could have arranged for your passage home, too. I could have used a good man to help me guard all that priceless amber. So, do I have your cooperation, or not?"

Through all that he said, even through his white smiles and his smooth laughter and total confidence that I would meekly do exactly what he said, I knew that one day, in an unimaginable tomorrow's world to which I knew I might never belong, I would see him again and pay him back in kind for everything he had done. For a moment the threat of some nebulous future revenge tried to form itself in my mouth and I even took a breath to give these futile words air. Instead, recognizing my impotence, I said nothing and I even think I must have nodded my quiet and spineless assent. The things you do for a woman.

Hennig buttoned up his tunic and then fetched his greatcoat and his cap.

"Shall we go?"

SIXTEEN

FRENCH RIVIERA
1956

The red beam from the lighthouse tracked across the Villa
Mauresque as if searching the blue night sky for an enemy
bomber to target but finding only me and Somerset Maugham
seated side by side, next to the almost motionless swimming pool,
and alerting each of us to the possibility that one of us might
bring some as yet unknown harm to the other. He remained very
still, and whenever the red light crossed his creased features, turning them the color of blood, he reminded me of a sort of vampire.
I had been silent for a long moment and the old Englishman
was sensitive enough to see that I had been much affected by the
telling of this painful story—more affected than I could have

imagined. It had been more than ten years, after all, and I hadn't even got to the good bit.

"It's been a while since I talked about it," I told him. "If it comes to that, I don't think I've ever talked about it. Frankly, it's not the sort of thing you bring up over a beer and a sausage."

"I'm sorry," he said.

I tapped a fingernail against the cocktail gong. It sounded just like my heart. Or so I wanted to believe. How else was I going to finish my story? I swallowed hard and kept on going.

"Königsberg was surrendered to the Russians on April ninth, nineteen forty-five, after which I and ninety thousand other German soldiers were marched off into captivity. Me, I was one of the lucky ones. Someone helped me to escape, in nineteen forty-seven. Most of us died, however. I believe General Lasch was only repatriated about nine months ago. Meanwhile, the city was renamed Kaliningrad in July nineteen forty-six, in honor of some murderous Bolshevik, and cleansed of its entire German population. Many of those people unfortunate enough not to have fled the city were just forced into the countryside, where they starved or died of the cold. Today the only Germans left there are probably the statues of Immanuel Kant and Schiller."

"But what happened to Irmela? What happened when she reached Germany? You can't end the story there. Surely you haven't finished."

"I have if you want a happy ending."

"I don't like happy endings. I like an ending to be ambiguous because that's the way life is. But wait a moment. Where's the happy ending in you being sent off to a Soviet labor camp? That doesn't make sense."

"I'm still here, aren't I? That's about as happy as this story gets, I'm afraid."

Maugham nodded. "Beginnings are much more enjoyable, it's true. I sometimes think that novelists should never be allowed to write their own endings. Because this is where fiction p-parts company with reality. In real life we never actually recognize when something has truly ended. Which makes wrapping up a book in just one or two chapters almost impossible."

I nodded and lit a cigarette. I'd smoked too much and my throat felt dry—too dry to continue speaking, but I knew he wasn't going to let me stop there. I poured another gimlet from the pitcher and swallowed it—for medicinal purposes, of course.

"Nevertheless," he said, "we both know there's another ending to your story that you haven't yet shared with me. After all these years there has to be."

I nodded again. "Yes, there is."

"I think you'd better tell me, don't you?"

I took a breath and dived in.

"All right, sir. After Hennig and I met with Irmela and persuaded her to send the unencrypted signal—which was more difficult than might have been thought—he lent me a car and I drove her from Königsberg to Gotenhafen, a distance of about two hundred kilometers, along a road that was sometimes jammed with civilians trying to escape from the Red Army. Some even chose to take a shortcut across the frozen sea, often with disastrous results. Meanwhile, the weather grew steadily worse with strong winds, snow, and below-freezing temperatures. Conditions on the road were so bad we almost didn't reach the ship before it set sail, so there was little time for a proper good-bye. I wish I'd said more to her. You always do. I suppose given the speed with which we coupled, it makes just as much sense that we should have uncoupled so quickly. Everything we did back then was done in a hurry. A last-minute thing. She kissed me quickly and then bounded up the gangway of the *Wilhelm Gustloff* while I stood there like a useless capstan feeling a horrible mixture of relief that she was on board and real fear that I might never see her again.

"Not that the ship looked to me to be anything but seaworthy, although I'm no sailor. Much later on I learned that for the best part of five years the *Gustloff* had been docked at the pier in Gotenhafen, where it had been used first as a hospital ship for German soldiers wounded in Norway, and then as a floating barracks for trainees in the submarine division of the German navy. Consequently, the ship's engines hadn't been in operation for all that time and most of the skeleton crew wasn't even German, but it was only supposed to be a three-day voyage, so this didn't seem like a problem for a ship launched in nineteen thirty-seven. And certainly not as much of a problem as the sheer number of people who had boarded her. It was hard to say how many had crowded onto the ship to escape the Russians, but some estimates put it as high as twelve thousand, including a crew of one hundred and seventy-three. Back in the day it had been designed to accommodate fourteen hundred passengers and four hundred crew. So you can imagine what the scene at Gotenhafen was like. A vision of hell, perhaps. A Doré wood engraving of the *Inferno*. It goes almost without saying that there were not enough lifeboats, nor were there enough life vests, and in all respects, the ship was woefully ill-prepared for any kind of emergency. With so many people on board, nearly all of the exits and gangways were blocked and there was no time to practice any emergency drills. Also there were only two escort vessels to provide some sort of protection against Russian submarines. Because of the extreme cold, one of the two escort vessels—a torpedo boat—developed a crack in its hull and was forced to return to Gotenhafen. Which left just one escort vessel. The *Löwe*. Not only that, but a group of German minesweepers operating in the area of the Bay of Danzig was deemed to be in danger of colliding with the *Gustloff*, and so a decision was taken to turn on the ship's navigation lights. Which went against all naval practice in wartime.

"Of course, all that would have been bad enough, but after the unencrypted message that Hennig forced Irmela to send on an open radio channel, there were already three Russian submarines heading for the area when the *Gustloff* set sail. At the submarine base in the Finnish port of Turku, they'd heard the same open-microphone message regarding the *Gustloff* and the Amber Room as the Russian Baltic naval headquarters in Kronstadt, and confusion now reigned about exactly what to do next. Eventually, the captain of one Russian submarine, the S-13, sighted the *Gustloff* lit up like a Christmas tree, radioed HQ for further instructions, and was ordered to shadow the ship but hold fire. Because it was night, the S-13 felt safe enough to surface, and then awaited clarification regarding the *Gustloff* and its priceless cargo from Kronstadt HQ, which had itself been desperately seeking a final decision from the Kremlin. Finally, the Kremlin responded: At all costs the *Gustloff* was not to be sunk.

"Unfortunately, the captain of the S-13 was a drunk named Alexander Marinesko, who was already facing a court-martial for a previous bender. He was probably drunk when he decoded the message from Kronstadt, and in the decryption of his orders it seems that he must have made a fatal flaw, probably omitting the word 'not' from his plaintext message. Minutes later, at eight forty-five p.m. on January thirtieth, nineteen forty-five, he ordered four torpedoes loaded into the S-13's forward-firing tubes. At nine fifteen he gave the order to fire, and three of the torpedoes hit their target.

"I can hardly imagine what it must have been like. The snow, the cold, the freezing water, the high seas, the dark. All of the naval auxiliary women, including Irmela Schaper, were quartered in the empty swimming pool on the ship's lowest deck, and they were probably killed instantly by the second torpedo. Others were not so lucky. Thousands of passengers were drowned inside the ship as water flooded in through the damaged hull. Thousands more jumped into the water and were drowned or quickly succumbed to hypothermia and died. The ship sank to the bottom of the Baltic Sea less than an hour after the torpedoes hit, with the loss of over nine thousand lives, making the *Gustloff* the largest single loss of life in maritime history. Eight thousand of them were women and children. By contrast, just fifteen hundred people were lost on the *Titanic*."

"Good God," said Maugham. "I had no idea. I mean, I've never even heard of the *Wilhelm Gustloff*."

"Two thousand people survived, among them Captain Harold Hennig—obviously—and many of the *Gustloff*'s worthless crew, including the ship's captain, Friedrich Petersen. Hennig was one of almost five hundred men who managed to get into lifeboats and who were rescued by *Gustloff*'s escort vessel, the *Löwe*. Within less than forty-eight hours, these people were all safely landed in Kolberg, some two hundred and fifty kilometers to the west of Danzig. As for the Amber Room, it's by no means certain it was on the ship. Later on there were rumors that this was just a lie—disinformation to try and dissuade the Russians from sinking the ship—and that the Amber Room was actually transferred onto a train for Germany. But if it was on the ship it went to the bottom of the Baltic Sea with all those people, including Irmela and her unborn child.

"Of course, if she hadn't been on that ship she might easily have died on any of the other ships carrying German refugees that were sunk in the winter of nineteen forty-five. The *Goya*, on which seven thousand people lost their lives. The *Cap Arcona*, on which another seven thousand also died. And the *Steuben*, on which three and a half thousand Germans died. Six months later, the S-13's captain, Marinesko, was dismissed from the Russian navy. And that's as much as I know, most of it from a book about the *Gustloff* that was published about four years ago, which is the factual account of a survivor. Until I saw Harold Heinz Hennig checking into the Grand Hôtel in Cap Ferrat under the name of Harold Hebel, that was the last I'd seen or heard of him in more than ten years. Now you know why I hate him so much. And what kind of man we're dealing with."

"And after the war? What happened to him? Why was he never brought to justice?"

"He was much too small a fish for anyone to bother with. The Allies were after more important Nazis. Believe me, no one gave a damn about Harold Hennig. And that is especially true now as the Federal Republic of Germany tries to move on and become a good partner for America and Britain in the war against world Communism. These days, justice takes second place to pragmatism. But Erich Koch was arrested in nineteen forty-nine and is in a Polish prison awaiting trial for war crimes. The Poles have a different attitude than the Bonn Republic about the deaths of half a million Poles. Frankly, I don't give much for his chances. My guess is that they'll hang him and good riddance. If ever a man deserved to be hanged, it's Erich Koch. Not that Hennig doesn't deserve to be killed a hundred times over for what he did, too."

"And yet in spite of what he did, you said you didn't want to kill him. I think under the circumstances—if I'd lost what you lost—I would have killed him."

"I didn't say I didn't *want* to kill him. I said I wasn't going to kill him. There's a big difference. I'm through with all that kind of thing. It's me I'm thinking about now, not him. My own peace of mind versus my own tawdry revenge. I have to live with myself. Even at the best of times I can be poor company."

"But if Hebel is Harold Hennig and was once a Nazi, how is it possible that he could be working for the Communists now? For Soviet intelligence? Surely they must know about his Nazi past?"

"The KGB or the HVA doesn't care about who you were and what you did any more than the American CIA does. What matters is how they can use you to their present advantage. After the war, the East German HVA—that's the foreign intelligence service of the GDR—recruited lots of Nazis at the behest of the Russians. They perfected many of the Gestapo's techniques. Almost nothing changed except the ideology. The fact is they're still the Gestapo in all but name. And if you're an enemy of the state who's facing the guillotine or ten years in a labor camp, there's nothing to distinguish between a Communist German tyranny and a Nazi one. It's the same Fascism but with a different flag. If the shit looks and smells the same as it did before, it's still shit."

"I suppose so."

"Take my word for it. I know these people." I smiled. "I should, since they're my people."

"You scare me, Walter. I know that isn't your real name but I can't imagine you'd feel comfortable with me using that, so I will just go on calling you Walter, or Mr. Wolf. But the world you describe isn't a world with which I am familiar. Not anymore. In nineteen seventeen it was all a bit of a lark, really—spying on the Russians. Look, what I'm saying is, I'd appreciate your help with all this. I'm an old man. And it strikes me that these people are playing a game I'm no longer qualified to play. My offer—that you should come and be my bodyguard—it still stands."

I wanted nothing to do with it all, of course. What did it matter to me what this Burgess fellow had said about the British SIS on the tape? I'd never cared much for the English. In two wars against Germany I'd seen how they were capable of fighting to the last American. And yet in spite of my commendable moral stance on the subject of Harold Hennig, there was a part of me that wanted to see this vile man brought down, and for good. I liked the old man and I think he liked me. If I could help him defeat a blackmailer like Hennig then that would be some kind of payback for what he'd done to Irmela and, in a smaller way, to me.

"I don't think so, Mr. Maugham. But I'll be happy to partner you in this rubber. That's the least I can do. But in return you can do me a favor and say hello to a lady friend of mine who's keen to meet you. She's a writer, too."

"All right. I'll be glad to. If she's a friend of yours."

"So, tomorrow, when Hebel gives me the tape, I'll bring it straight here to the villa and you can listen to it and decide what to do then. And if you think I can still be of service to you—well, let's wait until tomorrow, shall we?"

After telling my story I got back in the car and went away with a hole inside me where before a heart and stomach had once been coexisting. That's the thing about the past; it never quite belongs as much to the past as you think it does. I hadn't thought about Irmela or her unborn child in a long time, but I still bitterly regretted their passing. The idea that I could have talked about them both with impunity now seemed risible. Time hadn't healed anything, and I think people who say time makes things better really don't know what the hell they're talking about. For me, it was an inoperable tumor that I'd managed to ignore for more than a decade; but the tumor was still there. Probably it was going to stay with me until I died.

You could say I was feeling a bit sorry for myself and perhaps I was also a little drunk because instead of driving straight home I somehow found myself ignoring the lobster pot where I lived and heading out of town and up the hill toward Anne French's villa. I told myself that if you spend enough time around homosexuals, you begin to feel the need to redress the balance with the company of a congenial woman. It's not much of an excuse for what I was doing but I couldn't think of a better one.

I stopped in front of the gate posts, lit a cigarette, and stared along the drive at the house. The lights in her bedroom were on and for a moment I just sat there, imagining Anne in bed and wondering if I was about to make a stupid mistake and spoil everything between us. What would a woman like her want with a man who owned as pitifully little as I? Apart from bridge lessons.

I almost turned around and drove away. Instead I drove slowly up the drive and stopped the engine. Discretion might be the better part of valor, but it has no business between men and women on a warm summer's night on the French Riviera. I hoped I wouldn't offend her, but being drunk I was willing to take that risk. So I opened the car door, stepped out, and cocked an ear. Coming from the guesthouse was the sound of a large radio and someone trying vainly to tune it to a more reliable frequency. A few moments later the radio was turned off, the door opened, and Anne came outside wearing just a short, almost see-through cotton nightdress. It was a very warm evening. The cicadas showed their appreciation of her cleavage and shapely legs with an extra loud click of their abdomens. I certainly felt like giving my own abdomen a bit of action, too.

"Oh, I'm glad it's you," she said. "I thought it might be the gardener."

"At this time of night?"

"Lately he's been giving me a funny look."

"Maybe you should let him water the flower beds."

"I don't think that's what he has in mind."

"The heat we've been having? He's in the wrong job."

"Did you come here to mow my lawn, or just to talk?"

"Talk, I guess."

"So, what's your story?"

"I'm all out of stories tonight. Fact is, Anne, I'm feeling just a bit sad."

"And you thought I might cheer you up, is that it?"

"Something like that. I know it's a bit late."

"Too late for bridge, I'd have thought."

"I'm sorry, but I just wanted to see you."

"Don't apologize. Actually, I'm glad you're here. I was feeling a little sad myself." She paused. "I was listening to the BBC World Service news on the shortwave. And now that I have I wish I hadn't. Apparently the Egyptians have nationalized the Suez Canal and closed it to all Israeli shipping."

"What does that mean?"

"Well, for one thing, it means the price of oil is going to go up. But I think it also means there's going to be a war."

"When we haven't finished paying for the last one? I doubt that."

She shrugged. "A last throw of the dice from Britain and France to prove that these old colonial powers still matter? After all, it's them who administer the canal. Of course. Why not?" She smiled. "But you didn't come up here to talk international politics, did you?"

"We can if you like. Just as long as I don't have to vote for anyone. That never changed anything. Even in the good old days."

"How old?"

"Very old. Old enough to be good. Before the Nazis, anyway. Speaking of the very old, I spent the evening with Somerset Maugham. At the Villa Mauresque."

"How is he?"

"Getting strangely older by the minute, if that were humanly possible."

"Makes two of us."

"Not that I've noticed."

"You'd be surprised. The longer I stay parted from that fifty-thousand-dollar publishing advance, the older I feel."

In the car, I'd resolved to tell her everything; if I was going to risk my neck for the Englishman there had to be something in it for me, and that something had started to look like it might just be Anne French.

"Then it's good that I'm here. I've got some news that should make you and your publisher very happy. I've persuaded Somerset Maugham to meet with you."

This was making more of my effort on her behalf than was perhaps warranted, of course, but it sounded like the sort of thing she probably wanted to hear, which, for obvious reasons, was the kind of thing I was keen to tell her.

"When?"

"Soon."

"Really? That's fantastic."

"I wouldn't be too sure about that. Frankly, I think he is a kind of vampire."

"All authors are a bit like that."

"I wouldn't know. But I feel like I lost a lot of blood up there tonight. I feel drained."

"Then you'd better come in the house and let me mix you a transfusion."

"I think I've had enough to drink already."

"Something else then. Coffee, perhaps."

"Are you sure? It is late. Maybe I should go."

"Look, Walter, I've never been one for knowing what I should and shouldn't do. I always wanted to be good but now I realize I should have been a little less specific. Especially now you're here. Now I think I just want to be wanted." She shrugged off the nightdress like an extra skin and stood there naked in the moonlight. "You do want me, don't you, Walter?"

"Yes."

"Then let's go in before I change my mind, or I get bitten by something while I'm standing here naked. A mosquito, perhaps."

"Not if I get there first."

SEVENTEEN

The subject of the tape was printed on the box, which now lay on the refectory table beside the tape machine. "Interview with Guy Burgess, May 28th, 1951, SS *Pamyati Kirova*." I carefully threaded the leader onto the Grundig, lit my fifth cigarette of the day, poured some coffee from the brightly polished silver pot that Ernest the butler had brought for me, and, under the eye of a tomato-colored nude by Renoir, sat down to await Maugham's delayed arrival in the elegant drawing room. On the lawns the garden sprinklers were already spinning around like dervishes and the chauffeur had washed the car again. The

nude was a bit too pink and chubby for my taste; she only lacked
a lollipop and a Teddy bear to be wholly unsuitable. I was tired
but in an almost pleasant way, suffering a little with the equivalent of a hangover from an excess of sex, if such a thing is possible for a man living alone. My balls felt like they'd spent the
night on a beer-hall billiard table. I closed my eyes for a moment
and opened them again as Robin Maugham came into the room
and sat down heavily, more like an old housewife after a day
trailing around the shops instead of a man wearing a blazer who
had only just finished breakfast. He smelled strongly of cloying
cologne and false courtesy. I sensed that he had started to dislike
me almost as much as I disliked his cologne.

"My uncle is going to be another five or ten minutes. He had
an uncomfortable night. The heat, you know."

"I had a bit of a rough night myself."

"Well, I always say, there's nothing quite like a bit of rough."
Robin smiled at his own little joke. "Anyway, he's just getting
dressed."

I nodded. "Fine."

"You know, every time I open a door in this house these days
it seems you're there, Walter. Why is that?"

"Does that make you nervous?"

"No. It makes me wonder, that's all. I mean, what's in it for
you, that kind of thing. What do you want from this house,
Walter?"

"You asked me to come here. To play bridge. Remember?"

"No, what I mean is, why are you helping my uncle now?"

THE OTHER SIDE OF SILENCE

"Because he asked me to."

"Oh, come on, Walter. I'm not a fucking idiot. Everyone wants something from the old boy. What's your angle?"

"Would it make you feel a little more comfortable if you thought there was money in it for me?"

"Yes, I suppose it would. I mean, it's like Dr. Johnson says about being a writer: No man but a blockhead ever wrote except for money. Well, surely the same is doubly true for a man who used to be a private detective like you."

"Who told you that?"

"What?"

"That I used to be a private detective?"

"I suppose my uncle must have mentioned it."

"No, he didn't. I asked him to remain silent about it. And he gave me his word he wouldn't mention it to anyone."

"He and I have no secrets. You should know that by now."

"That's not true, either. I'm not sure your uncle Willie trusts you as much as you think he does, Robin. Plus, your uncle Willie's word actually means something. Which means someone else mentioned it to you."

"Like who?"

"Why don't you tell me? Who knows? You might appreciate a little confession. No?" I smiled patiently. "Besides, I am getting paid. That's what's in it for me. Since you ask. Your uncle promised me five thousand dollars. Or maybe he didn't tell you that, either."

"That was to handle the money transfer at the hotel. But

you've done that. This tape business seems to be a lot more complicated."

"All part of the same Grand Hôtel concierge service."

"Yes, I suppose one could look at it that way."

"I do."

"Good of you. Thanks."

"Will you be joining us to listen to the tape?" I asked.

"Yes. Of course. I wouldn't miss it for the world. Have you listened to it, yourself?"

"Not yet. It's really none of my business. And it seemed more courteous to wait until your uncle was present. He's the one who's been asked to pay two hundred thousand dollars for the tape, after all. Besides, I'm not sure any of it will mean very much to me. My English is good but it's not perfect. I still have a problem working out what any of you people really mean. English is very different from German in that respect. In German people say exactly what they mean. Even when they would prefer to say something else."

"Oh yes. Of course."

It was time for me to play out a hunch I had.

"Maybe this is a good opportunity for us to talk frankly, Robin."

"About what?"

"I was hoping you might volunteer something about this whole dirty business."

"I don't understand."

"Sure you do."

Robin smiled and feigned patience even as he fidgeted with his gold cuff links, nervously. "No, actually, old boy, I don't."

"By all accounts your uncle's old friend and companion Gerald Haxton had some quite substantial gambling debts. At the casino in Nice, it turns out. I checked with a friend of mine who was the manager there for a while. Gerald was up to his gills in debt."

"That doesn't surprise me. About Gerald, that is."

"Previously it was Gerald who put Louis up to blackmailing your uncle. To make some money for them both."

"Yes, perhaps. Louis wasn't my friend, exactly. He was Gerald's."

"Nevertheless you also went to bed with Louis. At least according to your uncle. Gerald as well, probably."

"What of it?"

"Only this: I think Gerald gave or perhaps sold you some letters and photographs before he died. As a sort of legacy or insurance policy, I don't know. And you decided to copy his example and use them as a way of making a bit of extra money now and then. When you needed to raise a bit of cash for a new toy like that Alfa Romeo you're driving."

"Are you suggesting what I think you're suggesting?"

"Didn't I make it clear? You're a blackmailer, too, Robin."

"Nonsense. I'm a writer. And I make a good living as a writer. A few years ago I wrote a novel called *The Servant*, which has done very well—look, I don't have to sit here and be insulted by you."

"You do unless you want me to tell your uncle exactly what you and Harold Hebel were arguing about the first time I saw you both at La Voile d'Or."

Robin Maugham paused, blushing to the edge of his hand-made shirt collar, and then lit a cigarette, trying to affect a non-chalance that plainly wasn't there. "No secret there," he said. "I should have thought that was bloody obvious. He had a compromising photograph involving my uncle and I was rather keen to get it back."

"In my experience people don't normally behave like that with a blackmailer."

"Is there a correct way to behave? Don't be absurd."

"Usually people are very meek because they're afraid."

"Possibly because they're the ones being blackmailed."

"According to the manager at the Voile you and Hebel met for a drink. More than once. Your name is in Hebel's address book. And his diary. I searched his room at the Grand the other night. I think it was Hebel who told you that I was a private detective. And I think your argument was because you were very anxious to know exactly how he came by that photograph."

"From Louis Legrand, of course."

"No. That's what Hebel said. But it's just not possible. You see, Louis Legrand has been in prison in Marseilles for several months. I checked with the police, in Nice. Hebel couldn't possibly have met your little friend Loulou."

"I don't like your tone."

"I don't like it myself. You're right. It makes me sound like a queer. Like a bitch. Maybe I should paint my toenails, buy a silk shirt—then I could fit right in at the Villa Mauresque. Either way I don't think your uncle will have any trouble believing me. Even without lipstick I can make an attractive argument about this to him."

Robin Maugham sighed and then stared up at the ceiling as if hoping he might find the answer hanging off the dusty wooden chandelier. The French windows were none too clean either; bright sunlight showed up cobwebs like giant fingerprints on more than one pane of glass, and in the lost domain that was one corner under the refectory table was a champagne glass containing a cigarette end. Maybe I did belong somewhere like that; I wasn't exactly gleaming myself.

"Don't get me wrong, Robin. I'm no better than you. In many ways I'm worse. Long ago I concluded I don't have a soul of my own. Not anymore."

"Look, if I tell you the truth, will you promise not to tell my uncle?"

"Perhaps. I don't know. It all depends on what you tell me."

"I'll pay you to keep silent about this."

"I think you're mistaking me for another double-dealing bastard, Robin. I'm not a blackmailer. And I agreed to help your uncle, not help someone else to put the squeeze on him."

"Look, I've made mistakes. I'm only human. But you must believe me, I'd never do anything to hurt my uncle Willie."

"Not consciously, perhaps. So. Why don't you tell me? How did Harold Hebel come to be in possession of this photograph?"

Robin Maugham got up and went to close the drawing room door. Then he lit a cigarette, quite forgetting there was one already burning in the ashtray, and walked around the room nervously for a few seconds before sitting down again. It wasn't yet eleven but already he was sweating profusely.

"I'm not exactly sure, to be honest."

"Take your time. I'm in no hurry. I took the whole morning off."

"There's a man in London who used to be a friend of my uncle's. Chap named Blunt, Anthony Blunt. He's queer, too."

"Blunt's one of the naked men in the photograph that was taken here at the Villa Mauresque, right?"

"The one taken in nineteen thirty-seven, yes."

"Go on."

"He's now a very prominent art dealer. Very well connected. Surveyor of the Queen's Pictures. Director of the Courtauld Institute of Art. Anyway, I was a bit short of cash and so the last time I was in London, Anthony and I met for lunch at my club and I offered to sell him the photograph and some letters from him to Gerald. You see, Blunt's a friend of this fellow Guy Burgess, too. In fact, I think they even shared a house during the war. Naturally, it would mean that Blunt would have to resign from all his offices if that picture ended up in the newspapers. Under the circumstances, it wasn't a fortune I was asking. Just a thousand pounds, that's all. Cheap at the price in view of how much Hebel is asking for it."

"So what happened after you started blackmailing Blunt?"

"Steady on, old boy. I wouldn't call it blackmail, exactly. I mean, I never threatened to send the letters and the picture to the newspapers or anything like that. You might even say I was trying to help the poor fellow out. To stop them from falling into the hands of anyone else. To give him peace of mind. Yes, I could have destroyed them, but then he might always have wondered what became of them, and if one day they might come back to haunt him. You do see the difference."

"You're a much better blackmailer than you think you are, Robin."

Robin Maugham leaned forward and stubbed out his cigarette with fury, as if he wished the ashtray had been my eyeball.

"Fuck you, Walter," he said.

"I'd rather you didn't. So, then; Blunt bought what you were offering so very cheaply. Prints, negative, letters, the whole package wrapped with a nice pink ribbon. Cash?"

"Yes. Cash. He moaned about it quite a lot but yes, eventually, he paid. So, naturally I was more than a bit surprised when this fellow Hebel turned up here with the photograph asking for fifty thousand dollars. I mean, fifty thousand dollars? Jesus. That rather puts my amateur effort in the shade."

"Have you spoken to Blunt about this?"

"Yes. He says the photograph was stolen from his flat at the Courtauld Institute soon after I sold it to him."

"Do you believe that?"

"Yes. Maybe. His place is always full of rent boys. Any one of them could have pinched it. Besides, I can't see why he would hand the picture to someone who might easily blackmail him. It strikes me that Anthony Blunt has as much to lose as my uncle."

"But a lot more to gain, perhaps. Is Blunt rich?"

"No, not especially. I mean, he has some rather valuable pictures, and some rich friends, but not much money of his own."

"So, not as rich as your uncle Willie?"

"Lord, no. Not many people are."

"So then. Has it occurred to you that Blunt and Hebel might be in this together? After all, Blunt could hardly threaten to send the picture to the newspapers himself. Your uncle would never believe he would risk doing that. But he would believe someone else was capable of it. Someone like Hebel, with nothing to lose. This might also explain how Hebel came to be in possession of this tape recording of Guy Burgess. Perhaps the friendship between Blunt and Burgess extended to more than just sharing a flat. We don't know for sure that it was recorded on this Russian ship and not at a flat in London."

"Yes, I suppose it's possible. I can see Blunt using a picture in the way you describe. But this tape is something else again. My uncle will only buy it if the secret service is prepared to underwrite the cost of the purchase. And they won't buy it without listening to it themselves. Which still leaves Blunt in the shit because of the photograph, I'd have thought."

"Not really. Your uncle has the photograph now."

"Yes, he does, doesn't he?"

"So, unless Anthony Blunt's name is on that tape, he's in the clear. More or less."

"Anthony Blunt?" Somerset Maugham came into the room and helped himself to some coffee. "What's Anthony got to do with any of this?"

Robin Maugham blushed again, this time to the roots of his dyed hair, and stammered an answer. "I was just telling Walter that Blunt used to share a flat with Guy Burgess in London. And that now and then you had him bid for pictures at art auctions in London. Isn't that right?"

"Yes, that's right. Old Masters are his special thing. Poussin, Titian, not really my cup of tea. And too damned expensive. But over the years he's spotted a couple of good buys for me. Impressionists, mainly. He has a good eye, Anthony."

"And yet he didn't seem to notice he was sharing a flat with a Russian spy," I said.

"You didn't know Guy Burgess," said Maugham. "He was a very charming rogue and a most unlikely spy. Everyone thought so."

"That's the thing about the English," I said. "You think charm excuses almost anything, including treachery and treason."

"Yes," said Maugham, lighting a pipe. "That's quite true. It's a failing of ours, to find excuses for people. Of course, charm only works for Germans when it seems to have been divinely conferred."

"When was the last time you saw Guy Burgess?" I asked.

Maugham paused for a moment. "Probably Tangier in nineteen forty-nine. Got himself into a bit of a scrape in Gibraltar beforehand, I seem to recall. But that was the thing about Guy; he was always getting into scrapes. Frankly, his behavior made him a most improbable spy. Often drunk and outrageously homosexual—when he defected, nobody could quite believe how he managed to pull it off for so long. I suppose you might say it was the perfect cover, to seem so indiscreet that people couldn't possibly think you might be a spy."

Maugham set his coffee cup down and moved to a chair.

"Are you ready?" I asked.

"As I'll ever be."

I stood up and walked over to the Grundig. In its green Tolex carry case, the tape machine resembled the forgotten layer of an old wedding cake. I twisted the gold switch and slowly the two reels began to turn.

EIGHTEEN

Like most Englishmen of my recent acquaintance—at the Grand Hôtel and the Villa Mauresque—Guy Burgess spoke with a plummy, nasal voice that seemed to contain a slight speech impediment, although that might just as easily have been the effect of too much alcohol. What else is there to do on a three-day voyage to Leningrad but get drunk? Suave, reptilian, and dripping with disdain, as if the whole business of being debriefed by his Russian handlers were beneath him, the voice reminded me of an English movie actor I'd once seen called Henry Daniell, who had seemed to me to be the screen personification of the sardonic, well-bred villain. As I listened to Burgess, it was as if the man were with us in Maugham's drawing room, searching his memory and perhaps his conscience for the best interpretation of his actions—indeed, he seemed every bit as mannered as Somerset Maugham and as full of whinging self-justification as the great writer's nephew. The recording was a good one, and occasionally, in the silences, you could even hear the dull, rhythmic throb of what might have been the ship's engines but could as easily have been the slow breathing of some unseen leviathan.

"My name is Guy Francis de Moncy Burgess and I was born in Devonport, England, on the sixteenth of April nineteen eleven. For the purposes of verification, in nineteen forty-four I was running a Swiss source for MI5, code named Orange, who, I'm afraid to say, met with a sticky end in Trier. MI5 is, of course, Britain's domestic secret intelligence service. My father was a naval officer and I myself attended the Royal Naval College at Dartmouth before going on to Eton and then Trinity College, Cambridge.

"Today is the twenty-eighth of April nineteen fifty-one and I just turned forty a couple of weeks ago, which seems incredible and rather horrible to me. Currently I am aboard a Russian freighter which must remain nameless, I'm afraid, and on my way to Leningrad in the company of my Foreign Office colleague Donald Maclean, with a collected edition of Jane Austen in my bag and a new raincoat from Gieves in Old Bond Street. But I can tell you that Donald and I reached Saint-Malo on the *Falaise*, from Southampton. And that prior to this, I hired a car from Welbeck Motors in Crawford Street to make the journey to

Southampton. I think it was an A-forty. Cream color. In Saint-Malo I paid a taxi driver rather a lot of money to drive his empty taxi to Rennes and to buy two tickets to Paris in our names. Meanwhile, we boarded this Russian ship. Because the fact of the matter is that I've decided I want to live in the Soviet Union because I am a socialist and it's a socialist country. And I think Donald feels the same way that I do. In fact, I know he does.

"The reason I'm saying all this on tape now is so that my Russian friends can send the recording to the BBC in London in the hope that they might broadcast it and let people back home in England know for themselves the truth about my decision and not what they've been told by the British government. I expect the newspapers are already calling me a traitor, but of course I'm nothing of the kind. That's a lot of nonsense. No more is it true of Donald Maclean. Besides, I really don't know what this word means anymore. I did what I did for conscience sake, for something I believed in, and which I happen to think is rather more important than some outmoded notion of loyalty to king and country. As it happens, I do love my country very much indeed, I just think it could be governed rather better than it is. (But for my poor eyesight I would very likely be a serving naval officer right now, like my late father.) But I still have family back in England and at some stage I would rather like to be able to go back for a month or so, and see them again, but I couldn't ever do that, of course, unless I knew for certain that I could get out of England again and come back to Russia.

"My critics will doubtless see this recording as a confession;

I prefer to think of it as an explanation. As Voltaire once said, 'Tout comprendre, c'est tout pardonner.' And whilst I don't expect to be forgiven, I do hope that my actions might come to be better understood. Consequently, I think it only right to place this explanation firmly in the context of my early life. So I suppose I ought to begin by mentioning that when I first went up to Cambridge in the summer of nineteen twenty-nine I found that most of my friends had either joined the Communist Party or were at least very close to it politically. Indeed, by nineteen thirty-two, the atmosphere in Cambridge was so febrile and the issue of Fascism so horribly pressing that I joined the party myself. It seemed to me inarguable that the Western democracies had taken an uncertain and compromising attitude toward Nazi Germany and that the Soviet Union constituted the only real bulwark against European tyranny. I believe that during the war the Soviet Union was never treated as a full and trusted ally by Britain and America in spite of the fact that the sacrifices made by the people of Russia were greater than those of all the other Allies put together.

"After I joined the Communist Party, like most young men I did a lot of talking and not much else. But by January nineteen thirty-three, with the election of Adolf Hitler as chancellor of Germany, that no longer seemed enough. Perhaps if I'd come down from Cambridge in the summer of nineteen thirty-seven, I might have gone to Spain to fight in the civil war, but in the summer of nineteen thirty-three I felt obliged to look elsewhere for some means of making my new beliefs seem at all relevant.

224

Then, in December nineteen thirty-four, I met a Russian called Alexander Orlov who recruited me into the Russian People's Commissariat for Internal Affairs, the NKVD—the forerunner of the KGB, Russia's foreign intelligence service. It was he who persuaded me that I could best serve the cause of anti-Fascism by resigning from the Communist Party and spying for the Soviet Union.

"Orlov introduced me to another man called Arnold Deutsch, code-named Otto, who urged me first to join the BBC—where I was a Talks Assistant; and then as war approached, MI6, which is Britain's foreign intelligence service. Indeed, so keen was Deutsch on my achieving a perfect cover for my future espionage activities within the British establishment that he actively encouraged me to try and wed Winston Churchill's niece. Can you imagine? Me, married to a Churchill? I did as I was told and pursued her for a whole month even though I did have some rather obvious disadvantages as a prospective husband for the girl. We were quite friendly for a while. I think I even took her for a weekend to stay with Dadie Rylands and his family in Devon and I may have introduced her to them as my fiancée. Clarissa Churchill is, of course, now the wife of the current British prime minister, Anthony Eden.

"It was Deutsch who gave me the code name Mädchen— the German word for 'girl'—and in retrospect it's clear to me that Arnold must have had a great sense of humor. My first major task—if it can described thus—was to make friends with as many people in government and the civil service as possible, and you

225

PHILIP KERR

might almost say that I became a sort of talent spotter for the
NKVD. I made a pitch to everyone who was anyone. The histo-
rians G. M. Trevelyan and Stuart Hampshire, John Maynard
Keynes, Noel Annan, the poet W. H. Auden, Anthony Blunt,
Maurice Bowra, Isaiah Berlin. All of them pillars of the British
establishment now. And I wasn't exactly subtle about it. I'm not
saying I tried to recruit all of these people as spies, not a bit of
it; I was trying to chivvy out people who were sympathetic to the
Russian cause, and who might be persuaded to speak up for
Russia and for the Communists—which is of course a very different thing. It's often forgotten that men as famous as George Ber-
nard Shaw visited the Soviet Union in nineteen thirty-one and
became enthusiasts for Russian Communism. And yet until his
death last year only his most virulently right-wing critics were
inclined to call him a traitor.

"I think it must have been in nineteen thirty-seven—around
the time of the Spanish Civil War—that I went to stay with the
writer Somerset Maugham at his fabulous villa on the French
Riviera. There were five of us, I think. Dadie Rylands, Anthony
Blunt, Victor Rothschild, Victor's girlfriend Anne Barnes, and
me. Victor had a smart new Bugatti and we drove to the Cap
from Monte Carlo, where we'd been staying. I think I may have
tried to sound him out as a potential recruit to the cause but
Maugham wasn't much interested in politics; he was much
more interested in boys, and I remember I had a rather marvel-
ous time as his guest. Certainly after Victor and Anne left. For a
young and highly impressionable queer like me, it was like peek-

226

ing through the keyhole at Trimalchio's party and an insight into what it might be like to live quite openly as a practicing homo-sexual. God, how I envied that man. We all did. Anyone who was queer, that is.

"From the French Riviera I went to Rome and from there to Paris, which both the GRU—the GRU is Russian military intelligence—and the KGB were using as a recruitment and clearance center. It was a chance for me to meet my controller in a more relaxed environment, which is to say, far away from the risk of surveillance. I even made a pitch to Edouard Pfeiffer, Daladier's *chef de cabinet,* who at the time of my proposition was playing ping-pong across the body of a naked young man in lieu of a net. I stayed on in Paris until just before Christmas nineteen thirty-seven. The Paris Bureau of the Comintern introduced me to all sorts of interesting people, many of them sympathetic Englishmen, such as Claud Cockburn and John Cairncross. Meanwhile, Arnold Deutsch took me out to dinner with all sorts of strange folk, not all of them obvious recruitment material. People who had no languages. People who hadn't even been to university. Some of them were downright dull. Not to say stupid. I remember a very uninspiring young English salesman recently returned from China, where he'd been working for a tobacco company. I mean, this chap hadn't even been to university, let alone Cambridge. All he could talk about was tobacco and the Chinese and about some awful bloody girl he'd married back in Somerset. And I remember thinking, what's the point of trying to recruit a chap to the cause who's going to be happily married and selling cigarettes? Are the Russians so desperate for spies that we're willing to fund the local tobacconists? Not that he took Arnold's ruble, so to speak. Anyway, ours not to reason why and all that rot. Of course, lots of these people are dead now. Killed in the war. Disappeared. God knows.

"In nineteen thirty-eight, I got back to London from Paris and joined Section D of MI6, before joining MI5, who sent me back to the BBC and while there, I interviewed Mr. Winston Churchill, in September nineteen thirty-eight. This was, of course, the time of the Munich crisis, which upset me greatly and resulted in my subsequent resignation from the BBC. Anyway, I had a Ford V8 of which I was inordinately fond, and one morning I drove down to Westerham and Churchill's house at Chartwell. I told him I was in some despair about what had happened and he showed me a letter from Prague, signed by Edvard Beneš, which ran as follows: 'My dear Mr. Churchill, I am writing to you for your advice and perhaps your assistance regarding my unhappy country.' Churchill looked at me and said, what advice, what assistance should I offer, Mr. Burgess? I am an old man, without power, and without party; what help can I give? And I said, don't be so downhearted, sir, offer him your eloquence; awaken people in this country with your speeches. He was rather pleased by that, I think. We then shared a bit of mutual hatred about Neville Chamberlain. Having finished discussing Munich, he then presented me with a book of his speeches, which he inscribed for me and which I still have. You and I know that war is inevitable, he added; if I am returned to power—and it seems likely that I shall be—and you need a job, come and see me, present this book, and I will make sure that you are suitably employed. I then went outside to my car and drove home. But it's an interesting story, I think—certainly of interest to listeners to *The Week in Westminster*, which is the show I used to produce for the BBC. The point of me telling this story now is to demonstrate to any listeners I might have that while I may be a Communist and allegedly a traitor, I am still enough of a patriotic Englishman to admire an old Tory grandee like Winston Churchill.

"From the BBC I went to the news department of the Foreign Office, and after the war I became an assistant to Hector McNeil, the current secretary of state for Scotland, who was then a junior minister in the F.O. and who sometimes stood in for Ernest Bevin, the foreign secretary, which meant there were lots of MI6 papers that came my way.

"I was handing over top secret stuff to the Russians on a weekly basis after that. Looking back on this time, I think he made it easy for me since he was always disappearing up north to his Glasgow constituency. Greenock, I think. Somewhere ghastly like that. I went with him on more than one occasion and felt like a foreigner since I could understand nothing at all of what was said to me. I'm not for a minute suggesting Hector McNeil knew what I was up to. But frankly, my work couldn't have been easier. People always imagine that spies live lives of derring-do and intrigue. It wasn't like that at all. No guns, no invisible ink, no disguises. I just lifted the files out of poor old

Hector's filing cabinet, or the yellow boxes that arrived from MI6, took them home in the car, and a chap from the KGB spent all night in my bathroom photographing them; I then placed them back in poor old McNeil's filing cabinet the following morning. I even had my own key so that I didn't have to bother him when I needed access to his papers. Once, I accompanied McNeil to the United Nations in New York and I pinched some papers from his ministerial box and had them photographed during his liquid lunch hour. These were mostly cabinet papers, government policy documents—Britain's position on this, Britain's position on that, and, rather horribly, which major Russian cities we might bomb if we decided on a first strike against the Soviet Union. The point is that nobody got hurt by what I was doing. Nobody.

"The last thing I want to say is this, and it's important. What I did really didn't require much nerve or ingenuity; nor was I required to take any great risks. In the beginning I was nervous, but after a while it became routine. Frankly, if someone such as I could get away with spying on His Majesty's Government for almost fifteen years, then anyone could. And in my considered opinion Britain is not well served by its security and intelligence services. Not well served at all. It's small wonder that the FBI doesn't trust MI6 and MI5. Which is hardly surprising as MI5 and MI6 don't trust each other one inch. They're great rivals. Not only that but our security services are riddled with so-called traitors and . . ."

Burgess stopped speaking at this point as someone else said something, possibly in Russian, and a few seconds later the tape ended. I turned off the machine and perched on the edge of the refectory table to await the old man's considered verdict.

"He's got a bloody nerve," said Somerset Maugham. "It's largely thanks to Guy Burgess and Donald Maclean that the Americans don't trust us anymore."

"So you do think it's him?" I said. "The real Guy Burgess."

"It's been a few years since I saw him, and many others would know better than me, but it certainly sounds like him, yes. As to whether it was actually recorded on that Russian ship, as he and Maclean fled London for Leningrad, I have no idea. Your guess is as good as mine."

"Hot stuff, some of it," muttered Robin. "Don't you think? All that stuff about Trimalchio's house. You wouldn't want that to come out, Uncle Willie."

"I suppose not," said Maugham unhappily.

"Though some of it was really quite amusing, what? All that stuff about Clarissa Churchill?"

"The urgent question is, of course," insisted Maugham, "where the fuck did this tape come from? And how did Harold Heinz Hebel come by it? Did the KGB send a copy to the BBC? If they did, it was obviously never used. I can't imagine the circumstances in which they would have broadcast the whole thing.

I think we'd have heard about that by now, even down here. If it was sent to the BBC, then has the BBC already shared the tape with the intelligence services? And if not, why not? Is it possible that the tape was stolen from the BBC? On the other hand, was the tape given to Hebel by someone in the KGB—someone who is intent on making more mischief in our security services? Or is it someone who just wants to make a ton of money from our security services, as Walter here suggested before? Is it worth two hundred thousand dollars to the British government to stop that tape from being sent to an American radio station?" Maugham relit his pipe and puffed it thoughtfully. "And even more importantly, is it worth two hundred thousand dollars to me? When you buy a tape recording, how do you know there isn't a copy?"

"To that extent, it's no different from buying a photograph," I said. "Even if you buy the negative there's no way of knowing how many more prints there are."

"Those are all good questions," said Robin. "And I wonder how on earth we can answer them?"

"I don't know," said Maugham. "But I do know someone who might."

NINETEEN

I went to the Grand Hôtel in Cap Ferrat, slipped on my black morning coat, and immediately I felt as if proper order had been restored to the world. It was as if I'd become a decent man again; polished and humanized, civil and courteous, and without any time for the darker shadows of feelings that pass for thoughts. Helping guests with their trivial problems, finding room keys, exchanging money, organizing porters, answering the telephone, fixing staff rotas—it was all a reassuringly long way from the tawdry world of homosexual blackmail and Soviet spies. It's easy to believe civilization still has a bright future when you're behind the front desk of an expensive hotel. I think

I may even have managed a smile. Through the tall French windows at the far end of the lobby the cloudless sky lined the sea like a blue-edged invitation to be calm and collected. I took a deep breath and smiled again. What did I care what Guy Burgess had said to anyone about anything? None of these people mattered to me. Not even me particularly mattered to me.

In the late afternoon the hotel's swimming instructor, Pierre Gruneberg, stopped by my desk on his way home to tell me that my second swimming lesson would have to wait a while because of the numbers of Medusa jellyfish that were presently in the bay. For some reason I had never learned, not properly, and Pierre was reputed to be an excellent instructor; he'd taught everyone from Picasso to David Niven and he'd promised to teach me, in the sea—it would never have done for me to have used the hotel pool. He always started the first swimming lesson the same way, by asking his students to put their heads in a salad bowl full of water. 'Learn to swim without getting wet,' he would say; it didn't sound any more strange or perverse than what was happening up at the Villa Mauresque.

I didn't see any sign in the hotel of Harold Hebel, but Anne French showed up for afternoon tea at around five and, by largely ignoring each other, we pretended that the intimacy that had taken place between us hadn't happened; although it had, of course. I could still recall the turbulent emotions that had poured out of her sensuous mouth and onto the pillows of a capacious brass bed. After I'd watched her cross the floor of the lobby I opened the newspaper and looked for some sedative story that would take my mind off her naked body and what it looked like when she was bent over in front of me like the keenest entomologist. I didn't find anything that did the job and twenty minutes later I was still marveling at my own erotic good fortune.

At just after eight o'clock I finished work. It would have been my bridge night but instead of going to La Voile d'Or to play cards, I drove east along the Grande Corniche to Èze, whose situation on a height dominating the coast makes it seem more like Hitler's seaside Berghof instead of a medieval village largely abandoned by its natives. Then again, I'm probably the only man in that part of the world who'd ever be reminded of the Berghof. Sometimes it's hard to forget about Adolf Hitler. Maybe the history of Germany might have been a little different if our great men had spent less time on mountaintops and a bit more on the beach. In fact, I'm more or less sure of it.

A little farther inland was the village of La Turbie, where Jack and Julia Rose had a villa the size of a modest French hamlet. I parked a little bit short of the cliffside house, lit a cigarette, and settled down to smoke it. Jack's cream-colored Bentley convertible was in the drive and I wanted to see if I'd remembered his habits correctly; on the nights when he and Julia didn't turn up for bridge he usually went to the casino in Monte Carlo, where he liked to play baccarat. By Spinola's account, he was pretty good at it, too. His was a fine house on a quiet, winding road, and it was easy to see why Jack and Julia lived there, quite apart from its proximity to Monaco. None of the homes on that road were any less exclusive than a summer palace. A couple of

motor scooters buzzed by very loudly, like angry hornets, star-
tling me a little; but as dusk arrived, things quieted down a lot
and I closed my eyes. I dreamed about Anne, and my wife,
Elisabeth—and for some reason I even dreamed of Dalia Dres-
ner, the movie star, who was staying along the coast in Cannes,
at the Carlton. I don't remember much of what happened in the
dream except that it left me feeling sad and wistful. These days
all my dreams leave me feeling sad and wistful, probably because
they're only dreams.

About ten o'clock the closing of a car door woke me. The
cream-colored Bentley was lit up like a television set and already
on the move in the Rose drive. In the moonlight it resembled a
boat in the harbor at the Cap. I waited until it had disappeared
up the road and then got out of my car and I walked to the front
door. There was no knocker but I saw a brass handle the size of
a horse stirrup that I was supposed to pull. I pulled it. The bell
sounded as if there should have been a cow attached to it, probably in a Swiss meadow. Julia came to the door holding a martini glass, which was maybe why she seemed pleased to see me.

"Walter. What a pleasant surprise. But if you were looking
for Jack, I'm afraid you just missed him."

"That's a pity. Never mind."

"He went to play baccarat."

"I can never understand that. Bridge requires skill. Baccarat
is all luck."

"Jack's always been lucky. Don't underestimate luck."

"Oh, I don't. Not for a minute."

"Now that you're here, would you like to come in for a drink? I just mixed a jug of martinis."

"I thought you'd never ask."

She stood aside with a smile and ushered me through a wide hallway into a huge drawing room. The French windows were ajar and a light current of air blew through the room off the sea, just enough to stir the petals that had fallen from a vase of roses on a table. Julia Rose was wearing a ruffed white shirt and tapered wafer-colored pants; there was a little red clasp on her fair hair that was shaped like a cherry; she looked like an ice-cream cone. She poured me a large one from a tall glass pitcher and we sat down on one of the several sofas there were to choose from.

"Nice room. You should send out a missionary sometime. See what new plants and undiscovered tribes he comes home with."

Julia smiled. "It is kind of large, I guess."

"But I like Èze and La Turbie. The view of Monaco is the best there is."

"Nietzsche thought so. He used to stay down the road in Èze."

"That explains it. Why I feel so very much at home here. It's the kind of place that mad Germans take to."

"We like it."

"You're English. You're almost as mad as us Germans."

"But you always seem so very sane, Walter. I'm afraid I find it hard to imagine the concierge at the Grand Hôtel in Cap Ferrat doing anything mad at all."

"It's usually the sanest people who turn out to be the craziest, Julia. Who do the most insane things. That's how history is made."

"I can see I'm going to have to keep a close eye on you, Walter."

"There's a flip side to that."

She lit a cigarette and smiled a little nervously. "Oh, you needn't worry about me, Walter. I come from a family of Lloyd's insurance brokers. Who are all notoriously sane. And there are very few opportunities for going crazy in Èze."

"Unless you're Nietzsche."

"Did he go insane? I don't actually know much about Nietzsche."

"He was mad but not noticeably. At least not in Germany." I glanced around the room again. "Anyway, it's a lovely home you have. Living up here must be like heaven. It's close enough, after all."

"Have you been here before, Walter? I can't remember."

"Once. With Antimo. To play bridge when the Voile had closed for the summer. We lost."

"Poor Antimo," she said. "That was awful what happened to him. The police were here, of course. Asking their questions. Did we know anyone who might have had a grudge against him? As if. They asked a lot of questions about you. Yes, they seemed quite interested in you. But Antimo was such a dear, sweet man. I shall miss him enormously."

"Me, too."

"Do they have any idea who did it, yet?"

"No," I said. "Not a clue. But I do."

"Really? You surprise me. Who?"

"You shouldn't be surprised. It was you who shot him, Julia."

"Me? Don't be ridiculous."

"No, it's not ridiculous. You were having an affair with him and you'd threatened to put a hole in yourself when he gave you the cold cut. Spinola took your gun—or at least a gun—away from you to stop you from doing it. I still have that gun at home somewhere. I guess he never figured you might own more than one firearm. Or that you might just shoot him instead of yourself." I sipped my drink. "This is a good martini, Julia. You're quite a cocktail barman."

"From the sound of things you've had quite enough to drink already, Walter. I don't know. What you said—it's rather offensive. I think you've outstayed your welcome. Perhaps you should go now."

I said nothing.

"Or do I have to call the police?"

"Yes, let's call them, if you like."

Now it was Julia who stayed quiet.

"The police found a green chiffon scarf at the scene of the crime," I said. "Poor Spinola was holding it in his hand when you shot him through the heart at close range. There's a dress in your closet that's the perfect match for that chiffon scarf. You wore it one night at La Voile d'Or. Maybe you remember that I picked it up when you dropped it on the ground and gave it back to you. I even caught the name on the label. It was Christian Dior. Same as the dress, I'll bet money on it. Although not as much as you spent buying it. I'm sure the police will find it very interesting. It's very hard to shoot someone at close range and not get blood on yourself."

"I think you're mistaken." But her eyes were welling up with tears.

"No, I have a good memory. Believe it or not it's part of my job to know what a lady is wearing. In case she needs to go shopping for something important. Like a new chiffon scarf. I wouldn't advise it now. The cops will be paying attention to that kind of thing. In fact, I'd steer clear of most of the expensive ladies' shops on the Riviera for a while, in case someone remembers you. Besides, green is really not your color, Julia. Take it from me. Blue would be much better on you."

Julia Rose let out a sigh that sounded like a diver checking his breathing apparatus.

"Oh Jesus Christ," she whispered. "What am I to do?"

"Do? There's nothing to do. All you can do now is tell me what happened."

I let her cry for several minutes.

"I'm so sorry," she sobbed.

"I can imagine. But you don't need to apologize to me. Even if he was my bridge partner. And a damn good one, I might add."

"I loved him. I loved him so much. He was the love of my life. I don't think I'll ever get over this as long as I live."

"I believe you. But how long were you lovers?"

"Three years. I wanted to leave Jack and marry Antimo, who wouldn't hear of it. He said he couldn't afford to get married and that he preferred things the way they were. Easy to say if you don't live with Jack. I told him I didn't care about money, but he didn't believe me.

"Then, out of the blue, he wanted to end things between us for good. I found myself unable to handle that. I was going to shoot myself in his apartment. That was the plan. I know it sounds stupidly, ridiculously melodramatic, Walter. You must think I'm mad. I suppose I was mad. Still am, if I'm honest. But love does that to people sometimes. I loved him so much I'd decided I couldn't live without him. I wanted him to know that. I mean, really know that. It was late and I let myself into his apartment with the key he'd given me when we were lovers. He was in bed and got up when he realized I was there. We started to talk, I asked him to change his mind, and he refused. Then I took the gun out of my bag. I never meant to shoot him at all. Not for a minute. You must believe me, Walter. I tried to press the gun against my heart and pull the trigger but he wrestled it away and then it went off. Just once. And killed him. After that I just panicked and ran away."

I nodded. "Do you still want to kill yourself?"

"No. I don't think so. I'm not sure. Frankly, I try not to think about it."

"No, please don't ever do that. Listen, forget about what the priests and psychiatrists tell you. Take it from one who knows. Sometimes it's only the thought of suicide that gets me through the night. It can be a real consolation."

"I never know when you're joking."

"I have the same problem. Tell me, does Jack know anything about this?"

"No. If he suspects anything he hasn't said as much."

"You're sure about that?"

She nodded. "Jack drinks a lot. He doesn't notice very much at all. Except the cards he's been dealt. Somehow he always manages to pay attention to them."

"What happened to the gun?"

"I still have it upstairs. And there *is* blood on the dress, you're right."

"Go and get the gun and the dress. Oh, and Spinola's apartment key if you still have it."

"Are you going to turn me in to the police?"

"Why? It was an accident, wasn't it?"

"Yes. But I feel so guilty that it's almost like I meant to do it. That I really am a murderer."

"Why don't you let me be the judge of that?"

"I feel sick. They still send people to the guillotine in France, don't they?"

"Yes, but that's not going to happen in this case. Look, if you can keep your head about this, then you can keep your head, I promise. Now, go and get those things like I told you."

She went out of the room and returned with a small Beretta

and her green dress in a carrier bag. She handed me the key, which had a small paper label on it that helpfully read "Spinola," and I slipped it into my pocket.

"What are you going to do with those?"

"The gun and the key I'll throw in the sea, probably. The dress I'll burn in the incinerator at the hotel."

"I suppose you want something for your silence. Is that how this works?"

"You think I'm going to blackmail you?" I smiled and shook my head. "I am not going to blackmail you, Julia. Most murderers only ever do it once, but blackmailers do it all the time. Which is why blackmail is a worse crime than murder. This is the first and last time we'll ever speak of this, Julia. The next time we see each other we won't even mention this evening."

"But why? I don't understand. Why are you doing this? Why are you helping me? I don't understand. We're acquaintances. But we're not really friends. I've never even thought that you liked me very much. You don't owe me a thing."

"You're no murderer, Julia. I knew it the minute I looked in your eyes. Take it from one who knows about these things. Besides, the law of murder doesn't mean the same as it used to. Not since murder became the continuation of politics by other means. That's von Clausewitz. Well, it is since nineteen forty-five. Nothing would be gained by sending you to prison. And certainly not in France. And it won't bring back my bridge partner, either."

"What about the police?" she asked.

"The police? Listen to me, Julia. The police are just ordinary men. It's only with the gun and the dress and the key that the impossible becomes possible and the possible probable, and the probable ever stands up in court. Not even the police can perform miracles, no matter how long you wait to see one. They need evidence. Without evidence there's nothing. Nietzsche said that. Clearly he wasn't nearly as mad as a lot of people make out."

TWENTY

Somerset Maugham is being blackmailed," I told Anne French over a late dinner at her house. "And not for the first time, I think. Previously it was just a few injudicious love letters. But this is much more serious. There's an old photograph of him and various naked men, some of them now quite well known, I believe. And a tape recording. I can't give you any details but it's all very compromising to the old man. There's a lot of money involved, too."

"And what's your role in this affair?" she said. "If you don't mind me asking. Because, I'll be honest, this sounds to me to be a little beyond the duties of a normal hotel concierge. Whatever they are. I'm never all that sure."

"I'm not so sure myself. Mostly I just answer stupid questions. Steal the occasional piece of lingerie from a guest's room. Throw away a room key now and then. Look after a gun or two. Dispose of a bloodstained dress. The usual stuff. But now and then I try to help people out."

I'd spent the evening doing quite a bit of that already. Julia Rose's gun and the key to Spinola's apartment were safely in my jacket pocket, and as soon as Julia's green dress was in the hotel incinerator, she'd be in the clear. I wasn't even looking for a tip.

"Is that what you'd call your role here? Helping out?"

"Sure. I'm a sort of go-between. A human fender, like you see dangling off one of those nice white boats in the harbor down the hill, to stop the paintwork getting scratched against the dockside pontoon or another boat. Only I'm hanging between Maugham and the blackmailer."

"How did you get that job?"

"I answered an ad in the *Nice-Matin.* Wanted: Dumb German. Look, it doesn't matter. But years ago, in Berlin, I was a cop. So this kind of thing isn't exactly new to me. People have been disappointing me for a long, long time."

"You certainly give that impression."

"It's my face, I know. I worry I'm on my way to looking like Somerset Maugham." I shrugged. "I don't know why, but I feel sorry for the old man. Almost everyone around him is looking out for themselves and their bank accounts."

"And you're not?"

"No more than is normal for a guy like me."

"Is he going to pay the blackmailer?"

"It looks that way. Some people are flying down tomorrow from the Foreign Office in London to help verify the tape recording."

"The Foreign Office? Goodness. It certainly sounds serious."

"It seems to be."

"Not to mention dangerous. One reads about this kind of thing in the Sunday newspapers. Demanding money with menaces requires—well, menace, doesn't it?"

"Usually. That's certainly true in this case."

"So please, be careful."

"I think I'm in no danger. But I'll let you know for sure, the day after tomorrow."

"No, really, Walter, if I can help in any way, please don't hesitate to ask."

"Sure. But I really don't see what you can do."

"You don't have to hide your hand from me. Is it that you think I can't be trusted? We are sleeping together."

"I know you're itching to write this biography and I will introduce you to him when all this is over, perhaps in a couple of days. But I can't betray his confidence. He's not a bad fellow, I think. I mean, for an Englishman."

"I thought the Germans were supposed to admire the English."

"That's just a story put around by a lot of guilty Englishmen who stay awake nights worrying about how they dropped bombs on children in Dresden and Hamburg."

"You started it."

"Strictly speaking, it was Neville Chamberlain who started it."

We were seated at the table on the terrace. In the dark we could hear some wild pigs snuffling around in the trees behind a wire fence. They came down from the hills in the dark to forage. Many locals regarded them as a nuisance but Anne was fond of them. There was even a nice bronze of a wild boar on the sideboard in her drawing room. She was fond of describing me as her own pig, which suited me very well.

"Come with me, *sanglier*," she said. "I want to show you something."

We left the terrace and crossed the garden to the guesthouse. The wild pigs heard us and ran away, squealing a little. They were French, after all. Meanwhile, Anne switched on the light to reveal a large room that had been perfectly set up for a writer. There were pots full of pencils, lots of bookshelves, several filing cabinets, and, on a table, a pink Smith Corona Silent Super typewriter. Next to this was a smaller pink portable, lying on its open carry case. It looked like the sweet daughter of the larger one. Against one of the walls was another table on which stood a Hallicrafters shortwave radio. Anne was a keen listener to the BBC World Service, where she got most of her news.

"This is my office," she explained. "Where I do my writing." She touched the big pink Smith Corona and a ream of paper next to it fondly, almost as if she were wishing she could sit down and start work right then and there.

"Nice. Very nice. I like it a lot. Yes indeed. You know, I think I could write in here myself."

"I'd like to read that book."

"Not a book. Too long. Your horoscope, perhaps."

"And what would my horoscope say?"

"That there's going to be a handsome man in your life. You just met him. He's a little older than you're used to, perhaps, but you're going to want to see a lot more of him. Hopefully naked. Just as soon as you've told him exactly what's bothering you."

"You're good. You should write for a magazine. As a matter of fact, there is something bothering me. The fact is that I owe you an apology. I haven't been entirely honest with you, Walter."

"I read that in your horoscope, too."

"No, really. I am sorry but I haven't been honest at all."

I felt the sincerity of what she had said, but it made me uneasy all the same, as if she'd played me like a hand of cards. Not that it mattered, particularly. I always liked my women a bit slippery. And it wasn't as if she'd used me to get close to Somerset Maugham. When first she'd approached me I hadn't even known the old man. All she'd wanted was some lousy bridge lessons. Besides, she didn't know my real name, so I was hardly in a position to feel aggrieved at *her* lack of honesty.

"That's not exactly an exclusive club, Anne. I wouldn't worry about it too much."

"When I told you I had an offer of fifty thousand dollars from Victor Weybright to write Maugham's biography, I didn't mention that I'd already signed the contract."

"Congratulations."

"The fact is, I've been working on the old man's biography for several months. I'm sorry, Walter, but I probably know more about Somerset Maugham than you do. Than you'll ever know."

While she spoke Anne pulled out one of the drawers in the cabinet, removed one of the red envelope files, and handed it to me. There was a printed title in the corner that read "MAUGHAM, SYRIE née Gwendoline Maud Syrie Barnardo."

"These are my research files. For example. This is all about his wife, Syrie."

"I thought he was— I mean, I didn't even know he'd been married."

"When they met, she was Mrs. Wellcome, the wife of a wealthy American pharmaceutical manufacturer. They married in 1914. It was probably Syrie that put him off women for life. They divorced in nineteen twenty-eight. But she never married again so he was obliged by the terms of his settlement to support her financially. She died last year. And not a moment too soon as far as Maugham was concerned. By all accounts he hated her. I think he felt she'd trapped him into marriage. That she'd used him as a way of getting rid of Henry Wellcome."

Anne showed me another file. It was titled HAXTON, GER-ALD FREDERICK.

"This name I recognize," I said. "He was friend and companion number one, I think. Another homosexual Englishman. It's something to do with the weather they have in England, I expect. They can hide a lot in that fog. Anyway, he sounds like a piece of work."

"He was. Only he wasn't English, he was American. From San Francisco. Maugham met him during the first war when Gerald was with the American Red Cross. He visited England only once, for less than a week, in February nineteen nineteen. He went to London, hoping to see Maugham, but was picked up and deported. Never went back."

"That explains a lot, I guess. I mean, why Maugham has stayed down here for so long."

"What I want to say to you now, Walter, is this. I really *can* help. If there's anything you need to know that you think you can't ask him, then ask me. The chances are I will know something about it. Like you, I'm an admirer of his. Albeit for different reasons. You just like the man for himself, perhaps. I happen to believe he's one of the greatest writers of the twentieth century. I know I haven't been very honest with you about all this but for what it's worth now, I give you my word that anything you tell me will be in confidence until after he's dead. Or at the very least until you give me permission to use it. Is that fair?"

"I suppose so," I murmured uncertainly. "I don't know."

"I'll pay you for your help, of course." She paused. "To cover your expenses."

"All of a sudden there are so many people trying to pump money into me. I feel like a cigarette machine. And all of them

English, too. The odd thing—to me at least—is how little I want it. Look, I'm not doing any of this for money, Anne. Not really. The old man is paying me a basic fee to help him out of a tight spot, and that's it. And between us, well, what I'm saying is that I'd prefer there was no money at all. If I help you—and I haven't said I will, yet—it will be because I like you and only because I like you. Nothing else. Money complicates everything. Especially between lovers."

"Of course. I get that."

"Do you? I wonder."

"Look, the files are there if you need to use them. All you have to do is ask."

"There is something I'd like to know about," I said.

"Name it."

"His service with SIS in nineteen seventeen. What can you tell me about that?"

"Actually it was through Syrie that the intelligence connection came about. One of her girlfriends was the mistress of a man in the secret service by the name of Major John Wallinger. It was Wallinger who offered Maugham a job and sent him to Switzerland, in nineteen fifteen. By nineteen sixteen, Maugham was an invaluable field agent working for Sir Mansfield Cumming, who was head of the foreign section of the British secret service and for whom Maugham was running a whole network of spies in southern Germany from the Hotel d'Angleterre in Geneva. Not everyone can do something like that. By nineteen seventeen, after the February Revolution in Russia, he was working out of

the British embassy in Petrograd, where he met Alexander Kerensky several times. Kerensky was the leader of the Mensheviks.
By now Maugham had several hundred secret agents under his
sole control. He left Petrograd two days before the October Revolution, which brought the Bolsheviks to power and which ought
to tell you something: that Maugham's intelligence antennae
were very good. Not everyone managed to get out safely. Since
then it's anyone's guess how much work he's done for the British,
but there's no doubt that being an internationally famous author
is always good cover for a lot of spying. China, Central America,
even the United States—Maugham has always maintained a
strong connection with his old pals in the British secret service.
In many ways he was the ideal agent: He's an extraordinarily
perceptive man, not to mention naturally secretive. He even
wrote a novel about spying called *Ashenden*. I'll lend it to you if
you like."

"Yes, I'd like to read that."

She went to the shelves and quickly found me a copy.

Feeling the heat, I took off my jacket and hung it on the back
of the door to one of the bathrooms. "I'm impressed," I said. "At
how much you know about him."

"That's my job. Tell me, these people from the Foreign
Office. Did he say who they are?"

"He mentioned two names. Someone called Sir John Sinclair."

"Never heard of him."

"And a man named Blunt. Anthony Blunt."

"Now, him I've heard of. He works for the Queen."

"Yes, but which one? There are so many queens in this story. I get confused which one's which."

She smiled and put her arms around my neck. In the lamp-light her brown hair wreathed her face like a lion's mane. I pushed some of it aside as if it had been a curtain, kissed her tenderly, and pushed my hand between her legs. Gentlemen prefer blondes, alleged a recent movie I'd seen; it was just as well I was no gentleman. She gasped a little and pressed down on my hand. Outside the wild pigs had come back. I could hear them snorting in the trees as they snouted around blindly in the dirt. At least I thought they were the wild pigs; in retrospect they must have been my brain cells.

TWENTY-ONE

Under a salmon-pink sky the following evening, Somerset Maugham, Robin, Alan Searle, and I waited for the old man's chauffeur to fetch the British from their hotel on the Cap. A cold buffet dinner had been prepared and was being laid out on the terrace by the cook, Annette, while the four of us were in the drawing room with cocktails and cigarettes. The Grundig tape recorder remained on the refectory table, ready for action. The atmosphere was tense and expectant and, as usual, more malevolent and cattish than the chorus line in an old Weimar cabaret.

"Look at that sky," said Robin. "It's Leander pink, isn't it?"

"More Garrick Club pink, I'd say," remarked his uncle. "Not that you'd know the difference, dear."

"I've never been to the Garrick Club," said Alan. "Willie's never taken me. Although he is a member."

"You're much too young for the Garrick, love," said Maugham. "You're not allowed through the door until there is a significant amount of hair growing out of your ears and nostrils. In fact, it's a condition of membership."

"Then you ought to be the club secretary," said Alan.

Maugham turned in his chair to address Annette. "Make sure we use the Victorian champagne glasses," he instructed her. "One of these men who are coming tonight is a knight of the realm."

"Oh? Who?" asked Alan. "Who are these people, Willie?"

"Sir John Sinclair and a chap called Patrick Reilly," said Maugham. "Sinclair's the current director of MI6 and Reilly's a Foreign Office mandarin. I believe he used to be chair of the Joint Intelligence Committee. The people who oversee MI5 and MI6. They're going to make sure I'm not about to buy a pig in a poke and, hopefully, underwrite my purchase."

"So why if they're so damned important are they staying at the Belle Aurore?" asked Robin.

"Because it's a lot cheaper than the Grand or La Voile d'Or," said Maugham.

"Why aren't they staying here at the villa? It's not like there isn't plenty of room."

"They've brought some thugs from Special Branch with

them. Just in case this is all some sneaky Russian plot to kidnap two of our top spooks. But as usual, Her Majesty's Government is also being tight with money. Besides, Sinbad will much prefer staying at the Aurore. It's rather more modest and low-key than those other hotels."

"Who's Sinbad?" asked Robin.

"Before he was director of MI6, Sir John Sinclair was a major general in Royal Artillery," said Maugham. "But prior to that he went to Dartmouth Naval College and for two years he was a midshipman in the Royal Navy. Sinbad the sailor. And that's how I know him. He served with the Murmansk force in northern Russia and for a while, in a small way, was one of my field agents."

"I don't even know where the Belle Aurore is," Searle said peevishly.

"It's on Avenue Denis Semeria," I explained. "Just down from the Villa Ephrussi."

"I say, listen to the hotel concierge," said Robin.

"On the main road to Villefranche?" said Alan.

I nodded. "I drive past it almost every day."

"Sounds a bit noisy to me," said Alan.

"Guy Burgess went to Dartmouth Naval College, didn't he?" I said. "At least that's what he said on the tape."

"Yes, he did," said Robin.

"Sinbad is much older than Guy Burgess," said Maugham. "About fifteen years older, probably. So there was no chance of an overlap there. Besides, Burgess isn't Sinbad's type at all."

"You don't mean he's queer?" said Alan.

"No, I don't. Sinbad is happily married."

"Stands to reason someone must be," I said.

"To Esme, I believe. For many years."

"Anyone married to someone called Esme for many years must be queer," said Robin.

"I find it hard to imagine that anyone who was a midshipman in the Royal Navy isn't a bit queer," objected Alan. "If they'd ever put it on the recruiting posters that the traditions of the Royal Navy were rum, sodomy, and the lash I'd have joined immediately. But instead I ended up in the army. In fucking Yorkshire. That's enough to cure anyone of homosexuality, for life."

"Is this all you people ever talk about?" I said. "Who's queer and who isn't?"

"It's that or bloody Suez," said Alan, "and right now I think I'd rather not talk about Suez."

"No, indeed," murmured Robin. "The gyppos are going to drop us all in the shit again."

"Don't think for a minute we haven't discussed you in the same vein, Walter," said Maugham. "Before the Nazis, Berlin was a poof's paradise. I find it very hard to imagine that you are not without something more interesting in your extremely secret history than a couple of unfortunately dead wives."

I shifted uncomfortably on my chair, lit a cigarette, and told myself that the sooner I could leave the Villa Mauresque the better. The atmosphere always made me uneasy, as though it had been calculated to make me feel as if I were the queer one. Perhaps I was at that. A fish out of water, certainly; out of water, and out of oxygen. I helped myself to another drink and tried to remain affable.

"I don't know that I'd call it a secret history," I said. "I think I told you quite a bit already, didn't I?"

"If you were a fictional narrator, my friend," said Maugham, "I should say that you were a narrator who was not to be trusted. Like Tristram Shandy. Please don't get me wrong. That's not a bad thing. Not in his case, nor in yours. It's merely entertaining."

Robin frowned at me and then looked irritably at his uncle. "What's Walter doing here anyway? That's what I'd like to know. He's a German. Surely an evening like this should be Brits only. I can't imagine someone like Sir John will welcome a Jerry at a meeting like this."

"You're right, of course," said Maugham. "An Englishman has an instinctive knowledge of what's right and wrong. And can always be relied on not to let the side down, unlike some fucking kraut. Especially someone who went to Eton and Cambridge. Someone like Guy Burgess, perhaps."

Alan laughed.

"Besides, Sinbad isn't the only one who can put on a bit of maximum security," said Maugham. "So can I."

"Well, I think he's a little too old to be a bodyguard," sniped Robin.

"Isn't that right, Walter?"

I slipped the automatic Spinola had given me back at La Voile d'Or out of my trouser pocket for a moment to let everyone see it, but mainly the sight of the gun was for Robin's benefit.

"So that's what it is," said Robin. "And here was me thinking that lump in his trousers might be his cock."

I smiled calmly; it seemed a little more socially adept than whipping him across his pink, sweaty face with the gun. But there's more than one way to slap a bitch hard.

"Perhaps, sir," I said to Maugham, "your nephew might be interested to know that Anthony Blunt is also coming tonight."

"Blunt? Coming here?" Robin Maugham was agitated. I didn't blame him. It must be awkward to meet someone socially when you've been blackmailing them. He stood up, red-faced and puffing like one of the carp in his uncle's ornamental pond, and flung away his cigarette. "No one told me. Why the fuck is Anthony Blunt coming here as well? I don't understand. Who asked him anyway?"

"Sir John suggested he might join us," said Maugham. "Blunt knows Guy Burgess as well as anyone. Besides, during the war Anthony worked for MI5. Which makes him doubly qualified to be here. Alan, please go and retrieve that cigarette end before it starts a fire. Everything in the garden is so very dry right now. Do try to be more thoughtful, Robin."

Alan stood up, found the cigarette, and returned it to the ashtray while Robin continued to sound off on the subject of Blunt's imminent arrival.

"Thank you, Alan."

"I didn't know he worked for MI5," said Robin. "I thought he was an art historian, not a fucking spy."

"Art historians make good spies," said Maugham. "In art as in life, things are never quite what they seem. During the last war I myself did some work for MI6 in Lisbon. And then, in New York, I helped Bill Stephenson run British Security Coordination from the Rockefeller Center. But I'm still not allowed to say too much about that."

"Is there a queer in London who doesn't work for the security services?" Robin Maugham whined. "That's what I'd like to know. Well, I wish someone had told me he was coming, that's all."

"I'm telling you now," said Maugham.

"If you're planning to be around when they get here," I told Robin, adding to his now obvious discomfort, "maybe now would be a good time to tell your uncle what he doesn't know. I mean about you and Blunt."

"Good Lord, you haven't fucked him, too," said Maugham, and started to laugh his gravelly old laugh. "You little devil."

Robin Maugham regarded me with pinpoint hatred.

"Perhaps before Blunt tells your uncle himself. Which he might well do, don't you think? It's just a suggestion, Robin. To save you any needless embarrassment."

"You bastard."

"He *has* fucked him, hasn't he?" Maugham was still laughing delightedly in his almost Satanic way. "Do tell."

But Robin had had enough and marched off the terrace like

an angry terrier. A few minutes later we heard his Alfa Romeo take off.

"Now I really am fascinated," said Maugham, continuing to cackle. "What on earth's the matter with the boy?"

It was time. I told the old man about the photograph, how his nephew had used it to blackmail Anthony Blunt and how Blunt had alleged it had later been stolen from his flat in London. "It might just be that Robin and Harold Hebel were in cahoots to make some money from you," I explained. "Fifty thousand dollars, if you see where I'm going."

"Yes, I do see. Oh dear. Poor Robin. No, it's not funny at all, is it?"

Composing himself again, Maugham sipped his martini, ate the olive, and then sighed. "Look, Walter, I don't expect you to understand this in the slightest, but for men like me and Robin and Alan, silence about who and what we are is not a choice so much as a matter of constant vigilance. In fact, it's nothing short of an obsession. We inhabit a dog-eat-dog world of extortion and blackmail the way some people live with religion or politics. Blackmail infects us to the extent that we're not merely its victims but, just as often, its perpetrators. Lovers spurned become our most painful tormentors. Boys we fondly kept in toys and treats and money—always lots of money—turn around and bite the hand that once fed them so generously in the name of their own freedom. Letters we've written are the tools of our own torture and potential downfall. It would be easy for me to condemn my nephew's actions out of hand, but I'm not going to. As you yourself no doubt remember, I myself blackmailed you to come and help me out with this business. So, you see, I'm just as rotten and unscrupulous as Robin is."

"I think you're making excuses for him," I said.

"Of course I am. Robin is my nephew, and in spite of his manifest failings I'm very fond of him. I'll always be making excuses for him. He is the only member of my family I like. No, that's not quite true—I have a niece, Kate, my brother's daughter, of whom I am rather fond. But Robin is a weak man. And needs me. 'Need' is a more important word than 'love,' Walter. Especially at my time of life. Although perhaps it always was. It's good to be needed. Perhaps one day you'll realize that."

TWENTY-TWO

Sir John "Sinbad" Sinclair crossed his long legs and straightened the perfect creases on the trousers of his summer-weight suit. His polished brown shoes gleamed in the lamplight, while his short, gray hair sat on top of a long head like an army beret. He looked exactly like what he was: an ex-general in the British army, one of those paternally minded and probably much-loved generals who regarded his men as his sons, and his junior officers as younger brothers. While he listened to the tape, he made notes with a fountain pen and occasionally rubbed a broken nose that was bent toward the left side of his face. He was a handsome man, about sixty years old and rather more vigorous than the other Englishman accompanying him. Patrick Reilly was younger than Sinclair by more than a decade, and while he was probably as tall as Sinbad, he was altogether less physical, with the beginnings of a double chin and a posture that belonged in a plantation chair on the veranda of some Indian bungalow. Where Sinclair's expression was lively and adventurous, like a well-trained gun dog, Reilly's was altogether more feline and wary, with small, searching green eyes and a mouth as tight as a Frisian miser's purse. Neither of them had said very much, but Reilly already struck me as the more intelligent of the two. Both men regarded me with strong suspicion and were more than a little surprised—as was I—when Maugham had earlier introduced me as his "private detective."

"Winston had one, when he came to stay here at the Villa Mauresque," added Maugham, by way of explanation and justification. "Can't remember the fellow's name."

"Walter Thompson, I think," said Sinclair. "Like the advertising agency."

"No, that was the previous one," said Reilly. "Don't you remember? Obtuse sort of chap. We had all that trouble when he wanted to publish a book about his experiences guarding Winston."

"Oh yes."

"Well, my detective is also called Walter," said Maugham. "And he's here with us tonight because he's been helping me to deal with this blackmailer, Harold Hebel. I trust you have no objection to his being here because I've rather come to rely on his judgment. In any event, I prefer him to remain. Just as I'm sure you feel safer with your two chaps from Special Branch. If that's what they are." Maugham nodded in the direction of the French windows, where two largish Englishmen with guns were blundering around in the gardens and trying to look inconspicuous.

"I've no idea where they're from." Reilly looked at Sinclair. "Do you?"

"Not my department. I drew them both from stores. Standard issue for an excursion like this. They're from Fort Monckton, I believe. Portsmouth muscle."

The third visitor from London seemed to belong at the Villa Mauresque in a way Sinclair and Reilly could never have done. Obviously homosexual, Anthony Blunt was about fifty, tall, as thin as a Giacometti bronze figure, with a shock of boyishly combed gray hair and the look of a man who had just tasted a rather indifferently blended sherry. He wore an open-necked white shirt with short sleeves as, unlike the other two, he had removed his jacket since it was a very warm evening. The deep laugh lines around his slit of a mouth were in frequent use. His dry sense of humor was deployed often and he struck me as a man both charming and highly intelligent, albeit deeply untrustworthy. The idea that this man had ever been a spy in MI5 seemed preposterous, but he didn't look like a blackmailer and I quickly discounted the idea that he might be in cahoots with Hebel to extort money from Maugham. I doubt he could have demanded his morning newspaper with any real menace. He, too, was making copious notes, and when we'd finished listening to the tape for the first time it was Blunt who spoke. His voice was probably as familiar to the English Queen as her own, and I assumed it was probably the way she herself spoke.

"I think the answer to the most obvious question right now— is this Guy Burgess speaking on the tape?—is categorically yes; in my opinion, it is. The details and dates he gives of his early life are, of course, accurate. As is the code name of the Swiss source he was running for MI5 back in nineteen forty-four: Orange. Only Guy and one or two others, including myself, would have known that name. Known, too, that poor Orange did indeed meet a sticky end with the Gestapo in Trier. That's one thing in favor of this tape's authenticity. And here's another, which is paradoxically confirmation by way of a perverse delusion, it being Guy's perverse delusion, of course.

"In spite of the weight of experience he had behind him to form a contrary opinion, I have to say it was entirely typical of Guy that he might actually believe the BBC would even be capable of broadcasting this tape recording. Guy was always extremely critical of the BBC and all its works. He believed, as I do, that the BBC is one of those institutions that trivializes the serious and it's impossible to imagine that they would have treated this tape as he could ever have wished them to. I can only assume he must have supposed some left-leaning soul at the BBC, intent on embarrassing the government, would leak the tape to a newspaper such as the *Manchester Guardian* in order that they might publish an extract from the tape. But even they would have been subject to a Defense Advisory Notice forbidding publication on the grounds of national security. The idea that open criticism of the security services is now permissible in our media is laughable, to say the least. Nor is his admission of the ease with which he helped himself to sensitive files something that could ever be allowed to be heard by the great British public."

"Yes, that's very damaging," admitted Sinclair. "It makes us look like incompetents."

"The story about Guy driving down to Chartwell to interview Churchill is true," continued Blunt. "I'd heard it before, of course, and the story is well known, I think. Guy told it often enough in the Reform Club, especially when he was drunk. What is much less well known is that Guy did indeed pursue Churchill's niece, Clarissa—now Mrs. Anthony Eden. I was vaguely aware of it at the time and of course I was surprised, to say the least, for the obvious reason. I certainly had no idea that he'd been put up to it by his Russian controller, Arnold Deutsch, code name Otto."

"MI6 has, to the best of my knowledge, never heard of a Russian handler called Arnold Deutsch, code name Otto," said Sinclair.

"Nor have I," admitted Reilly. "He might have been one of the great illegals, I suppose. Those Trotskyist Communists not born in Russia who believed in the Comintern. But I thought I'd heard of all of them. No such man as Deutsch, Otto or Arnold, exists in our files. I'm certain of it."

"How about you, Anthony?" asked Sinclair. "Ever heard of him?"

"No. I've never heard of him. Certainly there was no one I

remember at Cambridge who fits that description. And none I remember who crossed Guy's meandering, not to say erratic, path."

"Of course," added Reilly, "the Russians might readily own up to him now if he's dead, murdered by Stalin back in nineteen thirty-eight—a few years after Guy says he was recruited to the NKVD—like most of the illegals. So that would make sense."

"To me, the stuff about Hector McNeil is very damaging," said Sinclair.

"Especially as he was a government minister at the time."

"Certainly to the Labour Party if not to McNeil himself. He died last year."

"Really?"

"Yes. He was only forty-eight."

"Christ. Scots, of course. Working-class Glasgow. They never seem to live long, do they?"

"The information about Britain having a list of which Russian cities we might bomb in a preemptive strike is also damaging," said Reilly. "The British people don't like to think of themselves as aggressors. That could never have been broadcast. Not in a million years."

"I would like to know who this man was that Deutsch and Guy met in Paris," said Sinclair. "The one he says Deutsch was looking to recruit for the comrades."

"The ones who'd just come back from China?" said Blunt. "Yes. That was rather interesting."

"It sort of rings a bell with me somewhere," said Sinclair. "But why?"

"He'd been working for a tobacco company, so it shouldn't be too hard to find out," said Reilly. "But what interests me more is where the tape comes from. We need to find out from the BBC if they ever received it. And if they did receive it, who gave it to them and what happened to it. One can hardly imagine they wouldn't have been aware of its importance."

"On the other hand, if this chap Hebel was given the tape by someone in the KGB," said Blunt, "the question is what the Soviets can hope to achieve by letting us have it now, five years after Burgess and Maclean went to Russia. Disinformation or disclosure? It's rather a dilemma."

"Quite."

"Walter has an interesting theory about the tape," said Maugham. "Don't you, Walter?"

"Yes, sir." And I quickly told them about Hebel and his history as a practiced blackmailer in Germany. "This just may be a case of blackmail, pure and simple. If so, I can't imagine anyone better equipped than Hebel to handle it for the Russians."

"Yes, but what could they want?" asked Reilly.

"Money," I said. "What else? The Soviet Union is desperately short of foreign currency. And they know how sensitive Anglo-American relations are right now. How anxious you would be to prevent the Americans from having ears on the tape. There's no telling what's on the other tapes being offered as part of the deal."

271

"They could be even more embarrassing," said Reilly. "Yes, I do see what you mean."

"Under the circumstances," I said, "two hundred thousand dollars looks cheap compared with the diplomatic cost of this tape and others like it appearing in the pages of the *New York Times* or on some foreign news network."

"If Walter's right, then clearly someone in Russian intelligence has a sense of humor," said Maugham. "The idea of the British government paying off the KGB to stop it from leaking secrets about its number one defector is nothing short of hilarious. At least, it would be if it wasn't me who was being asked to pay up."

"Quite," said Sinclair.

"And Hebel is the man who was in possession of the incriminating photograph that Anthony bought from Willie's nephew, Robin," said Reilly. "Is that right? For a thousand pounds."

"Yes," said Maugham. "I'm sorry about that, Anthony. You must let me give you the thousand pounds you paid him for it."

"Please don't concern yourself too much, Willie," said Blunt. "As you know, this is not so much an occupational hazard as a constitutional one. The picture and the negative were both purloined from my flat several months ago. In my work as director of the Courtauld Institute I have to entertain a great many students. Sadly, I think one of them must have stolen it and sold it to this awful man. I do have half an idea of who it might have been. An Austrian boy. Which makes it even more disappointing. He's one of my most promising students."

"You know this fellow reminds me of the chap in the Sherlock Holmes story," said Sinclair. "'The Adventure of Charles Augustus Milverton.'"

Reilly smiled calmly. "Yes, of course. The king of blackmailers. Rather a good tale that one, I always thought."

"Milverton was based on a real blackmailer, by the way," added Blunt. "A man called Howell who was blackmailing the artist Dante Gabriel Rossetti. Howell was found with his throat cut and half a sovereign in his mouth. Which seems fitting, somehow."

"I wish someone would cut this man Hebel's throat," said Maugham. "I suggested to Walter that he should kill him, but alas he declined. Why don't you have your two friends from Portsmouth pick him up and go to work on him with a red-hot travel iron. It seems to me that you could get all the answers you need from him that way."

"I don't think the French would like that very much," said Reilly. "We're getting on rather well with them right now, what with all this Suez business. Which makes a very pleasant change. For once we're on the same page. They wouldn't like it at all if we acted in such a high-handed fashion as you describe, Willie."

"Besides," added Sinclair, "we risk Hebel's masters responding to that by simply sending one of the tapes to the Americans. Which would be a disaster. That's the risk you take when you call the blackmailer's bluff. That the whole thing goes pear-shaped."

"If this is just an attempt to raise a bit of extra money, then it's rather clever," said Reilly. "Willie pays the blackmailer—and pays quickly—to avoid personal embarrassment. We pay him—though rather more slowly, as is typical of government departments—to avoid placing Willie in the invidious position of wondering how to recover his money. And Walter is right, I think. These tapes have been keenly priced. Two hundred thousand is just enough to make it worth their while but not too much to stop Willie from buying them."

TWENTY-THREE

We listened to the tape recording again, and this time, when it was finished, we left the whitewashed drawing room and stepped onto the terrace and had champagne and a cold lobster supper under the stars. Later on, Sir John Sinclair excused himself and went to make a telephone call to "the friends" in London, he said, to set in motion the laborious process of raising Maugham's money from the cash-strapped British government. Robin Maugham continued to stay away from the Villa Mauresque, which suited his uncle, and, bored I think, Alan Searle drove off somewhere in his car, leaving Reilly, Blunt, Maugham, and me still talking over cigarettes and brandy. Then, with arms folded across his chest like an Egyptian mummy, and glasses perched on the end of his long, beaky nose, Blunt excused himself and set about surveying the old queen's pictures. From time to time we could hear him utter some adjective to punctuate his breathless appreciation of Maugham's collection, which, later on, he declared to be "as good as any he had ever seen in private hands," pleasing the writer to no end. He himself was again in a good mood; the prospect of risking a large sum of money with no guarantee of reimbursement had been troubling him a great deal.

"Well, that's a relief, I must say. About the money. I was thinking I might have to postpone the purchase of a nice little painting I've found by Stanislas Lépine. It is rather expensive. Icing on the cake, as it were. Or perhaps even the cherry. At my time of life, it's a little hard to tell. By the way, the money will be available from Hottingers, my bankers in Nice, tomorrow morning at eleven."

"You were quite right to call us, Willie," said Reilly. "Thank you. Thank you so much. There's absolutely no question we have to stop these tapes from falling into the wrong hands. And if Mr. Wolf is agreeable, we'll ask him to handle the exchange, I think. We wouldn't like to spook this fellow Hebel by introducing anyone new to the proceedings at this late stage. Having said that, perhaps our chaps from Fort Monckton could ride shotgun with you for some of the time and help keep an eye on the money."

"That's up to Walter," said Maugham. "He and Robin are the only ones who've met this fellow Hebel."

"The roads being what they are, the exchange is to take place on a boat," I told Reilly. "In Menton. It's my guess he's planning to make a quick getaway as soon as he's counted the money. I'll drive straight to Menton from Nice."

"Why Menton?" asked Reilly.

"Because it's on the Italian border," said Maugham. "He can be at one of those joke banks in Ventimiglia within an hour of receiving the money."

"Of course," said Reilly, "there's no real guarantee that we're going to put a stop to any of this by paying up. Once we've bought one job lot of tapes featuring the Cambridge Two, there's potentially no end to it. This is how blackmail works, of course. In no time at all, we could find ourselves obliged to buy more compromising material. In fact, I should go so far as to say it's a cast-iron certainty. Donald Maclean was based in Washington for four years, from nineteen forty-four to nineteen forty-eight, after which he was a key official in our Cairo embassy. It goes without saying he can make things very difficult with the Americans. Right now, J. Edgar Hoover regards us as a very leaky ship indeed. He looks at Burgess and Maclean and the state of MI6 and asks, what's the point of sharing any more secrets with the Brits? But the trouble Maclean could make for us with the gyppos while this Suez business is going on doesn't bear thinking of. I mean, he could really put the cat among the pigeons. We've been propping up King Farouk and allowing U.S. planes to land and refuel in the Canal Zone on their way to practice bombing missions over the Soviet Union. All of which makes General Nasser's demands look pretty damn reasonable. So you see we really do have to buy what they're selling or risk enormous embarrassment."

"Yes, I do see," said Maugham. "As soon as I listened to the tape I knew how damaging it was. Not just for me, but also for Her Majesty's Government. To my mind it's not just the English laws against homosexuality that provide a blackmailer's charter; it's the Official Secrets Act, as well. With anything where one places a premium on privacy there's always the possibility that people are going to take financial advantage of that."

"You know, this might even get you your knighthood," Reilly told Maugham.

"Do you really think so?"

"Why not? I shall certainly say as much to Selwyn Lloyd when next I see him."

"The British foreign secretary," said Maugham, in my direction. "And, as it happens, a bit of a fan of mine."

"The trouble is," Reilly continued, "these two—Burgess and Maclean—can now make any amount of mischief with impunity. Guy Burgess can repeat more or less whatever he likes and even if it isn't true, the Americans are going to believe him. He and Maclean look like better and more effective spies than they were, perhaps, merely by virtue of the fact that they got away with it so long."

"Isn't that the definition of a perfect spy," I said. "Getting away with it—in their case for almost two decades?"

"Walter's right," observed Maugham. "It's hard to imagine how they could have been more successful than they were."

"The net was closing in on them when they defected," argued Reilly. "I can't say too much about that but I'm quite certain we'd have caught them before very much longer."

"I'm sure that's of enormous relief to Mr. Hoover," Maugham said pointedly. "He'll sleep more soundly knowing that they were about to be caught. Before they managed to do some real damage to Britain's relationship with America."

I lit a cigarette and grinned. I liked the old man's sense of humor. In many ways it was a lot like mine—sharp and bitter and sometimes hardly funny at all. The kind of black humor that nearly always got you a big laugh in Berlin.

"Of course," he added, "one does wonder if these two were the only spies at the heart of the British establishment. When I was listening to Guy Burgess describe going up to Cambridge in nineteen twenty-nine to find that most of his friends had either joined the Communist Party or were at least very close to it in that febrile atmosphere of anti-Fascism, I asked myself if there were not others who, like Burgess, betrayed their country. Perhaps several others. In which case Burgess and Maclean are merely a sample of what you can expect from now on."

"I went to Oxford myself," said Reilly. "New College. Came down the same year as Burgess. Never a sniff of any Bolshiness there. Funny thing about people who went to Cambridge University. Hard to like any of them, really. I think it must have something to do with the inclement weather in that part of England. Very cold in Cambridge, you know."

"Even now," persisted Maugham, "there may be other Cambridge men like Burgess and Maclean who are handing over the family silver to the Russkies. Have you considered that possibility? I hope so, Patrick. I hate to sound like the witchfinder general, but one would hate to think that there is more that could be done to find out just how deep this treason goes."

Reilly smiled thinly as if such a thing were inconceivable—which only served to make the rest of us think that it was—and changed the subject with undiplomatic dexterity. "Tell me about yourself, Mr. Wolf," he said. "You interest me more and more."

"There's not a lot to tell. Less of a novel and more of a short story, you might say. And not a very interesting one at that." I gave Reilly the blue-penciled, redacted version of the kind he was probably used to sending in triplicate to his political masters. Just about every bit of it was untrue, apart from the fact that I'd once been a cop in Berlin, and every time I repeated it I was almost convinced I had as much talent for fiction as Somerset Maugham himself. Maybe I did, too; being a writer always looks like a good job to have when you're as dishonest as I am.

"*You're* not a Communist, I trust?" said Reilly. He said the word as if such a thing would have been impossible among civilized men.

"No, I always hated the Communists. Especially after nineteen seventeen."

"Still, I expect you were probably quite left-wing when you were a young man back in Germany."

"I was a Social Democrat when the Nazis came to power, if that's what you mean. They thought that was left wing. Then

THE OTHER SIDE OF SILENCE

again they were Nazis. Interestingly the Communists thought Social Democrats were as bad as Nazis. Being a Social Democrat in nineteen thirty-three wasn't a political choice so much as a predicament."

"Where are you now, politically?"

"Same place. Middle of the road. Neither fish nor fowl. As far as that goes in a country like France. Given the French love of empire, I'm not sure there can be any center ground in a country like this." I shrugged. "Mind you, the same could be said of England."

Reilly nodded patiently. "What do you usually do when you're not working?"

"Play bridge. Drink too much. Stay out of the sun during the day. Read a lot. I'm more suited to the night, I think."

"Been back to Berlin lately?"

"No, and I can't see myself going, either. Not since they surrounded it with the GDR, a lot of barbed wire, and a tissue of lies."

"Pardon me for asking this in your presence, Willie. Have you ever been queer, by any chance, Mr. Wolf?"

"No."

"What about spying? Ever done any of that?"

"Spying?"

"What I mean is, have you ever undertaken any clandestine activities?"

"Only at the Grand Hôtel. When I'm not muscle for Mr. Maugham I work as a concierge. I'm often to be found looking through keyholes. I like to keep an eye on blondes to see if they're natural or not."

"What's the verdict?"

"These days most of them are faking it."

"Walter has had a tough time with the ladies, I think," observed Maugham. "I think his heart has been broken once too often."

"There's nothing like an unhappy love affair to give you a good laugh," I said.

"Righto," said Reilly in a cheery sort of way. "I just wanted to make sure you can be trusted. I'm sure you can appreciate why we need to do something like that. Things being what they are, right now. Everyone in Whitehall is more than a little paranoid."

"Sure, I get it." I smiled uncertainly, wondering if I had just been vetted; and the possibility that Patrick Reilly had cleared me as a security risk was enough to make me understand for the first time just how easy it had been for Burgess and Maclean to spy successfully for the Russians over such a long period of time. Burgess hadn't exaggerated. A retarded child could probably have been as effective a spy as he'd managed to be. If Reilly could have cleared me he might just as easily have cleared Julius and Ethel Rosenberg.

"Anyone know the score in the test match?" he asked brightly.

TWENTY-FOUR

Sir John Sinclair came back from the library, took Reilly aside with some urgency, and then moved him smoothly into the drawing room, leaving me alone on the terrace with Somerset Maugham. The MI6 director's face had been flushed and was anything but its usual inscrutably English mask. Clearly he had learned something from London that had alarmed him. After a moment or two, he came back and closed the French windows firmly, as if the utmost discretion was now required.

"Hello," said Maugham, "something's up, I think."

I helped myself to another brandy. I was drinking too much but when the brandy was as good as that being served at the Villa

Mauresque such considerations hardly seemed to matter. Besides, I was bored. That's the thing about the British, even when they're spies they're so very boring.

"Oh Lord," said Maugham, "I do hope they're not going to start quibbling about the money." His snake eyes narrowed. "Look here, I've decided. I'm not going to pay if there's any question of them not reimbursing me. Sorry, Walter, and rest assured I'll pay you what I agreed to pay you. But I shall copy the Duke of Wellington's example and tell this German bastard to publish and be damned. I'd rather say to hell with them all than lose that Lépine. After all, what can the press do to me down here? I'm already an exile. It will be tough on my brother, but we've never been close and he'll just have to ride out the storm."

From the place where he'd left them, on the refectory table in the drawing room, Sinclair collected the notes he'd made when listening to the tape and consulted them impatiently; then, giving up, he tossed the notebook aside, turned a knob on the Grundig, and wound the tape back to the beginning.

"I don't think it's a problem with the money," I said. "I'd say there's a problem with something Burgess said."

"You don't suppose they think the tape is a fake?" Maugham asked.

"You heard Blunt. He's certain that it's Burgess talking. And according to all of you, he's the one who knows Burgess better than anyone. Whatever that means. No, this is something else. Something factual, perhaps. If only we could hear what's happening in that drawing room."

"Shit." Maugham turned a full circle on his heel and then stamped his foot irritably.

"There's nothing to do except be patient," I said. "We'll find out soon enough."

"Soon enough might be too late." Maugham shook his head. "Look here, Walter," he said, "there is a way someone can eavesdrop on what's happening in there. But you need to be a lot younger and quicker than I to do it. I was going to use this method in *Ashenden*, but my editor didn't believe it would work. But it does work, I can assure you. At least it does at the Villa Mauresque. If you go up to my study and then climb along the roof a bit, you can hear almost everything. The fireplace in the drawing room acts like a giant ear trumpet and conducts all of the sound straight up the chimney. The number of times I've stood up there and listened to what my guests really thought about me. I shall never invite Diana Cooper again. Well, go on. I'll follow you up to the study."

I went inside the villa, through the cool hall, grabbed the wrought-iron banister, and started up the stairs two at a time. The eagle atop a ten-foot-high gilded wooden perch on the corner landing eyed my swift progress with detached interest. There was something vaguely Nazi about that eagle, and I would not have been surprised if it had once been marched triumphantly through the Brandenburg Gate, at the head of an SA troop and a military brass band, in some midnight torchlight procession. Sometimes I miss Berlin more than seems appropriate.

I reached the second floor and climbed the wooden stair

onto the flat roof. On the other side of the freestanding structure that was Maugham's study was a short pan-tiled Moorish roof, and at the far end of this, a large square chimney, about the height of a man. I stepped gingerly onto the tiles and walked as quickly as I dared to the chimney, then took hold of it.

I hadn't expected it to be quite so easy, but Maugham had not exaggerated. The fireplace was like a large microphone and already I could hear the plummy sound of Guy Burgess speaking on tape. I didn't know it yet, but by sending me up there Maugham had effectively saved my life.

TWENTY-FIVE

The Paris Bureau of the Comintern introduced me to all sorts of interesting people, many of them sympathetic Englishmen, such as Claud Cockburn and John Cairncross. Meanwhile, Arnold Deutsch took me out to dinner with all sorts of strange folk, not all of them obvious recruitment material. People who had no languages. People who hadn't even been to university. Some of them were downright dull. Not to say stupid. I remember a very uninspiring young English salesman recently returned from China, where he'd been working for a tobacco company. I mean, this chap hadn't even been to university, let alone Cambridge. All he could talk about was tobacco and the

Chinese and about some awful bloody girl he'd married back in Somerset. And I remember thinking, what's the point of trying to recruit a chap to the cause who's going to be happily married and selling cigarettes? Are the Russians so desperate for spies that we're willing to fund the local tobacconists? Not that he took Arnold's ruble, so to speak. Anyway, ours not to reason why and all that rot."

Then someone—Sinclair, I assumed—turned off the tape and walked around for a moment. His stout English shoes on the stone flags sounded almost military, which they probably were.

"Well?" said Reilly. "Why all the flap? I must say you are looking very excited about something all of a sudden."

"I am," said Sinclair. "I've had this itch after I heard that remark Burgess made about China. So I scratched it."

"And, what?"

"I called the office and had one of my chaps telephone someone at MI5 who owes us a favor. And he did some deep checking in the personnel files at Leconfield House. Formerly the Ardath Tobacco Company, British American Tobacco's most popular brand in China was State Express 555. In June nineteen thirty-seven, prior to his wedding in July the same year, and at Wells Cathedral no less, BAT appointed a new assistant foreign manager to sell State Express to the chinks. But almost as soon as he arrived in Shanghai, in August nineteen thirty-seven, the Japanese army invaded the city and BAT's new assistant foreign manager was obliged to abandon his nice new villa in the Bund and skedaddle home to London, via Paris." Sinclair paused for dramatic effect. "That man was none other than our own dear friend Roger Hollis."

"Jesus Christ," said Reilly. "You're not serious."

"Oh, but I am. And it gets worse, I'm afraid. Just a few days after he's back in London, Roger Hollis quits his job at BAT and applies to join MI6; he's rejected, thank God. But he does manage to join MI5 just a few months later, in January nineteen thirty-eight, as a probationer under training. Apparently he was introduced in August nineteen thirty-seven by Jane Sissmore following a game of tennis at the Ealing Tennis Club, where he also met Dick White. That's what they used to call security vetting, I think. A game of fucking tennis. And here's something else. In October nineteen thirty-seven, Hollis gives a lecture at the Royal Central Asian Society in London on the subject of the recent conflict in China. Guess who else is a member of the Royal Central Asian Society? Our old friend Kim Philby."

"That is interesting, I agree. But look here, John, MI5's Peach investigation still shows that nothing has actually been conclusively proved against Philby. He's been cleared of being a Soviet agent."

"Only officially and in public. And only for the benefit of Anglo-American relations. You know it. And I know it. Who else but Kim Philby could have tipped off Burgess and Maclean that they were about to go in the bag? There was no one else it could have been." Sinclair paused. "Unless it was Hollis, of course."

Sinclair paused again.

"It's even possible that fingering Hollis leaves Kim Philby in the clear, retrospectively."

"I know that this is exactly what you chaps in MI6 would like, Sinbad. Something that leaves your man Philby in the clear and points the finger at your rival service, MI5. So be careful what you wish for, eh? Because you're suggesting that Roger Hollis, the current deputy DG of MI5—the man who's been the head of our Soviet espionage section for the last ten years—is a Soviet agent," said Reilly. "Is that any better than Philby being a Russian agent? I don't know that it is, really."

"But there's more, I think. Perhaps you've forgotten it was Roger Hollis who tried to see off MI5's investigation of John Cairncross in the wake of the Burgess defection. If you remember, it was thought that Cairncross might be the Soviet agent code-named Liszt. He's been under suspicion ever since."

"But he admitted it, didn't he?" said Reilly. "Which is more than Philby ever did."

"Yes, but it would certainly explain a lot about Hollis, don't you think?" said Sinclair. "Come on, Patrick, I'm not the only one who has had suspicions about Roger Hollis. Ever since the Gouzenko business the Canadians have suspected he might not be quite right. Back in nineteen forty-five, when Hollis interrogated Gouzenko in Ottawa, it was a travesty, by all accounts. And it was also Roger Hollis who cleared Klaus Fuchs, the Russians' top atomic spy in Britain. *Hollis.* God only knows who else he might have cleared. It might also explain how the Russians knew about Commander Crabb's mission last month and were undoubtedly waiting for him when he got in the water to take a covert look at that Russian ship. How? Perhaps Hollis told them. Look here, Patrick, Hollis could have been recruited to the general Soviet cause while he was still selling fags in China, back in nineteen thirty-seven, and then more specifically by the Comintern, in Paris, as described so carelessly by Guy Burgess. The comrades encourage him to give up BAT and join MI6 or MI5. And because this is all starting to make perfect sense, I admit that I do think there's a possibility that yes, this might, after all, clear Kim Philby of being the comrades' top agent 'Stanley.' Why not? With Roger Hollis at MI5 the Russians would have known everything we were doing before we thought of it ourselves."

Reilly sighed loudly. "Yes, but here's the glaringly obvious flaw in your brilliant theory, John. If Hollis is an important agent of the Soviet Union, why would Guy mention him on the tape, even obliquely?"

"Guy always did talk too much when he'd been drinking. So, no change there. But I think he just forgot that the boring little tobacco salesman who got married in Wells Cathedral was actually Roger Hollis. That would be typical, too. Besides, Hollis is, as everyone knows, quite self-effacing and anonymous. He's so underwhelming that people often forget all about him. He doesn't speak any languages. Doesn't even speak Russian. Imagine a head of the Russian counterespionage section who doesn't speak Russian. How does that happen?"

"All right," said Reilly, "suppose I accept that it's just imaginable Guy overlooked that he was mentioning a man who—if you're right—was Russia's top spy in England. How is it possible that the Russians themselves could have overlooked this particular detail? Which they would have to have done if they wanted to blackmail us with this tape."

"I take your point."

There was a longish silence, during which I shifted to a slightly more comfortable position on the chimney. Anyone looking at me in the moonlight would have mistaken me for a burglar or perhaps an off-duty Santa Claus. Ludicrous, really. All I really wanted to do now was leave the Villa Mauresque and go see Anne French in Villefranche and climb into bed with her. Down in the garden I could hear the two English agents talking about football and I smelled their cheap cigarettes. I wouldn't have minded one myself but for the fear that the men in the drawing room might smell my tobacco smoke coming down the chimney. I glanced around and saw Maugham now seating himself in the large square full of bluish light that was his study. He looked like an extinct species of tropical fish, most probably poisonous. But certainly he could have been no more poisonous than the relationship between MI5 and MI6, which reminded me strongly of the rivalry that had existed between the German Abwehr and the SD. I had direct experience of just how lethal a rivalry like that could become. I had no idea of who Kim Philby or John Cairncross were, but it was quite clear to me that Somerset Maugham had been entirely right when he'd suggested earlier that Burgess and Maclean might not be the only Soviet spies in Britain's so-called intelligence agencies.

"But suppose that's exactly what did happen," continued Sinclair eventually. "Look here, Occam's razor and all that. The simplest explanation is the most likely. Guy was always a fearful snob and typically dismissive of this tobacco salesman he's just met—so dismissive that the Russians didn't even notice that he could only have been referring to Roger Hollis. But here's a rather more persuasive explanation, I think. We've always strongly suspected that the Soviet GRU and the KGB both run separate networks of spies in England but don't keep each other in the loop about what they're up to. We even believe they're forbidden to consult each other without specific permission from the GKO—the State Defense Committee, in Moscow. This was a corollary of Stalin's paranoia. It was he who decreed that ideally UK Soviet counterespionage should be covered by both a KGB agent and a GRU agent, so that they could always double-check a source. Well then. Suppose Guy Burgess was being run by the KGB and they spirit him out of England and while they're doing it, for whatever reason, they record this tape. Suppose Hollis on the other hand is being run by the GRU—by Russian military intelligence. That would explain the oversight. The KGB don't know anything about Hollis because he's GRU. It was a cock-up, pure and simple. Too much security can be just as bad as not enough."

"Yes, that might explain it."

"Not only that: The GRU military intelligence chaps were running spies in China long before the KGB was even dreamed of. When Jim Skardon interrogated Klaus Fuchs in nineteen forty-nine for MI5, Fuchs said he'd been recruited by the GRU and that these two agencies disliked and distrusted each other even more than MI5 and MI6. Apparently when Fuchs was transferred to the KGB, the GRU made an almighty row about it in Moscow with the State Defense Committee. Their man, working for the competition."

"Christ, when you put it like that, Sinbad, the comrades sound even more disorganized than we do."

"Except that we don't happen to have an agent who happens to be the deputy chairman of the Soviet Committee for State Security. I'd give a great deal to be as disorganized as that."

"Yes. Think what it would be like to have a man like Alexander Shelepin working for MI6."

"If Hollis is working for the GRU, he's just as important as someone like Shelepin, Patrick. And just as big a traitor as Burgess or Maclean. Bigger. He has the power to stifle any investigation into any Soviet agent working in England right now. Klaus Fuchs or John Cairncross, perhaps. Or he might subtly encourage the belief that Kim Philby is a Soviet spy. It might just be that Philby has been fingered by Hollis all along. That all his protestations of innocence have been entirely justified."

"So what's our next course of action?" asked Reilly.

"Obviously we need to buy the tapes. I've already put in a request to the banking section in Melbury Road. The first tape's existence is already the subject of some speculation back home. Christ knows what's on the other ones. If indeed there are any other ones. This one tape is quite bad enough. So we have to have it, and soon."

"Guy Burgess speaks. Yes, I can imagine. It's sensational stuff all right. And Maugham is right. The American media would have a field day with this stuff. The FBI would never talk to us again. We'd be the pariahs of Western intelligence. If we aren't already."

"Patrick, I'd also like to ask my people at Broadway to get cracking with a full belt and braces investigation into Hollis. Tonight."

"To do that you're going to need the nod from the Joint Intelligence Committee and Sir Patrick Dean. Perhaps also the minister. What about Dick White at MI5? Are you going to tell him?"

"He's too close to Hollis. As I said before, it was White who was supposed to have vetted Hollis. For all we know he might be a GRU agent himself. The last thing we want to do is to spook Hollis into doing a bunk like Burgess and Maclean. Which this just might."

"No, I can't believe it of Dick White. He wanted to resign from MI5 when Percy Sillitoe left in the wake of those defections. Sillitoe talked him into staying on and taking over the corner shop. No, I can't see the comrades would ever have contemplated even allowing White to resign if he'd been theirs all along. Besides, he was at Oxford, not Cambridge."

"Fair enough. But still, Hollis and White are as close as a fat lady's thighs. I think we'd best leave him out of the loop for now. Everyone knows that Dick White always agrees with Hollis."

"All right. I'll call Patrick Dean tonight. And you call your people in MI6. But not here, eh? We'll do it back at the hotel. Much as I admire Somerset Maugham as a writer I just don't trust the old bugger. Or any of these awful queers he surrounds himself with. Least of all that fucking German, Walter Wolf. He may not be queer but he's got the look of a Nazi. And let's not forget that Maugham is an old Russia hand. He was running agents in Russia when you and I were in short trousers. Not just in Russia. But in Washington, too. Perhaps it's no accident that Guy Burgess was here, in this house, back in nineteen thirty-seven."

"So was Anthony Blunt."

"That doesn't fill me with optimism, either. The GRU-run Comintern was based in Paris. But they were almost as active down here on the Riviera, recruiting Communist refugees from the Spanish Civil War in Marseilles. Anyone shopping for suitable agents in the South of France would certainly have been interested in some of the men who were guests of Somerset Maugham in nineteen thirty-seven. After all, most of them were already leading very secret lives because of their sexual predilections. That's always been something attractive to the Russians."

"Blunt again."

"He's been interviewed by MI5, hasn't he? As a possible suspect."

"Several times. The FBI has had him in their sights for a while. But Courtney Young—who interrogated him—insists Anthony Blunt is innocent. That it's just guilt by association. Still, we've only Anthony's word for it that the photograph was stolen from his flat at the Courtauld in London."

"Perhaps one of the queers who were here in nineteen thirty-seven was already a Red. I think we should ask Maugham if we can see this picture, don't you?"

"If he'll let you. He's a cagey old sod."

"Do you think he could be a Russian agent? He wouldn't be the first Communist to own a fucking Picasso."

"Including Picasso."

TWENTY-SIX

Maugham was seated at the table in his brightly lit office. He tossed me a towel with which to wipe the soot off my hands, which had been clinging on to the chimney for the best part of twenty minutes.

"You were right about the chimney," I said. "I heard every word. They're going to pay you the money. There's no question of that. But I wouldn't believe a word they say about anything else. Those two are properly rattled by that tape."

Maugham nodded grimly.

"Sometimes I think I'll probably die at this desk," he said quietly. "Like a spavined horse in harness. With a half-finished novel or play on the go. I often think of starting a new book just so I can make that possible, like Dickens. At other times I look at the painted bedstead in my bedroom and imagine what I'll look like when at last I'm lying there dead, laid out like Miss Havisham's wedding breakfast. Not good, I think. Not good at all, I'm afraid."

"Is there a good way to look when you're dead?"

"The embalmers would have you believe that the best way to look when you're dead is alive. Healthy pallor, red cheeks, pink lips. Which I must say seems rather creepy to me. You'd think it wouldn't bother me. But every morning when I awaken I look in the mirror and I can't believe how much like a corpse I already am."

"I've seen a lot of dead people in my time. More than is good for me, frankly. On the whole, the dead don't mind what they look like. And I'd have thought having a face like shit is the best guarantee that you've had a full life. That's what I keep telling myself, anyway."

"By that standard I've lived at least two lives, both of them like Dorian Gray's picture. Then again, all bodies are imperfect, aren't they? Even those that we mistakenly idealize. Take that picture on the wall there. *Eve* by Paul Gauguin. You know why I bought her? To remind me how ugly I find women. That and because she has seven toes on her left foot. It's almost as if Gauguin wants to remind us just how imperfect we all are. How fundamentally none of us is ever to be trusted. Imagine if she was wearing a nice pair of court shoes. You might never know she's not all that she seems."

I looked at the picture and nodded. "She's not my type," I said. "I do know that. I like my women to look more like women than Wallace Beery. That's why high heels were invented, isn't it? To stop women looking like us."

"And you wonder why your relationships go wrong? Take it from Gauguin. You can't trust Western ideals of beauty, Walter. Every angel is really a devil. And every woman is a whore."

"Not every woman. Only the ones who ask for money."

"They all want money."

"Are your boyfriends any different?"

"They're not whores. They're cruel because the world we live in has made them that way. Women choose to be whores because it's just easier to take money from a man than to make some themselves."

I shrugged. "Who can you trust? Not anyone, maybe. Not the British, that's for sure. Certainly none of those characters downstairs. And especially not Sir Lancelot and his squire." Momentarily I thought of Anne and felt better knowing that at least there was a sense of trust building between us.

"All right, what else did those bastards say?" he asked.

"Right now they seem to think that Guy Burgess may have accidentally revealed the existence of a spy at the very top of MI5—one they didn't know about."

"You're joking."

I told him all I'd heard about Roger Hollis at MI5 and how Reilly and Sinclair suspected that, like Guy Burgess, he, too, had been recruited by the Russians in the thirties.

"Roger Hollis? Never heard of him," said Maugham.

"In my experience, it's no good being a spy if people know your name."

"I take your point. Although I am the living proof of the opposite argument. On and off I've been a British spy for as long as I've been a writer. And the more famous I've become the more effective a spy I've been."

He came around the desk, sat down beside me on the sofa, and patted me on the knee. Not that I minded. He meant it kindly.

"Another spy, eh?" he said. "If this gets out the British can say good-bye to the 'special relationship.' Burgess and Maclean were one thing. But this is something much worse. A spy at the top of MI5 is nothing short of a catastrophe. Hoover would have a heart attack at the very idea."

"That was certainly the tenor of the conversation I just overheard."

"They'd have to purge everyone in the British intelligence community. MI5 and MI6, from top to bottom. *If it's true.* You said it's only suspected that this chap Hollis is a spy."

"Look, I was certainly convinced even if Patrick Reilly wasn't. Not that either man impressed me as particularly good at his job. In my opinion, civil servants make the worst kind of spies. To people like Sinclair and Reilly, it's just a schoolboy game. A way of moving up the Whitehall ladder and getting a knighthood. But you can't win that way. The British are at war with the Russians but they don't know the Russians at all. Not as a people. That's bad. They think the Russians are just an ideology. But they're much more than that. I know. I spent almost two years of my life in a Soviet labor camp."

"In Petrograd I got to know the Russians pretty well myself," said Maugham. "Of course, I still made mistakes. Once I even killed the wrong man. But most of the time I knew what I was doing. I'm not sure that the people who run things these days do. People like Sinclair and Reilly. The Russians make excellent spies. Much better than us because they lie so well. And of course they lie to themselves most skillfully of all. Which is the key to all effective lying. You have to convince yourself, first of all. The English are hopeless liars by comparison. We're too honest about ourselves. Too self-effacing. Lying shocks us. That's why the English were so horrified by Burgess and Maclean. Because they were such unusually good liars. Like me—and you, I suspect. I think perhaps you are the best liar of us all, Walter. But then, maybe you've had to be."

"Over the last twenty years I've found truth to be a very over-rated virtue when it comes to staying alive."

"Isn't it? Well, I've spent my whole life lying for a living so I'm bound to agree with you. What are their plans now? Sinclair and Reilly?"

"I think they're going back to their hotel," I said. "To make more telephone calls to London in private. To set a rather urgent witch hunt into motion. After which, if you don't mind, I'll go home, too. I'll be back the day after tomorrow to take care of the handover of the money. Until then, you know where I am if you need me."

Maugham nodded. "Thank you for everything, my f-friend."

"Once that's done I'm just going to hunker down at the hotel. Safely behind my hotel desk, answering stupid questions for clueless tourists. It's what I'm best at."

Maugham smiled his inscrutable smile. "You don't fool me for a minute, Walter. You're just like me. A survivor. The only difference is that you're not as old. Not yet. But, of course, if you live long enough, you will be."

"Now, that's the hard part, isn't it? Nobody wants to get old, but then nobody wants to be dead, either." I shrugged. "To be honest, I never thought I'd make it this far."

After the English spymasters had returned to the Belle Aurore I drove back to Villefranche. The road home took me straight past their hotel and for a while I parked outside the entrance and contemplated sneaking into the little cliff-top garden to eavesdrop some more. All of the lights on the upper floors were burning brightly and I even caught a glimpse of Sinclair at the window, with the telephone pressed to his ear. But I'd had enough of spies and blackmail for one day. I was tired and all I wanted to do now was go to bed with Anne. There was that and the fact that at least two of them were carrying guns.

Although it was well past ten o'clock I found her typing in the guesthouse on her big pink Smith Corona. But the Hallicrafters radio was still on. I could hear the BBC World Service chattering away in the background.

Disaster was in the air, but it wasn't the kind everyone else was expecting. This was to be a rather more bespoke, disastrous kind of disaster, created just for me.

"What's the news?" I asked. "About Suez. Have the British invaded the zone yet? The French?"

"No. But it's not looking good."

She was wearing a crocheted white dress, with little flowers on the hem. Her feet were bare. In retrospect I ought to have counted the toes on her left foot just to make sure she didn't have seven. She wasn't wearing makeup and seemed smaller than I remembered, and just a bit more vulnerable, too. Even a little sad. She opened a bottle of wine and we drank some of it on the terrace. I told her I'd been back to the Villa Mauresque. She was quiet, unusually so, almost hermetically self-contained. And smoking a lot, too; there were at least a dozen cigarettes in the ashtray.

"Where's the body? Floating in the pool? Or lying on the bedroom floor?"

"You're looking at it."

"I thought as much. Is something wrong? Only you seem a little tense."

"Nothing serious. Just a little rigor mortis. It's infectious when you're researching a man like Somerset Maugham."

She touched my face with the neatly manicured tips of her fingers and suddenly I realized how much I wanted her. I ached for her inside and I realized how much I'd missed her. And now that I had the scent of Mystikum in my nostrils, everything seemed all right; just about.

"Were you working on the biography all day?" I asked.

"Yes. I've been on my own too much, really. I should have gone into town, or to the Grand Hôtel for a swim, but I didn't. And it's still in my head a bit, that's all. Books are like that sometimes. They get jealous of time spent doing other things. A bit like husbands, I suppose."

"Do you have many of those, too?"

She smiled sadly but didn't answer, which left me to draw my own conclusions. Had she been married before? I realized I didn't know and resolved to ask her everything about herself when she was feeling a little more forthcoming. Perhaps.

"How's it going? The book, I mean."

"Well." She paused and lit another cigarette, inhaling it fiercely. "As well as can be expected, I guess."

"Sounds more like a crash victim."

She shrugged. "It's never easy."

"You've had a better time than me, at any rate. I've spent the whole evening at the Villa Mauresque. It's been difficult, to say the least."

"What happened? More hijinks?"

"You could say that."

I hesitated for a moment, wondering for the first time just how much I could really trust her.

"Look, I hate to bring this up again, but you haven't forgotten our deal," I said. "That you won't write about this until after he's dead. Or unless I say otherwise."

"Of course I haven't. A deal is a deal. I'm surprised you need to ask."

She shrugged. "But don't tell me if you don't want to. I shan't mind in the slightest. Really. I was only making conversation." She smiled thinly and looked into the distance.

"It's just that things up at the villa are getting serious now. Maybe even dangerous. Not just for him. Perhaps me, too. And anyone close to me." I paused to allow that one to sink in. "Meaning you, of course."

"The plot thickens. Tell me more."

"I'm serious."

"I can see you are. But you needn't worry about me, Walter. I can look after myself."

"I do worry about you. I've just realized that. Maybe more than I should."

"No one knows about us, do they?"

"No."

"Well then." She sounded calm—so calm that I felt there was something she had nailed down very tightly indeed, like the escape hatch on her one-man lifeboat. "There's nothing to worry about, is there?"

"There is when there are men with guns on the scene. Up at the villa. Muscle types. Ex-army probably. The kind that shoot people and think of questions later. If they think at all."

"But why are there men with guns? Somerset Maugham doesn't strike me as the dangerous sort."

"I'm not so sure about that. I thought *I* had a past. He's had several. And all of them secret. You'll have a hell of a book on your hands when you've finished it. What happened tonight would make a very long chapter on its own."

Then I told her about the two spymasters from London and how, as a result of listening to the Guy Burgess tape, they thought they'd identified yet another spy working for the Soviets at the heart of the British intelligence services.

"I take it you don't mean Somerset Maugham."

"No, not him. Someone else."

She laughed. "Jesus Christ, not another one. This is more than a scandal. It's an epidemic. Who's the spook this time?"

"Someone called Roger Hollis."

"Never heard of him."

"You're not supposed to have heard of him if he's a spy."

"God, is he queer, too? Like the other two?"

"I don't think so. He's been married for almost twenty years."

"That doesn't mean anything."

"It used to mean that you liked women enough to want to spend your life with one. That's how it always was for me, at any rate."

"You surprise me. Anyway, not in England. Lots of queers

get married just for show. Look at Somerset Maugham. He was married for a lot longer than twenty years."

"Yes, I'd forgotten about his wife."

"He didn't. He couldn't. Although he did his level best to forget her. Poor Syrie. I think she must have had an awful time with that miserable old bastard. I feel so, so sorry for her." She sighed crossly. "Christ, I hate men."

"Leaving that aside for a moment—on account of the fact I happen to be a man myself, last time I looked—I thought you admired the old buzzard."

"As a writer, yes. But as a human being? No. Not for a minute. At least, that's the conclusion I've come to. Where are they now? The two English spymasters."

"At the Belle Aurore Hotel. In Villefranche."

"They're not staying at the Villa Mauresque?"

"No. Lucky them."

"Why not? I thought he asked them to come here from London."

"He did, but they insisted on bringing their own personal security with them. The men with guns I was telling you about. Two thugs from Portsmouth. I expect they're just nervous travelers. French waiters can be quite intimidating."

"How long are they here for?"

"A couple of days, I'd have thought. Until this affair is concluded. Frankly, Patrick Reilly seemed rather more interested in a cricket match."

"England versus Australia."

"That's something else I don't understand. England is about to send troops into Egypt and everyone who's English is more interested in a cricket match."

"What's the other thing you don't understand?"

"You, of course. I think there's something you're not telling me."

"Oh?"

"And I suspect that when you finally get around to it I'm going to find it just as hard to comprehend as a game of cricket. Perhaps harder."

"Cricket's really not that hard to understand. And nor am I."

"I'll take your word for it."

"I'm just tired, I guess."

She went to bed, or so I thought. I stayed downstairs for a while longer to empty the ashtrays and fetch a couple of bottles of cold mineral water, and a little vase in which I'd placed a single flower from the garden. As I entered the bedroom she came out of the bathroom, still dressed and now avoiding my eye, rather ominously.

"Room service," I said, and placed the bottle and the flower on her bedside table. "I'd have brought a chocolate for your pillow but you're all out of chocolate. You're out of a lot of things actually. There's almost nothing in your cupboards. Like you're going away somewhere." I turned down her bed. "You know, anyone looking at me now could get the very wrong idea that I liked you a lot. That and the fact that I've had extensive hotel experience. Did I ever tell you I used to own a hotel? It was a dump in Dachau. Yes, that's right. Dachau. It's no place for a hotel. Not anymore. But that was all a long time ago."

"Leave that," she said.

"And risk losing my job? I don't think so." I smiled. "Would you like fresh towels?" I was talking too much because I didn't want her to say anything that might be something I wouldn't like. I was right, too.

She didn't undress. She sat beside me on the bed, with her knees drawn up underneath her chin and looked thoughtful and then very awkward. She reminded me of an unhappy schoolgirl.

"Stop fussing, please. Sit down. Listen."

I dropped down on the bed and found my stomach had beaten me to it. Suddenly the scent of Mystikum made me feel sick and I had the sense that for me, from now on, it was always going to be the scent of disaster.

"What is it?"

"You're right. There is something I'm not telling you. Please forgive me."

"That's easily done."

"I wasn't going to tell you tonight but since you've raised it, perhaps now is best. Well, it's like this. I'm sorry. But I just can't do this anymore."

"Do what?"

"Be with you, Walter. Sleep with you. Fuck you. Be your lover."

I stiffened. "I'm sorry to hear that, Anne."

"I'm sorry, too."

"Is there anything I can do to change your mind?"

"Look, I've decided to go back to London."

"I'll take that as a no. What about your book?"

"I'm going to give the advance back."

"Why's that?"

"I've decided it's not—it's not what I want to write anymore. I don't think it ever was. Anyway, it's not working for me. None of this. So, I'm leaving here. Soon. The sooner the better. Tomorrow. Probably first thing."

I made a fist and bit my knuckle; it felt a little kinder than punching my own thick head. "Then I guess my usefulness is at an end," I said. "Yes, I can see how that might work."

"It wasn't like that."

"No?"

"No."

"If you say so." I paused, trying to shepherd my thoughts, but it was no good, they were now scattered like so many lost sheep across the barren hillside I called my life.

"Yes?"

"Forgive me, but it's a little hard to talk right now with all my teeth kicked out."

"I'm sorry. Really I am."

"Do you want me to go?"

"I think it might be best, don't you? To avoid any awkward scenes in the morning."

"No, we certainly wouldn't want that." I smiled as gamely as I could manage. "Especially not after the awkward scene we've had tonight. You know, you should have telephoned the Villa Mauresque, left a message, and saved me the journey up here. I know you've got the number. I saw it on one of those neat files of yours in the office. Then again, maybe you thought it was kinder to do it in person, to spare my feelings."

I went downstairs and walked through the lush garden back to the car in a silence that was already roaring in my ears like the sea hitting the beach on the Cap. In a way I'd seen it coming and been stupid enough to ignore what my keener senses had already told me. Not that it really counted for very much in the scheme of things. It was nothing more than just another tragedy, in a long line of tragedies of the kind Bernie Gunther was already well used to. If anyone had the constitution to take it on the chin, that person was him, I told myself. Maybe that's what all ordinary human life amounts to. One tragedy heaped on top of another like sharp gray layers of shale. What did it matter anymore than the death of the lobster I'd eaten for supper or the leaf of tobacco now burning in my cigarette? Not a damn thing. If ever you stopped to think of just how much pain there was in any one life it would surely kill you, just as surely as if someone had put a bullet through your heart at close range with a little automatic.

TWENTY-SEVEN

There were two bottles of twenty-year-old Schinkenhäger I'd been saving for a special occasion, and as soon as I got home I knew instinctively that this was it. The special occasion. Deep pain creates its own singularity. I opened one of the bottles and stared at the first brimming glass, feeling nothing less than a categorical imperative to get drunk: an absolute, unconditional requirement that had to be obeyed and was justified as an end in itself. There's a central philosophical concept for you. I drank one whole bottle before I went to sleep, and the other almost as soon as I woke up again. And somewhere in the middle I called the hotel to say I was sick. Not that I really was sick.

Nobody calls that being sick except the poor nurse who has to pump the alcohol out of your stomach and even then her pity for your illness is alloyed, rightly, with a strong sense of disgust. Well, I was almost as sick as that. I hadn't drunk like that—with real malice aforethought—since the day I learned the *Wilhelm Gustloff* was lying at the bottom of the cold Baltic Sea.

A while after I made the call to the Grand Hôtel, I awoke with the vague idea that the doorbell rang. A stupid, drunkenly deluded, childishly eager part of me thought it might be Anne French come to apologize and say she'd made a dreadful mistake, and thinking that I might just find it within myself to forgive her, I persuaded myself to pick myself off the floor. Of course I would forgive her. I was drunk.

With two bottles of good schnapps inside me it was all I could do to crawl across the tiny bedroom in my lobster pot and stumble downstairs to open the door. I have no idea what time it was but it must have been the late afternoon or early evening of the next day. I opened the door to brilliant sunshine, which dazzled me painfully, or at least that's what I thought. Instead it was a fist on the end of a very strong, red-faced Englishman's arm and it hit me more quickly than the schnapps, squarely under the chin, dumping me on my backside like a puppet that was suddenly and stupidly without any strings. I sat on the stairs, legs splayed in front of me, with my ears singing a very loud tune, and thought hard about puking. I was still thinking about it when the same Englishman picked me up, bounced me off the wall a couple of times, and then punched me again.

"If there's one thing I've always liked," he said—I think it was probably the last thing I remembered hearing for a while—"it's hitting fucking Germans in the face." He laughed. "And to think I get paid for this. Fuck me, I'd do it for free."

For a moment or two I felt light-headed. I was back up on the roof of the Villa Mauresque, eavesdropping on the two spymasters. The next I was falling backward down the chimney with all sense of self-awareness left behind alongside the gene-deep certainty that life was actually worth the struggle. It wasn't. That much was obvious. The light at the end of the tunnel that was the sun framed by the chimney grew smaller by the second until it was no bigger than a dim and distant star in some remote galaxy. I'd gone missing and it was likely that I was going to be missing for quite a while, perhaps permanently. Back in Berlin, even before the Nazis, looking for missing persons used to cost the city millions of marks a year. Did any of it ever matter? Perhaps it was even possible that I would never be found, as those before me had not been found. When the darkness of the chimney closed around me I had the strong sense that life was over as surely as if I'd sat in my car once again and tried to asphyxiate myself with carbon monoxide. I took a deep breath of my present oblivion and hoped my useless, tired mind was no longer required. I didn't want to know anything anymore. What difference did it make anyway? There was no need to hold on to life so tightly. So I let go. I let go. The Englishman had done me a favor. I welcomed the darkness as a child welcomes Christmas morning.

TWENTY-EIGHT

I stared at the yellow lightbulb on the dark green ceiling for a long time. It never went out. The yellow wasn't just yellow but orange and sometimes green and perhaps more than just a simple lightbulb. It looked like the evil eyeball of some almost invisible Cyclops that was trying to stare into my soul in order to decide if I was worth devouring. Once or twice I tried to stand, thinking to smash it, but the ceiling must have been at least twelve feet from the bare wooden floor on which I lay. The room was as big as a ballroom, but stiflingly hot and oppressive with the smell of vomit—my own—and the sound of flies now enjoying this unexpected repast. I was covered in sweat and my

salt-stained shirt stuck to my back like a butter wrapper. If I'd
been wearing any shoes I would have thrown one at the bulb
because I couldn't see a light switch anywhere. Louvered shutters as big as the garden gates at the Villa Mauresque were closed,
and even without opening them I knew the windows were
barred and that I was a prisoner. Not that I had energy for doing
anything as strenuous as throwing a shoe or opening a window.
Besides, my hands were tied painfully behind my back. My jaw
ached as if I'd tried to chew my way out through the skirting
boards below the blood-red walls. Even the hair on my scalp
seemed painful. Most of all I was desperately thirsty. I shouted
for water but no one came.

There was an old French clock on the dusty marble mantelpiece and, as time passed, I realized it was permanently stuck at
ten past twelve, like my life, it seemed. I guessed I was in some
disused or vacant villa close to Villefranche-sur-Mer. I could
hear the sound of the ocean, which helped to calm me, and I
imagined all of the places I would go if I'd been given a ship and
my freedom. Scotland? Norway? Kaliningrad? The Cape of
Good Hope? Good hope was something in very short supply,
and so that felt like a good place to go. Beyond the louvered
shutters it seemed to be dark, but with the pain behind my eyes
I couldn't be entirely sure. I'd stared at the bulb for so long most
of my vision was just a negative afterimage. Something negative,
anyway. Like everything else. At ten past twelve I heard a key in
the lock on the doors and the two Englishmen from Portsmouth
walked heavily in and hauled me to my feet.

"Pissed himself," said one, his nose wrinkling with disgust.

"Saves us taking him to the bathroom. What are you complaining about?"

"The boss won't like it."

They dragged me to another room, almost as large, and sat me on a dining chair in front of a long table. There was a glass chandelier immediately above my head but the shutters were closed and most of the light came from some standard lamps in the corners and an Anglepoise on the desk.

The pale-faced man behind it was wearing a seersucker suit and thick glasses and seemed more interested in the contents of his cherrywood pipe than in me. His hair was thin and so were his nose and mouth and, to my way of thinking, his blood, too. At the far end of the room the door was open, and while I could not see who was in there I was certain from the clouds of tobacco smoke that the room was occupied by more than one person. Perhaps the two spymasters from London.

"Did you bring some clothes from his flat?" the pale-faced man asked the other two.

"Yes, sir."

He nodded. I'd never seen him before, but he was English and very still and deliberate, like a monk from a nearly silent order.

"He smells. Wash him, give him something to eat and drink, and then bring him back here wearing a change of clothes."

Fifteen minutes later I was back in front of the monk, who stared at me with polite indifference, as if he'd been watching a dull game of cricket. When I sat down the monk stood up slowly and from a wallet file removed some papers and then placed them on the table in front of him as if they were evidence. I couldn't yet see these clearly from where I was sitting but I had a strong idea that they were to form the basis of some serious accusation against me that might easily cost me my liberty or my life. In the monk's hand was my passport. The one Erich Mielke had given me.

"You are Walter Wolf," he said. "And you work at the Grand Hôtel in Cap Ferrat as the hotel concierge."

"Yes. And I must protest. Why have you brought me here?"

"But that's not your real name, is it? Your real name is Bernhard Gunther, is it not?"

"No."

"Your real name is Bernhard Gunther and this passport was provided by the state security service of the German Democratic Republic, also known as the Stasi." His tone was almost apologetic, as if he regretted bringing me inside on such a warm day.

"No."

"You are in fact an agent of the Hauptverwaltung Aufklärung, the foreign intelligence service section of the East German Ministry for State Security. Is that not so? You work for the Communist HVA, don't you, Herr Gunther?"

"No."

"Before this, you were an officer in the Nazi secret security service. The SD. But in nineteen forty-six you were a prisoner of war at the MfS prison camp at Johanngeorgenstadt in East Germany, where you were first recruited to the Stasi."

"No."

"It was the condition of your release from that prison camp that you should work for the Stasi, was it not?"

"No. I was a POW, yes. And they—I don't know what their names were—they did ask me to work for the Stasi. I refused. But later on, I escaped."

"Escaped? That was very intrepid of you," said the monk.

He was tall, blond, well spoken, with a deep, mellifluous voice, and now it seemed the look of a very old schoolboy, or perhaps a young schoolmaster, and certainly not a spy—there was nothing athletic or physical about him. A killer he was not; this man had been chosen for his intelligence instead of his ruthlessness. Unlike the two thugs from Portsmouth, he was more used to punching holes in paper than in the faces of men. A lot of the time he remained silent, puffing his pipe, as if he was offering me the opportunity to provide a better answer than the inadequate one I'd given. I'd have preferred someone who was a violent bully, who shouted at me and slapped my face, the kind of interrogator who tries to beat and sweat the truth out of you. You knew where you were with an interrogator like that. But this one would try to be my friend and make me dependent on him, psychologically, until he became Jesus—my only source of salvation and redemption.

"There weren't many German POWs who were imprisoned

in Russia and East Germany who escaped from labor camps, were there? To my knowledge, hardly any at all."

"I don't know. Not many, perhaps. I saw an opportunity and took it."

"You were lucky, Bernhard."

"I've always been lucky."

"Oh? How's that?"

"I'm here, talking to you, aren't I?"

He smiled and looked at his fingernails before relighting his pipe.

"One might say that the kind of luck you enjoyed was very much the kind described by Seneca," he said. "A case of opportunity meeting preparation. Your opportunity. But it was almost certainly someone else's preparation. Erich Mielke's preparation."

"Seneca? Who's he?"

"A Roman Stoic and an adviser to the Emperor Nero."

"That's a relief. I thought he might be another East German spy I'm supposed to know."

"It's interesting. You ask who Seneca is. But you don't ask who Erich Mielke is."

"I assume he's not a Roman Stoic."

"No indeed. Comrade General Erich Mielke is the deputy head of the Stasi."

"I've not heard of him. But then I haven't lived in Germany for several years."

"He's a Berliner, just like you, Herr Gunther."

"I don't care if he's from Fucking, in Austria. You've made a mistake. I'm not whoever it is you think I am. I was helping you people, remember? You've a strange way of showing your gratitude. And I really don't have time for this. I'd like to leave. Now."

"We've got plenty of time. I can assure you."

"In which case, might I have some water and a cigarette?"

The monk nodded at one of the thugs, who stepped smartly forward, as if he'd been on the parade ground, put a cigarette in my mouth, lit it with a cheap lighter, and then fetched me a glass of water.

"Thanks," I said. "Now, where were we? Oh yes. I was telling you I haven't a clue what you're talking about. You've got the wrong man. That much is obvious, anyway."

"Then let me refresh your memory, Herr Gunther. We checked your name with our friends in the CIA. And I think that you are the same Bernhard Gunther who was part of an elaborate Stasi operation to snatch three of their agents from the French zone of Berlin in nineteen fifty-four. Those three American agents believed they had employed you to help them kidnap Erich Mielke in return for an American passport and the sum of twenty-five thousand dollars. Instead, you betrayed them to Mielke. Two of them are still in an East German prison. Did you know that?"

I shook my head. "You're mistaken. My name is Walter Wolf. I'm the concierge at the Grand Hôtel. And I haven't the first idea what you're talking about. I've never met anyone who was working for the CIA. And once again I don't know anyone by the name of Mielke."

"It's quite an elaborate operation you've mounted here in France, isn't it? A lot of time and effort and money have gone into this little scheme."

"I haven't seen any of it. The money, I mean. You've seen the flat where I live. You can check my bank accounts. I have very little money. I spend what I earn at the Grand Hôtel. I'm certainly not on the East German payroll."

"We have someone who says different. A witness."

"Then that person is mistaken or a liar."

"Since you've mentioned bank accounts," said the monk, handing me one of the papers on his desk. "This is a copy of a letter from you to the manager of a bank in Monaco, the Crédit Foncier, dated February nineteen fifty-six. It states that Harold Hebel is to be a joint signatory on this bank account with you. It seems that there is more than twenty thousand francs in this account, Herr Gunther. The money appears to have been paid into this account by the Schönefeld Export Company of Bonn, in West Germany. We believe this company to be one owned by the Stasi."

"I've never even heard of this bank until now."

"Was this money meant to cover your expenses?"

"Look, I didn't write the bank any letter. That isn't my signature. And I've certainly never heard of the Schönefeld Export Company of Bonn."

"But you do know Harold Hebel, don't you?"

"Of course I do. If you've spoken with Somerset Maugham

THE OTHER SIDE OF SILENCE

you'll already know that. He'll confirm what I already told him: that Harold Hebel is a professional blackmailer from before the war. He's the man who's been blackmailing Maugham. And now, it seems, the British secret service. And I've been helping Mr. Maugham at his request. Ask him."

"I'm afraid that's not possible. He's had a mild stroke."

"Look, I didn't ask to be involved in this. Until he asked for my help I was minding my own business at the Grand Hôtel. And now if you don't mind I'd like to go back to the hotel and resume my duties."

"Harold Hebel. Real name, Harold Heinz Hennig, formerly of the Gestapo and now working for the Communist HVA, too."

"That certainly wouldn't surprise me. I guess it was them who supplied him with that tape. And before them, the KGB. Is Hennig your witness?" I shook my head. "The man's a liar. I wouldn't trust a word he says."

"But you and he were working together here on the Riviera. From the very beginning."

I sucked my cigarette and blew some smoke at the chandelier in the hope I might deter a large spider that was now abseiling down a length of gossamer toward my head.

"No. I hate him. I'd kill him before ever working with him. He and I have a long history of enmity."

"Whose operation was this? Mielke's? Or your namesake's?"

"My namesake's? I don't know who you mean."

"Major General Markus Wolf."

"I've never heard of him, either. All these generals I'm supposed to know. The next thing you'll be telling me is that I'm a general, too."

"Our information is that Markus Wolf is head of the East German HVA and reports directly to Mielke."

I glanced up at the spider again, which had been only momentarily deterred.

"How well do you know Comrade General Mielke?"

"I already told you. I've never heard of him, either."

"Come now, Herr Gunther. Elisabeth Dehler—the woman who was living as your wife here in the South of France until quite recently—she knows Erich Mielke very well, doesn't she? From way back. And what's more, she also works for the HVA."

"Elisabeth?" I smiled. "I doubt that very much."

"Most assuredly she does work for them. And she's now safely back in Berlin."

"That much I do know." I shrugged. There was nothing I could have said about that other than the fact that it was true. Elisabeth did know Erich Mielke. They were old friends from before the war, when Mielke was just a young KPD thug with a gun, but I hardly wanted to admit as much to my English interrogator. Certainly not until I knew of what I was being accused. "Look, she left me, a while ago. Couldn't stand the heat. Couldn't come to grips with the language. She missed Germany more than she figured she'd miss me, I guess. What she's done since she got back home—I really have no idea. She hasn't written to me in a while."

"Let's talk some more about the operation, shall we?"

"I'm not sure what you're talking about."

"I'm talking about a put-up job by Karlshorst to frame Roger Hollis, the deputy director of MI5, as a spy working for the Soviet military intelligence—the GRU."

"Karlshorst? I know the area, in Berlin. But I've no idea why you mention it now, as if it means something to me."

"It's where the HVA is based these days."

"MI5. The GRU. The HVA? You'll have to remind me."

"The Hauptverwaltung Aufklärung. The East German foreign intelligence service. The equivalent of the British MI6. Or the American CIA."

"There you go again. You learn something new every day, I guess. Look, until a day or two ago, I'd heard of Guy Burgess. I'd even heard of MI6. But I'd never heard the name of Roger Hollis. And if he is a spy for the Soviet Union then good luck to him. I don't care. None of this has anything to do with me. All I've done was act as a middleman between Hennig and Somerset Maugham. You make it sound as if I'm the one who has suggested Hollis is a spy. I didn't. And I've certainly never mentioned him to Sir John Sinclair or Patrick Reilly."

"You didn't have to. That's what was so damned clever about it. A small, almost insignificant detail in Burgess's so-called taped confession that Erich Mielke and Markus Wolf hoped we would spot. And we did. We fell right into the trap. The Shanghai connection, let's call it. British American Tobacco. You really did have us chasing our tails about this. I have to hand it to you.

329

You've no idea the kind of panic this has produced in Whitehall. But for the timely defection of one of your own people, poor Roger Hollis would now be under a very large, very dark cloud of suspicion."

"So what do you want from me? A reference for him so that he can be completely exonerated? Fine. To the best of my knowledge Roger Hollis is actually a very nice man and was never a Russian spy. Is that what you want me to say? Sure. Give me a piece of paper and I'll write a letter to the Queen on his behalf and recommend him for a knighthood. You British seem to hand those out much more frequently than brains."

"A confession would be preferable to a letter. It would save us a lot of time."

"In other words, you haven't any proof. If this was a game of bridge I'd say you were bluffing."

"Since you mention bridge, Somerset Maugham's nephew, Robin—"

"Robin isn't very reliable, you know. Why don't you ask him where the photograph came from?"

"Oh, we have. He freely admits selling it to Anthony Blunt. But when Harold Hennig turned up here with the picture, he felt he had no choice but to go along with what Hennig wanted him to do. Robin says it was Hennig who suggested that Robin invite you up to the Villa Mauresque to play bridge. He was most insistent. And of course it was Hennig who suggested you as a suitable go-between in the blackmail. As a disinterested and apparently reliable person who could be trusted not to lose his head. But from the start you two were partners in this whole covert operation, weren't you?"

"No bid."

I leaned forward to avoid the spider that was now a few centimeters above my head and stubbed out my cigarette in an ashtray on the table. I was tired. All I wanted to do was sleep. But as I leaned forward the monk placed a photograph in front of me, and then another. In both photographs I was wearing a Stasi uniform. To me they seemed like obvious forgeries, but I could tell that the British wanted to believe the pictures and that made a big difference.

"How do you explain these?" said the monk, showing me another photograph.

This one I'd seen before; it was a picture of me taken in Prague with SD General Reinhard Heydrich, just a short while before he'd been murdered by Czech assassins.

"You've had an interesting life," said the monk. "No doubt about it. I expect you're an excellent hotel concierge, able to provide all sorts of information. Not just about local restaurants."

"What are you—a spy? A cop? A civil servant?"

"Something like that."

"Put me in a room with Harold Hennig," I said. "And let me ask him some questions. You'll see just how unreliable your star witness really is. Frankly, it's just his word against mine."

"Perhaps."

"Look, I can see that this man, Erich Mielke, and the Stasi—they've been to a great deal of trouble here. But ask yourself this:

If they went to all this trouble to discredit your man Hollis, how is it that their plan now falls apart so easily? How is it that Harold Hennig is possessed of pictures that are incriminating to me, if he's supposed to be on an operation with me? That makes no sense at all."

"He's a blackmailer. You said so yourself."

"Think about it. How is it that you're now able to discount what was in Burgess's confession so quickly? So conveniently?"

"You'll understand everything soon enough. We've decided that it would be quickest to assemble all of the interested parties here in this room, to go over all of the available evidence and to hear what the various people involved have to say. A chance to clear the air. That's fair, isn't it?"

I glanced at the open door at the end of the room where someone had coughed.

"Are my judges in there?"

"Judges?"

"What you're describing here sounds suspiciously like a trial," I said.

"I suppose you might say that, yes."

"And if I'm found guilty?"

"That's a very good question."

"Maybe you'd like to answer it."

"I think it's you who needs to think very carefully about your answers, Herr Gunther. We're asking the questions. And I would strongly advise you to cooperate. You'll find life is so much easier for you that way."

TWENTY-NINE

The two thugs took me back to the red room with the green ceiling and handcuffed me to a cast-iron radiator that looked like a giant silver anaconda. Unlike the lightbulb on the ceiling, it wasn't switched on, fortunately. They gave me a pint glass of water and another cigarette and I felt as if life was almost worth living. Almost. I had a bad headache, but that was hardly surprising given two bottles of schnapps and two equally powerful punches. On the whole, I'd preferred the schnapps. It's a much more effective means of cauterizing raw feelings, although when the stuff wears off it does leave you a little depressed. When the effect of two bottles finally draws to a close you just want to find a nice shallow grave and crawl inside. The way things were shaping up with the British, they'd probably find one for me or even dig it themselves. I had little faith in the fairness of British justice when it was just a kangaroo court convened in some disused villa on the Riviera, and I had no doubt that my life was at stake. I'd seen enough evidence of the brutality of the British army during the first war to know that these people were more than equal to the task of killing me in cold blood. The Tommies thought themselves fair, but they were just like Germans in that respect. Nearly every man I'd known in the trenches could tell stories of killing prisoners he could not be bothered to escort back to his own lines. That was just as true of the Tommies as it was of the Germans. I was a prisoner now, and I could hardly see how these particular Englishmen were going to transport me safely to a cozy jail in England without risking some sort of diplomatic incident with the French. Murder is a lot easier when the alternative is a lot of very time-consuming paperwork. I tried to sleep but without much success. It's only the guilty man who can sleep when he's wearing manacles.

They fetched me back to the room with the chandelier a couple of hours later. I figured something was wrong because Harold Hennig was already there and wearing handcuffs, like me; there was a large bruise below his eye and his shirt was torn. It seemed like a strange way to treat your star witness. They made us sit at opposite ends of the room. I tried to ignore him and he paid me the same compliment. There were now three men behind the desk, including the monk. One of the other men looked like a duchess who was aware of a bad smell under the floorboards. In that house, there probably was. The other man was an avuncular type with large ears and irregular teeth. Around his neck was a striped tie that matched the monk's and I wondered if it meant they'd been to the same school, or if they just went to the same boring tie shop in London. The two thugs from Portsmouth were also there, but now they were accompanied by others of similarly anthropoid stature. And once again I had a strong sense that there were yet more people listening to these proceedings through the open door in the next room. From time to time I could hear matches being lit and chairs creaking.

"Well, we all know why we're here," said the monk.

"I wish I did," I remarked.

"So let's get started, shall we?" He nodded at one of the thugs who was standing by one of the other doors. "Would you fetch the witness in here, please?"

"So this is a trial," I said.

The thug went out, and when he came back in he was followed by Anne French. I felt my stomach turn. And while I wasn't yet able to understand why she was there, I was increasingly certain that I was facing something calamitous. Not least because she avoided my eye. That wasn't so surprising, I suppose; it was what Harold Hennig said that really caught me unawares.

"Anne, my love. What are you doing here?"

"You took the words right out of my mouth," I said, already wondering just how intimate they might have been while I was on duty at the Grand Hôtel.

She didn't answer Hennig any more than she looked my way. Me, I don't believe in the devil but I'm still scared of him, and I was now possessed of an uncomfortable feeling deep in my guts that he'd arranged for something doubly unpleasant to come my way.

Anne French sat down on a chair beside the table and stared straight ahead of her. She was wearing a sober-looking sleeveless blue dress. Her hair was gathered at the back of her head in a knot. She looked like an innocent schoolgirl. By now I could smell the cloying scent of her perfume, and I suddenly remembered where the red wallet file I had seen on the table in front of the monk must have come from. It was one of her research files from the cabinet in her office in Villefranche.

"What is your name?" asked the monk.

"Anne French."

"Would you please tell us why you're here?"

Imperfect and partial evidence that she was about to betray me swiftly became something much more concrete.

"I'm an author by profession." She smiled a rueful smile. "Not a very successful one, I'm afraid. It's a job that enables me to travel to lots of different places and provides excellent cover for a spy. Like Somerset Maugham himself, you might say. Until recently I was also a member of the Communist Party of Great

Britain and an agent of the HVA—the East German Hauptverwaltung Aufklärung."

"What's your connection with East Germany?"

"Originally my mother was German. From Leipzig."

"Do you speak German?"

"Fluently."

All of this was news to me. Not once had she ever given me
to suspect that she could speak my own language.

"And for how long have you been an agent for the East
Germans?"

"I joined what was later to become the HVA on a trip to
Leipzig in nineteen fifty; since then I have been involved in a
number of clandestine operations here on the Riviera. Most
recently I was asked to befriend the French minister of defense,
Monsieur Bourgès-Maunoury, who was staying at the Grand
Hôtel Cap Ferrat. I was to become his mistress so that I might spy
on him for the HVA. This, however, was not successful. He's a
happily married man with two sons. Not long after this I received
new orders from Berlin to—"

"Did you receive any special training for your work?" asked
the monk.

"Some. I attended a few classes at an espionage school in
Tschaikowskistrasse, in Berlin-Pankow. But to be honest it was
mostly teaching table manners and social behavior to young
East Germans who lacked social niceties. That wasn't much
good to me since I already had those manners. I was trained to
use a radio transmitter, however. And a gun."

"How did you receive your orders from Berlin?"

"Mostly by radio."

Suddenly Anne's devotion to her Hallicrafters and the BBC World Service took on a different meaning.

"I'm sorry, my dear. Do go on with your story."

The "my dear" was nice; it helped me understand that they already believed whatever it was she had to tell them now, and told me to prepare for the worst.

"Not long after my abortive attempt to become the mistress of Monsieur Bourgès-Maunoury I received new orders to join an operation with two agents of the HVA I'd met in Berlin. Bernhard Gunther and Harold Hennig."

"Bullshit," muttered Hennig. "What is this?"

"Can you identify these men?"

"Yes," she said flatly. "There they are."

Anne duly pointed us out, just in case there was any doubt about who we were. This was one of the few times in the proceedings that she ever looked at me, but she might as well have been looking at the postman.

"Can you describe the HVA operation, please?"

"Yes. It had been something that was planned at the highest level in the HVA by Comrade General Mielke himself. In short, it was a covert black operation designed to entice MI5 into eliminating or at the very least neutralizing the deputy director general of MI5, Roger Hollis. To persuade the British secret service that one of their most efficient and loyal spymasters was in fact a long-term spy working for Soviet military intelligence—the

GRU. Gunther was already working in a deep cover position as the concierge at the Grand Hôtel where, originally, it had been hoped he would help me carry through the honey trap for the French minister. But when this plan failed, the plan to discredit Roger Hollis—code-named Othello—went into immediate effect."

"Can you explain how the plan was to work in detail?" said the monk.

"This is all a lie," said Hennig.

"You'll have a chance to speak," said the monk. "Please allow Miss French to finish."

Anne nodded patiently. "Thank you. Well, Comrade General Mielke's idea was inspired by Shakespeare's play *Othello*, he said. Iago sets about blackening the name and reputation of Desdemona, with a great show of reluctance and almost incrementally. Which was what was supposed to happen here. So, Harold Hennig arrived at the hotel posing as a businessman. His job was to blackmail Somerset Maugham with a compromising photograph featuring Guy Burgess, Anthony Blunt, and Maugham himself. The photo had been sold to Anthony Blunt by the author's nephew, Robin, and then stolen from Mr. Blunt's flat in London, and sold to Hennig."

"Stolen by whom?" asked the avuncular man with bad teeth.

"By an agent of the HVA. One of Blunt's students in London, I believe. At the Courtauld Institute. I'm afraid I don't know his name. He gave the picture to Berlin, who passed it on to Hennig, and when Hennig arrived down here, he contacted Robin

Maugham, who rightly identified the photograph as the one he himself had used to blackmail Blunt. Consequently, it was a relatively simple task for Hennig to pressure Robin Maugham, first to invite Gunther to the Villa Mauresque, and then for Somerset Maugham to use Gunther as a reliable courier between himself and Hennig. The plan was that Gunther should ingratiate himself with Somerset Maugham by obtaining the photograph for no money, at which point Hennig would reveal the new material with which he was going to blackmail Maugham, and by extension the British secret service. Carrying out the blackmail down here was perceived to be a lot safer than attempting such a thing in London, where almost certainly everyone involved would have been arrested."

"Tell us about the new material," said the monk. "It was a tape recording, was it not?"

"Yes, a tape recording of the Soviet agent Guy Burgess explaining how he came to work for the KGB. General Mielke believed that as soon as Somerset Maugham heard what Burgess had to say he would understand the vital importance of the tape to his old friends in MI6. Also, it was believed that Somerset Maugham had the financial means to buy the tape himself on behalf of the British secret service. Of course, the Burgess tape— which is perfectly genuine, it is indeed Guy Burgess speaking, although the tape was recorded in Moscow, not at sea—contained a small, almost insignificant detail that was to be the equivalent of Desdemona's handkerchief, I suppose; something small and almost insignificant. It was this: that Burgess had met someone in Paris in nineteen thirty-seven who had recently worked for British American Tobacco in Shanghai, and that this same person had been recruited by the Soviet GRU. Mielke hoped that someone in British intelligence would eventually make the connection between the tobacco salesman and Roger Hollis. After which MI6 and MI5—already feeling deeply paranoid after the recent defections of Burgess and Maclean—would do all the heavy lifting work of discrediting Roger Hollis themselves. He was quite convinced that just to plant the seed of doubt about Hollis would be more than enough to scupper the man. In the same way that Iago lets Othello do most of the hard work of distrusting Desdemona by himself."

"Did Mielke have to take the Othello plan to the KGB for operational approval?"

"I believe so, yes. It was to be the HVA's first big operation to prove it had come of age as an intelligence service to Moscow, as it were. You see, the HVA is a comparatively new service still trying to win the trust of the Soviets."

"Did the KGB give the tapes directly to the HVA?"

"No. For the purposes of establishing some sort of provenance they were first given to the BBC's Berlin office on Savignyplatz. I believe one of the BBC's local correspondents works for the HVA and he was ordered to sell them to Hennig, as if he'd considered using them for broadcast and then decided to make money from them instead."

Anne paused and asked for a glass of water, which was duly provided, before she continued with her bravura performance.

"My job was to meet with Gunther and Hennig and to report their operational progress to my controllers in the HVA by coded messages on a shortwave radio. Gunther and Hennig were to extract a large sum of money from Maugham and by extension the British secret service, and to hand over yet more tapes containing other false and misleading information about other secret service personnel. I believe there are other tiny details on the other tape recordings that might also help to discredit Hollis. I'm afraid I don't know what those are. Any money they made from the blackmail operation was to be split between the three of us as a reward for loyal service and to fund future operations in this theater."

"And these are the tapes you've provided for us. The ones you were keeping in your office at your rented villa in Villefranche-sur-Mer."

"That's right."

Anne lied so smoothly, so expertly, that I almost believed her myself. She never hesitated, not for a moment, and I wondered if she had ever considered the possibility that the British might actually shoot me or Harold Hennig. Her voice was even and, it has to be said, sexy, too; a couple of times there was even a quaver in it, as if what she had to say was upsetting. She was very good. Mielke had chosen his Judas very well indeed. I doubt if Jean Simmons or Deborah Kerr could have given a better performance in that room than Anne French. But the hardest part of listening to all that was knowing that I loved her.

"And what was it persuaded you to change your mind about

your involvement in this elaborate plot?" The monk was smiling kindly at her now, as if he pitied her for being used so egregiously by such unscrupulous people as Erich Mielke, Harold Hennig, and me.

Anne sighed.

"Take your time, my dear. There's no rush. We don't want to make any mistakes here." The monk's tone was solicitous, as if Anne was finding it difficult to betray me and, it had to be faced, Harold Hennig, too.

"Yes, take your time," I said. "But if it helps you can kiss me on the cheek."

She didn't flinch.

"I joined the Communist Party because I believed in the absence of social classes and the state, but more particularly because I believed it was the best way of opposing British and French imperialism of the kind we can see happening now at Suez."

"Let's not get into that, shall we?" said the man with irregular teeth.

"No, well, I'm an idealist, you see," continued Anne. "Like my father. Or at least I was. But during my association with these two men, Gunther's wife, Elisabeth, told me that during the war he and Hennig had both been Fascists working for the SD and the Gestapo. It was she who gave me the photographs you've seen. And it was this that caused me finally to question my loyalty to the party and to the HVA. The notion that the German Communist Party could use former Nazis like these two men to further its ends still seems abhorrent to me. I asked Gunther about it once and instead of denying it or feeling any shame about it, he actually boasted about his Nazi past. He said that there was no difference between the Gestapo and the Stasi. That Fascism and Communism were coterminous. That their uniforms were still made by the same tailors and that even the same concentration camps were in use for today's political prisoners. When I protested about this he seemed to think that was very funny and told me he thought I was extraordinarily naïve. Well, maybe I was. In fact, I'm sure I was."

I tried to will her to catch my eye, but it was no good, and she carried on giving her deceitful evidence in a flat, steady voice.

"By the time he told me that some British spymasters had arrived on the Cap and were staying at the Belle Aurore Hotel, I'd already decided I didn't believe in the party anymore—I mean, I couldn't anymore, you do see that, don't you? I felt completely disillusioned. As if the scales had fallen from my eyes."

"Was it always the aim of the operation to have Maugham summon some friends from MI6 down here?"

"Yes. It seemed unlikely that he would buy the tape without some expectation that the British would underwrite its purchase. Nor that at his age he would wish to travel to London. Comrade Mielke always believed that the British would come here. And listen to the tape themselves."

"And when Gunther told you that these spymasters were coming, what did you think?"

"I thought this was my chance to switch sides. To redeem myself. So I went to see them in person, threw myself on their mercy, and told them absolutely everything I knew about the plot to discredit this man Roger Hollis." She sighed again. "Look, I won't go to prison, will I?"

"That's not up to me. But under the circumstances, no. I don't think so. Provided you continue to cooperate, Miss French."

"Thank you."

"Is the HVA yet aware that you've told us all about Othello?'

"No, not yet. I made my last scheduled transmission two nights ago."

"And your next scheduled transmission is tonight, I believe."

"That's correct."

"At which point you will be required to report on the progress or lack of it on Othello? Is that right?"

"Yes."

"Thus the urgency of these proceedings," said the monk. "But you're quite happy to resume contact with the HVA and assure your controllers that the operation is still progressing. Is that correct?"

"Yes. Of course."

There were many more questions like this, but it was already agonizingly clear to me that as soon as Elisabeth had returned home to Berlin, Erich Mielke must have squeezed her for as much information about my life on the Cap as she was able to provide. Probably she wouldn't have even known he was asking the questions in pursuit of an HVA operation. At the same time, any pictures and files on me would have been easy to find for a man like Mielke. Nearly all of the police records at the presidium on Berlin Alexanderplatz had been captured by the Russians and were now the property of the Stasi. But I still couldn't bring myself to believe that Elisabeth could ever have worked for the Stasi, although of course that was rumored to be their greatest skill—they were much better than the Gestapo at blackmailing people to spy on their nearest and dearest. By comparison the Gestapo had been amateurs. Possibly they had something on Elisabeth I didn't even know about.

As for Anne French, I could see clearly now that I had no one to blame for what had happened but myself. I'd walked straight into Gethsemane as if a taxi had driven me there from an upper room on Mount Zion. She must have known how easy I'd be to snare after Elisabeth had left me. From the first minute Anne French had spoken to me at the hotel she'd been acting on Mielke's orders and had used me with not much more thought than she'd used the swimming pool at the Grand Hôtel.

At the same time, I now understood the whole ghastly little trick that was being perpetrated by Mielke. And I had to admit it was a nice operation. The point of the whole scheme must have been to bolster Hollis's reputation in MI5. What better way of doing that than to expose an ingenious scheme to discredit him? And just listening to all that Anne had said, the conclusion I'd come to was that Roger Hollis was indeed a spy, and a spy who must have been under a cloud of suspicion, too. After this operation, however, Hollis was surely in the clear. No one would ever suspect him now. Which was a lot more than I could say for myself. The case against Bernhard Gunther already looked water-tight. Denying everything seemed pointless. I had no illusions about the probable fate that now awaited me. Thanks to Anne, I was as good as dead.

THIRTY

I stood up slowly, wearily, willing myself to become much smaller in their eyes, as if resigned to my probably ignominious fate. And in a way I *was* resigned to it, but a moment's reflection had persuaded me that, as in a game of poker dice, I didn't have to pick up and throw anything myself. All I had to do was close the lid on the cigar box handed to me by Anne French and make a bid that improved on the one I'd tacitly accepted. Sometimes, when you have nothing and you've got the stone face and the balls for it, those five dice in a closed box can get you much further than you might think is even possible. She was a pretty good liar, but, as Somerset Maugham had recently observed up

at the Villa Mauresque, years of practice born of simple neces-
sity had made me a damned good liar, too; perhaps an even
better one than Anne French. That now remained to be seen.

"All right," I said, staring unhappily at the monk, "you win,
Englishman. You said before, when you were interrogating me,
that you wanted a full confession. Well, I'll give you one now.
All of the dirt. The full unexpurgated version. Names, dates,
everything. I'll write it all out and sign it. Whatever you want." I
rounded my shoulders, lowered my battered head as if in peni-
tence for what I had done, and pushed a hand through my greasy
hair. I'd seen enough broken men in my time with the Murder
Commission at the Berlin Alex to know the full pantomime for
a true confession. "It was a put-up job, just like the bitch has
said, to discredit Roger Hollis. To take your top man in MI5 and
make him smell of yesterday's shit."

I let out a sigh, and shook my head as if in pity of the hopeless situation now affecting me. At the same time I was very
careful to avoid her eye, just in case I was deflected by the incre-
dulity I knew I would certainly meet there. This little performance was going to take all my powers of invention.

"What are you saying?" demanded Hennig. "She's lying,
you stupid idiot. Look, I don't know what's going on here but I
think there's been some sort of mistake."

"Of course there's been a mistake," I shouted. "We got caught,
thanks to her. Look, Harold, it's no good. Don't you see? The
game is up for us now."

"What game? There is no game."

"The stupid bitch has betrayed us both. She's told them almost everything now, and quite clearly they believe her. So, what's the damned point of maintaining the fiction any longer? Eh? Answer me that. We might as well put our hands up to the whole thing. The party isn't going to save us now. Nor the Stasi."

"What the hell are you talking about, Gunther?"

He didn't realize it quite yet, but his using my real name suited my purpose very well.

"And what's more she's right and you know it. The masters we work for in Germany today, they're just as rotten as the bastards we served before. Perhaps worse. At least Hitler tried to be popular. This lot we have in Germany now, they just don't care one way or another. Because they don't have to. No one knows who the hell they are, anyway. They're just a lot of faceless bureaucrats in Karlshorst."

"You bloody fool, Gunther. Just shut the fuck up, will you? You're going to get us both shot. Do you know that?"

"Can't you see? The double-crossing bitch has done that already. Me, I've had enough of the whole damned business. I'm tired—so very tired. I think the best thing is if we just give them what they want and get this circus over with as quickly as possible. Come on, man. What do you say? Let's make a clean breast of it and hope for the best."

Hennig's manacled hands were clasped tightly on his knees, as if in earnest prayer, and I could see his knuckles turning white as I was speaking. His jaw was shifting furiously, like two small tectonic plates, and his nostrils were flaring as wide as an emptying hot water bottle. He looked as if he wanted to strangle me. And this wasn't so very far from the truth, as a moment later he stood up abruptly, ran across the room, and, screaming like Krampus, launched himself at my head in imitation of one intent on hauling me down to the underworld. Fortunately, one of the thugs from Portsmouth intervened just in the nick of time and sent Hennig sprawling on the threadbare carpet with an upper-cut that would have floored Floyd Patterson.

"Get that bloody man out of here," yelled the monk. It was the first and only time I heard him raise his voice. "Lock him up and keep him locked up until he's learned to behave." He might have been speaking about some unruly schoolboy instead of a blackmailer and probable Stasi spy.

I smiled because in the exclamatory, violent chaos of the moment I had seen Anne French staring at me, her face ugly with suspicion about what I might actually tell the British secret service men when the thugs had finished dragging Hennig's semi-conscious body out of the room. Given all that she had said already, she could hardly contradict my own full confession now. It was, I hoped, the one thing her cynical masters in the Stasi could never have anticipated. That I might actually agree with her. Every word *and more.* And for the first time since I'd met her at the Grand Hôtel in Cap Ferrat there was real fear in her lovely eyes.

THIRTY-ONE

"Give me another cigarette," I told one of the thugs still in the room.

He looked at the monk, who nodded back at him. He took out a silver cigarette case, opened it, and pulled a face as I took two, slid one behind my ear for later, and then let him light me. I took a lungful of smoke, which wouldn't have tasted any sweeter than if I'd been facing a firing squad.

"There's not a great deal to say," I began.

"For your sake, I hope that's not true," said the monk.

"The damn woman is right, of course." I was looking straight at Anne when I said this and smiled as she tried to conceal her discomfort. "It was a put-up job from the start. And it would have worked, too. It would have worked if she hadn't opened her stupid trap. It's the one thing you can never anticipate in any clandestine operation—someone having a crisis of conscience and turning themselves in. No, indeed. So then. I'll tell you everything. From the beginning."

"If you don't mind."

"Operation Othello was run by Erich Mielke. I've known him for years—since before the Nazis came to power when he was just another KPD cadre with a gun and a Lenin cap. Put a lot of weight on since then. I mean, he wouldn't recognize himself if the Erich Mielke from nineteen thirty-two was to meet today's Erich Mielke. He murdered a couple of Berlin cops that year and I helped him to get away from the city before he could be arrested. I helped him escape from Berlin to Antwerp, where he and another Communist called Zimmer were smuggled onto a ship to Leningrad, just like your friends Burgess and Maclean. I wasn't a party member then myself, but I hated the semi-Fascist government of von Papen and was determined to do all I could to stop Mielke from going to the guillotine. Besides, those two cops had it coming. Everyone said so. I also helped him to escape from a French internment camp at Le Vernet in nineteen forty when I was in the SD. I'd been sent there to try and identify him."

"How does someone who had helped a KPD killer to escape end up working for the SD?"

"The same way that Burgess worked for MI5, I suppose. I was what they used to call a beefsteak Nazi: brown on the outside but red in the middle. Besides, I wasn't the only Red working for the RSHA. Heinrich Müller—Gestapo Müller—he was a Red, too."

"What were your duties in the SD?"

"Mostly I worked for General Reinhard Heydrich," I said. "The so-called Protector of Bohemia. You might say I was a kind of troubleshooter. If I saw any trouble, I shot it." I smiled at my own little joke. But no one else did.

"And when did you next see Comrade Mielke?"

"He helped me escape from that labor camp in nineteen forty-seven, which was when I did join the party and the Stasi. Yes, he and I—we've been looking out for each other for almost twenty-five years. My ex-wife has known him even longer than that because she helped to raise the young Mielke after his real mother died. He'd do anything for Elisabeth, but the same is not true for me. He's not my friend. You can't be friends with a man like Comrade General Erich Mielke. He'd shoot me just as soon as have a beer with me. The same as Heydrich, really. Two chips off the same block of dirty ice."

"Tell us about the tape," said the monk. "Whose idea was that?"

"The tape was mostly Markus Wolf's idea, I think. Unlike him, Mielke is not a man of great subtlety. More of a bully boy, really. A man of action. You want someone beaten up, intimidated, interrogated, killed, tossed into a labor camp, and forgotten, then Erich Mielke's your man. He's what you might call the blunt instrument of German Communism. But if you want an intellectually sharper approach to a problem, then you speak to

Markus Wolf. Wolf's the chess player. I met him only twice, in Berlin, before that business with the Americans in nineteen fifty-four, and we actually sat down and played a game together. He's Jewish, and of course you know what they're like. Scheming, clever, bookish—I swear he thinks everything out several moves ahead like a grandmaster. Brought up in Moscow, of course, where a lot of those German émigrés were weaned on chess and spying. Not for nothing is he known as 'The Admiral' around Stasi HQ in Karlshorst—after Canaris, of course, who was Hitler's famous spymaster and whom I also met, but only once."

By now I was lying so fluently I was starting to feel as if I might have missed my vocation. Maybe I could have been the German Somerset Maugham. Anne French must certainly have thought so, and, to me at least, she couldn't have looked more uncomfortable knowing that mostly I was still agreeing with her entirely fictitious version of events. But like all good lies, this one had a reasonably substantial basis in fact. The best lies are always partly true.

"Anyway," I continued, warming to my Münchhausen task, "Wolf had the bright idea of using Guy Burgess and Donald Maclean to blackmail the British secret service almost as soon as they defected to the Soviet Union in nineteen fifty-one. But he needed Mielke to help him sell the whole idea to the GKO—the State Defense Committee—in Moscow. One thing you can say about Erich Mielke is that he's a seasoned old party hand and knows his way around the Kremlin. Well enough to escape the big purge of nineteen thirty-seven, when a lot of those old

German Communists were killed or sent to labor camps. Of course, Mielke was lucky enough to be out of the way in Spain then. He was a party commissar with the Republican faction.

"It was three or four years ago when he and Markus Wolf went to Moscow. The two Englishmen were already under suspicion. Moscow thought they'd been allowed to escape to Russia and that, in return for allowing Burgess and Maclean back in to England at some time in the future, the British planned to use them to supply all sorts of disinformation to the Soviets. Stalin even considered having them both liquidated just to be on the safe side, or sent to some far-flung corner of Siberia where they could do no harm. Gratitude was never Uncle Joe's strong suit. Anyway, kinder, wiser counsels in the GKO prevailed and they remain alive and almost at large. But consequently neither of them has ever been given much more than a nominal role in the KGB or GRU. Markus, however—he showed the GKO that Burgess and Maclean were still an important and valuable intelligence resource, and that the British continued to be just as afraid of them as perhaps the Russians were. He showed them how that fear could be turned into paranoia and exploited to our advantage.

"The tape recording was made at the main studio of Moscow Radio. It was quite a production. Sound effects, everything. Maclean made one or two tapes, I think, but it was Guy Burgess who revealed that he had a real talent for the microphone. Of course, having been a radio producer with the BBC may have made it easy for him, especially with the help of a bottle of good whiskey. And it was Burgess who had the idea of the tapes being designed for submission to the BBC. According to him, there were lots of lefties at the BBC who thought the same way as he did—especially in Berlin. One or two of them are even on the Stasi payroll."

"You're saying that there are BBC employees in Berlin who are the agents of the Abteilung?" This was the man with the irregular teeth speaking now; while he spoke he nervously adjusted the cuff links on his shirt. Meanwhile Anne gave a loud sigh and reached for her handbag, from which she took out a packet of cigarettes and then lit one impatiently.

"That's right," I said. "Guy Burgess told Wolf that if ever they'd had the same opportunity as he'd had—to spy, that is— they'd have done exactly the same as he did."

"So why did they choose Roger Hollis to target and not someone else? Someone in MI6 perhaps."

"As a matter of fact, in the beginning the KGB weren't convinced that Roger Hollis *was* the right man to go after. But Wolf convinced them that it was the apparent ordinariness of Hollis that made him so effective in counterintelligence; that and the fact that as number two in MI5 he was also Wolf's principal opponent, so to speak. Wolf liked things like this. It appealed to his sense of spying as a game of chess, I think. The whole thing was a bit of a game, really. To have some fun embarrassing the British secret service. Also, Guy Burgess really had met Hollis in Paris in nineteen thirty-seven, although purely by chance. Anyway, that was to be the key to the whole operation. Of course,

Hollis never was approached by anyone from the GRU. He was quite beneath the radar, having no foreign languages nor any interest in socialism, and not even having been to university. Later on, when Guy Burgess saw that Hollis had joined MI5 and risen quickly through the ranks, he came to regard Hollis with a new respect and to believe that his complete lack of ego made him probably the most effective man in the whole of British counterintelligence. That was also the opinion of Major General Markus Wolf. According to General Wolf, it was Hollis being so unremarkable that made him so remarkable. You see, Wolf believes that spies are like works of art that have been painted by master forgers. It's usually the smallest things that give them away, but only to another expert. A careless brushstroke here, an initial letter on a signature improperly formed, a dealer's number incorrectly sequenced on the back of a picture frame. You had to treat Hollis in the same way and imagine some art expert looking at the man's life as if he were investigating a priceless work of art. Which meant finding some tiny bogus detail that most ordinary people would overlook—something so small that someone else might very well miss it—and inserting it into the man's whole historical narrative, retrospectively. Like using cobalt blue instead of Prussian blue, he said. And it was clever to have Burgess snobbishly dismiss the man he'd met in Paris as a no-account little tobacco salesman."

"But why involve Somerset Maugham in this whole scheme?" asked the monk.

His tone was completely neutral and gave me no clue as to

whether I was on the right track or not. Like one who was trying to focus on what was true and what was not, I took a long pull on my cigarette, narrowed my eyes, and stared into some amorphous, intellectual space above Anne's brunette head where deep thoughts and ideas were floating around in her cigarette smoke.

"Again that was Wolf's idea. He decided to use Maugham because Maugham was rich and, in spite of his age, perceived to be extremely well connected, albeit historically, to the British secret services. Many of the men who worked with him in Russia were still involved with the service. He was the soft underbelly into MI6 and, of course, easily compromised because of his homosexuality. Wolf spent a long time looking for that photograph of Maugham and Burgess, which Guy Burgess had told him about. Yes, I forgot to mention: Wolf spent several weeks talking to Burgess at the Hotel Metropol in Moscow, noting hundreds of details like that. And as soon as he found the photograph, the plan went into action. By then I was living down here and working at the Grand Hôtel, where a number of French ministers are fond of taking their holidays and mistresses. Anne's wrong about the minister, however. Operation Othello was always accorded a much greater operational importance than entrapping one French minister of defense. Almost the minute Wolf had the photograph in his possession we knew we were finally in business. The photograph was perceived to be the best way for me to secure the old man's trust and confidence. And the whole scheme would have worked, too, but for the girl's crisis of conscience. I told Wolf we should have used a native German, someone with family still in East Germany whom we could have pressured if she'd even thought of defecting. That's how the Stasi works, see? You don't ever have a choice. You work for them or something bad happens to someone you care for. They lose their job, or worse, they get sent to a camp. Or in my case, they threaten not just to keep you in a camp, but to put you on hard labor. At the camp I was in at Johanngeorgenstadt, they put me onto a detail mining pitchblende rock, for their uranium enrichment program. I'd have been dead within a few weeks of that if I hadn't agreed to join the Stasi. But Wolf was convinced that Anne's background as a writer made her perfect for his plan. Frankly, I think he was sleeping with her."

"Nonsense," said Anne. "You bloody liar. That's just not true."

"Isn't it? You seem to have slept with almost everyone else— me, Harold Hennig, an American millionaire at the hotel, your gardener, and for all I know that French minister. If I'd suspected the bar had been set so low, I would have avoided your bed and kept things between us entirely professional."

I turned back to address the monk. "But as it is, I fell for her even though I always suspected she was ideologically unsound. Perhaps *because* she was ideologically unsound. I don't know. And not that it really matters now. We're all for the high jump, I expect. Even you, Anne. I can't imagine what kind of deal you think you've cut with them, but you're quite deluded if you think you're just going to walk away scot-free from this room. That there aren't going to be any consequences for you back in London."

361

"Never mind that now," said the monk. "Tell us about Harold Hennig."

I was enjoying myself now and plowed on. I was sure that if my story had sounded completely implausible to anyone except Anne, by now they'd have silenced me the way they'd already silenced Harold Hennig.

"Harold Hennig I've known since before the war, when I was working as a policeman at the Police Praesidium on Alexanderplatz and he was working for the Gestapo in Berlin. He was attached to the Queer Squad. He had a very profitable sideline in blackmail even then. The master blackmailer, we used to call him on the police force. I mean, what better cover for a blackmailer than being a policeman? It was Hennig who was behind the scheme to blackmail General von Fritsch into resigning from the Wehrmacht in nineteen thirty-eight. That was on Hitler's orders. And no one understood blackmail better than Adolf Hitler. I was the one who brought Hennig into the Stasi in the first place. That was one of my major functions in the beginning; to track down men from the RSHA and cajole or pressure them into working for the Stasi. Anne is quite right, again: Half of the Stasi has some sort of background in the old Reich Main Security Office. Most of us cut our teeth in the RSHA. That's what younger ideologues like her can never understand. That the dictatorship of the proletariat requires the working class to be even more ruthless in the administration of that dictatorship than the Fascists. No one is forbidden to join the organs of the state merely by virtue of their former political allegiance. Men were Nazis. Men are reeducated in socialism. I was. Anne was wrong that I told her that I thought this was funny. My English always lets me down when I try to make a joke. Just ask my employers at the hotel."

Anne was still shaking her head. If she'd had a gun she'd probably have shot me.

"You'd thought it all out, hadn't you?" said the monk. "This scheme to sell us the idea that Hollis was a mole."

"No," I said loudly. "Wolf hated that word. Moles make mole-hills, he said. There is no subtlety in that. What Englishman doesn't notice molehills on his beautiful lawn? Wolf preferred to think of this as his cryptic egg scheme, which is something that *kuckucks* do. I'm sorry, cuckoos. A cuckoo is a brood parasite. It lays an egg that's just like all the rest in the host bird's nest, to persuade it to bring up the cuckoo chick as its own. Wolf's idea was that you could equally be persuaded that you had been bring-ing up a cuckoo chick all along." I shrugged. "Well, now you know the truth. Hollis was your egg, not ours."

"If what you say is true," said the monk, "then perhaps you know of other cryptic eggs in our service."

I lit my second cigarette with the butt of the first, which I stubbed out in a glass ashtray the monk had shoved in my direc-tion. On purpose I didn't put it out very well and, to his irrita-tion, the cigarette butt continued to smoke for several more minutes.

"The HVA is a new service," I said evasively. "It takes time to lay an egg like Hollis. So far, only the GRU and the KGB have had the opportunity to do this. I daresay Wolf is recruiting people in your service as we speak. But they won't hatch for a while."

"How about Russian eggs," said the monk. "Perhaps you heard a mention of someone's name when you were last at Karlshorst."

I thought quickly, recalling the names of the two men I'd overheard Sinclair and Reilly mention while I'd been eavesdropping on their conversation on top of Maugham's roof, and wondering if the old man had told them about that. Perhaps not if he really had suffered a minor stroke. This was the moment I'd been hoping might come along—when the British, already paranoid about Soviet agents in their service, would ask me for names. But I had to play things carefully now. If I was too reluctant to give them any names, they might decide I knew nothing; but if I was too eager, they'd assume I was making it up.

"Perhaps," I said carefully.

"Maybe you'd care to share a name with us now."

"In return for what?"

"We could make a deal."

"What kind of a deal?"

"The kind of immunity deal that gives you back your liberty, perhaps."

"How do I know I can trust you to keep your word about something like that?"

"You don't. But we're holding all the cards here. Quite frankly, Gunther, I think your only chance is to come clean with us and hope for the best." He paused. "The way I see it, you've got noth-

THE OTHER SIDE OF SILENCE

ing to lose. You're burned. Finished. Useless to the Stasi now. We might easily let you go on the basis that you probably won't last five minutes when they find out you've told us everything. Of course, you might survive. Stranger things have happened."

"Yes, that might work, I suppose." I nodded thoughtfully. "There is a name I can give you. Two names, actually. For a while they were the two most important Soviet agents in MI6. The question is, which of us is prepared to share them with you now? To some extent I'll only be confirming what you know since one of them is already in the public domain. But the other should prove I'm telling the truth, all right. Although once I've given you these names, I'll have effectively told you what this operation was really about. That this whole operation was set up by the HVA not only to blacken the name of Roger Hollis but more importantly, to salvage the reputation of someone else. Someone even more important, perhaps. Someone who might yet still make a comeback as the KGB's top man in MI6. Someone who was always a better spy than Roger Hollis."

"I've already explained what this is about," insisted Anne. "What are you talking about, Gunther? This is complete fantasy."

"Herr Gunther, we both know you don't really have a choice here," insisted the monk. "I'm sure you know the difficulty you are in. The difficulty we are both in. There is no legal process available to you, or for that matter to us. Then again, we can hardly let you go, can we? Unless and until we're convinced that you've told us everything, I'm afraid I can't answer for the consequences. Some of my more muscular colleagues favor taking you out to sea and dropping you over the side with a weight around your ankles. Ever since the defections of Messrs. Burgess and Maclean, morale has been low in our service. I'm afraid that killing you and Herr Hennig would help to restore a sense that the balance has been redressed. I sincerely hope it doesn't come to that. For your own sake I urge you to cooperate fully."

"All right," I said. "But I have to say there's something I don't understand."

"What's that?" asked the monk.

"Why hasn't she told you this? I don't understand you, Anne. Why are you trying to protect him? It's all over for me and you and Hennig. The best we can hope for is to try and cut some deal before they throw us all in jail."

"This is fantasy," Anne told the monk again. "Look, I've told you everything there is to know. The whole bloody operation. I'm not holding anything back. But for me, the deputy director of MI5 would probably be suspended pending an investigation. Wouldn't he? It's only because of me that you know anything at all. But for me, you'd be in the dark about all this."

No one spoke. Anne looked furtive now, even a little desperate. The trouble was that everyone believed her lie, which meant she could hardly contradict mine without compromising her own.

"Why on earth would I hold something back now?" she said. "It makes absolutely no sense. He's making this up to try and make me look bad in your eyes and to save his own skin. That much is obvious."

"Anne French is telling you she doesn't know this man's

name," I said. "But I have to tell you now that she and I have had more than one lengthy conversation about him. While we were in bed. So I'm afraid she's lying when she tells you she doesn't know what I'm talking about."

"What? That's a load of crap," said Anne.

"Is it?" I asked smugly. "Look, the last time I saw her I had absolutely no sense that she was experiencing any crisis of conscience about her actions. None at all. She was cool and very collected. If I'd had even half an idea that she was going to betray Hennig and me I'd have put a bullet in her head without a moment's hesitation." I frowned and wagged a finger in her direction. "When last I met with Anne French all of her questions were about Sir John Sinclair and MI6, not MI5. Was it possible that proving that Roger Hollis was a Russian spy would help to put our man in the clear again? That kind of thing."

"Tell me you're not going to believe any of this Fascist bastard's nonsense," said Anne.

"I don't know," confessed the monk. "Really I don't. It's a most intriguing picture you paint, Herr Gunther. It is as if you really do have the names of two men who have spied for the Soviet Union in MI6. Do you? I wonder."

"Look," said Anne, "it's perfectly obvious he's just going to give you the name of Sir John Sinclair or Patrick Reilly. Or that other queer who was at the hotel. The art curator. Blunt. He's bluffing you, like this was a game of bridge. There is no Soviet agent in MI6, I tell you. At least none that we know of."

"Look, we all know that there's an easy way to prove who's

telling the truth here," I said. "We should both agree to write down two names at the same time. Then you can decide for yourself what her real intentions are here, gentlemen. To help, or to hinder. If these names are not under some suspicion in the British secret service, then I'll be the one facing a midnight boat trip, not her. I've already put up my hands to everything of which I've been accused. So, I've nothing at all to lose, have I? Can this beautiful lady honestly say the same?"

The monk handed me a pencil and a sheet of paper. "Very well," he said. "I'm going to do what she's been urging me to do for several minutes. To call your bluff. Write it down, Gunther. Write down the names. But woe betide you if you're wrong, my German friend."

"With pleasure."

I tore the sheet of paper in half, wrote the name JOHN CAIRNCROSS, and handed it to the monk.

"This first man has already confessed to being a Soviet spy," I said. "However, his name is not yet known outside of MI6. So I couldn't possibly have known about him unless someone in the HVA had told me. Agreed?"

The monk read the name and passed it to one of his colleagues.

I prepared to write the second name, uncertain now of how to spell it. English has such peculiar, idiosyncratic spellings. The Christian name was short and obvious. But the surname was something else, like a type of felt hat beloved of English gentlemen. If I made a muck of it I was a dead man, without question.

For a second or two I considered beginning the name with an "F" but changed my mind and, praying that Maugham had not mentioned to the spymasters my having listened to the conversation of Sinclair and Reilly while I was up on the roof, I wrote it with a "Ph," like Philip. When I finished, I handed the paper back to the monk. On it was written the name KIM PHILBY.

"I suspect," I said, "that restoring the reputation of this second man was, perhaps, what this operation was always all about."

The monk looked at the name without betraying a flicker of recognition and then showed it to his two colleagues, whose reactions were equally gnomic.

"Now then, Miss French, I wonder if you'd mind doing the same as Herr Gunther," said the monk, handing her the pencil and another piece of paper. "Take your time. But write down the names of anyone who was spying for the KGB in MI6, if you can."

Anne stared at me for a moment with tight-lipped malevolence. Her early cool demeanor was gone; she'd even started biting her thumbnail.

"I already told you," she said evenly. "Are you deaf? I don't know the name of any Soviet agents in MI6." She tossed the pencil away and crushed the paper into a ball, which she now threw at me. "I can't tell you what I don't know, can I? He's lying. Neither of us knows the name of any Soviet agents in MI6."

"Anne French ought to be the one person you people can trust because she's already betrayed the HVA's Hollis operation to you," I said. "And, of course, it's perfectly understandable that you should trust her. Christ, I know I would. Anyone would. At great personal risk she's told you everything about Othello and in considerable detail. That's undeniable. Did you hear me deny it for very long? No. I've confirmed it and so has Harold Hennig. Well, more or less. But if I have supplied the names of two men who've been Soviet agents in MI6 and she says she can't, then where does that leave your opinion of her? And of me? Clearly she's demonstrated her loyalty to her own country and to you, and yet she says she knows nothing at all about any Soviet agents in MI6. It's puzzling." I looked at her and smiled kindly. "You might as well tell them, Anne. I really don't think that either one of those names is going to be such a surprise to them."

"Fuck you," she hissed.

"You already did, sweetheart. In bed. Several times. And then in here. But do let me know if I've forgotten somewhere else."

THIRTY-TWO

The thugs from Portsmouth took me back to the red room, only this time they didn't chain my hand to the radiator, or leave the light on, or even hit me, for which I was grateful. So I wandered round the room for a while, for the exercise, stood at the window, opened it, and then pushed at the louvered shutters. I was glad of the fresh air, but the shutters themselves didn't shift a centimeter, not even with all my weight against the center gap. It was dark outside and I had no idea what time it was. I could hear and smell the sea and I longed to be outside. I felt sick and terribly tired. My jaw still ached and I was longing for a bath.

"Be careful what you wish for, Gunther," I said to myself.

"They might take you for a bath in the sea. The kind of bath for which you won't need any soap. Just a pair of concrete overshoes."

I went to the red room's door, held my breath, and listened. I could hear nothing but silence, but I didn't doubt that they were probably talking about me; I'd given the Englishmen a great deal to discuss. And even if they didn't believe a word of it, at least I'd managed to upset Anne French. That alone would have been worth the effort. After a while I lay down on the floor by the window and closed my sore eyes. I'm not sure how long I slept but it was still dark when I awoke and for several pleasant minutes I stayed there with no knowledge of who or where I was. According to *Betty Cornell's Popularity Guide*, you should always be yourself, but a lifetime's experience had taught me differently. With my background, being yourself can easily get you killed. Minutes passed and I got up and made a token effort to push the shutters again, but they were just as unyielding as they'd been before. So I walked back to the radiator and managed to find what was left of the water they'd given me earlier. I drank it and returned to the door and listened. This time something was different. The house remained silent but now I felt a cool draft of air on my feet and when I dropped down onto my stomach to peer under the doorway I felt it on my face, too. A door was wide open somewhere. The front door perhaps. And an old prisoner's instinct told me that if the front door was open then maybe another was, too. I stood up, grasped the brass handle, turned it gently, and pulled. The red room door was unlocked and opened with barely a creak. At the end of a long, unlit corridor I'd paid little attention to earlier, the main door was standing wide open. I waited for several long, frigid moments to see if someone came in, but I had a strong feeling that no one would and that the British had gone. I walked to the front door as quietly as I could and stepped outside onto the terrace, into the overgrown front garden, still half expecting that someone would emerge from the shadows and hit me, or worse, put a bullet in me. But nothing happened except I learned where I was. The house was situated somewhere on the slopes of Mont Boron, just to the south of Villefranche and overlooking Nice, to the west. It was a typical three-story bastide with peeling yellow walls and blue shutters. There were no lights on in any of the windows and no cars parked on the drive. The place looked deserted, almost derelict. For a moment I considered making a run for it down the graveled drive. Instead, curiosity got the better of me and I went back inside the big house. The room with the cobwebbed chandelier was deserted now except that my shoes lay on the table, next to my watch, a packet of cigarettes and some matches, and a set of small keys on a ring. I put on my shoes, grabbed the keys, and started to explore. Gradually it became even more obvious that the house was empty. I even risked switching on some lights, and it wasn't long before I found Harold Hennig, chained to a radiator in one of the larger bedrooms up on the first floor like some forgotten prisoner in the Bastille. I decided that if I looked anything like him I was in bad shape. He was unshaven and had a blue eye the size of a beet-root from when he'd been slugged.

"So this is where you've been hiding," I said.

"What the hell are you doing here?" he said, blinking uncomfortably at the light.

"I don't know. Maybe I'm supposed to be the caretaker. They're gone, you see. The English. And I don't think they're coming back. Dunkirk all over again. There's no one here but you and me and—for all I know—the man in the iron mask."

"Are you sure?"

"The longer I stay here talking, the more sure of it I am." I dangled the keys in front of his face. "I found these on the table in the room next door."

"So?"

"Nothing. But I've an idea they might fit that bracelet you're wearing."

"How come you weren't chained up?"

"Somebody had to release you, I suppose."

"They obviously don't know us very well," he said.

"It's best you don't remind me of that," I said. "I'm just liable to change my mind about this."

I tried the key on the handcuffs he was wearing. The lock opened.

"Why are you helping me?"

"I'm not sure anyone else would come and find you here. The place looks more or less disused. I guess I'm not the type who can leave a man to die like that. Chained to a radiator like an abandoned dog. Even if it is what you probably deserve."

"Thanks."

"I'd be grateful if you didn't mention it."

"If the English spies left you unchained they must have believed something of what you said."

"Perhaps." I thought about Kim Philby, the Soviet agent in MI6, and reflected that but for my remembering his name, the English wouldn't have believed a word of it.

"More than I did. I could see what you were up to, Gunther. And I congratulate you. That was quite a performance, the way you took the wind out of her sails with your story. I thought the best thing I could do—the only thing, to help your crazy story along, I mean, and fuck her up—was to try and hit you." He moved his jaw in the palm of his hand. "I just didn't realize that English bastard would punch me so hard. He knocked me out cold."

"I appreciate your thoughtfulness."

"But this has to be a trap," said Hennig, rubbing his wrist and flexing his hand. "The English will probably shoot us when we try to walk out of the front door, don't you think?"

"Why would they do that?"

"I don't know. But why would they let us escape, either? It doesn't make sense."

"Perhaps it makes more sense than you think," I said. "As far as they're concerned, we're an embarrassment to them. And no use to the Stasi. I doubt Comrade General Erich Mielke would ever believe that the British secret service just let you escape, would he?"

"No, he certainly wouldn't."

"In which case the British think we're both burned. As good as dead. There's no need to kill us if they think that the Stasi will do it for them, in time. Presumably Hollis has been cleared of suspicion, and you and I are of no further use to them. So letting us escape is the simplest, least embarrassing, and most diplomatic solution. I wouldn't be at all surprised if that's what happened to Guy Burgess and Donald Maclean. That the Brits let them escape to Russia. To avoid a scandal. The British just hate scandals."

"Any sign of Anne French?"

"Not so far."

"That double-crossing bitch. I'd love to catch up with her again."

"You were sleeping with her, too, then?"

"Of course. From way back. I'm afraid she was using you, old boy. I suppose we both were. Sorry about that. Comrade Mielke's orders." He stood up and rubbed his jaw again. "You really think they're just going to let us walk out of here?"

"Yes, I do. But I still think we should get moving in case someone else shows up. The local police, perhaps. Or even the real caretaker."

Hennig followed me out of the house, through the unkempt grounds and along a quiet main road that took us down Mont

Boron and toward Villefranche, with me glancing over my shoulder from time to time to make sure he wasn't carrying a rock with which to hit me on the head. I wouldn't have put it past him. By now Hennig and I knew the road we were on was going to lead us right by Anne's villa, but neither of us said anything about that. We didn't need to. It was almost dawn when we reached the place on Avenue des Hespérides, and although the front gates were locked with a heavy chain, neither of us hesitated for a moment; we climbed over the gates and walked up the drive, but it was soon apparent that the villa was empty. There was no sign of her car, either. Hennig insisted we make sure she was gone and even clambered up to peer through the windows of her bedroom to check that she wasn't hiding in there.

"The closets and drawers are all open," he called down to me. "Looks like she packed in a hurry."

"I'll bet she did."

He dropped down onto the terrace beneath her window and let out a sigh. "Bitch," he said. "To treat me like this after all we went through together. I can't understand it."

"She must have left with the British," I said, ignoring the pang of regret I felt at his casual mention of their earlier intimacy. "Perhaps she's gone with them to the Belle Aurore Hotel on the Cap."

"Maybe," said Hennig. "But my guess is that they're already on a boat to somewhere further along the coast. Or on a private plane back to London. Either way it doesn't look like she's coming back here soon."

He knew where a key to the guesthouse was hidden in the garden and let us in through the front door. He switched on a light and found a cigarette in a drawer and then a bottle in a cabinet.

"You seem to know your way around," I observed grimly.

"I've been staying here when I wasn't at either of the hotels on the Cap," he explained. "I kept the tapes here. Want a cognac? I know I need one."

I thought about the state I'd left my stomach in after two bottles of schnapps; I was only just over that particular hangover.

"Sure," I said. "Make it a large one."

"Is there any other kind for men like us?"

He handed me a fist-size tumbler like his own and we both downed the brandy in a couple of gulps. Meanwhile I glanced around the room, noticing first that Anne's portable typewriter was gone and then that the Hallicrafters radio had been put beyond use with a hammer that now lay on the stone-flagged floor like a murder weapon.

"Looks like someone has been in here, too," I said.

"Looks like."

"Her?"

"More likely the British. Just in case either of us felt like radioing Berlin."

"I wouldn't know how."

"No, but I would. As soon as they find out that she's betrayed this operation, she's dead anyway. They'll send a squad of killers after her."

"Why?"

"Because that's what they do."

I went into the bathroom for a pee and saw my forgotten jacket was still hanging on the back of the door where I'd left it on the night I'd come from Julia Rose's house in La Turbie. That seemed a long time ago now. Because the early morning air was cool, I put the jacket on. When I came out of the bathroom Hennig was pacing up and down like a neurotic bear, with another drink in his hand. There were even tears on his cheeks and I almost felt sorry for him, he looked so like the way I felt myself.

"It's a pity," he said. "I really would have liked to get even with that damn woman myself. I feel really angry about it. Jesus, I think she affected me much more than I realized."

I shrugged. "Get used to it. I have."

"No, really." He put down his tumbler, picked up the hammer, and hefted it meaningfully for a moment before tossing it onto the sofa. "I think bashing her brains in would make me feel so much better. I don't know how else a man is supposed to heal after something happens to him like that."

"In this particular case, getting away alive is the best revenge, don't you think?"

"Says you. Me, I think I'd prefer to bash in her brains. But slowly, you know. I'd like to take the time to enjoy it. One blow a minute."

"You're just saying that. And you think it will be sweet. But take it from one who knows. It isn't. It never is."

"What are you? Hamlet? Look, Gunther, don't try to handle me. I know what I want, okay?"

"Then it's just as well she's not here, I guess."

"It makes no difference," he said. "One day I will catch up with her and I'll pay her back."

"You mean that, don't you?"

"Of course I do. She'll walk into a hotel room and I'll be there, waiting behind the door, with a garrote in my hand."

I shrugged. "Have it your own way."

"You really don't feel the same? She betrayed you. She played you like a hand of cards. Believe me, if anyone should want to kill her, it's you, Gunther."

"Maybe you're right."

"Of course I'm right."

"As a matter of interest, what were your orders, Hennig? Just to help discredit Roger Hollis, I suppose."

"That's right. It was a good operation, too. And it would have worked but for Anne French. She's got a mad streak, don't you think? Either that or the woman is made of steel. Probably both."

"Of course, it's perfectly conceivable that it wasn't Anne who betrayed you, but Mielke and Wolf. That the whole operation was really meant to put Roger Hollis back in good odor with his Whitehall masters. That she was told to do it from the outset."

"I don't understand."

"Don't you? I'm afraid I've formed the opinion that she was always meant to betray your operation. Yes, from the very beginning. That those were General Wolf's orders. I'm afraid I really didn't buy all that stuff about falling out of love with the Communist Party. It would certainly explain why Wolf picked her and not someone with family back in the GDR, who could be threatened with reprisal. No one like that would ever have done what she did."

But Hennig wasn't having any of it. I didn't blame him; it sounded madly convoluted to me, too. Just madly convoluted enough to be the kind of thing that people in the secret services might actually think of.

"Nonsense," he said. "What you're saying—there's no way I wouldn't have known about a plan like that. Mielke and Wolf would certainly have said something."

"Why? Because you're that important? Nonsense. The whole operation worked all the better if you were ignorant of it. Anne's betrayal now puts Hollis in the clear. And forever after, probably. Which can only mean MI5's deputy director was Moscow's man all along and will remain so. That Othello was never meant to discredit Hollis but actually to achieve the exact opposite."

"No, it was Anne who betrayed me. Not them. Wolf isn't that clever. Nobody is." He clenched his fists and walked around the room cursing Anne and swearing to a whole variety of ugly revenges on her. I almost felt sorry for him. And in a way for her, too.

"Kill the goldfish in the pond or burn the house down if it makes you feel any better," I said.

"What would be the point of that? It's not hers. It's rented. She's not coming back here. If I thought there was even half a chance of that happening, I'd wait here and burn the house down with her in it."

"You know, there's a difference between revenge and vengeance," I said, putting my hand in my jacket pocket.

"Is there? I can't say I appreciate the difference very much, or even care."

"Revenge is personal. An act of passion. An injury is revenged. But I think vengeance is about justice. That's something very different. Crimes are avenged, don't you think so?"

"Does it matter which it is when you're the one being shot?"

"Probably not," I said, and brought my hand out of my pocket. There was a gun in it. Julia Rose's Beretta 418. The one that had killed my friend Antimo Spinola.

"That's the second time you've pointed a gun at me," he said. "There better not be a third, Gunther. What's the idea this time?"

"You're going to have to try very hard to convince me why I shouldn't kill you, that's all."

"You're sore about the girl. I can see why. Look, she was sorry about that. She really liked you, Gunther. She liked you more than she liked me. She told me. She didn't have to go to bed with you. That was her choice."

"Sure."

"Listen, Gunther, there's ten thousand francs in my toilet bag at the Grand Hôtel. That's for you. And don't forget that there's a bank account in Monaco. At the Crédit Foncier. That much is true. There's another twenty thousand francs more in that account that was meant to finance this operation. You're already a signatory. All you have to do is show your passport to the manager and the money is yours. We could go there right now. Get the cash. You needn't ever see me again."

"No."

I worked the slide on the little gun and put one of the little twenty-five-caliber bullets in the chamber. It wasn't much of a gun to kill a man, but at a range of less than two yards it didn't have to be. Hennig knew that, too, and started backing away.

"You're not the type to kill me, remember?" He was starting to sound scared now. "You said so yourself, Gunther. You're a decent man. I knew that the first time I met you."

"No, I said I wasn't the type to leave a man to die chained to a radiator, like an abandoned dog. But this is different." I pointed the gun at him.

"This is for those nine thousand people who died on the *Wilhelm Gustloff* in January nineteen forty-five. It's been eleven years in coming, and for them this is an act of vengeance. But for Captain Achim von Frisch, Irmela Louise Schaper and her unborn child—my unborn child— it's revenge, pure and simple."

And then, as he was probably about to speak again and beg me for his life, I shot him in the chest five times and then once more between the eyes when he was oozing blood down on the floor.

I stepped outside the guesthouse for a moment and lit a

cigarette to help slow my pounding heart. The cicadas were quiet now, holding their breath probably, shocked that human emotions could make other, more intelligent living creatures such as ourselves behave in such a barbarous fashion. What did they know about real tragedy anyway? Without emotion, pain is just pain; it's human feeling that makes pain such absolute agony. I had no regrets about killing Harold Hennig, but I was wrong about revenge, of course. It was sweet, after all. And I wasn't finished with it yet. Not by a long way.

I went back into the house, wiped my brandy glass and the little Beretta clean of fingerprints, and tossed it onto the floor next to Harold Hennig's dead body. Then I placed the keys to Spinola's apartment near the front of Anne's desk drawer. I also wrote his address onto a card in her Rolodex, in block capital letters. It wasn't much in the way of evidence for the police, but in my experience you don't need to be a Georges Simenon to frame someone for murder, just a corpse and a murder weapon and a set of keys and perhaps a woman who's suddenly left the country. The police love things to be neat like that. This one had crime of passion written all over it. I told myself I might even stay around the Cap just long enough to answer their questions and recall Anne and Herr Hebel in the bar at the Grand Hôtel and perhaps remember something important I must have forgotten, about how Spinola had once mentioned a writer in Villefranche he was seeing sometimes and how he'd had a fight with her new German boyfriend. Threatened him. Either way I could easily cause enough trouble for Anne French to make sure she could never return to France. Or perhaps she would be extradited back to face a murder trial. But to carry off a story like that I would need to speak to someone else first. I would need to speak to a master storyteller. I would need to go and see Somerset Maugham.

THIRTY-THREE

I walked home, washed and shaved, changed into my working clothes, flung a suitcase into the back of my car, and drove up to the Villa Mauresque. It was still early and little was stirring at Maugham's beautiful house, certainly not the great man himself, or his nephew, or Alan Searle. Only the butler was up and around, and he seemed not at all surprised to see me again, even with a large bruise on my jaw and the suitcase in my hand.

"How is he?" I asked.

"Who?"

"The master, of course."

"Oh, him. Much better, sir. It was only a mild stroke, I'm happy to say."

"Good." I meant it, too.

"Have you come to stay, sir?" he asked, checking the buttons on his white jacket.

"Not this time," I said, as if nothing much had happened since the last time we'd seen each other. "Mr. Maugham isn't expecting me, but he'll want to see me nonetheless. It's all to do with the events of the other night. When all the other Englishmen were here."

"I understand. Would you care for some breakfast?"

"Yes, I would."

I sat down in the whitewashed dining room where the makings of breakfast had been laid and pretended as if I were prepared to eat it; but as soon as Ernest had left to make some fresh coffee I grabbed the suitcase again and went upstairs to the master bedroom, where I found the master sitting up in bed with a newspaper and a cup of tea in his unsteady hand. He was wearing white silk pajamas and half-moon glasses, and with the Chinese prints on the walls he looked like an older and rather less compassionate version of the goddess Kuan-Yin, whose imposing statue stood on the black floor of the downstairs hall.

"You don't look like someone who's had a stroke," I said.

"I'm not," he said coolly. "I feigned that in order to be rid of everyone. I'd had enough of the whole business. And now that they've all returned to London, I can return to normal."

"I might have known."

"Well, this is a surprise. I certainly didn't expect to see you again, Herr Wolf. Or perhaps I should now say Herr Gunther. Have you come to shoot me?"

"Oddly enough I haven't."

"Pity. At my time of life one craves a little excitement. I rather think that being shot might have a very stimulating effect on my book sales, which, lately, have been in decline. Just as long as one didn't die, of course. That would be too sad. Then I should miss the thrill of seeing myself once again at the top of the *New York Times* bestsellers list. 'England's Greatest Writer Shot by East German Spy.' As a headline it has a certain news-worthy ring to it, don't you think?"

"Yes. But as it happens I don't work for East German intelligence. Or for that matter any other intelligence service. I'm sorry to disappoint you, sir, only I'm not a spy. I'm afraid your friends in MI6 were sorely mistaken on that score. And I do mean sorely. I've got the bruises to prove it. The fact is, I'm just a citizen with a past."

"Aren't we all, dear. Aren't we all. But you have come to settle a score, have you not? With me."

"Actually, I've come to do you a favor," I said.

"Really?"

"I was hoping you might do me one in return."

"This sounds suspiciously like a rather more subtle, slippery kind of blackmail. A squid pro quo, so to speak. Is it? Are you intending to blackmail me, Herr Gunther?"

"I said I was hoping you might do me a favor, sir. I wasn't even thinking of demanding one with menaces."

"Good point." He nodded at a comfortable chair beside the bed. "And I beg your pardon for my presumption. Please. Sit down."

I sat down a little too gratefully, leaned my head back, closed my eyes, and let out a sigh.

"You sound tired. And you look terrible."

"I just want to go to bed and sleep for a thousand years."

"I do hope you're not planning to do that here," he said. "At the Villa Mauresque."

"Why would you think so?"

"That suitcase, of course."

"That suitcase contains files about you. Lots of them. Compiled by someone called Anne French, who worked for the Stasi—the East German secret service—and who was, she alleged, planning to write a biography of you for some American publisher."

"Oh, which one?"

"I'm afraid I don't know. I don't even know if it's true—about the biography, I mean. Actually, there's very little I do know about this woman that's true, probably. But the files are real enough. There was a whole drawer full of them in her filing cabinet. And now they're all in this suitcase."

"She's the woman who Sir John said had been working with you and Harold Hebel all along. To blackmail me and, in turn, the British secret service."

"That's right. Only with you I was on the level. Which is more than I can say of her. Frankly, the idea that she and I were working together was painful news to me. Exquisitely painful. I thought we were just sleeping together now and then. I found out otherwise. It seems that she had her own clandestine agenda."

"That's fish for you."

"Fish?"

"Sorry. Queer slang for women."

"Oh. Right. Anyway, a great deal of what's in those files is quite detailed and for all I know there may be something that you'd prefer never saw the light of day. You being a very secretive, private man."

"I'm quite sure that's true. I loathe the idea of a biography as another man might loathe the attention of a Harley Street proctologist. Especially at my time of life. So. What do you want for these files? Money, I suppose? There's very little else I can give a man like you."

"No. I've got some money." I was already thinking of the ten thousand francs I planned to take from Hennig's toilet bag at the Grand; there was no point in letting the French police have it when, eventually, they came to search his room. "No, all I want is something that you of all people should easily understand, Mr. Maugham."

"What's that?"

"I just want to be left alone."

"Ah. Privacy. That's the most precious commodity there is. You do know that, don't you?"

"Now that your friends in MI6 have returned to London, there's only you and Alan and Robin who know who and what I am. Or at least what I was. I want your word that you'll be silent about me and all that's transpired involving me, here, on the Riviera."

"Most assuredly I do understand. You have my sympathy. And you want my silence? Very well. You have it."

"All that has transpired and all that has yet to transpire."

"You intrigue me. I had hoped that this whole sorry affair was now concluded. Robin was assured it was. Pray what has yet to transpire?"

"The fact is I murdered Harold Hebel a couple of hours ago."

"Good God."

"He was shot and killed at the house of Anne French in Villefranche-sur-Mer. The bitch has gone back to London, I think—I'm not sure. But I'm sort of hoping the police will find the body and think it was Anne who murdered him."

"Two for the price of one. The revenger's bargain, as it were. Yes, I do like that symmetry. Very Jacobean."

"I've certainly made sure that all of the evidence points her way."

"So. You killed Hebel, after all. Fascinating. Might one ask, what changed your mind?"

"He did, actually. The bastard kept talking about how he wanted to get even with Anne and he had so many reasons to do it, I guess he just persuaded me."

"Well, that's a first, I must say."

"You notice I said 'murdered' because I won't try to justify what I've done. Not to you. And certainly not to myself. It's true there were more than nine thousand good reasons to kill him. All those people on the *Wilhelm Gustloff*. But when it came right down to it there were only two that made me pull the trigger." I shrugged. "And you know who they were. By the way, there's nothing at all that connects the dead man with you. So you can relax. Enjoy your house in peace. I doubt the police will come asking questions about him up here at the Villa Mauresque."

"I'm pleased to hear it. We like to discourage visitors."

"That's just one of the secrets I want you to keep for as long as I try to stay working at the Grand Hôtel."

"It seems to me that your secrets are inextricably bound up with mine." He sighed. "And I can hardly talk about Harold Hebel without talking about the photograph, and the tape, and the British secret service, can I? The leisure moments of an ill-spent life have made me every bit as vulnerable as you are. But is this course of action wise, my friend? Given what I've been told you are. Sir John said he thought there might be some men who would come looking for you. More spies. Guests at the hotel who might turn out to be assassins. He told Robin he thought you and Hennig would probably make yourselves scarce as quickly as possible. I must say, this shrimp pool we call Cap Ferrat has never been so exciting."

"Perhaps they will come. Perhaps they'll shoot me. I don't know. People have tried to kill me before and I didn't cooperate.

I'm still here. Or at least some of me is. But I'm tired of running. This particular *Flying Dutchman* needs to put into port and make substantial repairs. None of what your friends in MI6 said about me was true anyway—well, perhaps some of it was—so, maybe the Stasi will leave me alone. But down here on the Cap, I'll leave you alone and perhaps you can do me the same courtesy. On the subject of each other we will be silent."

Maugham nodded. "I understand. After this rather unwelcome period of tumult in your life you wish to subside, gently into cheerful peace. With a real future as opposed to an imaginary one. Am I correct?"

I nodded. "Something like that, I suppose. I can't be more particular than that right now."

"That's not unusual. And I can certainly be silent regarding you, Herr Wolf. Yes, let us return to using your nom de plume. But I can't guarantee that my nephew Robin can do the same. He is what is descriptively called a blabbermouth."

"But I do think you can control him. Especially since his whole financial future is largely dependent on you."

"Yes. That's true." The old man smiled his inscrutable smile. At least I think that's what it was. There were too many creases and wrinkles on his face to be sure. He gave a great throaty chuckle.

"All right. It's a deal."

I got up and walked to the door of his elegant bedroom, helping myself to a cigarette from the box on the sideboard. It was made of amber and rather hateful.

"I like you, Herr Wolf," he said. "For what it's worth, I would dislike it very much if some m-men did come from East Germany to try to kill you. But I think you're a very dangerous man to know. In fact, I'm sure of it. So, please, be kind to an old man, and don't ever come here again. I don't think my nerves could stand it. Besides, you're a terrible bridge player."

I didn't stay for breakfast, after all. I went quickly down the staircase of the Villa Mauresque and out to my car, ignoring Ernest and his offer of the silver coffeepot. The clipped lawns and carefully tended hedges of pink and white oleanders contrasted sharply with the wreckage that was inside me, almost as though the gardens had been carefully designed as a poignant reminder of what a hollow man I was and how empty I felt. Brilliant blue dragonflies hovered over the surface of the swimming pool like flying sapphires. The scent of orange and lemon blossom might have originated in an extra heavenly part of paradise itself. Everything in the garden looked and felt precious. Everything except me. I didn't belong there. But that was all right. In my eyes the absolute perfection of the Villa Mauresque was imperfect. I could never have belonged somewhere like that, among men without women. They were risky creatures, women, but that's what life was for—to take risks. I got into the car. It didn't start the first time, or the second, but on the third attempt the engine wheezed into life like old lungs and I steered slowly down the gravel drive. In the rearview mirror I caught sight of Somerset Maugham watching my departure from the wrought-iron balcony in front of his bedroom. He would die soon. He knew that. He looked dead already. His thoughts were always on death now. But whether he would die before me remained to be seen.

I went to the Grand Hôtel, put on my morning coat, straightened my tie and my cuffs, adopted a smile, took up my station behind the desk, and waited.

AUTHOR'S NOTE

ERICH KOCH was captured by British forces in Hamburg in 1949 and extradited to Poland. He was tried in 1958, found guilty of war crimes, and sentenced to death. His sentence was commuted to life imprisonment because of ill health, although many believe the Polish government came under pressure from the Soviet Union, which believed Koch had information regarding the whereabouts of the Amber Room of Tsarskoe Selo Palace, near Leningrad. Salvage attempts to find the Amber Room on the wreck of the *Wilhelm Gustloff* have so far revealed nothing. Koch died in prison, in November 1986.

The sinking of the *Wilhelm Gustloff*, while almost unknown today, remains the greatest maritime disaster in history. Nine thousand four hundred people died, many of them children.

Formerly KÖNIGSBERG, Kaliningrad is the administrative center of Kaliningrad Oblast, the Russian exclave between Poland and Lithuania on the Baltic Sea. It is the only part of the Russian Federation that—geographically, at least—is entirely within the EU.

W. SOMERSET MAUGHAM really was a British spy and did indeed control a large network of secret agents in Petrograd in 1917. He died, aged ninety-one, in Nice, in December 1965. The Villa Mauresque, now Le Sémaphore, is to be found at 52 Boulevard du General-de-Gaulle, Saint-Jean-Cap-Ferrat. It is owned privately and, unlike the excellent Grand Hôtel Cap-Ferrat, is not open to the public.

GUY BURGESS, Clarissa Churchill's former suitor and Soviet spy, died in Moscow, in 1963, aged just fifty-two. He and Anthony Blunt were both guests of Somerset Maugham at the Villa Mauresque in 1937.

ANTHONY BLUNT was knighted in 1956. He confessed to being a Soviet spy in 1964, and in return for this confession was granted full immunity from prosecution. His life continued as normal and he remained Surveyor of the Queen's Pictures until 1973, and director of the Courtauld Institute of Art until 1974. His spying activities were not revealed to the general public until November 1979. He died in 1983.

KIM PHILBY was revealed in 1963 to be a member of the

spy ring now known as the Cambridge Five; JOHN CAIRN-CROSS was finally revealed to be a KGB spy in 1979.

SIR JOHN SINCLAIR was fired from MI6 by Prime Minister Anthony Eden in July 1956. He was replaced as director of MI6 by Sir Dick White. Sir Dick White was replaced as head of MI5 by Sir Roger Hollis, who after being director general of MI5 for nine years, from 1956 to 1965, died in 1973.

Formerly private secretary to Sir Stewart Menzies, then chief of MI6 PATRICK REILLY was chairman of the Joint Intelligence Committee from 1950 until 1953. He was knighted in 1957, when he was made British ambassador to Russia.

According to Selina Hastings's definitive biography of Somerset Maugham, in 1959 ROBIN MAUGHAM was offered $50,000 to write his uncle's biography by an American publisher. On learning about this project, W. Somerset Maugham sent Robin a check for $50,000 on the strict understanding that he drop all plans of writing about him. As Hastings writes: ". . . Maugham had no trouble in recognizing blackmail when he saw it."

SIR ROGER HOLLIS was cleared of being a Soviet spy by Prime Minister Margaret Thatcher in a statement to the House of Commons in March 1981. However, Ray Cline, the CIA's deputy director of intelligence from 1962 to 1966, concluded that there was "a high percentage of probability that MI5 had been penetrated at a high level and that, among the possible candidates to be a Soviet agent in that category, Roger Hollis was the best fit to be matched with all the evidence concerned." Robert Lamphere of the FBI has also stated: "To me, there now remains little doubt that it was Hollis who provided the earliest information to the KGB that the FBI was reading in their 1944–45 cables. Philby added to this knowledge after his arrival in the US but the prime culprit in this affair was Hollis." Senator Malcolm Wallop, a long-serving member of the Senate committee in charge of U.S. intelligence, told the British author Chapman Pincher that William Casey, the CIA chief from 1981 to 1987, was convinced that Hollis had been a spy. Victor Popov, Soviet ambassador in London from 1980 to 1986, agreed with this assessment. Pincher states in his exhaustively detailed and very readable book *Treachery: The True Story of MI5* (2011): "In summary, if one imagines a magic compass that could be placed over any suspicious set of circumstances affecting MI5's countermeasures to the Soviet intelligence assault, the needle almost invariably points to the man who served in the agency for twenty-seven years and became its chief. The extraordinary concatenation of dates and circumstances all fit. Hollis's serial culpability for security disasters, whether due to treachery or to sheer incompetence, can no longer be in doubt. Except when events outside his control took command, almost every recommendation he made and every decision he took benefited Soviet intelligence." That is also my own opinion.

Bernie Gunther will be back in 2017 with *Prussian Blue.*